Hattie Rising

A young woman's search for joy and happiness using work, wits and talents.

George Graft

Revised Edition

Cover picture courtesy of Rebecca and Madison Peterson

THE HATTIE SERIES:

Hattie Rising
Fire Walking
Stone Music
Hattie Heads Home

OTHER BOOKS BY GEORGE GRAFT:

Door 101

COMING IN 2014:

The Ballenger Seeds
Southern Surprise

COMING IN 2015:
Oaken

First Revision August 2014 © George Graft

Disclaimer

Acknowledgements

I wish to express my gratitude to my dear wife for her loving patience, support, comments, editing, and encouragement during the process of creating this book. I wish to thank Lianne Vroustouris for her skillful editing and helpful suggestions that helped to make this book more interesting and readable. I wish to thank Heather Brinkerhof for information concerning self-publishing and for cheerful cheerleading. Thanks to Madison Peterson for inspiring my vision of Hattie and all the other kind people who encouraged me to take this leap of faith and put my beliefs on paper.

I wish to thank those loyal readers who plowed through my rookie mistakes in the original edition. I hope the elimination of hundreds of typos, grammar mistakes, and punctuation errors creates a more readable book for future readers. Hattie's message remains the same. Talent, training, work, and truth will trump adversity every time.

Dedicated to all my Grandchildren
From their Grouchy Old Grandpa

Prologue

Salt Lake City, Utah,
1 August 1913

Bishop David Rasmussen gently laid the frail fingers that he had been holding on top of the coarse hospital sheet and checked for a pulse. He had not detected a breath for over a minute. He arose quietly from the stern old lady's bedside noting that the drive, fire, and determination previously contained by the thin alert face had given way to a look of peace and repose. The strikingly dark eye brows that reminded him of Fourth of July rocket trails rising from the apex of the slim patrician nose and disappearing into the wisps of white hair were still there—rising ever rising. The effort to sit up and greet him when he visited her yesterday had sapped her strength. Today she had only managed a smile and seemed resigned to pass peacefully.

He moved into the hallway and called to the nurse at the duty desk. "Would you come and check her? I think she has passed on, and it should be confirmed."

He turned to reenter the sparse, lonely room. Who was this woman? He had noted the special attention she received from the staff. He had visited other patients at this hospital but never observed this level of special treatment before, almost like visiting royalty. Her short two-day stay had not allowed time to gather more information about where she had lived before coming here.

He glanced at the box Hattie had asked him to take with him and open after she was gone. He picked it up as the nurse entered the room.

She moved to the bedside using a stethoscope to confirm what he already knew. Opening the box, he found an envelope containing a will, with the letterhead of a prominent local attorney; a contract with a local mortuary marked "Paid-in-Full" for all funeral and burial expenses and a note to him appended to a hand written funeral program showing songs and speaking topics. He sighed, wondering how could he ask members of his Ward to take time from their busy lives to speak or sing at the funeral of this unknown old woman.

The hospital had only recently accepted her as a patient and she had never been to a church meeting. He wondered why his first funeral had developed so many complications. The will left any remaining assets to the new Primary Children's Hospital. The box also contained a smooth polished board wedged tightly along one side and a number of journals. The one on top was ragged and worn, held together with a piece of twine. As he picked it up to examine it, the twine broke and an old envelope slipped out of the pages and fell to the floor at his feet. The faded address was barely ledgible. He picked it up to take a closer look, but could barely make out the name, Mary Grant at some strange place in England. Time and weather had obliterated the rest. He began to read the letter.

My dearest Hattie,

I'm a dying and me Priest sez I must write to you and tell you these things afore I kin go in peace to me God. Mary and Will aint yer real parents. Yer wuz born in February 1838. Yer muther were a good kind lady. Her name wuz Catharine. I came with her when she married yer Father. Everone luvd her espeshly yer father. We all call yer father Mr. Kirkland but his Christian name be Thomas. Ye have a twin sister, her name is Anne. The Priest were there that nite and christened ye with the name Helen Marie Kirkland. My daughter Mary and me agreed to call ye Hattie soz no one cud find yer. At the time I feared fer yer life. Yer sis lives wit yer fater. Yer muther is dead. She died givin berth to ye girls but not afore she made me promise to take care of ye. We all thot ye wuz gona die too. Wen ye com out ye wuz all twistet up together. You getin the worst of the twistin. Yer father ordered me to get rid of ye but I cudna do it.

Mary took ye home wit her. She had come to me fer the birthin of her own first child. That child died the morning before ye wuz born. I tooked ye to Mary and she took ye home with her. We put her ded wee wun in the coffin wit yer real mum. I be askin Mary to giv ye this letter wen ye old enuf ta unnerstan. She tells me most uf yer twistid legs and back be better now. I hope ye fergiv an ald lady fer eny trubil I cozd ye.

All me luv,

Tillie

After reading the letter, the Bishop skimmed through some of the journals. He recognized the handwriting that identified it as Hattie's personal life story. He wanted to read more. He needed help to prepare the eulogy he would give at the funeral service outlined in the program. With a last sad look at Hattie, he gathered the items given to him and left to carry out the arrangements she had so carefully prepared for him. On his way home he stopped by the newspaper and was just in time to get the announcement in the obituaries before the evening edition went to press. The special attention from the chief editor puzzled him but he was thankful for his cooperation. He then visited with his Relief Society President to make sure women would be available to help dress the body.

Once he arrived at home he helped his wife prepare the kids for bed. After family prayer he decided to read parts of the journal to help him prepare his talk. The story he found described a life full of adventure and trials that were hard to believe. He became so involved that he couldn't put it down. He couldn't count the number of times this woman had started over with nothing but her wits and the skills she had learned. He doubted if the Salt Lake City library had as many books as she claimed to have read. Adventures with Indians, (both kinds), shipwrecks, and train wrecks filled the pages. He read all night.

He arrived late at his office downtown the next day and was surprised when his partner whispered that he had a real important visitor. He thought he heard "What have you been up to now?" But, when he turned around his partner had disappeared.

He found one of the most influential men in the Church sitting in his office. When Dave entered his visitor arose and extended his hand with a warm smile and greeting.

"I see from the morning paper that the funeral for Sister Hattie is scheduled for this Saturday. I would be honored if you would permit me to sit on the stand with you and possibly say a few words."

"Of course sir I would be most grateful for your support and I am sure Hattie would be honored," replied Dave trying to act nonchalant with his guest. "I was privileged to read a little of her life story last night and my respect and admiration for her has grown in the last few hours."

"Yes indeed. She was truly a remarkable lady and I only know a portion of her story. I do know that there will be many who cannot make it on Saturday because time and distance to travel will keep them away. I am sure that they will send prayers in her behalf. Well then, we all have lots to do this week. I will see you Saturday, Bishop. I only hope there will be room." With this remark, he shook Dave's hand and gripped his shoulder with the other hand and, with a pensive smile and a twinkle in his eye left Dave standing in his office wondering if he should run after his visitor and see about reserving the Tabernacle.

The visitors that next knocked on his door created almost as big a surprise. When all were seated and comfortable, and introductions concluded, he asked, "What can I do for you sisters? I could sell you some new living room furniture but I am not convinced that is the reason for a visit from three members of the Tabernacle Choir to the office of an overpaid furniture salesman."

"You are right."

"We want to sing at Sister Hattie's funeral."

The third lady said, "She was a very special person. She is the reason the three of us are where we are today. She truly motivated and inspired us to work beyond our potential and reach a higher level of performance. If you were to ask for testimonials from the congregation on Saturday we would probably be there until Church starts on Sunday." The others nodded in agreement.

"She mentioned that she taught school for a while. Were you her students?" Dave asked.

"Yes we were all her students. She taught us to love music. She was an excellent teacher, but I always felt that she had more to say. It seemed that she had actually been there, and had lived many of the stories she told. Her exciting adventures illustrated how we could succeed in life through hard work and proper execution of the skills, abilities, and intelligence that God gives to us all."

Bishop Rasmussen chuckled as he said, "I'm not sure the stories weren't true." Everyone smiled as they thought about the stories they had been told and Dave remembered some of what he had read the night before. He then stood up to signal a close to their meeting not wanting to become too maudlin this early in the morning.

He indicated a song that Hattie had chosen. *"Nearer My God to Thee,* I wonder why she chose this song?" He asked. The blank looks resembled those he might expect from one of his children caught with their hand in the cookie jar. He felt confident that the music for Saturday's program would be tastefully and beautifully accomplished. Had he detected a wink passing between the three ladies as they left his office? He wondered if anyone remained alive who really knew the whole story of Sister Hattie.

Chapter 1

Hattie's Journal

21 April 1853: I was admiring this journal the day I had the fight with Bart Janes. I hit him with it. I was already at Mam and Pap's before I realized I was still carrying it. I was 15 years old when I left home—an outlaw!

The rain drove cold silver needles into Hattie's shoulders. Her lungs felt on fire as she pushed her way through the dense brush and last year's weeds. Her feet slipped on the wet clay and mud on the hillside.

She stopped.

She didn't know how long she had been running. Her side ached and her bad leg dragged in the mud. She really wasn't running anymore. Her movements resembled a fast slog. Great balls of the muddy clay from the English hillside encased her slippers causing her to slow down and wipe or kick the mud free before stumbling on. She glanced back briefly but rain and tears smeared her vision. She shivered, chilled by the cold wet wind as it penetrated her wet clothes. Wiping her face with her fingers and pushing her hair from her eyes, she stumbled on.

She moved deeper into the trees instinctively searching out the roughest terrain. She knew that the immediate pursuit would consist of servants and farm laborers from Janes Manor many of whom were friends of her family. She hoped those clever enough to look in this direction would remember her as a friend. Maybe her enemies would pick the search areas that followed the well-used roads and paths all of which led in other directions. A line from one of the many books she loved to read came to mind. "Hope for the best but plan for the worst."

She paused to catch her breath in the bushes surrounding a giant oak tree that had fallen that past winter. Her dark clothing blended with the bark from the wet oak. It was early spring. She could smell last year's wet leaves mixing with the scent of new grass. Trees and bushes in the warmer parts of the forest were already showing buds and new spring growth. The leaves that still clung to the fallen oak's branches shielded her from view as well as providing some protection from the wind and rain. Hattie allowed the bag she had been carrying to slip from her shoulder and drop to the ground. Exhausted, she sat on the oak log to rest.

Using a broken branch, she cleaned the mud from her slippers, instinctively knowing that if spotted, any hope of a fast escape would depend on being able to move quickly. That would prove impossible with a ball of mud on each foot the size of cook's unbaked bread loaves. She checked to see what was in the bag Pap had fetched from the barn as they scrambled to help her get away. The canvas bag they used to gather fruits and vegetables consisted of nothing more than a heavy cloth strap sewn to the top of a piece of canvas stitched on each side leaving an open top.

She discovered the journal resting inside. She had seen Mam put an envelope inside the cover. It couldn't contain money. They didn't have any. At least none printed on paper. She found her work shoes, and decided to stick with the slippers for now. They were already muddy and she could run faster in them. Her spare dress and a knitted shawl held what little food Mam had been able to find. She found two loaves of bread, a chunk of dried cheese a little bigger than her fist, and two wrinkled apples. She decided to leave the food wrapped up as it was for now. The shawl would provide her little warmth or protection from the rain, so she might as well keep it as dry as possible for later.

The rain stopped while she rested. That would make traveling easier but would also make hunting for her easier. A whiff of breeze carried the scent of a barnyard toward her. She remembered Pap saying it was spring when he could smell the barnyard. Would she ever see him again or feel a hug from those strong arms? With a mental shrug, she picked up her bag and took a more difficult, but hidden route deeper into the undergrowth ahead of her.

Hattie stopped for the evening before the sun set. One of the books she had borrowed from the Janes' library to read after work had been an adventure novel. The hero had always tried to locate a good place to stop for the night well before dark. He would find a place that offered concealment and protection from the weather. She followed his example by climbing the tallest tree around. She wanted to spot any pursuit, and to map out in her mind one or more escape routes should it be necessary to leave quickly during the night. She couldn't see anything behind her except trees and more trees. She heard no shouts or noise of any kind. She was able to see a small stream winding along approximately parallel to her direction of travel. She decided to carefully go over to the stream and drink. The same book mentioned that camping near water was an open invitation to capture or visits from unfriendly night animals. She shuddered, imagining what might be hunting her for dinner. She stopped for the night in the jumble of rocks ahead of her. She found several boulders leaning close together forming a tent shaped cavity. Winter winds had piled up leaves between the rocks. Many of those imprisoned under the rocks had escaped the rain and were relatively dry. She could snuggle into them and pile more around her to keep out the cold.

But first she needed a drink.

As she carefully crept up to the creek, she spotted a large water worn boulder that lay in the streambed creating a small pool. She climbed carefully over the rock so as not to disturb the ferns and water plants growing nearby. She took a large satisfying drink, washed her face and hands, and carefully returned to her camp.

She had walked to the stream barefoot in hopes that it would prove easier to cover her tracks. Upon returning, she used grass and leaves to clean the mud off her feet and slippers. She decided to put the heavier shoes on the next morning. She found a pair of dry woolen stockings jammed inside her work shoes. She put them on and then wiggled into her rock cave, rolled up the extra clothing for a pillow, covered her head and shoulders with the emptied bag, and settled down to rest. For the first time since leaving, she thought about the events that caused her to run for her very life, filled with terror and sheer panic. Not wanting to deal with those emotionally charged moments right away, she let her thoughts drift all the way back to her earliest childhood memories.

Pain. What is it about pain or some other strong feeling that imprints those first memories on our minds? Her memories came from the pain of being tied to the sticks, boards, and straps that Pap had made based on directions received from old Mora, the healing woman that lived out in the woods. In fact, old Mora's hut was not that far from where Hattie was camped right now. By the time her first memories developed, she had grown accustomed to the pain and the foul smelling baths Mam dunked her in when she removed the braces. Hattie seemed to remember that they ended about the time baby Andrew came along. That happened sometime before her fourth birthday. By that time, she already knew her sums and letters and was reading from the books Mam said she had used as a little girl. She remembered taking her first few, pain filled steps at the same time baby Andrew started walking. After that she pretty much fended for herself. Mam was popping out a new baby once a year for a while there and had little time to help her. In fact most of the helping with the kitchen chores landed on her shoulders.

She remembered helping with the little ones. Another pain filled memory came to mind. She and Andrew had been fighting over whose turn it was to gather the eggs. Andrew had pushed her. She tried to balance on her bad leg. Little Josh, he must have been two at the time, had come running to join the fight and crashed into her. They fell in a tangle both crying. Mam, pregnant again, had rushed in and scolded *her,* as usual. She, being the oldest, should know better. She had grabbed the egg basket conceding the argument to Andrew and ran outside to her favorite spot.

A low, stone wall ran alongside the house and marked the boundary between the house and the chicken yard. When the sun was out, it would warm the stones. She had previously arranged some of the rocks into a makeshift seat. Sitting there on the sun-warmed stones eased the pain in her twisted back and leg. She sat there crying in frustration at not being able to control her brothers or her own emotions—just plain feeling sorry for herself.

The warm rocks did nothing to ease the pain of rejection. She felt lost and alone, as if she didn't belong to the family. She sat sobbing quietly, then a pebble hit her on the head and another landed on her back. Andrew and Josh began pelting her with rocks. She just didn't care. Take it out on misfit-sister she thought, stone me to death like they tried to do to the girl in the Bible before Jesus stopped them. She felt hated, lost, and alone.

Trying to catch the boys and make them stop had proved useless in the past. That's what they wanted her to do since both could easily outrun her. So she just sat there ignoring them, praying they would go away. The chickens began acting funny. One old hen was just sitting on the ground while all the others would come over and peck at her. As she watched, she realized they were pecking the old hen to death. The other chickens wouldn't leave her alone. That old hen just lay there. It was like that with Andrew and Josh. They wouldn't leave her alone. Wasn't she better than some old hen in a chicken yard? She needed to break the cycle by not letting them know they were hurting her. She must endure the pain and stop the fighting. *Take control Hattie, rise above it!*

Outside her struggles with Andrew, the early days at home included many good times. They sang songs and played games, and Mam read them stories from the books Mrs. Janes brought them. Hattie would take over the reading when Mam had other chores. She learned to hold her feelings inside where no one could hurt them. Mam and Pap taught her many important lessons about living, especially how to work. She never lost the feeling that she belonged somewhere else, but with time that didn't seem to matter.

The smell of rain-wet flowers near her rocky tent reminded her of Margaret Janes. She always smelled like flowers when she came and brought gifts to the family. Hattie liked the soft cool touch of her hands not rough and worn like Mam's. Sometimes she would sing to them in a soft cultured voice, not high and screechy like Mam's. Mrs. Janes always brought special sweet treats and new storybooks when she came to visit.

She remembered the first day Mam brought her to work at Janes Manor. Mam had so many youngsters to look after by then that she placed Hattie in service when she was only eight. Fear of the unknown and so many strangers with strange customs imprinted that day on her mind. For the first few weeks she worked in the kitchen cutting vegetables and scrubbing floors. They assigned her a room in the topmost level of the manor house and she worked long hard hours on her knees, which hurt her bad leg and back. One day Margaret Janes noticed her limping and ordered no more scrubbing on her knees. She dusted and cleaned the common rooms in the main

wing of the house. These included the library, boys' classroom, parlor, and
Mr. Janes' study. Hattie, smart enough to recognize that this was special
treatment, bit her lips and worked through her pain doing her very best to
keep the wooden panels glowing and the floors shining. No one ever found
a speck of dust on any of *her* books or furniture.

She heard the other servants talking about the little girl baby that Mrs.
Janes lost the year after her son Peter was born. Hattie figured she and the
baby must have been about the same age. Maybe that was why Mrs. Janes
treated her special. Whatever the reason, Hattie worked harder than ever
to show her gratitude.

Hattie, like all the servants, received one day a month off. She also
attended Church with her family in the village chapel. She liked to go and
listen to the music. That was her favorite part. She didn't think much of
the shouting preacher. That was her least favorite part. Later when she was
older she found him difficult to understand. Why would the God of Love
she read about in the Bible want all his children to end up in some burning
pit? Maybe one day she would figure it out, but right now all she could do
was work and learn all she could. Maybe sometime in the future she would
be smart enough to figure out God.

Hattie smiled as she thought about those early days at home with
Mam and Pap and the later visits on her days off. That was when she
learned the basics of reading, counting, and doing simple sums. Hattie
picked up every piece of paper she found in the manor and made a game
out of sounding out the words and trying to make sense of the ones she
didn't understand. She practiced writing the way Mrs. Janes did with her
beautiful curling letters all strung together to make each word. She even
learned to read Mr. Janes' scratches that looked like tracks from a chicken
yard.

Hattie smiled as she remembered a very special time. It was autumn
and the leaves were beautiful. The sun was warm and bright that morning
when she opened all the heavy draperies covering the windows in the boys'
schoolroom. She had planned to clean the windows that day so she started
earlier than usual. She was just squeezing the water and vinegar mix from
her rag when the door banged open and the most beautiful boy in the world
bounded into the room! The morning sun spotlighted him, and he glowed
from his wavy blond curls to the glossy shine on his riding boots. He,
likewise stood frozen in surprise and admiration, locked into immobility

by the angel in the white pinafore surrounded by a halo of early morning sunlight behind her.

"Eee," Hattie exclaimed dropping her cleaning rag with a plop, right back into the bucket creating a splash.

"Whoops!" came his reply at almost the same instant, followed by, "Who are you?"

"I'm the one what cleans up your mess in here every day. Usually I don't start here this early, but today I wanted to get at the windows so I could see the smudges in the sunlight." She answered, wringing out the water in her rag and mopping up her spill.

"Well, I'm Peter and this is my classroom. That is, mine and my brother's."

"Aye, I know who you are. My name's Hattie." She mumbled keeping her head down and continuing to clean up the spilled water as she looked him over more closely through her hair.

"Well, well, and my name is Bartholomew, Bart Jr. or just Bart to my friends." came a mocking voice from the doorway. "I thank you for stopping my brother here long enough for me to catch him and get my riding crop back," he said as he jerked the crop from the smaller boy and ran laughing from the room.

"It's really my riding crop. He thinks it's more fun to chase me and beat me up than look for his own," Peter muttered mournfully with a look on his face that indicated he would like to smack his brother. "I guess I'll just have to find his or use one from the stables. Nice to meet you though," he said, smiling as he left. Distracted and dreamy eyed by that smile Hattie took twice her normal time to do a special job cleaning the windows hoping *he* might come back to watch her.

Another week would pass before Hattie saw Peter and Bart again, and the circumstances would be different indeed. It came about as she was polishing the large wooden panels in the library. Several panels showed bad scuffmarks, and she was rubbing extra hard to make that area shine. Suddenly, the panel began to move into the wall! At first she stopped, convinced that she had caused some really bad damage. She looked around fearing discovery then examined the boards more carefully. She could find no damage. She pushed harder on the panel with her foot and soon it swung open far enough for her to look inside. There was a passage! Ever the curious sort, she silently squeezed through the opening.

She discovered a short passage from the library to Master Janes' study. Her excitement mounted when she realized that the passage went behind the wall of the schoolroom, and she could see and hear old Mr. Simkins droning on. His dreary voice washed over a sleeping Bart Janes while Peter gazed out the window. Learning new things excited Hattie. She couldn't understand why they looked so bored. What would happen if she looked in, listened and learned?

Because of her special relationship with Mrs. Janes, Hattie could pretty much set her own schedule as long as she finished all her work. She didn't want to do anything to ruin that arrangement. She wasn't sure if two hours each day in the classroom was all Mr. Simkins could handle or if it was all that the boys could stand. Either way she could easily remain in the secret passage for most of the two hours each day. She worked out a system. She could easily hear anyone that came into either the study or the library looking for her. If they entered one of the rooms, she would quickly enter the other and be busy at work with no one the wiser. Spying on the boys represented great sport to Hattie. It would indeed break up the daily drudgery, and then there was Peter to look at! She couldn't make up her mind, which was more interesting, learning or just watching Peter.

While the infatuation with Peter continued, Hattie began to take a real interest in what was being taught in the classroom. One day, Bart pitched one of his famous temper tantrums and threw his slate and chalk across the room breaking them against the wall. Later, she put the pieces in the secret passage when she cleaned the schoolroom. She left the larger piece of slate in the passage and took the smaller one to her room in the attic. Finding chalk for her slates presented no problem since the boys were always throwing it at one another and leaving it all over the classroom. With the chalk and slate, she began to follow the arithmetic exercises that Mr. Simkins taught the boys. In the evening, she would complete more exercises using the slate she kept in her room.

While cleaning the library, she came upon more of the same books the boys were using. She would take the appropriate book with her and read along silently as the boys read aloud. She soon passed Peter and was keeping up with Bart. The day arrived when the teaching came to an end. It was also the end of Hattie's ability to worship Peter from afar. Margaret Janes, unhappy with her boys' progress, took charge of the situation. Mr. Simkins was dismissed and the boys were sent off to boarding school.

Hattie's quest for knowledge could not be quenched. She continued to spend the two hours each day in the passage first reading books from the schoolroom and later from the library. She would borrow books from *her* library and read them at night in her room, then bring them back the next day. Many books contained controversial subjects and she wished there was someone available to discuss or argue different viewpoints. She silently shrugged to herself thinking you can't have everything.

Hattie lived in a small dormer room high in the manor. She had a problem sleeping, not just once in a while but every night. Her crooked bones still bothered her, especially when she tried to sleep. The pain would keep her awake until she reached total exhaustion. She discovered that it was easier for her to relax and sleep sitting up. She folded her straw tic mattress halfway against the wall of her room, but the mattress kept slipping down and she would end up flat on the floor in pain again the next morning.

The smell of smoke aroused her one night. It was coming from the other side of the wall! She kicked at the wall anxious to investigate the smell. Looking through the hole into the partitioned-off space, she saw the brick chimneys from the three main bedrooms rising to the roof, but no fire. Bricks protruded into three sides of the room. Between the chimneys there was more space than in her little cubbyhole. She crawled inside and found the source of the smoke-smell. One of the chimneys had a crack in it. She decided to fix the crack herself so as to keep the room a secret. Later from her reading, she discovered that being that far up from the fire below, the crack did not present a hazard to the safety of the house. She was not going to burn up. She would only smell the smoke when conditions were just right, as they had been on the night when she found the room.

She learned that she could make a suitable patch from wet mud. To make this patch, she had to take out the bricks around the crack and clean them. While doing this, she happened to hear the Master and the Missus in conversation through the chimney. The acoustics from the fireplace below and up the chimney worked just right. Being naturally curious, to the point most would call nosy, she listened to their conversation. It proved very boring. But, she reasoned that she might gain knowledge that affected her, so she decided to replace the brick in such a way that it could be removed easily. She kept up with what was going on in Peter's life when the parents discussed the boy's progress at school. It was her interest in Peter and what he was doing that kept her curiosity aroused and her ear to the hole in the chimney.

She decided to move her mattress into the chimney room. That winter, she found out the real benefit of her discovery. Hattie had taken the boards from the wall and wedged them against the bricks at an angle that kept her straw mattress from slipping to the floor. She could nestle down between the warm chimneys and the heat would warm her back and ease the pain.

It wasn't long after her discovery of the chimney room that Master Janes bought new furniture for the manor. In a magnanimous gesture of good will, he let the servants have some of the old furniture. One of the items was a narrow wing back chair with velvet padding. When she discovered that the servants were to have a claim, Hattie immediately ran to the library and pulled the chair into the hidden passage to prevent the other servants from claiming it. Because it was small and narrow, she was later able to pull it up to her room and place it between the two largest chimneys in the hidden room. She anchored it at a slight angle by placing wooden blocks under the front legs and propping the back against the chimney bricks. Replacing the boards each day, prevented discovery of the chimney room. This arrangement allowed her to sleep in relative comfort. The space was warm in the winter and surprisingly cool in summer due to the updraft from the fireplace flues. As her thirst for knowledge grew she would "borrow" books overnight and sit in her chair reading until she ran out of candlelight or was exhausted enough to sleep through her pain.

With the boys off to school, Margaret Janes grew lonely. She knew she had way too many servants for the work required to keep up the manor. She reasoned that they were needed when she gave parties or when guests came to visit. In truth, she just couldn't bring herself to let anyone go. She kept herself busy by keeping the servants busy. *Not a very rewarding life* she thought to herself. She needed a project, something with a reward.

Her husband was definitely finding his rewards. For years, he had obsessed over steam engines and locomotives. He was sure that soon tracks would run all over England bringing growth and prosperity to everyone. He invested heavily in railroads and served as a director on several companies involved in railroading. His plans and ideas began to pay off, but his obsession was costing him. His absences from home and family became longer and more demanding each year. He reasoned that there was money to be made, and, fortunately, it involved something that was fun and personally rewarding for him. Between school for the boys and his business, he very seldom had time for his sons. Any common interests they might once have had evaporated like a pot left to boil and burn on a hot stove.

One of Margaret's early pleasures involved playing the piano. What if she were to open the music room and take up the piano again? The next evening happened to be one where her husband was home between business trips. She ordered his favorite meal prepared along with a large bottle of his favorite wine and at the prime moment suggested her plan. She explained how bored she was with nothing to do out here away from the city. Would he mind if she did some remodeling and arranged for a special live-in tutor to help her improve her expertise on the piano?

Soon Hattie found herself busy packing up books, maps, and rulers along with all the other items in the schoolroom. She took the dust covers off the piano and the chairs in the music room and gave them a good shaking before using them to cover the desks. Hattie asked, "May I stay and watch when the piano man comes ma'am? I want to know how to keep it clean and nice."

"What a marvelous idea, Hattie," exclaimed Mrs. Janes, "I want you to know that this piano is very special to me." *Me too* thought Hattie to herself.

She listened very carefully as the piano man used his special instruments called tuning forks to tune the piano. "Interesting how the fork vibrates at the same frequency as the piano string when it is tightened just right." Hattie murmured to herself trying to remember what she had read about audible resonating frequencies.

"What did ye say?" asked the piano man giving her a quizzical glance.

"Oh, I was just jabbering to myself." Hattie replied skipping towards the windows at the back of the room with a grimace for an expression. What had she done now! But the man was busy selecting the next tuning fork from the box he had brought with him and was ignoring her again. With a sigh of relief Hattie returned to her dusting and cleaning.

She was interrupted later as the man said, "Would you like to try playing it?"

"Oh no, sir. It's me Mistress's most precious thing. She would whip me bottom something awful if I did that!" she replied with a look of horror on her face.

"Well then you better run get the missus 'cause someone needs to try it, if I'm fer getting me pay," he replied.

Hattie ran off, as fast as her game leg would let her travel only to meet Mrs. Janes coming down the main hall.

"Has Mr. Dugan finished yet Hattie?" She asked not waiting for an answer, or for Hattie to catch her breath. She continued down the hall to the music room. Hattie being as interested as Mrs. Janes quickly followed.

Mrs. Janes paused just inside the door. A look of pleasure covered her face. She moved slowly toward the magnificent piano. Its highly polished surface gleaming in the sunlight. "Isn't it beautiful, Hattie?" She exclaimed. "I had it imported from Austria. That's where the great composer Mozart lived. But then you probably don't know who Mozart was." She smiled condescendingly at Hattie. She directed Mr. Dugan to turn the piano so that the light from the windows would fall at just the right angle on the music rack. "Hattie," she said, "go over to that shelf where I had you place all the music sheets earlier and bring me something to play." Hattie brought her one of Mozart's piano concertos. She almost bit her tongue in two to keep from smiling at the look of surprise on Mrs. Janes' face.

Hattie knew all about Mozart. She also knew about Beethoven, Chopin, Bach, Haydn and many of the other great composers. She had read about them in the books in Mrs. Janes' own library. But, of course she wasn't about to let her mistress know that.

They both listened carefully as Mr. Dugan explained the care required to keep this beautiful instrument in perfect order. He concluded by presenting Mrs. Janes with his bill and an admonition to invite him back at least once a year to keep the piano in tune. Then with a bow to Mrs. Janes and a small wink at Hattie, he left them alone to admire the beauty of the instrument that would become the centerpiece of the music room and of Hattie's immediate future.

As Margaret Janes sat playing the piano a thought entered her head. Why not see if she could teach Hattie to play? There were certainly enough servants about that Hattie could be spared for an hour each day for a lesson and allowed, no ordered, to practice an additional hour. She sensed that Hattie was different. Even with her bad leg, she carried herself with a certain grace, an almost flowing motion. It was as if she was born with a royal pedigree and not born to the stout and sturdy Grant clan. They were good people and she admired them for the hard work and loyalty they always showed to her and the rest of her family. But, Hattie didn't have the same build or features. She was tall for her age and growing taller. Even at what, twelve years old, she guessed, Hattie was nearly as tall as she was herself. Her thin aristocratic face, long graceful neck, and those dark but thin curved eyebrows made her simply stunning! Margaret needed a project, something to occupy her time. And here it was gliding toward her stopping with a slight graceful curtsey.

Looking at Hattie always reminded Margaret of that terrible time in her life when she lost her daughter. The pregnancy happened too soon after Peter was born. She was bedridden for almost seven months to no avail. She had an early labor and the child was born dead. It had been a girl. She had been devastated. On the pretext of recovering from labor, she had remained in bed sobbing for her lost child. As she began to recover, she heard about the little girl born to Mary and William Grant. The Grants lived on one of the tenant farms. Margaret made a point of paying a visit to all of the tenant families when a child was born and again on Christmas Day. Fighting through her own pain and depression, she made her way to the Grant's small cottage. Her visit coincided with one of Mora's. She felt great respect for the healing powers of the wise old woman who helped those who couldn't afford the services of a doctor. Margaret secretly believed that Mora's ministrations could prove to be more effective than those she had received from the expensive London physicians she herself had visited over the past year. As she held the crooked little body and watched the stubborn will to live surging through her, Margaret's spirit began to recover. She found herself visiting often. A strange transformation began to occur. As she gave love to the tiny infant her own pain and suffering abated.

A few days later, Hattie approached Margaret while she was doing the household finances. "Madam, there is a woman in the parlor waiting for you. Here is her card." Hattie said as she handed the business card to Mrs. Janes. Margaret looked up from her figures with a gleeful glint in her eyes.

"Oh, yes. This is the lady I wish to engage to tutor me at the piano. It's been so long since I have played seriously, and I do so want to improve what little talent I have. What do you think of her, Hattie?" she asked with a secret twinkle in her eye.

"She seems to be a little stern and pompous for just a teacher, ma'am." Hattie answered.

"Hmm, well she is not *just a teacher*. She is a performer and writer of music as well with an excellent reputation in the city. I understand from mutual friends that she wishes to find some quiet time away from the city to work on her music and to compose. She has developed a bad cough that persists despite the ministrations of some of London's finest physicians. Perhaps we can induce her to take a rest here with us in exchange for music lessons for me," she paused and then added with a smile, "and for you." With that unexpected remark, she arose from her writing desk and left the room and a completely stunned Hattie standing with her mouth open.

There were no words to express the absolute shock and bewilderment Hattie felt. She, *always* knew what was happening around the old manor. That is to say, she had her secret passage, she listened to the other servants gossip, and she had her secret brick. This news came out of nowhere. She had to find out what was happening!

Margaret Janes put on her best face and manner as she entered the parlor to greet her visitor. "Miss Flower, I'm so glad you accepted my invitation to visit. How was your ride out from the city?" She asked, as she moved toward her visitor with arms open and a smile of welcome on her face. Eliza Flower remained seated on a small brocaded chair. She had fair hair and a rather plain face with a pallor portraying illness. She was dressed soberly as befitted a woman raised in a home dominated by those who preached the Word of God.

"Please call me Eliza." Her guest replied rising to meet her. She smiled in an attempt to show higher spirits than she possessed at the moment. "It is beautiful here in the country and you have a lovely home. It is so quiet and peaceful here." She added wistfully.

They continued to exchange pleasant conversation until lunch was ready in the small dining room. Both women moved to sit at a table set with the finest crystal and china available at Janes Manor. As they were seated, Margaret smiled to herself when she saw that Hattie, not usually available, but certainly capable of serving them, began to do just that. Seems that curiosity caused Hattie to worm her way in she thought to herself.

After a very nice lunch, Margaret set aside her dessert plate and adapted a serious attitude. "So Eliza, to the business at hand. I understand that for reasons that you don't need to share with me, you are looking for a quiet restful place in the country. While I, on the other hand, have decided to renew my interest in music and become more accomplished both for my own enjoyment and possibly the enjoyment of others. I wish to invite you to join me here at Janes Manor as my guest for as long as you choose to stay in exchange for music lessons for me and for my protégé."

"I don't understand. I anticipated your invitation thinking that you might want to improve your own talent. But, I was not aware that there would be a need to teach any one else. Who is this protégé?" she asked.

"Did you notice the young girl that served the luncheon?"

"Yes"

"It is she." Margaret answered smiling. Eliza almost dropped her tea-cup as she stared openmouthed at Margaret in total and obvious surprise. What possible reason could this woman have for wanting to teach music to a serving girl? It just wasn't done! Eliza, decided to go along with the idea since she really wanted the position being offered.

"That could be arranged." She replied, recovering quickly from her sur-prise at the news. Having settled on the basics of their agreement, the two ladies toured the manor and the grounds. Eliza found the living accom-modation more than suitable. Both were in full agreement on all points when Eliza parted later that afternoon. She promised to return the follow-ing Monday prepared to take up residence and begin work.

Margaret turned from watching Eliza depart to speak to the butler holding open the door for her. "Please have Mrs. Morgan and Hattie accom-pany you to my study in an hour. We have some business to discuss."

When they entered she looked up and said, "Let me get right to the point. I think it is obvious to all that I have a special soft spot for Hattie. At first I wanted her to be able to find work in spite of her injuries. I think we have all done well in protecting her and at the same time finding useful work for her. I have a concern that the other servants may resent her special treatment."

"That not be a problem Ma'am," piped up Mrs. Morgan. "Hattie is a good girl. And, she is always willin' to help the others. She pitches right in on all the dirty jobs too."

"That's good to hear," interrupted Margaret. "As I have already explained to Hattie and now to you, things might change. I want to give you warn-ing so you can make any necessary adjustments. Hattie may have to work extra hard so that others are not provoked by the appearance of favoritism. Starting Monday, Hattie will begin music lessons with my guest Miss Eliza Flower. She will also practice on the piano in the music room for one hour each day. Please fit this into her schedule and see that the others get equal time for personal business if necessary. I don't see a problem with the work. You should get everything done with the staff we have. Mr. Janes is traveling on business more and more, and the boys spend so much time away at school. We will just cut back on what we all recognize as work designed to keep everyone busy. I will expect everyone to jump to around here when Mr. Janes or the boys are home, but when it's just us mice around here... well, you know how to work it out I'm sure."

And work it out they did. Even those that didn't like change had to agree that everyone became better off. Hattie was in heaven. She loved her time with Eliza and the piano was easy to learn. Even Eliza was impressed with her progress and her natural talent. More than once she thought of Hattie as a female Mozart. There was one dark cloud. Eliza's cough refused to go away.

On a day during Eliza's second month at Janes Manor, Hattie knocked on the music room door and entered carrying a tea tray.

"Oh Hattie, that's just the thing I needed. Put the tray on that little table between the two visitor's chairs and we will enjoy some tea before your lesson." Eliza indicated a chair for Hattie. "Sit there and we will take tea together."

"Oh no Miss Eliza, this tea is special and just for you," said Hattie. "I found a remedy in a book. This tea is made from Goldenseal and Echinacea leaves. I think you should try it for your cough."

"Will it really work?" asked Eliza with more than a little disbelief in her voice.

"Well, it worked with a sick horse last winter," giggled Hattie as she poured. "That old horse drank a bucket full every day for a whole week. I don't think you will need that much, but I thought you might like to try it."

"Nothing has worked so far and I feel so bad I'll try anything," a look of skepticism still crossed Eliza's face. "I will drink this tea but you have to play your lesson at full tempo. If you make a single mistake, I will stop drinking. Agreed?"

To seal the bargain, Hattie sat at the piano and played perfectly until Eliza drained her teacup. Then Hattie jumped up and clapping her hands, exclaimed, "Now teach me some Mozart!"

A week later Eliza greeted Hattie at the door of the music room. "It worked! I have completely recovered from that dratted cough." She exclaimed. "I haven't felt this good in months! Hattie you are a miracle worker. Where did you ever come up with such a thing?"

"I found it in a book," Hattie replied, "I am so happy it really worked."

"Oh Hattie, now I feel so good I can return to my work. Listen to the new song I have written to go with the words to a poem sent to me by my sister. It's called *Nearer My God to Thee*. Let me play it for you. Then we can sing it together." She took a seat at the piano, and they began to play and sing together.

And, so it went. For the rest of the year, Eliza Flower taught Hattie piano and music theory. Both Hattie and Margaret enjoyed singing so Eliza also became their vocal coach. Eliza would arrange three-part harmony of church hymns and some popular songs of the day. The days passed quickly. The three became best friends in spite of age and station differences. Hattie peeked through the front parlor drapes, and cried the day Eliza left to return to London. She sobbed even more a few weeks later when Margaret told her that Eliza had died. Hattie blamed herself. She vowed to study harder and gain more medical knowledge so that she could help people like Eliza get well permanently, not just for a short time.

Years later, a series of events happened that would bring a drastic change in Hattie's life. The boys came home on holiday and even Mr. Janes returned from Europe after investigating a new locomotive design. Bart Janes quickly became bored with the Manor routine. His efforts to elicit an invitation to spend the holiday with his roommate had failed. Nothing about this dreary old place held his interest. It rested too far from the city, and his father had already refused his repeated pleas for permission to take the buggy into Sherborne. He even refused to allow Bart Jr. to go into the village to visit the local pub.

His father demanded that he participate in family activities. Bart found them boring. Why after all this time did his father suddenly insist on becoming his playmate? He had found a life for himself. Why did his father want to shackle him to the Manor? He wanted to have fun during his holiday, and nothing around this old block of bricks interested him.

One of the serving girls approached as he was leaving his room. He deliberately stepped in front of her, blocking the way. "Now what are you doing with that tray?" He asked, as he reached out to lift the frilly little cap his mother insisted all the serving girls wear. *How can I find a cute one when they all wear these silly caps and walk around looking down all the time?* He thought to himself.

Hattie looked up at him with a blank expression on her face. "Oh master Bart, I'm sorry I didn't see you." She had, but her training prompted her to make a suitable reply as if the meeting were her fault. Giving him the smallest possible polite smile allowed by proper serving manners, she headed off down the hall toward the back staircase.

He watched her leave. A slim, slightly crooked-backed girl, with a sort of pert, jaunty look about her. The back of her black skirt bounced the bow on her white servant's pinafore like the tail of a doe fleeing through the forest. *Maybe I can liven up my stay at the old manor after all,* he thought to himself snapping his riding crop against his leg. He turned and continued his walk to the stables with a smile on his face, and a little more spring in his step.

Hattie worked in the library dusting books. They really needed it. Earlier, she had talked her brothers into carrying the rugs out and beating them. They normally worked in the stables with Pap but he had supported her request for their help. Her deep cleaning had suffered recently, replaced by piano practice. Now the boys were home and she wasn't allowed to practice with them in the house. After Eliza left, Margaret and Hattie had continued to practice and play. They challenged each other to improve. The bond between them grew as they shared their love for music.

Hattie picked up a strange book from the shelf. It sported the same rich leather embossed design Master Janes preferred on all his books; but there was no title on the spine. The front revealed one word embossed in gold lettering, *Journal.* The book contained nothing but blank pages.

"Why such a baffled look on such a pretty face?"

The comment gave Hattie a start! She dropped the book in shock. Turning, she saw Bart Jr. standing in the doorway with a large, lecherous grin on his face. As she stooped to retrieve the book, Bart bounded across the room and caught her around the waist in one arm turning her towards him.

"I've waited a long time for this," he breathed as he spun her around under one arm. With his other hand, he closed the library door. "We are going to have a little party, just you and me."

His version of a party failed to materialize. Hattie wildly swung the book still clutched in her hand, catching him across the bridge of the nose. Letting go of Hattie, he grabbed his nose, and yelped in surprise and rage. He looked at his fingers covered in blood. "Ahh, you little wench, look at what you've done! You will *really* pay for this!"

He spun around making a wild grab for Hattie. But she moved too fast for him. She swung the book again, catching him on the left cheek. Letting her momentum carry her around, she darted behind a chair, grabbed a reading lamp from a table next to her and threw it at him. He deflected the lamp, but it fell to the floor, shattering the globe, spilling lamp oil and bits of glass all across the highly polished floor. Hattie moved toward the door across the room, but Bart lunged after her. His foot landed in the oil and broken glass. He lost his balance and flopped head first into the fireplace.

Suddenly, dead silence decended on the room. Hattie's gasping breaths became the only sounds. She flung open the library door intent on running away to hide. She turned for one last look. She saw him lying on the hearth, his neck cocked at a crooked angle with blood streaming from a terrible gash above his left ear. He was hurt worse than she thought. He looked... dead!

No one would believe her. He was the master's first-born son. She was but a lowly serving girl. Even Margaret—Mrs. Janes wouldn't save her from this. Gone were the good times, the songs, the music, the books left unread. She must run for her very life!

Chapter 2

Hattie's Journal

5 May 1853: *Hiding in the wilderness and living off the land is not easy.*

Ow! Her knee hurt, and some fly kept buzzing around her head. She opened her eyes to a blazing sun and a bright blue sky. Apparently, she had been trying to run in her dreams, and managed to bang her knee against the rock that formed one side of her shelter. Groaning silently, she inched her way out of the cave, pulling her meager belongings behind her. When she cleared the cave, she shook off the leaves and looked around, remaining as quiet as possible. No voices or snapping twigs broke the silence. She noted that it wasn't really that silent. She could hear the birds and the leaves as they moved on the wind in the branches overhead. She remembered from her reading that wild things went silent when something unfamiliar approached. *I guess I'm familiar* she thought to herself rubbing her knee.

Hattie reached into her bag, and pulled out the food parcel wrapped in the dress Mam had thrown into the bag during her hurried stop at home. She wouldn't let Mam and Pap give her anything that would show that they had helped her to escape. Breakfast had to be light since her food would have to last her for a while. She racked her brain for a bright idea as she munched on a crust of bread and one nibble of cheese. That hard old lump of cheese smelled delicious. It took all her will power to wrap up the remainder, and put it back in the pack. She needed a long drink from the pool near the rock where she drank last night. She considered the idea of not returning to the same spot but then it seemed to make sense to avoid too many different stopping places at the brook. That would only increase the opportunity for others to discover her tracks.

After her drink, she packed her few belongings and headed away from the direction of the manor using the morning sun as a guide. *Thank goodness for all the books I read,* she thought to herself as she moved carefully through the forest always on the lookout for dogs or people. From now on she would keep a steady pace and not flee in panic as she had done the day before. Now her movements must include stealth, as opposed to speed and distance, leaving as little trail as possible.

She brought to her mind the map of England that used to hang in the classroom back at Janes Manor. She knew the manor was near Sherbourne. The countryside east of Janes Manor was more rugged and less populated. Traveling through unfamiliar countryside undetected presented the biggest challenge but the best opportunity to escape detection.

She heard barking. *Dogs.*

They could see her and track her smell. They would be her biggest worry. She needed to head east while keeping away from farms with dogs!

With this plan in mind, she traveled for three days attempting to put as much distance between herself and her old home as possible. Then, she ran out of food. She needed to find something to eat without giving away her location. While crossing over a small rise, she spotted a village in the valley beyond. The layout was similar to that around the village near Janes Manor. A cluster of houses, a church, barns, and outbuildings associated with the raising of crops and cattle sat nestled in the valley. She couldn't see a manor house, but she knew it was there. Could she find food without being forced to steal? She didn't want to beg for food in a place this small. She was still too close to home and someone might recognize her or worse yet they might know she was wanted for murder.

Hattie waited for the sun to set before she began her descent into the valley. She traveled only a short distance before she rounded a nest of boulders and discovered an abandoned herder's hut. Since it was early spring, the hut stood vacant. She tried the door—locked! *Good grief* she thought *didn't any one trust anybody these days?* On a sudden impulse, she moved around to the side of the hut facing the meadow below. Sure enough, she found closed shutters indicating an opening. Picking up a rock, she broke the latch holding the two shutters together. She swung the shutters open, revealing a small opening. Fortunately, it proved large enough for her to wiggle through.

The hut, dug out of the ground, contained a dirt floor inside, much lower than the wall outside. She suffered a nasty bump on the shoulder as she fell inside. Looking up from her tumbled position on the floor, she surveyed her surroundings. A fireplace constructed from local stones filled the uphill side. A small table holding a candle and a food encrusted tin plate occupied the space between the fireplace and the door. A single narrow bunk covered by a straw tick mattress rested against the far wall, and a three-legged stool resting on its side near her feet completed the other things in the room that she could see. The fast approaching darkness prevented her from noticing anything else. There was just enough light left for her to stagger to the bunk before sleep and weakness overtook her.

Morning light streamed in the open window. She awakened feeling weak and dizzy from lack of food. Crawling off the bunk, she staggered to the table, managing to catch the edge before she fell. Leaning on the table, she made one last visual inspection of the hut's interior. Nothing had changed or magically appeared in the night. She picked up the tin plate, and stub of candle before she stumbled weakly to the window. She didn't have the strength or agility to pull her self up and crawl out. She moved the stool under the window. Standing on the stool, she managed to reach the window ledge, and lift herself up and over on the second try.

She closed the shutters and fixed the latch well enough to hold until she was long gone. She limped to a large flat rock that had obviously been used many times before as a seat from which to view the meadows below. She sat down to rest, and to think.

This hut sat quite some distance from the village she had seen in the valley. *Anyone staying up here, even overnight, would need to have a source of water at least.* There had been nothing in the hut used to store supplies. Something just wasn't right. Was there a spring or storeroom nearby? She sat very still listening for the telltale gurgle of water bouncing over the rocks or from a pipe.

Nothing.

She started her search all over again. There had to be something. She happened to glance to her left, away from the village, in fact it was the way she had approached the hut last night. Maybe that was why it took her so long to find the answer.

She arrived at the hut in twilight. As she crossed the ridge, her feet had quite naturally intersected and followed a dim trail, invisible last night, but plain to see now in broad daylight. Her eye followed the trail to the point where it curved down the hill among the rocks. She noticed something different about the grass. Not a greener patch, for the rains had been keeping all the meadow a brilliant green, but a longer, more mature growth filled one area.

Pushing herself up from the rock where she sat, she began to limp down the trail dragging her bad leg a little just too tired to make the extra effort she normally used to keep the limp unnoticed by others. Approaching the rocks, she could make out a door fitted into a man-made arch. This door was not locked, but was held closed by a large rock tilted against it. Hattie looked around and found a stout stick hidden in the rocks that had apparently been used before to pry the rock away from the door. The open door revealed stone steps leading down into a root cellar.

The cave-like room Hattie entered proved quite large, not as large as the hut, but big enough to have wooden shelves on each side and a workbench built across the back. The shelves were almost empty. She did find a partially full tin of black tea, another larger tin with maybe a quart of flour, and a third labeled *Sugar*. Empty of course, but the tight lids had kept the bugs out. She also found an empty whiskey flask. *Probably held about a pint* she thought to herself. Water seeping through the rocks had collected in a pool built beside the steps. She used the empty sugar tin as a cup, and scooped up a drink. It was so good and so cold! The tin, while appearing empty, still had sugar crystals stuck in the creases. It provided her with a sudden boost of energy, which immediately revived her. She wanted to drink another tin-full but chose to wait knowing that too much cold water on an empty stomach could cause a cramp. She might need to run for her life, and a cramp would be fatal.

The prize find stuck up from the top of the workbench. It was a butcher's knife obviously used by the herder to cut up meat and bread. A bucket also rested on the bench.

Probably used to feed the dogs.

The shelves on the opposite wall yielded a burlap bag containing a few small wrinkled potatoes. These she washed in the spring. She proceeded to rinse out the whiskey flask and the bucket, leaving them beside the spring ready to be filled with fresh, clean water from the spring. She made two trips up the path to the hut placing her treasure near her bag. On her return to the cellar, she filled the flask and sugar tin with water after taking one last long drink. She hobbled up the steps and closed the door. Returning to the rock near the hut, she packed everything in her canvas bag and sat down to think, munching on a couple of the raw potatoes.

She could head down the hill and across the meadows as she originally planned or take another route. Going down hill still posed a risk of discovery. Yesterday, she was willing to take that risk. Now, with the supplies she had found in the springhouse, she could look at other options. Should she stay in the hut for a while? It was deserted and might even be abandoned, but the herder and his dogs might return any day now. Also living inside, she would not be able to detect their approach. The third choice involved backtracking, up into the rougher country behind the hut. That direction also kept her moving east, the direction she needed to go to get away from Janes Manor.

With a sigh of resignation associated with the obvious choice of climbing the hill, she picked up her now much heavier pack and headed up into the rocks. Her slow going became slower still. The burst of energy from the sugar water, and the potatoes soon faded under the uphill struggle. She found it necessary to stop more and more often. She needed to find someplace where she could hide and rest soon. Leaning her pack against a rock, she sat there using it as a backrest. She watched the clouds moving across the sky, and tried to pick out puffy white faces and animals as she rested. She watched the clouds drift by. She imagined mansions and castles where she was a queen and not just a serving girl. The thought came to her that learning to serve others was not bad. Maybe serving was a part of learning to become a queen?

It was several minutes before she noticed the soaring black birds that moved beneath the much larger images in white. *A hawk?* Soon one was joined by another and then a third. She could make out as many as six or seven birds soaring and circling over one area. She watched for several minutes but the black birds continued to orbit about a point out of her sight, around the corner of the rocky ridge.

Hattie's ever-present curiosity overwhelmed her caution. Picking up her bag, she approached a point where she could get a look at what attracted the birds. All she could see was a large, dark object wedged among the rocks.

It appeared to be moving!

No, the birds hopping about were doing the moving. The object itself remained still, still as death. She shuddered in fear, but continued her stealthy approach.

It was a cow.

Probably lost its way and fell in the rocks during a winter storm. Now with spring coming on the decomposition had sped up and its smell attracted the birds. Closer examination revealed that a huge section of hide along the back from the neck to the hindquarters was still intact.

Hattie had helped Pap skin critters at home. It was deemed punishment at the time, but she had found the butchering process interesting since it allowed her to investigate the anatomy of the different critters she studied in her books. The breeze carried a terrible odor! But, it was not much worse than the smell in the slaughterhouse back home. Here at least, she could move away, up wind, and get a breath of air when it became too bad. She wanted that skin. Cow skin became leather and with leather she could make a sheath and belt for her knife, and new shoe soles. This rough ground was wearing holes in hers.

The hide proved too heavy to carry. She decided to just drag it behind her. After a mile or so, she stopped to rest. She discovered that dragging the hide over the rough ground removed the meat and fat. Seeing this, she swapped ends when she started out again thus scraping the entire hide as she moved across the rocks and gravel on the trail across the mountain.

Her timing proved more fortunate than she realized. She skinned the cow on the perfect day. Had she found the cow earlier, the hide would have been green and without the proper chemicals she could not have cured it herself. Time, the weather, and natural elements in the rocks around the carcass had promoted the curing process. The carcass would have rotted or baked hard in the summer sun if she had discovered it at a later time. The process, while not perfect, proved good enough to meet her needs.

Late afternoon found Hattie looking for a place to stop for the night. She noticed some trees down the mountain a ways that looked interesting.

She hid the hide and her pack and taking the knife with her began a slow approach. She discovered that a small stream falling from the rocks up above had formed a small pond. She lay on top of the rocks looking down, carefully scouting the area. The water rested in a dip in the hills that could not be seen from below. If the sunlight had not been just right, she doubted that she would have seen it from above. It was a tiny oasis surrounded by heather covered hills and large protruding boulders. After finding a way down to the pond, she returned to pick up her pack and hide. She moved slowly down through the rocks to the pond.

She found a small slip of sandy beach back under a ledge on the uphill side where past floodwaters had created a smooth area roughly six feet across. She dropped her belongings and flopped down to rest. The crystal clear water in the pond attracted her attention. She decided to take a bath. From the water she saw a patch of wild onions and some other edible plants nourished by the pond. After bathing, she picked them and brought them to her camping area.

Now all I need for a nice stew is a fat hare and a fire.

She worried over that problem as she sat munching on the plants. The pond was in an excellent location. She was exhausted from constant travel with little to eat. She needed a resting place. This was as good as she could hope to find. She would rest here for a few days. With that decision made she fixed a bed for the night and dropped into another dreamless sleep.

Singing birds awakened her at dawn. As she started to shake off the shawl, she caught a flicker of movement. She froze in place and looked more closely. At first all she saw was a large round eye looking at her. Soon, she picked out the shape of a hare. Even as she watched, it flicked its ears and vanished. Getting up from her bed, she walked over to where she had seen it. She could still make out its tracks in the mud at the edge of the pond. She turned and looked about hoping to see other animals but saw nothing.

Oh how hunger can change our attitudes she thought. Two weeks ago a hare was just a timid woodland creature, now it was dinner. No, it was more than that. It meant survival.

She needed a fire to boil water for tea. Oh, she so wanted a cup of tea! A fire, how could she make a fire, or catch a hare to cook on it? The heroes in the books she read always had a fire but no one explained how to start one without matches.

Hattie didn't know what made her open the tin with the tea in it. Maybe she just needed assurance that the tea really existed. Maybe she hoped that the smell of the rich heady aroma from the leaves would help to ease her desire. For whatever reason, she opened the tin holding the tea. She had scrambled about, moving in a hurry that day in the dark cellar. She noted the same brand cook always kept on the shelf in the kitchen. Not the good stuff they served to Mrs. Janes and her friends, but the more common mix purchased for the hired help. A quick glance that day in the cellar had been enough to verify there was indeed tea in the tin. Here in the daylight, she opened the tin and saw the corner of a small wooden box nestled in the tea leaves.

Matches!

The box was empty.

Hattie flopped to the ground, frustration bringing tears to her eyes. A glimmer of an idea began to enter her brain. Matches-Matchlocks? What came next in that book she had read about guns and gunpowder? Flintlocks emerged as the next generation of guns. The gunpowder ignited when the trigger was pulled releasing a steel hammer on a piece of flint. What if she could find a flint rock? She could use the back of her butcher's knife. It was made of steel. She could find a flint rock by striking the rocks around her camp. After considerable searching and testing, she finally found a rock that gave off sparks and her scratching finally produced a fire.

Hattie knew she still had a problem. Smoke from a fire would point right to her location. She decided to wait until darkness could hide the smoke. She laid back down both to continue resting and also to bring to her mind all she had read that might help her survive. She wanted—no— needed that hare. How did she go about catching a rabbit? She hadn't learned how from a book but from listening to Pap!

She remembered listening when he had taught her younger brothers how to build snares to capture small animals. Hattie had watched and listened but since building snares and capturing hares was considered unsuitable for young ladies she had never really made one herself. First she would need some type of strong cord. Maybe a strip from the cowhide would work. She tried that first. It wasn't working. The rough unseasoned cowhide would not form a loop that would close quick enough to catch anything. She sharpened the knife on a flat stone and carefully trimmed the rough edges from the rawhide strip. Then, she soaked the raw hide in water to make it more flexible. Finally, she rubbed the rawhide with wax from the candle picked up in the shepherd's hut. This helped to make the rawhide strip slippery and supple. Pausing for a moment, she decided that one snare might not do it. She had noticed several tracks in the pond mud at different locations and decided she would need at least three snares to increase the odds of success. Next, she rigged the snares the way she remembered Pap explaining it to the boys.

She found a patch of mint while searching out the best locations for her snares, and rubbed her rawhide cords with the leaves. She later returned to the mint patch and picked some more leaves taking them back to camp and laying them out in the sun to dry. She also spent time searching for other herbs that she had read about or used in the past that were good for pain and other ailments thinking that they might come in handy some time. She silently thanked old Mora for her patience in answering questions from a curious child concerning the herbs she collected. Finding some cattails, she picked them having read that they were edible. She knew she would have to soak the roots and boil them first before eating them.

She built a small fire that evening. Using the driest sticks and branches she could find, she kept the fire so small she could have made it in a teacup. But it did the job. She finally sipped on a cup of hot tea. After drinking the tea, she took some flour and fuzz from the cattail blossom and stirred it together with a small green stick. When she had a small lump of pasty dough on the end, she toasted it over her fire and ate it right off the stick. Building up the fire and using the dog bucket, she heated water and boiled the cattail roots and left them to soak.

Hattie stayed at the pond for five days. By the fifth day she had regained her strength at the expense of almost all her food including the three rabbits she was able to catch in her snares. By that time the rabbits had grown wary of her traps and her other supplies were nearly gone.

She kept busy. She cut the cowhide into new insoles for her shoes, and placed three extra pair in her pack. She used the rabbit entrails and sinews to make several long cords that would prove useful for future snares and tying other things up as needed. She also cut a belt from the rawhide and made a sheath for her butcher's knife. She made one more thing from the cowhide, a pouch to carry her journal. She tried to write a few brief words in the journal using a sharp stick dipped in wood ashes soaked in water.

The morning of the sixth day, she arose early and walked away from her pond feeling much more confident that she could make it on her own. The knowledge from the books she had read coupled with intelligent application of that knowledge, helped her to rise up and survive.

Chapter 3

Hattie's Journal

12 May 1853: I have a twin sister. She lives with my real
father. Aunt Tillie works for them. I wonder if they
ever think of me?

Anne Kirkland stretched and then kicked her legs to throw all her covers off. She let go with a scream so loud it hurt her own ears so she screamed again. Tillie heard the scream as she climbed the back stairs used by the servants to reach the second floor of the Kirkland home in London. She had been expecting the scream, but even after eight years, she still wasn't used to it. Lizzie, the upstairs maid, complained of not feeling well and tripped on the stairs and dropped the first breakfast tray. The poor girl thought she was going to lose her job. The entire Kirkland household staff was fully aware of the trouble Anne could cause. They also knew that Tillie would do everything she could to see that they kept their jobs. She was sensitive to the problem, plus she would have to find a replacement to put up with Anne's terrible tantrums—and smile while listening.

"Here we go, mistress Anne," she said, trying her best to sound cheery. She placed the tray on the side table and reached down for the bed covers Anne had kicked off earlier. "Do you want these on or off, dearie?"

"I don't care what you do with them. They are too hot and heavy in the morning and too cold at night. Get me some better ones," she screamed. She proceeded to jump to the floor, and crouch on all fours. "I guess I will have to eat here. You treat me like a dog so I will become one today." With that being said, she began to howl like a dog in pain.

Tillie was so tired of these games. Every day brought the same thing with all the new wrinkles a child's mind could invent, but what could she do. Mr. Kirkland left specific instructions that Anne was to receive anything she wanted. Her room had to be the nicest in all of London. It was probably more ornate and plush than Queen Victoria's. Pink velvet drapes over French lace covered the tall windows. The plush carpet was pale green and so soft and deep it covered Tillie's shoes. The bed and matching dresser were made from polished English walnut with ivory inlays of animals from the fairy tale books. The two bedrooms on each side had been turned into storage areas offering immediate access to every toy a child's imagination could conjure up. Tillie's orders were specific and she knew from previous experience that she would be chastised in front of Anne should she incur the little brat's disfavor.

"Do you want the curtains open or closed?" She had learned to pose questions that required Anne to decide between two options. Giving Anne more than two choices would provoke a scream indicating the choice was too difficult. A single choice invariably resulted in "no" for an answer. Asking Anne to make up her own mind would likely result in some infantile decision impossible to satisfy.

"It's a beautiful day. Maybe we can take a ride along the Thames today. Or would you prefer to go to your favorite pond near the park?" she offered. *Maybe you will decide to do all of us a favor and jump in,* she thought to herself.

Tillie wondered how the other twin was doing. It had been a long time since she had heard from her daughter. Her thoughts drifted back to that cold, stormy, February night. She had wrapped the other one in a blanket not much bigger than the doll blanket she was folding in Anne's room. The eyes staring at her from that trusting little face had seemed to say, "Give me a chance and I will make it on my own." Panic had driven her out the door. She feared Mr. Kirkland would see her as she crept down the back stairs to the servant's entrance and out into the cold, blustery night with the bent and twisted baby. The baby had not uttered a sound. Tillie feared she had died. Placing the still, small body next to her daughter, she had whispered a few words of comfort to both of them. She scooped up her daughter's dead baby and hurried back to the house to see to Anne. With her mother dead, Anne would need nourishment. They would need to find a nursing mother that could supply milk. With so many things on her mind, the fate of that other twin rested with her daughter.

A letter had arrived several months later indicating that her daughter had asked old Mora the healing lady that lived in the hills behind their farm to see to "Hattie." The soaks and braces were working and it looked like the baby would be able to walk after a fashion. It would take longer than normal, but Mary indicated she was making progress. The child showed signs of an early wit and intelligence. Her ability to communicate by talking and acting out her needs more than compensated for her inability to walk or crawl about.

Anne's strident demands interrupted Tillie's thoughts. "I have decided to play by myself in my room today. I want all my dolls set up. We will be having tea at ten, cucumber sandwiches for everyone at twelve and tea again at four. I will then dress for dinner with Papa at seven. Where is Lizzie? I want her here all day. I will need her to help with the dolls."

"Lizzie, ain't feelin so well today miss. I can send Dora or Francis. Which would you like?" asked Tillie.

"Both will do just fine." Anne answered as she began to pick at her now cold breakfast. Fortunately, that's the way she liked it. Probably because by the time she settled down from her morning tantrum it was always cold. *And so begins another day jumpin' to the foibles of Anne Kirkland*, thought Tillie to herself as she left to give Dora and Francis their instructions.

Walking back to the kitchen, Tillie had time to think back to the promise she made to Caroline Kirkland before she died. Caroline seemed to know even before her labor started that she would not survive. She made Tillie promise to take care of the baby just as she had promised Caroline's mother that she would take care of her. Tillie loved Caroline as if she were her own child. She had raised her and accompanied her here when she married Thomas Kirkland. An intense wave of guilt and despair drifted over her as she realized that she was failing to meet Caroline's expectations. Not only had she abandoned one baby to a life of servitude, she was raising the other as a nightmare.

Anne crawled back into bed after Tillie left. The rug on the floor did not keep the cold away from her bones. It also hurt to lay there even if it was the softest rug in London. Anne became bored just sitting in bed, but the thought of doing anything about it brought immediate revulsion to mind.

What if father could hire a puppeteer to sit behind a little theatre? A box as big as an armoire aught to do it. The puppets could put on a show for her while she lay in bed watching. If she didn't like the show, she could ring a bell like the one used to call the servants during meals. The puppeteer would then start a different show with new puppets and new costumes. It would be glorious fun and she would never be bored again. She would ask father to see to it when he came home.

Thomas Kirkland arrived home at 5:30. He had stopped off at the club as usual and had imbibed more than a few of his new favorite drink composed of gin and bitters. Jensen the butler met him at the door, deftly catching the hat and cane tossed to him by Mr. Kirkland as he passed through the foyer. "I will be in the study Jensen, have Tillie call me when Anne decides it is time to dine."

"Sir, Miss Anne indicated she would be dining at seven. But of course, that was this morning."

"Call me anyway. I may take a short nap. I've had a busy day."

Jensen smiled to himself, almost laughing out loud. How busy could one be if one's only occupation was squandering the family fortune on ridiculous ideas that never amounted to anything, except to waste money? Jensen believed that even with his limited education, he could achieve a higher success rate than Mr. Kirkland. But then, he hadn't lost his wife and killed a daughter all in the same night, like his employer. That story remained as common gossip among the household staff. Mr. Kirkland had never been convicted of the crime, but there were no secrets here concerning that awful night eight years ago. Kirkland's heart was already dead. It was a race to see if his alcohol pickled body would go before his fortune.

People asked Jensen why he stayed with Kirkland. He had several pat answers, he usually just answered by saying, "Loyalty, I guess." The real reason involved his system. He collected a cut from several businesses that he used to purchase all the extravagant toys, games, food, and distractions Anne Kirkland insisted her father buy for her. Everyone knew that her father doted on her. That Jensen made a small percentage on each purchase, remained his personal secret. He skimmed just enough to slowly build up an "inheritance" for his retirement. Thomas Kirkland, constantly befuddled by alcohol, would run out of money long before he caught on to the scheme.

Dinner that evening started in the usual manner. The servants moved busily about bossed by Anne's demands. The table sparkled with crystal and silver reflections off glowing candles. A direct contrast to the large quantities of dull tasteless food Anne preferred. The servants appeared more intent on avoiding Anne's reprimands than pleasing the diners. Thomas Kirkland dozed in a drunken slouch at the head of the table and watched with an annoyed look on his face.

What kind of a monster have I created? There must be a useful diversion she can master. She can really be a sweetheart when she tries. She could be so like her mother. My little girl, my sweetheart is slipping away! He needed to step in but didn't know how to do it.

Sitting up and leaning forward, elbows on the table, he spoke to Anne. "Sweetheart, I want you to begin learning the things all young ladies of good breeding are expected to know. I will instruct Tillie and Jensen to begin a search for a competent governess to instruct you and help you become the charming young gentlewoman I know you to be." With this announcement he stood from his chair and left the dining room.

Run away as usual you coward thought Tille as she continued clearing the table. *Leave the dirty work for me.*

Anne pretended to not hear her father's announcement. She felt confident in her ability to wear him down. If nothing else worked, she could always terrorize any governess they sent to her and send her packing. She smiled to herself. *Just let them try to make me do anything I don't want to do.*

She frowned.

She had missed her opportunity to ask her father about the puppet box. He was in one of his dark moods anyway. She needed to tread carefully when they came on.

It soon became obvious that Kirkland was serious. Anne would need to have some breeding beaten into her if nothing else. He needed to feel certain she could find a suitable marriage as soon as possible. Then his responsibility would end. Maybe he could start a new life? Driven by guilt and baffled by her belligerent attitude, he needed help to avoid careening down a road to disaster.

After Anne's many arguments and tantrums failed, they drafted a suitable advertisement. Jensen dropped it off at the newspaper office on his way to visit his bank where he deposited the latest payment into his retirement plan. He double-checked all the documents stored in the safety deposit box. Everything needed to create his new identity rested inside, ready for the day he would leave Kirkland and never return. He added the new stock certificates to his growing portfolio. Kirkland poured money down worthless ventures based on what he perceived to be solid investments in proven, but unfortunately dying, industries. Jensen placed his capital in modern businesses driven by the industrial inventions that were creating growth opportunities throughout the civilized world. He was getting rich while poor Kirkland was heading for disaster, while attempting to find a solution to his problems in the bottom of a bottle.

It took over a year and a long line of governesses before Thomas Kirkland admitted to Tillie that shaping Anne into a socially acceptable young woman was beyond their capability. The struggle had simply strengthened Anne's ability to berate and bully any and all around her to her own will. He would just have to accept his fate. Giving in to Anne's demands might well become his lifelong punishment for killing the one person he had ever truly loved.

Tillie could do nothing to help Mr. Kirkland this time. She was tired. The pain that had started in her belly, moved to her back. Now she noticed her legs going numb. She suspected and rightly so that she was not long for this life. She talked to her Priest and made her peace with God by writing a letter to her daughter. In it she enclosed a second letter to be given to Hattie. She died in her sleep a few days later.

The years passed slowly after Tillie died as Thomas Kirkland driven by depression drifted farther into the depths of drunken oblivion. He began to spend more and more time at home lost in his own dark thoughts. He found it difficult to hire competent help. Anne's tantrums abated somewhat, mainly due to his presence in the house and Anne's growing lackadaisical attitude or desire to sustain any emotional feeling. She slowly turned into a fat, slovenly, young woman totally dependent on others.

Anne drifted from one illness to another most brought on by lack of exercise, rich food or a vivid imagination. She had given up all desire for an independent life as one failed diversion after another drove her deeper into depression. Her demands came less often not because her wants diminished but because she just didn't have the energy to complain any more. Her father's business ventures continued to falter. The Kirkland home, never a happy place disintegrated into a dreary house inhabited by strangers bound together by guilt, greed, and apathy.

A park with a pond sparkled in the sunlight not far from the Kirkland home. One of Anne's few pleasures included a walk to this park. She would sit on a bench near the pond, and watch several varieties of waterfowl, including ducks, geese, and swans, as they went about living life. Anne would stare at the scene. The reflections of trees, sky, and the birds would constantly change with the weather. It was so peaceful here. She wished she could paint the picture, capturing the greens, the blues, the silver flashes as the birds took flight off the water. But, painting was too hard. She had tried it once. Her hands would not command the brush to please her. The colors always came out wrong. Her teacher was always so critical and demanding. Like everything else it became just too much effort. So, she must be content to just sit and watch and never do. Work, after all, was for servants.

On a day shortly before Anne's twentieth birthday, a solicitor visited with Kirkland at his home. The news signalled disaster. Creditors began to sense that the Kirkland name created by Thomas' father and grandfather was tarnished beyond recovery.

Jensen picked up enough comments as he served drinks in the study to know that the time had come. He left that night. Sobered by fear, Kirkland pulled himself together well enough over the next few days to sell off the remainder of the family assets. He and Anne left town the following morning. When the solicitor returned at noon the next day, he found only one lonely servant girl left to answer the door. She had no answers to the questions he fired at her. Others followed the angry solicitor over the next few days. On the following Monday morning, she too was gone.

Anne Kirkland started to complain almost immediately. "Father, I don't want to go for a drive at this ungodly hour. Why did you have Dolly pack my things in those trunks? I will need to wear some of those things."

"I know you will dear. That's why Dolly packed them. The trunks are safely secured in the carriage boot. Now you just relax and try to take a little nap," her father reasoned in an exasperated voice, "or just sit back and enjoy the ride. We will be out of the city in a little while, where we will need to change to another coach. We can have a lovely breakfast while our luggage is transferred."

"What! Another coach?" Anne screamed, beginning to realize that this trip was more than a ride in the park.

"And stop that infernal screaming. You know I can't stand it!" he hollered back at her

"I won't! I won't! I won't! I—I—I." Anne's screams dissolved to blubbering silence as he shook her violently. He finally stopped, gasping for breath. Seeing the look of horror on Anne's face, he let his hands move from their grip on her shoulders to a comforting embrace.

"I'm so sorry Anne. You just don't know what that screaming does to me. Every time I hear it I remember the night you were born and the horrible events that happened."

In a rare moment of sympathy for her father, Anne asked, "What really happened that night father? I have heard rumors and bits of servant's gossip all my life. Please tell me the whole story."

He bowed his head and wouldn't look at her. The silence stretched on. For a while, Anne thought he would remain silent on the subject as he had in the past. Her father began. "I was deeply in love with your mother. I found her and courted her rather late in life. It was one of those arranged meetings. I'm sure you know the kind I mean. One of her friends had married a business associate of mine.

We met at a party where she was the unattached female and I was the unattached male. For once the matchmakers got it right. We courted for several months, but we both felt right about each other from the start. We were deeply in love. Our marriage and time together was truly beautiful. It was the happiest time of my life. Knowing we were soon to have a child together, only increased my happiness."

"Then came that terrible dark night." he gasped a little and tears began to form. "First came those awful screams. Exactly like yours. I began to drink. I was taking a sip of brandy with each scream. I became quite drunk, and then the screaming stopped."

"Why father? What happened?" Anne interrupted.

For a time, Thomas Kirkland could only look at Anne with his face etched in sadness. "She died, Anne. She died giving birth to you and your sister."

"My sister?" screamed Anne in disbelief. She watched him wince once again. "I'm sorry father, please continue. I must hear about this sister!" Anne continued to stare at her father her curiosity aroused by the story.

"She was your twin. I am not quite certain, but I think she died that night. Remember, I was quite drunk from all that brandy. People were rushing about. The doctor wanted to leave and was pestering me for his payment. Tillie was shouting orders at all the servants. As I recall, Father Jaimison was there. He christened you Anne Victoria. Your mother wanted you named after Princess, now Queen Victoria. You were the oldest by a few minutes and so received that name. The other, your twin sister, I named Helen Marie after our mothers. The last thing I remember before everything went blank was Tillie asking me what to do about the other one. I didn't want to know about the other one."

Kirkland continued, "She was not a healthy baby. She was grotesque as a matter of fact. Her crooked legs and back made her look like a gnome. She cried incessantly. I think I told Tillie to get rid of her."

"Why?" Interrupted Anne horrified at the thought that her father might have killed his own defenseless child.

"In my drunken befuddled state I felt it was she who had killed my beloved Caroline, your mother," muttered Kirkland.

"How?"

"I think the doctor explained it to me this way. As you and your sister grew in your mother's womb, you became entangled with one another. He said you were very lucky. Many times, babies actually grow together sharing a limb or other body parts. He called them Siamese Twins. In your case you were not connected just terribly tangled up together. This situation created the problem that killed your mother. She died before the doctor could get you separated and pull you out."

"It all sounds so terribly sad and ugly," said Anne quietly. "Did you ever ask Tillie what happened?"

"Indeed, it was exactly that, terribly sad and ugly. I tried talking to Tillie about it but she would always change the subject or just walk away. Her unwillingness to discuss what happened always left a question in my mind as to what really happened. You may have a twin sister somewhere but we will never know the truth with Tillie gone." They completed the remainder of the carriage ride in silence. Both lost in their own thoughts.

They stopped at a crossroads inn near Croyden for several days. Kirkland needed to find just the right transportation arrangement. He finally located a man driving a freight wagon who was returning home empty. He lived near the town of Wylye. He would be taking little used, out of the way roads. Kirkland had been looking for just this sort of opportunity. They loaded their trunks and bags in the back. "I think I will ride here in the back," said Kirkland holding on tightly to the satchel he had been keeping with him since arriving at the inn. "Anne, you can ride on the seat next to the driver. If you get tired later, we will switch and you will be able to rest back here."

A different much more silent and thoughtful Anne smiled at him and murmured, "Anything you say father." Unfortunately that compliant attitude was soon shaken out of Anne by the constant bouncing and rough language from their driver as he urged the team pulling the lightly loaded freight wagon towards home. What had started as silent annoyance soon elevated into grumbled moans and from that moved on to loud, vocal, angry comments on every hole and rock in the road. Even moving Anne to the back of the wagon where she could ride in cushioned comfort failed to quiet the constant complaining.

The noise from the back only strengthened the driver's resolve to push on. He cracked his whip over the backs of his horses, and made a fateful decision to drive through the night planning to rid himself of his annoying passengers as soon as possible.

The skittish snorting horses jerking the reins, failed to alert him to the impending danger.

Chapter 4

Hattie's Journal

10 May 1853: I had never met a man as strange as Kim Wang. He saved my life and I will always be eternally grateful.

H attie stopped—filled with indecision It wasn't the first time and she was sure it would not be the last. But this problem definitely held her attention. She had reached a river last night. Her first thought had been to just wade or swim across. She found a place to spend the night deciding to cross early in the morning. Here she stood with the sun turning the river to a glittering moving mass that looked more like molten metal than dirty water. It was much too deep and moving way too fast for her to attempt a crossing. The spring rains had turned the once peaceful stream into a raging torrent. The river had overrun its banks and formed a swamp full of brambles and brush that prevented her from reaching the main channel where crashing waves and large trees carried by the brown dirty water created a maelstrom impossible to cross.

Do I go upstream or down? To cross here is suicide.

Hattie chose to move away from the edge of the flooded area and turn upstream figuring the higher she went the less water would drain into the river. She followed a dim, rocky, mountain trail along a ridge-line that paralleled the raging torrent running below her. She decided to investigate every mile and look for a way to cross. Finally, she came to an area where high rocky banks on both sides held the river in a narrow channel. The river's banks compressed the flow and turned it into a chute, filled with dangerous rapids. *More suicide* she thought as she trudged along.

Above the rapids, the river formed a large calm lake. She might be able to cross here if she could build a raft to put her supplies on and then push it ahead of her as she swam across. With this plan in mind, she walked along looking for the right place to build and launch a raft. She found a large tree with a hollow place. She hid all her things except for her knife, and began to search for wood with which to build a raft.

She soon became totally engrossed in searching for broken branches the right size for her raft. She felt total surprise when a hand grabbed her by the shoulder pulling her back.

"Well, well what have we here."

The deep, hoarse voice seemed to come from the depths of a whiskey barrel. Hattie felt herself spinning around. Her butcher knife flew from her fingers. The smell that followed the harsh husky laugh from the hairy-faced man, confirmed her impression of the whiskey barrel. Hattie twisted and scratched at the man but his grip proved too strong. "Hey lads, c'mere and see what I've found for your pleasure," chortled the black hairy face.

Soon Hattie found herself surrounded by four more equally unkempt and bad smelling men. They were all leering at her and making vulgar but vivid comments concerning her immediate future. She never saw the blow coming at her. All she saw were streaks of light racing down an ever-narrowing dark tunnel of unconsciousness.

She woke to pain—agonizing pain! She half-remembered moments of being smothered by hairy, dirty, foul smelling faces, laughing, laughing, laughing.

More laughter brought a wave of remembered pain and nausea. Laughter and flickering firelight casting long ghostly shadows revealed drunken men cavorting and cussing as they partied nearby. No attempt had been made to tie her up. Why should they? Here she lay, a broken whimpering waif, wrapped in the bloody shreds of what was once the dress reserved for her Sunday best. The dress now as ruined as she was by these beasts from a world she had only read about in stories. The reality of lying there wrapped in rags and pain presented a completely and crudely different picture from the stories consumed by candlelight in her safe warm chimney room curled up in her velvet chair.

Why had they left her alive? The answer came on the heels of the question. *They weren't done with her yet!* With this thought raging in her mind, she forced her arms to drag her away from the fire. Her legs seemed paralyzed. They were no help, just dead weight draging behind her.

She didn't know how long she struggled to move silently through the grass. The fire was no longer visible. The shouts of drunken laughter had turned to silence. She noticed when her hands became wet. At first, she thought it was blood. Then she discovered the mud on her face. She must be near water. She pulled herself along one more body length and felt a coolness kiss her face when she stopped. The water revived her somewhat, giving her enough energy to pull herself further along. Her face and shoulders submerged for a moment. Finally, her whole body floated free, making it easier to keep putting distance between her and the men somewhere behind her.

Hattie floated along the edge of the lake as far out as she could go, and still pull with her hands in the mud and weeds along the lake bottom. She pulled and pushed herself along wanting to put as much distance as possible between herself and the ugly laughing men behind her. She felt numb from the waist down. Nothing worked except her arms and the natural reflex to keep her head above water. She found the log with her head. The painful bump broke it loose from its anchor of weeds and brush holding it to the shoreline. She grasped the log as it caught the current from the swollen river.

She couldn't touch the bottom! For a moment panic gripped her. She clung to the log with all her remaining strength. Parts of her torn dress had become entangled in the submerged branches of the log trapping her. It was pulling her into the slow, but ever-strengthening current. The lake quickly became a river. With the last of her failing strength, she knotted shreds of her dress around a branch on the log and slipped into oblivion.

Once again she awoke to pain. Pain and panic passed through her mind as she glimpsed a face smiling at her. But, it was a smooth face with slanted eyes, and a mouth full of large white teeth. She was so startled and curious she forgot her fear. A spoon moved in front of the face and the teeth said, "You dlink please." The warm bitter liquid tasted awful. She drifted into a gray fuzzy cloud, but the pain went away. She vaguely remembered the sequence repeating except it included several spoons full of what tasted like chicken broth before the warm bitter liquid returned her to blissful slumber.

Hattie opened her eyes and looked around. She still felt pain but it was more like a throbbing ache. The sharp knives no longer stabbed her. She tried to move and gasped. The stabbing pain returned in a rush. She took a shallow breath and cried out.

She tried to focus on where she was. She could see a small room painted white. One window with a canvas curtain provided a measure of dim light. Moving her head gently from side to side, she noticed a small table next to the bed. The table contained an oil lamp, a pitcher and a basin. Her searching hands found a soft bed covered by a light sheet. Further inspection seemed just too hard. She closed her eyes and returned to sleep.

The next time she awoke, darkness covered the curtain. A lamp, turned low, burned on the bedside table. A man in a strange robe stood with his back to her. He cast a large threatening shadow on the wall at the foot of her bed. She inhaled a frightened breath. He turned, revealing the same toothy grin and strange slanted eyes she remembered.

"Then I wasn't dreaming," she whispered.

"You see me when I feed you?" asked the face.

"Who are you?" she asked squinting, trying for a better look.

"For now, you call me Kim," he said, with a toothy smile, "you hungry? You eat more soup now." He lifted the bowl in his hand. Whatever it contained smelled delightful. He took that same big spoon she remembered and fed her spoonful after spoonful of delicious beef broth.

"Now you rest. We talk more in morning." Hattie drifted off to sleep before he had turned down the lamp and left the room.

Kim came into the room the next morning with the same grin on his face. He noticed that Hattie's eyes were open, but before she could say anything, he held up his hands. "I speak, you listen, save energy, after breakfast you talk."

"Several days ago, I drive home from visit to sick patient. I cross bridge and see you on log caught under bridge. I stop to see if you dead. You breathing so I bring you here, make you better. You have broken bones and you need operation. I look at old bone problem and fix some while you out. So good news, you walk better. But," the smile left his face, "you never make babies."

"That's for sure," muttered Hattie as she began to weep and grip the sheet until her knuckles turned white as she remembered the sight and smell of the dirty men covering her. It meant she would never have a child of her own. She would never know the pull of tiny fingers or a cry in the night for comfort. The family bonds of two hearts and one flesh would never be hers. She vowed that a man would never touch her like that again!

Stop it, Hattie! She had plenty to worry about without fussing over something she couldn't change. There were ways to find love and companionship without growing them inside you. She tried to imagine how she might tame a wild spirit such as herself. This thought made her smile and helped to calm the raging torrent of sadness mixed with anger boiling inside her.

"Now you eat. Get better." Kim ordered as he took extra pillows and placed them behind Hattie, raising her up. He left the room only to return in a moment with a large bowl of porridge with lots of milk, butter, and sugar mixed into it. Taking another pillow, he placed the bowl on Hattie's lap, gave her the spoon and left the room.

Hattie salted her porridge with tears of gratitude as she proceeded to eat every last bite. Nothing had ever tasted so good to her. She wondered if she could ever put the events of the past behind her? *No!* She told herself. *Don't put them behind you. Build on them, rise up! Make a better life by remembering but avoiding past mistakes.*

Later that day, she told Kim her entire story. She recounted why she had left home, and how she had survived in the hills of southern England. Kim just nodded and smiled. *He's pretty good at that nodding and smiling thing* thought Hattie. She decided that was a pretty good way to get people to talk out their problems. She would have to try it sometime.

Later that evening after Kim returned from visiting another patient, Hattie learned that Kim Wang came from Tibet. From early childhood until his eighteenth birth year, he trained as a "Guardian."

Whatever that was thought Hattie.

After completing his training, his grandfather asked him to accompany him on a pilgrimage to India. Kim realized he had a family obligation and accepted the opportunity to revere his beloved ancestor. The trip lasted two years. Kim had "many adventures." They ended when his grandfather died.

Left alone in India, Kim wandered about until he met a learned man of medicine. He became his apprentice and later companion. One day, he saved the life of an Englishman and they became good friends. The friend invited Kim to return to England with him. Kim accepted. His friend died in a duel and Kim found himself set adrift in another foreign land.

He wandered about for a while. Finally joining up with some gypsies. He learned the medicinal value of the local herbs from one they all called Oma. His medical skills eventually caused him to leave the gypsies.

He saved the life of a rich man's son trapped in a coach, wrecked along the highway, near their camp. To show his appreciation the man called "Kipring" gave Kim this house. Kim lived here and continued to provide medical help to those in the surrounding area that could not afford the services of a "real" doctor. Mr. Kipring continued to help Kim. He would send his young son, John Lockwood known as "Woody", to visit at regular intervals. He purchased food or medical supplies for Kim's practice. When Kim was not busy, he would regale young Woody with stories of his adventures in India.

"Where is Woody now?" asked Hattie.

"He move to Bombay in India," Kim replied.

Hattie, tired out from the day's activities, began to snore softly. Kim adjusted the pillows and sheet about her. The thought entered his head that this young lady had a very important mission in life. Her spirit was destined to touch many lives, but she needed to stand up to fierce struggles. She needed to survive, and he felt the strongest sense that he had to help prepare her for those struggles. With that thought in mind, he left her room to take his own rest.

Hattie's recovery moved at a slow and painful pace. As she returned to full strength, she was amazed to discover that she had more strength and agility than ever before. She attributed her recovery to the rigid set of exercises and physical workouts Kim developed for her. While she exercised, they discussed her situation. It would be difficult to prove that she was the victim of assault by Bart Janes. Wealth and power played such an important role in the English legal system. Hattie liked Kim's suggestion of hiding in plain sight, but how could she do that?

Kim came up with a suggestion, "Why not you become boy?"

Hattie felt shocked! "I can't do that!"

"No, no," Kim answered, "You just dress like boy and act like boy. I tell people you my apprentice. You work for me."

Hattie thought about this idea. "That might work, for a while anyway. I could wear boy clothes and cut my hair. It would make an excellent disguise. I like it."

They proceeded with the plan. Kim picked up clothes from different stores as he made his rounds. He coached Hattie on movements and mannerisms he observed boys making. Hattie, remembered back to the days watching Peter and Bart in the schoolroom. She quickly picked up on the male way of moving and talking. She discovered a natural talent as an actress. This helped to speed the process. Before long, she appeared in public as Kim's apprentice. She traveled with him and even did boy chores such as taking care of the horse and buggy, and cleaning the stable.

One day while they paused to rest after cleaning the stable and putting in fresh straw, Hattie asked Kim. "What did you mean the first day we talked. When you said you studied to be a Guardian?"

"Easier to show than to tell," Kim replied. "See stick we use to keep stable door crozed at night? Pick up, hit me, hard as you can."

"Oh, Kim, I can't do that. If I hurt you what would we do?"

"You not hurt me," smiled Kim. "No hit me, no get supper. You go bed hungry."

"Well, you asked for it," Hattie shouted taking a roundhouse swing at Kim. The stick flew from her hands and Kim stood smiling in front of her unharmed.

"You too easy," laughed Kim as he picked up the stick and handed it to Hattie. "You try again."

Hattie gripped the stick tighter, determined to make contact. She feinted with the first swing and then tried a backhand slap to Kim's rear. This time, because she had a tighter hold on the stick, she ended up flying head first into the manure pile. She managed to dig herself out, spitting manure. She looked up in time to see Kim laughing so hard tears ran down his cheeks. This infuriated Hattie, she came up from a sprinter's start ready to tackle him right there in the barnyard, and throw him in the manure pile! He dodged her rush, but as she went flying by he grabbed her, and prevented a nasty spill as she headed toward the carriage parked behind him. The lesson ended with both laughing hysterically.

"How did you do that?" exclaimed Hattie.

"That is what I learn as Guardian," Kim answered. "One resson verry important. Never hit attacker with hand. You save hands for helping people. You try hurt with hand you only hurt self. Hand full of small bone— hard to heal. We do enough for now you earn supper by making me raff."

"I want to learn how to do that!"

Part of each day, Kim and Hattie would train in the guardian arts of self defense. The other part involved training in medicine and surgery. At night, Hattie would read. Mainly she read medical journals and texts that Kim had acquired from his doctor friends, but she also studied history, philosophy, and law. When she finished reading an interesting article, she and Kim would discuss it's merits. Kim's input, based on centuries of far eastern philosophy would add interesting insights not mentioned in the modern texts she was reading. As they traveled around the country, Kim showed Hattie local herbs he used and taught her about the medicines he had studied in India. He also taught her other useful skills.

One such episode started when Hattie exclaimed, "Look there is a goldfinch!"

"Why you miss starlings, sparrows, nuthatch and wrens we pass in just the last mile or so?" Kim asked grinning at her.

"But they are not as pretty," retorted Hattie.

"Even your answer begs question. Do you see the wisdom in your answer?"

"Hattie remained silent for some time as she pondered his comment. Then she brightened and said, "First, I was not as observant as you great master," she said sarcastically bobbing her head at him. "Second, there were many birds with plain brown or gray feathers hiding in plain sight. One can become invisible in plain sight with the right feathers."

"Correct. You must rearn to hide in plain sight, my little goldfinch." And so it went day after day, lesson after lesson. What surprised and pleased Kim was that very seldom did Hattie need to repeat a lesson.

One day they traveled along a road that, while strange to Hattie, seemed somehow familiar. She turned to Kim and asked, "Have we ever traveled on this road before?"

He looked at her and then back at the road as he fussed with the reins. Finally when Hattie was almost ready to burst, he replied. "Just around the corner is prace where I find you under bridge."

Hattie stared at him in amazement. And then she smiled saying, "Of course, we eventually would have to go past here. It makes perfect sense."

"I avoid road many times in fear you would find it hard to come here again."

"Yes. I can see where you might want to spare me the pain of remembering. Do you suppose we could drive upstream along the river? There is something I want to find."

Kim turned the buggy along a dirt path that skirted the riverbank. They had only gone a short distance when Hattie raised her hand. "Will you stop here for a moment, please?"

Hattie gazed at the river and the hills surrounding their stopping place. She turned to Kim and said, "This is the place where I first encountered the river. I made the decision to turn upstream reckoning that the higher up the river I went the less water would drain into it and I would stand a better chance of crossing. Had I but known how close that bridge was I could have crossed over and been on my way. Kim, do you realize how that decision changed my life? I would not have encountered those scoundrels that ruined me! But, I also would never have met you and learned to protect myself, or learned so much about the art of healing."

Kim crouched on the seat, elbows resting on his knees with the reins held loosely in his hands. He turned his head toward her and grinned. "You make me feel bad and sad, same time."

"Oh Kim! That's the way I feel! One of Shakespeare's stories has this line, something about taking the tide and how that can change men's lives. I remember the moment when I stood here. My head told me to go upstream, but something kept whispering 'You may want to go another way.' What if I had listened? I might have found a good man like Pap and have a brood of brats hanging on me right now. That simple decision changed my life."

Kim slapped the horse on the rump with the reins and they continued on up the trail. He remarked, "Sometime we make decision with head and sometime with heart, every time better when we listen and follow resson learned from honorable teachers."

Hattie sighed as she remembered some of her teachers. Some added good, some bad but all had taught her something. She hoped the recipe was right when she baked up the story of her life.

They had traveled a considerable distance when Hattie exclaimed, "Stop here!" She jumped from the buggy and went running across the grass to a large tree. Kim marveled at how well she had recovered and was now able to move about. He felt certain other hands had helped him that night as he worked on her. The operation had taken many hours and he had been tired when he started. There had been moments when he had felt like a puppet being guided by a master's hands.

Kim couldn't see what she was doing behind the tree but soon she emerged carrying a moldy old pack. After throwing the pack into the buggy, she turned to Kim and said, "We can go on home now."

On the way home, she explained to Kim how she had left the pack in the hollow tree before being attacked. She wanted to recover a journal she had left in the pack. She hoped it had survived. Upon arriving home, Hattie found that the raw cowhide had hardened to the point that she had to break it to get the journal out. She borrowed pen and ink from Kim and retraced the entries previously written using the crude ink she had made from ashes and soot. Over the next few weeks, she wrote additional comments to bring the journal up to date.

Hattie awoke to rapid knocking on the cottage door. She stumbled out of bed and was nearly at the door in her nightdress when she heard voices. She paused and remembered that she must appear in public as a boy! Turning away from the door, she madly threw on her "boy clothes" and rushed into the main room in time to see Kim and another man, carrying someone inside.

Looking at Hattie, Kim ordered, "Fix table for examination."

Hattie went right to work. She found a clean white sheet and spread it on the table. As the men moved forward, a young woman squeezed through the door bumping against Kim in the process, causing him to stumble under the heavy load and fall, injuring his hand. The man they were carrying let out a terrible groan as he hit the floor and Kim grabbed his hand grimacing in pain. With Hattie's help, they placed the injured man on the table.

All the frightened young woman could do was stand wide-eyed grasping her elbows repeating, "I'm so sorry. I'm so sorry."

Kim looked at all of them. "Must do as I say, wrist broken or bad sprain. You lady, go heat water in kitchen. You," he nodded at at the man that had helped him. "Tell why you bring man here?"

The man answered, "My name is Jones. These folks are my neighbors. The missus there asked me to help bring her man to you. He had a bad bellyache, but he was able to climb in the wagon when we started. Now, he just groans and can't move by himself."

Looking at the patient, Kim said, "You take off man's shirt so I can see. Harry," the name he and Hattie had agreed to use in front of others, "you get me two inch bandage and small sprint." When Hattie handed him the bandage, he gave it back to her. "Wrap wrist and appry sprint."

With these tasks completed, Kim looked at Hattie. "Harry, we need more right. Go get more ramps." Hattie ran to do as she was told. Returning she saw Kim examining the man on the table. She placed two lamps on the little shelves built high up in the corners of the room especially designed for this purpose. She turned them up thus illuminating the man lying on his back on the table with Kim bent over examining him and pressing gently with his one good hand.

"This man need operation," muttered Kim looking up at Hattie. She moved to the special box where they kept the surgical supplies. She took out razor sharp scalpels, forceps, clamps, and the other instruments Kim usually asked for during surgery. She placed them in the wire basket they used for sterilization. She dunked them in the boiling water the young woman had prepared. Turning to place them near the table ready for use, she saw Kim with that silly toothy grin he wore when he was really in a serious mood. "You must prepare for surgery."

Hattie turned and took down a gown for herself and one for Kim. After donning her robe and mask, she turned to see Kim, with a mask on, holding his wrist. "Now you wash hands really good." She went to the kitchen to wash and it hit her. Kim was not dressing or washing! She turned to look at him wide eyed. She was going to operate not just hand him things.

"Is this lad really ready to do this?" asked the man when he realized what was going to happen. "He don't look old enough to spit let alone operate on someone." Hattie had to agree.

"He good apprentice learn much here. Besides, is emergency. I cannot do myself. Hand will not hold knife. I tell 'him' every move to make. This is only way. Appendix break soon, and man die quick. You take woman for ride to town get something to eat. Come back in couple hours."

They started with Kim directing Hattie's every move. Fortunately, the man survived the ordeal, and so did Hattie, although it was a near thing for both. After that, Hattie routinely assisted with surgeries becoming more and more adept and capable as the months passed. At first, she thought it strange that he would often ask her to do the fine stitches and close work. She passed it off as his way of teaching her the finer points of surgery.

Hattie was busy working in a closet near Kim's room one day. She was looking for the bolt of white muslin that she had put there the last time she cleaned the storeroom. They both needed new smocks, and she wanted to make more sheets for the operating table. Kim had told her, he had moved the material to the large closet next to his room, and she could use any material she found in the closet. She found the muslin on a chest right where Kim had said he put it.

She wondered what was in the chest? Kim had gone to Southampton to purchase supplies that were not available in the village. He would be gone all day. Feeling that old itch of curiosity, Hattie pulled the chest out into the middle of the room and opened it. Inside, she discovered several folded pieces of beautiful Chinese silk fabric. She found bright reds, yellows, greens and blues all in different shades and hues accented with black designs. She found one she especially liked, and set it aside. After all, he had said she could use anything she found in the closet. Christmas was coming and with the material she could make Kim a new tunic. When they were alone, he always wore his tunic and it was becoming dirty and even threadbare in places. She planned to have the new tunic ready as a special gift for him in time for Christmas.

They had celebrated the holiday the previous year even though Kim was not a christian. She had wanted to give him something special last year, but she had neither the funds nor the opportunity. She decided this year would be different. Taking his old tunic from the closet in his room, she traced out patterns on old newspaper. Laying the patterns on the beautiful new silk material, she took a deep breath and began to cut. She soon had all the pieces she would need. After hiding all the pieces of fabric in her room, she returned to Kim's bedroom to make sure that there was nothing he would notice to betray her secret.

She knew from past experience that he was a very observant fellow. She even checked the broom she used to sweep up when she was done. Several long strands of silk thread had unraveled from the material while she was cutting out the pieces. She carefully pulled them from the broom, winding them around her fingers as she did so. She wrapped the last couple of strands around the loop creating a colorful skein of silk thread. Walking back to her room, she impulsively picked up her journal and placed the thread between the pages creating a colorful bookmark.

When Christmas Day arrived Hattie felt sure her gift would be the best. Kim seemed truly amazed and pleased. He had been meaning to have a new tunic made and now he had a special one. He then produced a gift of his own for her. It was a metal box with a tight fitting cover and a handle much like a thin suitcase. Inside compartments lined with velvet, nested surgical instruments. The case folded flat so that both the top and bottom provided compartments for the instruments. Hattie remembered the silver at Janes Manor being kept in a similar type of box but one made of wood, without a handle. A velvet lid covered one part of the lower side of the box.

"You rift rid," grinned Kim. Underneath, a space appeared just big enough to hold her journal with a padded compartment for ink and pens. "This for you. Now you are real surgeon, have knowledge, skills, and tools. You rike gift?" asked Kim.

"Oh, Kim, it's beautiful. It's the best Christmas gift I have ever received. Thank you so very much!" Hattie replied giving him a quick hug.

Kim must have watched her writing in her journal. He must have realized that it was important to her. The space was deep enough that she could start another book or keep notes on medications and procedures. She turned and gave the old gentleman another hug. Then the impact of what Kim had said penetrated. He felt she was good enough to call herself a surgeon!

The older man just blushed and grinned. "I rike coat it just fit. How you know my size?"

"You, dearest friend, are not the only one here with secrets." Hattie responded as she went about clearing away wrapping paper and returning the teacart to the kitchen. She completed these chores with a certain lift to her shoulders as she tried to convince herself, I am finally a healer.

One cold blustery day in February as they were resting from a strenuous workout involving several complex guardian moves Hattie turned to Kim.

"I think today is my birthday. I am twenty, give or take a week or so. Most of the women I know that are twenty are busy having babies. Look at me," she said, holding her hands out to him as if for inspection. "All I'm good for is delivering them. And," she laughed, "if any man tries to take me in his arms, I can put him on the ground wondering how he got there." She thought as she said it how wonderful life would be if the right man were to try.

As they returned to the house, Kim looked at Hattie with the grin that told her he had something important to say. He started with some hesitation. "You become very good at guardian arts. You make me work to my rimit to not hurt you, but now is time for important resson. You must arways use only for defending self or helping others. Never use for power or selfish means or guardian power reave you. We must cerebrate birthday rater, friend coming on ship from India. He bling specaow medicine. We must meet ship. You harness buggy and pack." Kim said as he bustled about performing other tasks needed to close the house for several days.

"Where are we going?" asked Hattie, as she packed her limited wardrobe consisting of two pair of boy's pants, and a few shirts. She also packed her underclothes and a nightshirt, which remained more feminine.

"We take buggy for one day and then ride on ra'road to Bristol."

The thought of a train ride excited Hattie. She knew a lot about trains from listening to Master Janes pontificate, but had never ridden on one. Little did she know that much would happen before that first train ride.

Chapter 5

Hattie's Journal

11 March 1858: Today I met my twin sister and my father. How do I feel? Undecided.

When Thomas Kirkland awoke to the steady clip-clop of horses' feet and the jarring ride, he resolved that when this infernal torture wagon stopped, he would have gone far enough! He and Anne could continue by train to Bristol. The constant bouncing and jouncing accompanied by Anne's complaining outweighed the chance of discovery this far from home. He was aware of Anne sleeping next to him. He couldn't see her but every now and then the wagon would lurch in the right direction, and he could feel her heavy relaxed weight as it pressed against him in the narrow confines of the wagon bed. He tried counting the tree branches overhanging the road as they blotted out the few stars shining through the cape of clouds overhead. The darkness prevented him from picking them out. He shook his flask—empty again. His head ached, and if he couldn't sleep or watch the trees he might as well go talk to the driver.

Taking advantage of a change in movement that rolled Anne the other way, he arose from his position and sat down on a barrel located behind the driver's seat. Clinging to the seat back, he asked the driver. "How much longer before we stop?"

"Not far now, Mr. Kirkland. About another hour at the most. Then, we be pulling into Wylye."

"I understand one can catch the train there for Bristol?"

"Aye, ye can. Do you want to go directly to the station or to a hotel?"

"Take us to..." Before he could finish the sentence, a shot rang out! The driver gave a groan and slumped sideways on the seat. The startled horses, tired as they were, bolted in panic. Kirkland gripped the seat unable to do anything except hang on as the horses, feeling the reins go slack, continued at a dead run down the road.

Kirkland managed to pull himself up using the seatback for leverage. As he rose up attempting to climb over the seatback, he heard another shot and simultaneously felt a hammer blow hit him in the arm. Losing his grip on the seatback, he fell over backwards into the wagon box hitting his head on the barrel. The last thing he heard before he lost consciousness was Anne's infernal screaming.

The screaming probably saved their lives. The horses, hearing this high-pitched siren behind them, ran like the devil himself was chasing them. They quickly increased the distance between the wagon and the two dark shadows left standing in the middle of the road cursing and accusing each other of the inept execution of their plan to rob the weary, unwary travelers.

Kim and Hattie had just reached the intersection where their road met the road being traveled by the wagon bearing Thomas and Anne Kirkland, when they heard the first shot. Kim quickly pulled the buggy into the shadows under the trees. With a sharp command to stay with the wagon, he jumped down and faded into the night.

Hattie tied the horse to a nearby tree limb and moved several feet away from the buggy. She crouched down near the road just as the totally exhausted horses pulled the wagon to a stop near her hiding place. Hattie ran up to the wagon and used the spokes on the large wheel as a ladder to climb up and grab the seat pulling herself in. She could barely make out the slumped figure of the driver. She must have pressed on something that hurt, because he gave off a soft groan. She could hear a gasping, hoarse noise coming from the back of the wagon. "You back there, are you hurt?"

The noise stopped. She heard no answer. Crawling over the seatback, her foot encountered something soft that moved and groaned under her feet. She quickly adjusted her foot to another position and felt underneath her. She found another injured person wedged in among the boxes and barrels in the wagon bed.

A groan from the second victim brought renewed rasping and croaking from the back of the wagon. Lifting her head and straining to see, Hattie asked again. "Is there someone back there? I need your help. There are two people up here in bad shape, but alive. Now, I want you to answer me. I need your help."

"I can't talk," came a faint whispered response.

"You don't have to talk to help me lift this one. He's wedged between these boxes. We will need to be careful moving him and I can't do it alone," Hattie grunted as she tugged on the man's coat. She heard it rip from the strain.

"That's my father," whispered the voice from the rear.

"I'm glad to hear that, dearie. We will save the introductions for later. Right now, we need to get him situated where I can determine the severity of his injuries."

At first, Hattie thought the large soft woman that crawled up from the rear of the wagon was being overly gentle, but by the time they got him propped up on the boxes, it became obvious that concern was not the problem. For a large woman, she was terribly weak. *I'll wager this woman has trouble just moving around on a regular basis.* She thought as she stood up to stretch her back.

Hattie froze in a listening position, and carefully crouched back down in the wagon. "Shh," she whispered to the woman who was fussing noisily over the man in the wagon. "Don't make a sound. I thought I saw something moving out there!"

"You did," came a voice from her shoulder. Turning she saw Kim grinning at her.

"What you find here?"

Hattie explained as Kim began to check the pulse of the man on the seat. She realized that it was getting easier to see as dawn began to lighten the sky in the east. With a worried look on her face, she turned to Kim.

"What about the shots we heard?"

"No probrem, shooters run into trouble. They stumble in road, run into something I think." He grinned at her. "Now must help these peoples."

Hattie and Kim carefully moved the driver off the seat to the ground. Hattie went to the buggy to get Kim's medical bag and the box of supplies they always kept in the special compartment built on the rear of the buggy. After examining the driver, Kim climbed into the wagon to check on the man lying on the boxes in the rear of the wagon.

The weeping, snuffling woman cowered in the rear corner of the wagon box. She sat with her knees pulled up and arms crossed to protect her face." What kind of man are you?" she whispered hoarsely.

"I am healing man," he replied, giving her his best grin.

"Where do you come from?"

Kim tilted his head toward her and smiled. "I come from a place called Tibet. I live high in mountains. I learn to be good doctor in India. Do you know where that is?"

Anne had heard her father mention friends at his club that had served in the army in India. She had never seen anyone from there but this strange man could have said he was from the moon for all she knew, and here he was about to work on her father. She only felt capable of whimpering some more since screaming was out of the question. For the first time in her life, she felt the need to beg. "Please, help my father. Please, don't let him die!" she whispered in her hoarse voice.

Kim's examination of Thomas Kirkland showed that the bullet had passed through the fleshy part of the arm. While it was a bloody, ugly wound it was not life threatening. He was more concerned about the gash on his scalp.

"This no burret wound. You see what happen?"

"He fell and hit his head on that barrel when the horses bolted." Anne whispered as she pointed out the barrel.

Kim nodded. That made sense. They needed to make him comfortable, and get him to a place where Kim could make a more complete examination. He grabbed Kirkland under the arms and moved him as gently as possible, placing his head in Anne's lap. "Here, you hode honorable father. I rook at other man," he smiled his friendly grin and hopped quickly out of the wagon box.

Hattie had removed the driver's coat and shirt. She was inspecting the wound in his shoulder when Kim arrived. Kim applied a large square of clean linen cloth to both sides of the wound and wrapped it tight. Soon, the bleeding stopped. Hattie began bathing the man's face. He regained consciousness a few minutes later.

"What happened?" he asked, "Last thing I remember, I was about ready to fall asleep up on that wagon seat. Then, Thomas he said something and that's all I remember."

"You were shot by robbers, and your horses bolted. You were lucky we came along when we did. You have a bad bullet wound and possibly a broken shoulder. We need to get you somewhere close and fix you up."

The driver raised his head and looked around. "Are we at the crossroads?"

"Yes."

"My place is just up the road. Take us there."

"Can you get up in our buggy with my help?"

"I think so." He leaned heavily on her as they slowly made it to the buggy. They paused there to rest. Kim arrived in time to help hoist him onto the seat.

They agreed that Hattie would drive the buggy and Kim would follow with the wagon. They arrived at the driver's house in full daylight. They settled the driver in his own bed, and placed Kirkland in another room holding two narrow bunks.

"This room is used by our two boys. They can sleep in the barn for now," said the woman who had met them at the door. "I'm Maude Daniels. I am surely grateful to you for helpin' my man."

"The other gentleman may have to stay here for a while. He shouldn't be moved. We think he may have a brain injury. My friend here is a doctor," Hattie said, gesturing to Kim. "He comes from China but he really knows a lot about medicine. My name is Harry and I have been studying with him for the past few years."

"Who is the young woman hiding in the wagon?" Asked Maude eyeing Hattie with a curious look.

"Her name is Anne but she doesn't talk much. We don't know much about them. That's her father who got hit on the head."

They had been standing near Daniels' bed. He reached over and tugged on his wife's apron. "Don't you go letting Mr. Kirkland go until he pays for the trip."

At this news, Hattie jumped like she had been stuck with a needle! Mr. Daniels had called the other man Thomas earlier now he called him Kirkland. The man's full name must be Thomas Kirkland. Could he be her real father? If so, the young woman could be her sister.

Just then, Kim entered the room. Looking at both of them, he said, "I fix shoulder now. Harry, you stay with other man. Someone must watch." Looking at Maude he grinned. "You go see about getting young girl out of wagon prease?"

Maude moved immediately outside to the wagon and opening the tailgate said, "Well now, young lady, let's get you out of there so you can help with your pa." In her best motherly tone she coaxed Anne to leave the wagon. As Anne climbed down, Maude handed her one of the suitcases. "Here, no sense going inside empty handed."

Anne turned to her with a look of shock and amazement. She was still unable to talk. Maude just walked on by carrying more of the Kirkland's luggage. Anne squawked but nothing came out. She stood for a moment lost in disbelief. Soon, she shrugged, and staggering under the heavy bag set off after Maude who was fast disappearing into the cottage. Soon, the two of them had carried the remaining luggage into the boy's bedroom where Hattie ministered to Kirkland.

Hattie turned to Anne. "Your father has what we call a concussion. As Kim explained it to me, his brain took a nasty blow. He seems to have slipped into a coma. That means the brain has turned off some of the things that it does for us like walking, talking, and eating. The brain is trying to heal itself. Our job is to take care of father while the brain recovers. We must pray that he recovers before he dies from lack of food or water. One of us must be awake at all times. If he moves at all we need to drop liquid on his lips to try and keep him from becoming dehydrated. I can't be here to do this all the time. I will need some rest and I also need to care for Daniels. Will you do this for your father?"

Anne nodded.

"That's good," mumbled Hattie. "Kim has to go to Bristol and meet a ship coming from India. There is a man on that ship bringing medicine that he can only get from the Far East. The man will only be there a short time. If Kim doesn't make contact with him the man will leave and Kim will not get the medicine he needs. Many people might die without this medicine. Ministering to," Hattie hesitated "your father, is up to us."

Hattie had figured out who Thomas and Anne Kirkland were as soon as she heard Daniels utter the name, but she was not yet ready to confront Anne with the news. She wanted time to think. She had a good life now, living with Kim. Why make things difficult for all of them? In a few days, fate would decide the issue anyway. Either Thomas Kirkland would die or live. Why not leave the decision in the hands of God for now?

But, if her father died that would only deepen her dilemma. Who would take care of Anne? From what she had observed so far, Anne was totally dependent upon others for her support. Without her father to provide for her, she could find herself in serious trouble. On the other hand, if their father survived, it would raise other issues. What about loyalty and responsibility? Should she be loyal to Kim and stay with him? Or should she go with her father and sister and try to become a part of her real family?

The first night turned into the worst. Hattie felt exhausted from being up most of the previous night. Daniels continued to suffer from pain. The adrenalin had worn off, and he tossed and turned, threatening to open his slowly healing wound. Hattie felt sure he would break the stitches or tear loose from the framework of supports Kim had constructed to keep his broken shoulder immobilized. If that happened, she wasn't sure she could repair the damage. She had never done one like it before and Kim had put the framework together while she was tending to her father.

The slow rise and fall of Thomas Kirkland's chest as he breathed continued as the only sign of life left in him. From her reading Hattie knew that only in some cases did the patient breathe on his own. She would have to monitor him continually to make sure his condition didn't become worse. He could slip deeper into the coma and stop breathing altogether.

Both Maude and Hattie had to prod Anne to keep her focused and paying attention. Hattie needed to be with Daniels part of the time and she also needed some time to relax and catch a nap. Fortunately, she required little sleep. She had trained herself by reading long into the night at Janes Manor before arising early the next day ready to do her work. Still, the following morning found her totally exhausted.

Hattie sat at Maude's kitchen table having a cup of tea and some toast. As she began to relax, her eyes began to close and she drifted off.

Maude said, "Pretty tough on you aint it? You being a girl and all."

Hattie nodded in agreement. The impact of the statement failed to penetrate for a few seconds. "What gave me away?" asked Hattie, looking up at the smiling Maude.

"Oh, the way you move and your actions. I have me two boys you know. At first, I suspected that you was just 'different' if you know what I mean.

Then, I saw you was built like a woman under those bulky clothes you are a wearin."

"Do you think anyone else suspects?" Hattie asked, thinking of Anne and her father.

"No. My boys have been too busy working outside to pay much attention. As for mistress high and mighty in the other room, she is too fixated on her own troubles right now to pay much attention. She probably wouldn't notice anyhow. I've met some snooty rich folks in my time, but that girl beats them all, when it comes to lordin' it over other folks. But, back to you, my man back there, he will notice. He's got him an eye for the girls that one does," she winked at Hattie. "But, I know how to keep a check rein on him."

Hattie decided to try the story she had used a couple of times in the past. She told Maude how all her life she had wanted to study medicine and become a doctor. How being a girl closed all doors to her. She had finally heard about Kim and had decided to apprentice with him.

No one called him "Doctor Kim," because he had no certificates or degrees from a real university. He insisted that no one ever call him anything other than Kim. He was smart enough to know that to be called a Doctor would incite the medical community to action against him. As long as he remained just Kim, other doctors let him work on patients too poor to meet their payments. All he had was more knowledge and experience as a physician than any doctor in England and probably all of Europe as well.

She explained how they had come up with the idea of her dressing like a boy. It eliminated many questions and allowed her to assist in treatments and operations where a girl would never, otherwise be permitted. Everything Hattie said was true. It just wasn't the whole story.

Maude just nodded. Either she bought the story or decided to leave well enough alone. They finished their breakfast and went separate ways, each to the next task at hand. Hattie checked on her father and Anne.

She entered the bedroom and found Anne laying on her bed dozing. Hattie moved to the other bed to check on her father. She found him with eyes wide open staring at her as if he was seeing a ghost! "Caroline, what are you doing in those silly clothes?" he muttered questioningly.

"It's okay," Hattie smiled. "You are just having a dream." She reached across the table for the cup of broth she had put there earlier. "Here, drink this." She spooned the liquid and carefully allowed it to pass between his lips. She soon had him taking the broth as fast as she would give it to him, but he continued to stare at her with a mixture of fear, love, and hope.

With the soup gone, she turned to Anne. "Wake up, your father is coming around. I need you to fetch fresh water and some more broth from the kitchen."

"Go get it yourself I'm tired," Anne replied as she rolled her suety body to face the wall.

This became the final straw for Hattie. The last of her patience departed with her lost night's sleep. Taking one of Anne's shoes from the middle of the floor, she reached over and smacked Anne on the well-padded rump facing her. "I need your help now! Get up and do as I say! We will settle this between us when father is taken care of. Until then you will jump when I say jump. Do you understand?"

Anne did not say anything she just rolled off the bed and left the room with a strange look of curiosity modifying but not elimating her normaly sullen expression.

Kirkland opened one eye and said, "No one talks to Anne that way. It's true she needs to be told off just as you did, but soon we will all hear the screaming. And let me tell you, she can really scream!"

Hattie giggled as she said, "She can't scream right now. She can barely whisper. The other night when you were shot? She screamed so long and so loud that she overtaxed her vocal chords."

"I was shot?" he asked his eyes opening wide.

"Yes, both you and Mr. Daniels were shot by robbers. Kim and I found you and brought you here to the Daniels' farm."

"Who is Kim?"

"He is a very special man. I work for him and he teaches me medicine and other things. Before I met Kim, I studied a lot about science. Medicine allows me the chance to serve others by using science. I also use the special skills and knowledge of plants and herbs I have learned from Kim. Right now he is not here. You lie back now and take it easy. Anne will bring you some water and more broth and then we need you to take a rest."

"Are you a doctor?"

"No, I consider myself a healer."

"Is there a difference?"

Hattie pondered the question for a moment then smiled and said, "Sometimes."

Hattie stayed away so that Anne and her father could get caught up. She figured Anne would tell the story from her perspective, but that would be a good start. Kirkland needed to get things straight in his mind before Hattie dropped her news on both of them. That is, if she decided to do it. She still hadn't made up her mind. As it turned out, she didn't have much choice.

Later that afternoon while Hattie was checking Kirkland's pulse and temperature and changing his bandages, Anne got up off her bed and closed the door and leaned against it. She began. "There is something strange about you. My father and I have been talking, and we are confused about several things."

"What are you referring to?" asked Hattie. She had learned from her reading that if you wanted to stall for time and figure out a good answer, try answering a question with a question.

"Well for a start," quized Anne, "Who...no, what are you? Are you really a boy or a woman? My father has this crazy idea you may even be his wife, my mother returning from the grave."

Hattie sighed and mentally shrugged, deciding more deceit was not in her, she motioned Anne to sit on her bed as she took the stool next to Kirkland. "This could be a long story so you might as well get comfortable. To begin, you are both pretty good detectives but a little too superstitious. The short answer to your questions: I was christened Helen Marie Kirkland. I was born at the same time and place as you Anne. We are twin sisters. I don't have a picture of my mother, but if *father* here is any judge, I must resemble her somewhat, just as you do. Finally, yes I am a woman. I guess I can't hide that fact from anyone any more. Do you wish to question any of this before I continue?"

Both shook their heads.

"I have a signed letter from Tillie Mayfield, written shortly before her death confirming these facts should you require proof." I was not trying to intercept you or meet you the other night. Those events were pure fate. I have no desire to become a part of your life, unless you want me. I am quite happy and content to continue my education with Kim. Should you desire to have a relationship, I would consider it. After all, we are family. Judging from the blank looks on your faces you both need to digest this information. I would suggest Anne that you see to your father's needs. I must go check in on Mr. Daniels." Hattie smiled at Anne and with just the flicker of a curtsey to her father marched out the door.

Hattie walked into the kitchen and flopped down on a chair. She looked up at Maude and said, "Well I told them."

"Told them what? That you are a girl?"

"More than that. I told them they are my family."

"How can they be your family? I thought you told me the other night that you and Kim found them at the crossroads? I figured you had never laid eyes on each other before."

"That's true," said Hattie. "Well almost true. The last time my father saw me, I was only hours old. I have been separated from them since birth."

"That must be some story," remarked Maude, shaking her head and placing the bread loaves she had been kneading into the oven.

"It is, I guess. I'll tell it to you sometime." Hattie rubbed her eyes and used her fingers to comb through her short-cut hair.

"What about your little dress-up game? My guess from what you just told me that they must know you are a woman and not a boy?"

"Yes, that's a part of it. In fact, I think I could have gotten away with just telling them that much, but I really wanted them to know my past. I guess I have some secret desire buried inside me wanting them to know we are family. Maybe it was a need to make my father feel guilty. You know, pay him back for all my misfortune. Then, there are times when I feel this need for family. The need to know someone cares. Someone I can always count on. We may have disagreements and we may make each other angry with what we say or do but in the end we all need someone there to love us in spite of our shortcomings."

As they sat in Maude's kitchen, Hattie continued to think about what it would be like to have a real family. She knew from Tillie's letter that Mam and Pap were not family even though they loved and nurtured her. She loved them and cared about them, but she had left them. They had helped her when she couldn't help herself, but she had never felt a real family bond. As she looked back, she could see that the other kids always received special treatment. Events intervened to change that life. She had to rise above those events and create a life for herself.

"Oh, Maude, I don't know what to do! Suddenly I have this family. We are bound together by a bloodline but where is the bond of love? Here I am, just a poor serving girl, raised to serve those of their class. Yet, I feel like I am the parent of this new family. They both seem to live behind this wall of wealth that was built by others. What talents do they possess that will allow them to exist in the real world? Can they stand as productive people? What happens when the crutch of inherited wealth breaks? I don't know if what I feel is love or pity mixed with some misguided sense of responsibility. I don't know if this is a load I can or want to carry." Hattie paused for a moment and then continued, "and I'm sorry to unload on you almost a complete stranger and all."

"Look, child," Maude responded, "don't you worry none about me. Lots of folks tell me their troubles. I guess I'm just one of those folks with that for a gift. You just need to follow your heart and use that wonderful brain God has given you, and everything will work itself out. Live life one day at a time, doin' the best you can, that's my motto."

Hattie felt that getting involved in a new project might help take her mind off her current problems. "About the boy-girl thing? I don't suppose you would know where I could find some girl clothes do you? It seems I have matured to the point where playing a boy is too difficult to disguise any longer."

"Now that you mention it there are some things in the attic. I just couldn't part with them after I started having babies. You mind this here bread I got bakin while I go take a look-see." Tossing her apron to Hattie, Maude moved toward the narrow staircase that led to the attic. She returned shortly loaded down with clothing.

Later when she entered the Kirkland's room, Hattie received a blank stare from Anne and a tentative smile from her father. He opened the discussion. "That is a remarkable story..."

"It's not a story." interrupted Hattie, crossing to her medical case open on the table near his bed. She removed her journal and tossed the letter from Tillie at him. "Read it for yourself."

"I will if you insist," answered her father. "But, I was not questioning your honesty just remarking on how truth can sometimes be more interesting than fantasy."

Hattie could see from Anne's expression that she was not as convinced. Of course, Anne had the larger dose to swallow. She probably had no idea she even had a sister. Thomas Kirkland at least knew the truth concerning the beginning of the story. How much her father had glossed over the details concerning that first fateful night of their lives, Hattie could only guess. He probably spun the story to his advantage. Nobody wants to admit they ordered another's death, even if such a tiny deformed body might not have survived.

Hattie replaced the precious letter in her journal, and sat down on the stool. "Let me continue. I was raised by Tillie's daughter. We lived far from you. Of course that was the idea. I won't tell you where. You can find out I am sure, but I wish you wouldn't. Such knowledge would not do you any good, and could place you in a difficult position at some future time. Those reasons are connected with why I ran away and use this disguise when I travel with Kim. It is sufficient to know, there was trouble and I left."

Kirkland reached up and touched Hattie softly on the arm. "I want you to know that I accept you as my daughter and sincerely hope you can forgive me for any pain you have suffered."

"Oh no," responded Hattie, "I feel just the opposite. I had a good childhood. Yes it was hard work and even painful at times but I managed to rise above it. I had to work of course, but I had access to a tremendous library, and was able to educate myself in many areas. I seem to have a special gift. I remember everything I have ever read. I may never have developed that talent had I been a part of your family. I have read several books about identical twins and I truly believe that Anne has the same talents. She has just never had to use them. Perhaps they were smothered by over attentive servants or suppressed by guilt."

Anne looked up at Hattie. "I always wanted to paint, like an artist. I once had a teacher who said I had talent, but I would have to study, work, study, work. How can you study and work to become an artist? The books were too hard. I quit because they would not let me do what I wanted to do. I would show them the things I did and they would just laugh not able to understand what I was trying to do. I got bored. That ended that."

Hattie sprang from her chair and crossed to Anne and gripped her by the shoulders. "Oh Anne, you see. Even with all you have been given, life has not been kind to you. Maybe we can do something to change that for you." The two girls held each other for a long time, locked together as they had once been at birth.

Over the next week, Hattie began to see that her father and sister had many good points. She began to develop a close bond with both of them. Several times, she looked up to see Anne looking at her with a strange pensive expression. Kirkland and Daniels both continued to mend and require less nursing care. Hattie and Maude came to a smooth arrangement of sharing household chores and nursing their two patients. Anne moped around the house and farm, never going far. If asked or told to help with some task, she would grudgingly comply. It was as if she had to put on a show of not helping, but really wanted to be involved. But, she never offered to help or do any work on her own initiative.

In the evenings, the three women would sit in the living area off the kitchen and sew. They were busy making Hattie women's clothes from things Maude had worn as a young bride and from items donated by Anne from her abundant wardrobe. Anne would become bored with the work, but would sit and participate in the conversation. She had recovered her voice, but managed to suppress her desire to scream. Everyone seemed convinced that she was not happy with the present situation, but since no one would listen or seemed to care about her discomfort, she remained quiet.

Hattie began to assist her father in taking short walks. He would tire quickly, so they took frequent rest stops. He never complained about dizzy spells. Hattie remained concerned that he might become dizzy and fall causing a repeat of his injury, but she felt the benefit of moving around and regaining strength was worth the risk.

She especially enjoyed the stories he told her about her mother. She could tell that he had really loved and cared for her. She discovered that her mother had descended from French and Spanish royalty. He told her stories of Phoenician ancestors that crossed the Mediterranean Sea. Could this be the source of the strange rising eyebrows both she and Anne possessed?

At the edge of a field, stood a low, rock wall. When they first started their walks, Hattie made the wall a goal. Now it became a favorite stopping point even though they might continue on. They were sitting on the wall one afternoon when Kirkland turned and said, "Helen, I mean, Hattie, I must talk to you."

"Of course, speak whatever is on your mind." she said, taking hold of his hand.

"I need to speak frankly with you. Much of what I am going to tell you Anne does not know. She may suspect because I have failed to submit to her demands that we leave here, and return to our home in London," he paused and then continued. "There is no home to which we can return. I have burned all our bridges, so to speak.

"When I inherited the fortune made by my father and grandfather there seemed to be money to burn. We had several properties. The rental returns from those properties alone created enough income to keep us comfortable for life. The business was flourishing. Then things began to go bad. One could say there was a slump in the economy or make some other weak excuse but in the end it was just poor management on my part. I am sure my depressed state after your mother died and I," he paused, "lost you, along with my heavy drinking, accelerated the downward slide. I recently managed to convert my remaining assets to cash and some negotiable securities on European banks. When you found us, Anne and I were on our way to Bristol to find a ship to America."

"What do you plan to do there?"

"Invest in the growing economy and start a new life."

"What makes you think you won't make the same mistakes and loose the rest to some sharp American businessman? It takes research and skill to ensure you are investing in assets that will promote a healthy rate of return," Hattie paused, observing the look in her father's eyes as they began to gloss over. *Oh yes, I have seen that look before,* she thought to herself. It was that what do you know, you are just a girl look. In the past she would just shut up. This time the situation demanded a different result. This was her father. She needed to help him, but in such a way that her suggestions would appear to be his ideas not hers.

As soon as the thought entered her head, another followed it. Helping her father would not be a simple one-shot solution. It could not be done from long distance—across an ocean. The magnitude of the decision she must make began to grow.

Kim returned to the farm one evening later that week. The following day he carefully examined both patients. He declared Kirkland fit to travel, and modified Mr. Daniels' brace so that he now had some mobility. Kim was pleased with the exercises Hattie had prescribed for Daniels but he did increase the repetitions to ensure a full recovery. Daniels found that he could get up from his bed by himself, eat and sit in the chair by the fireplace. Hattie instructed Maude on the therapy and the schedule she should follow to restore mobility to her husband's shoulder. That evening, Kim declared, "Hattie and I will leave for home tomorrow."

Upon hearing this decision, Hattie's father asked her to come with him to their room. He indicated he had something to discuss with her in private. Upon entering the room, he motioned for Hattie to sit down. "Please have a seat Hattie. I wish to give you something." With this comment, he moved to the black leather satchel he kept under the bed. Hattie had observed him constantly checking to make sure it was still there on several occasions. He extracted a thick envelope and handed it to her. "Here, I want you to take these. This envelope contains several of the securities I mentioned the other day. I have endorsed them over to you. The Vicar witnessed them when he was here the other night to pay his respects to the family. You can exchange them for cash at any bank in England or on the continent."

Hattie looked up at him as he handed her the envelope. She was filled with gratitude for her father. She knew how much worldly wealth meant to him, and the sacrifice he felt he was making. She knew he was trying to make up for gifts he should have given her over a lifetime. With tears in her eyes she said, "Father you don't need to do this. I am an independent woman. I can make my way in the world. I don't need this."

"Maybe not, but it is the only inheritance I can leave you. Please take it so I can feel a sense of peace."

She smiled at him and slipped the envelope into her bag. Just then Anne entered. "Hattie, there is something I wish you to have." Both Hattie and her father looked at her and then at each other in amazement. This was not Anne! It was just not in her to want to give anything to anybody. Anne continued. "I have lost weight trying to exist on this terribly plain food I have been forced to eat. And, I have been forced to work like a slave! I plan to give Maude many of my things that will fit her, with a little fixing, and I have already donated much to you. You realize that a young woman, unlike a *boy*, must keep her things nice. You must have some place in which to carry your new clothes. You must have this traveling trunk that I have just emptied." Picking up the clothes she had been sorting through as she talked, she grunted, "These are going to Maude." With that statement, she opened the door and left.

Anne's intrusion had created a sort of comic relief. To Hattie's amazement she heard herself saying. "Thank you father. I may well never use the money but thinking of your sacrifice of something I know is like life itself will remain with me always. I may just keep them forever to remind me of this moment." After placing the envelope in her journal and returning it to the special compartment in her instrument case, she rose from the bed and crossed to her father. They met in the middle of the room in a loving embrace. The answer to Hattie's question concerning what she should do, came to her as she held her father.

Hattie helped Kim load the buggy the following morning. He buzzed around like an aroused bee anxious to leave. Hattie moved at a more sluggish pace so unlike her. Finally she said, "Kim we need to talk."

Kim seemed troubled. He mentioned a telegram he received in Bristol, indicating that one of his rich benefactors in Southampton was ill. He wanted to get started for home as fast as possible. He paused and studied Hattie just as the rising sun caught her standing by the door of the Daniels' cottage. He noticed that she was dressed as a young woman, not in her boy suit as he called it. Her tall regal form complimented by the stylish traveling suit cut down from one donated by Anne, had turned her into a woman of culture and means. He noticed her bags still sitting on the stoop.

The reality of what was happening finally penetrated. His shoulders slumped as if holding his head up had become impossible. Raising his face up, he met Hattie's gaze. For the first time that she could remember Kim was not wearing his silly grin. He seemed to age right before her eyes. How old is he? She wondered. For the first time she truly saw him as an old man. The vitality and vigor she had come to depend on were not there. He seemed to fold up and collapse as he turned to cling to the buggy behind him. What had she done! She ran down the path. Approaching him, she reached out to lift him and hold him. Their eyes met. Both wept openly.

Finally Kim blurted, "I see last night what happening. I say to self no, not true. But, it is. Maybe that is why I want to start early. We get out of here you forget. Life is good again. But, that is not so. I see now you must go with father and sister. I see they need you. You need them. That is your karma."

Hattie found no words to convey what she felt. He had said it all for her. She stood there by the side of the road watching the buggy bounce it's way out of her life. She didn't move until the last particle of dust had settled and all sight and sound from the buggy was lost in the trees. She turned, squared her shoulders and began to walk back to the cottage wondering if she had made the decision to stay out of love or loyalty?

Chapter 6

Hattie's Journal

25 June 1858: Today we set sail for America on the Susan Ganes. Father is apprehensive. Anne is disappointed. I am excited.

Maude's oldest boy, Johnny, drove the three Kirklands to the train station in Wylye. The train ride from there to Bristol proved uneventful but extremely exciting and interesting for Hattie. She marveled at the speed they travelled. The lurching, swaying motion forced her to hold on fearing that they would crash at any moment. Even the smoke and cinders flying in through the open windows failed to interfere with her excitement.

After they found suitable accommodations in Bristol, Hattie coaxed Anne into taking a walk with her before dark. Anne found the busy streets and noisy crowds of the seaport boring. She kept making up reasons why they should return to their rented rooms. Hattie, on the other hand could barely contain her excitement. She had never been among so many people all moving and jostling one another. Wagons and carriages of all kinds passed them rumbling by on the cobblestone streets. She found this surging mass of humanity intimidating but exciting.

As it began to get dark, the nature of the crowd changed. Loud talking seamen from the ships and painted ladies replaced the families and businessmen on the street. The shops they passed began to close for the night. She gave in to Anne's demands, and they returned to their room.

The next day, Hattie got up early. She and her father planned to go to the office of the shipping agent and arrange passage on the next available ship bound for the Colonies, as her father insisted on calling America. Hattie wanted to seek passage to New York City or Boston. When her father questioned her reasons, she simply told him she had read in a book about these two places. They had the best harbors and most opportunities for business and commerce. How could he argue with that since his objective was to invest in businesses exactly like she was describing.

Anne insisted on remaining in bed. She had begged Hattie to bring her a tray with a large breakfast. Hattie's response had been, "Go hungry or get your own." She smiled to herself as she went down the stairs to the lobby to meet her father. It felt so good to be a woman of independent means. She had the securities from her father and the money from Daniels, she felt free to do as she pleased for the first time in her life.

On the previous day, her father had paid Daniels the money he owed for the trip from Croydon to Wylye and for room and board while they lived with the Daniels family recovering from his injuries. Mr. Daniels had then turned to Hattie and given her money. "This here is what I owe you and Kim for fixin' me up so good. I met Kim as I was coming from town the day he left. He said to pay you. I would have paid earlier, but I had to wait for your father to pay me."

Hattie's father had a cab waiting at the curb. He gave the driver the address of the shipping agent found on the letter he had received confirming his earlier reservations. He believed funds were on file and that suitable passage would be arranged upon his arrival in Bristol. As they set off in the noise and confusion of the busy streets, Hattie felt relieved that someone else was driving and not her. After several stops and starts accompanied by shouted arguments at every intersection, their driver finally pulled up in front of a dreary building on a side street just off the wharves along the waterfront.

They were leaving the carriage when the driver leaned down to Hattie and whispered, "I sure 'ope your father knows wat 'esa doin'. These 'ere folks don't 'ave the best reputation in town, ya know." After saying his piece, he cracked his whip and eased his cab back into the traffic.

Hattie felt confident she could hold her own. One of the things Kim had drilled her on had been how to study human nature and anticipate danger at all times. She tuned all her senses and skills to the situation as she followed her father into the shipping office.

The place they entered had large, dirty windows facing the street. Both walls intersecting the windows were covered with handbills and advertisements for shipping lines. Most were old and yellowed, some even years out of date. They approached a chest high counter running the width of the back wall. Hattie could just see a bald head that seemed to float in a cloud of cigar smoke. As they approached the counter a cheerful voice greeted them. "A fine good morning to you folks. Can I help you?"

Her father replied, "My name is Thomas Kirkland and I believe you are in possession of correspondence from me concerning passage to the Colonies. In my original letter, I indicated that accommodations would be required for two passengers. It will be necessary to change our requirements to three persons on the next available ship leaving for New York City or Boston."

The smile on the bald headed man's face didn't change as he announced, "I'm sorry sir, but I have no record of any communication from a Thomas Kirkland."

"My good man, I have a letter here! I will have the Law…"

"And you, my 'good man' are mistaken," interrupted Baldy. "Why just yesterday there was an officer here from the sheriff's office. He was looking for a man named Thomas Kirkland. It seems there is a matter of money being owed to some London financier. Now, if you was to be that Kirkland fella that the law be lookin' for why maybe I should call for the Sheriff? But if you was to forget makin a certain deposit and just go on about your business. We could keep the law out of this and go our separate ways. Now what say you to that?"

Hattie could see her father getting red in the face, his indignation turning into rage. She calmly said, "Come father, perhaps we have the wrong address." She smiled sweetly at the grinning bald man and using one of the holds Kim had taught her, she quickly marched her father out the door and into the busy street.

Hattie decided it would be best if they walked off her father's anger. She quietly led him away from the shipping office. She noticed a park nearby and led him to one of the benches where they sat for some time in silence. Finally her father said, "Thank you, Hattie. If you had not led me out of there when you did, I would be in jail right now. And I would have added assault and battery to the charge of embezzlement that is probably hanging over my head right now. I am curious though. When you took my arm, I felt a most excruciating pain whenever I resisted. What did you do?"

"Kim once told me the name in Chinese but I prefer to just call it a 'come-along.' There are certain nerves in the hand and arm. If one knows where and how to press just right the other person just comes along with you no matter how big or strong they may be."

"It's very effective," her father mumbled as he rubbed his arm in an effort to ease his discomfort.

"You will be okay in a few minutes," she replied as she turned to survey the other people in the park. Baldy might forget his promise and call for the Sheriff and she wanted to make a quick but casual getaway should it be necessary.

As they rested on the park bench, Hattie noticed a group of people clustered around two men in long black coats. She turned to her father and said, "I think a cool drink might make us feel better. Why don't you rest here. I will go and see if I can find a suitable establishment." At her father's nod, she headed off across the park anxious to satisfy her curiosity and find out what the speaker was talking about that managed to draw such a large crowd.

She passed close to the crowd. Just as she walked behind the man standing on the box, she heard him say, "And so I testify to you that the true Gospel of Jesus Christ has been restored to the earth by the Prophet, Joseph Smith!"

What a strange thing to say, she thought to herself. Everyone knows there aren't any prophets around these days. The thought entered her head from somewhere, but it sure would be nice if it were true. She stopped for a moment as the speaker continued, "John the Baptist conferred the priesthood on Joseph and Oliver. With this restored authority, they baptized each other." She shrugged and walked off. Her curiosity satisfied, she continued to look for a place that sold cool drinks. She failed to find any place suitable for females. She did however, find a man selling apples and purchased two.

When she returned, she found her father in a talkative mood. "Here I am," he growled with a wry smile. "I have run out of ideas and you show up with an apple. Let's chew together and see if we can come up with a plan." As they ate their apples, Hattie continued to watch the crowd where the two men were speaking. The speaker got down off the box, and the crowd began to disperse just about the time they finished eating. Both Hattie and her father rose together and began to look for a trash barrel where they could place their apple cores. They naturally walked toward the ships moored to the wharf nearby. As they approached the water, Hattie noticed that it was full of garbage. Thinking nothing of it, they both tossed their apple cores off the end of the wharf adding to the refuse already floating there.

Turning back away from the water, Hattie noticed that the two men in long black coats were talking with two other similarly dressed men. She sidled close enough to hear them discussing something about passengers embarking on the ship moored to the wharf. She immediately became interested. Moving closer, she suddenly realized that one of the men was looking at her and smiling. He looked deep into her eyes and her breathing seemed to stop as the world spun around those eyes. She seemed to have a sudden start of recognition as if being reunited with a long forgotten friend. She reached out and grabbed her father's arm to steady herself. He jerked at the grip on his sore arm, and broke the spell that seemed to hold her.

"What brings a lovely young lady like you to such a busy place on this fine morning?" The man asked, cheerfully.

Hattie stopped, startled by his greeting. Had the man seen her staring at him? "My father and I were just taking a stroll." Kirkland placed his other hand over hers. They exchanged greetings and smiles all around.

"We are hoping to find passage on a ship bound for America. You wouldn't happen to know of any that might have room? Maybe there is room left on this ship?" Hattie inquired, gesturing to the ship moored next to them.

"Oh no," interrupted the man who had first spoken to Hattie. "They are full up. In fact we are presently trying to find enough room for the rest of our congregation on the ship loading tomorrow." Seeing the crestfallen look on Hattie's face, he continued, "There is another ship leaving shortly. We did not find it suitable for our needs. It's not really set up to carry passengers, but the captain is looking for a few people to cut his costs—or so he says. You might try him. The name of the ship is the *Susan Ganes*. It's moored down the wharf where they load the heavy cargo." He gestured behind them. "Please excuse me, I must join my companions. It was nice to meet you." He hurried to catch up with the other members of his group.

"Oh father, we must try to find the captain of this ship the *Susan Ganes*. We must leave town before the sheriff finds you. Let's find this ship and arrange passage."

After an exhausting search and several inquiries they located Captain Joshua Barnes emerging from a waterfront dive more than a little drunk. He pointed out the ship, and indicated that yes, he did have room for three more passengers if they were willing to share two staterooms. They made arrangements to board before eight o'clock, as he planned to sail when the evening tide turned. Hattie haggled as best she could on the price but the captain knew from Kirkland's actions that he was desperate to leave England. She knew they paid too much but at least she got Captain Barnes to agree to full payment after they were aboard, if they made it by eight o'clock that evening.

Returning to the hotel, Hattie ran up the stairs to the room she shared with Anne only to discover she was missing! She searched the dining room and the lobby, all to no avail. She saw her father in the bar off the lobby, and motioned for him to join her. "Anne is missing." She told him.

His face turned pale with shock at the news. "What? Have you searched...?"

"Yes, Yes, and Yes. I can't find her anywhere!"

By this time they were standing outside the main door. Hattie asked the doorman. "Have you seen a young woman leave here?" He shook his head as he turned to respond to another gentleman demanding his attention. Obviously, he was too busy at this time of day to be of any help.

"Hattie, you go that way and I will look up here. We will meet back here in an hour," her father called as he began walking up the road to his right.

That was fine with Hattie. She had a feeling she knew where Anne might be. And she would never go uphill to get there. Anne was gone, yes.

She had gone shopping.

Hattie entered a store selling women's hats. She approached the clerk and giving her a description of Anne, she inquired if such a person had been in the store that morning. The clerk told her that she remembered a young woman asking about a store that sold under garments. She gave Hattie the same directions she had given the other young lady earlier. In this way Hattie was able to eventually track Anne down.

She found Anne at the counter. She had just finished paying for the carefully wrapped package the clerk handed to her. "I have lost so much weight I just had to have a new corset!" she cried when she spotted Hattie entering the store.

Hattie was relating the morning's events to Anne as they walked back toward the hotel. She carefully avoided mentioning anything to do with the sheriff. She stopped and turned when she noticed that Anne was no longer puffing along beside her. She retraced a dozen steps and found Anne gazing at several dresses on display. She positioned herself between Anne and the display in the window.

"Anne! Please! We must hurry. Father is worried and we still have to pack and take care of several important items if we are to board the boat before eight o'clock!"

"I know, Hattie. But, they are so beautiful, and they are the latest style. I so want to look my best when we enter America," she said with a dreamy look on her face as if she were imagining entering Queen Victoria's throne room.

Hattie glanced away thinking, can I really put up with this the rest of my life? Just then she saw a familiar face laughing and talking with three ladies in a carriage passing by on the street behind Anne. She would recognize that face and that laugh anywhere! It was Bart Janes and he was alive! His ghost would not be laughing, talking or riding about in a carriage, flirting with three lovely young ladies. Fortunately, he had not been looking in her direction and even then she would have been hard to recognize standing behind Anne. *Sometimes larger is better,* she thought to herself. She needed to get off the street! She took a firm hold on Anne and began dragging her back to their hotel.

The remainder of the day passed in a blur for Hattie. She did what she was told. She even offered suggestions about packing and what to purchase to make the trip less unpleasant. They met a man in the hotel lobby who had just arrived from America on a ship. He made several suggestions including some things they might want to take with them that were in short supply in the Colonies. All Hattie could focus on was the face and voice of a living Bart Janes. Did this mean she was free to return to the Manor? No. Even with all the problems that came with her family they needed her and she wanted them.

They were standing on the pier at the foot of the gangway leading to the *Susan Ganes*. They had made it well before the appointed hour of eight o'clock. Hattie felt dwarfed, surrounded by their small mountain of bags and boxes.

A voice from the quarterdeck boomed down to them. "Well, quite a load you have there. Fortunately we have plenty of room in the hold for your belongings. Room in the cabin now, that's another story. We have a simple scheme that seems to work well. You can take all you can carry or drag in one trip with you to your cabin. Everything else must go in the hold. Since I'm feeling good natured this evening I will send two of me strongest men to make the one trip to the cabin for the ladies. My First Officer, Mr. Hapwood, will collect the money for your passage and then ye are welcome to come aboard."

Mr. Hapwood was a pleasant faced man. He was older than the girls but younger than their father. He wore a plain black coat cut in the mariner's style, but unadorned with piping or trim. His curly brown hair stuck out and around a well-worn officer's cap. The remainder of his uniform consisted of the same canvas trousers and pullover shirts worn by the two men who accompanied him. With the help of these three and much wailing and whining from Anne, the loads were reorganized and apportioned according to the captain's dictates. Mr. Hapwood explained that while the system seemed a bit cruel and awkward it was really necessary. They discovered the truth in his statement once they entered their assigned quarters.

Hattie and Anne found they would share a space not much bigger than a closet. *Sort of like my room at Janes Manor minus the chimney room* thought Hattie. A set of narrow bunks, one above the other, occupied the bulkhead across from the door. They placed one trunk on either side of the door and sat the other baggage they had managed to carry with them on top of the trunks. Mr. Hapwood showed them the ropes attached to the bulkheads that could be used to secure the trunks during bad weather. He showed them the basin latched to the back of the door. When lowered on its hinges, it served as a place to wash. Lowering the basin also revealed a mirror in a frame screwed to the door. He showed them how unlatching and lowering the basin locked the door. He explained that this prevented someone from entering when the basin was in use. *Clever, these sailors,* thought Hattie to herself. When all baggage had been stored, hardly enough space remained for both girls to stand. "Passengers find it more convenient to take turns when dressing or opening their trunks." With this final piece of advice, he touched the bill of his tattered cap and backed out of the space.

Hattie moved around Anne, and placed her instrument case at the head of the upper bunk. As she did so, she discovered two additional items Mr. Hapwood had failed to mention. First, she bumped her head on a lantern hanging from a hook set in the ceiling, no Mr. Hapwood had referred to it as the overhead. She needed to get used to talking sailor talk if she wanted to impress the crew and the rest of the passengers. She bumped into the second item with her foot. The chamber pot, with lid thank goodness, wobbled and rolled across the deck like a lopsided football. She picked it up and examined it.

"Dirty, as I expected," she looked at Anne. "Why don't you take the lower bunk and get yourself settled. I am going to see if I can clean this before we have to use it—ugh!" She left the compartment and stepped into the narrow passageway.

She was just in time to catch her father opening his door. She glanced in and noted that her father would be in a cabin the same size as hers, and that he had a roommate. "It looks like we will all be a little crowded on this trip. Who is your cabin mate?" she asked.

"His name is Beauregard Calhoun. He owns a string of cotton gins, whatever they are. He was here in England buying machinery to construct more of these gin things. Why on earth someone would name an infernal machine after my favorite beverage is beyond my comprehension."

"A cotton gin is a machine used to extract the seeds from the cotton bolls so that the cotton remaining can be spun into thread more efficiently. The name gin is a shortened, americanized version of 'engine," Hattie rattled off as if reading directly from a book, which was precisely the case. "I would be interested in seeing one of these engines. I wonder if I can talk Mr. Calhoun into showing me one sometime."

"How do you know what they are?" asked her father.

"I read about it in a book," replied Hattie, as she walked up the steps to the open deck.

Spying a sailor coiling a rope on the deck, she asked him where she could clean her chamber pot. He told her to wait until the ship cleared the harbour, and she would be able to clean her pot with fresh seawater. He indicated the pump but was quick to add, "Don't you be using the pump now ma'am. The water in this harbor is dirtier than that pot you be holdin' in your hand. I'd sooner drink from that pot than from this harbor!"

Hattie ignored his vulgar and earthy comments, but followed his advice. She returned to her room and discovered Anne wedged into the lower bunk like a trapped polar bear. She sighed to herself and being as quiet as possible, managed to make the necessary nighttime preparations without awakening the sleeping bear. She failed to fall asleep right away. The excitement of the day's activities and the constant noise and movement outside and above the cabin kept her awake for some time. Her final thought became, *Bart is alive. I am not a murderer.* She smiled in relief as she drifted off to sleep.

Hattie left her bunk early. The ship was moving. She could feel the motion and hear the sailor's cries as they worked aloft. As she finished dressing, she turned to Anne. "Come on sleepy head. It's time to get up. The ship is taking us away from England. Get up or you will miss the opportunity to say goodby to our homeland."

Anne just groaned. "I don't feel so good. Leave me alone."

"Come now, get up and get dressed and you will feel better." Under Hattie's cheerful prodding, Anne began to move. Soon both girls stood on the main deck amidst the seemingly disorganized chaos of moving men and shouted orders from the captain.

"Avast, young ladies step lively up here to the quarterdeck. There is room here out of the way. Hurry now! I can't have ye getting hurt before we even clear the channel!"

As they arrived on the quarterdeck, Captain Barnes indicated a corner by the railing. "Now you stay right there. You can watch but don't move about."

"How does the ship float and not tip over?" Anne asked.

"The walls of the ship, they call it the hull, form a large sausage shaped space. The weight of the ship pushes down on the hull and it pushes on the water. When the force from the water trying to fill the space is slightly greater than the weight of the ship pushing back on the water then the ship floats, provided the sides of the hull are tall enough."

"But just look up there at the masts and sails. Why doesn't the ship tip over?" asked Anne, pointing aloft to the masts and spars full of dirty white sails and shouting seamen.

"Well, Captain Barnes is very smart." *I might as well make him feel good,* thought Hattie, catching the captain listening to her description with a look of impressed amusement on his face. "He has loaded the heavy cargo like Mr. Calhoun's machine parts in the bottom of the ship, and has balanced them so that the masts are straight up in calm water. That means the center of gravity is low and directly over the ship's centerline."

"Who is Mr. Calhoun?" asked Anne an interested expression crossing her face.

So much for my lesson on buoyancy thought Hattie. "Mr. Calhoun is father's cabin mate and I think, the only other passenger on the ship."

"Father has a cabin mate? I thought he had a room to himself. I had hoped to put some things in there with him!" wailed Anne, stomping her foot and turning away to lean on the ship's rail.

"Did I hear my name mentioned?" said a deep baritone voice from behind them. "Beauregard Calhoun at your service ladies. I do indeed have the ah, fortune to share a cabin with your father. He has mentioned both of you with fondness."

Both girls turned to stare at the gentleman behind them. He was tall but seemed even taller due to his straight military bearing. A large buff colored planter's hat shaded piercing black eyes, a long straight nose, a thin moustache and small goatee. His face seemed to show a trace of hardness even cruelty despite the friendly smile on his lips. His clothes were new and in the latest fashion.

Probably purchased while here in England thought Hattie. She found it difficult to like this man. She pushed the thought aside reasoning that it was probably a result of her past bad experiences with strange men.

"I have prevailed upon our captain to allow me the use of his cabin for breakfast. Unfortunately, his attention must be on avoiding the rocks and shoals of the channel. Would you ladies care to join me? I have already invited your father and I have provided some delicacies from my private stores. This may be the last good meal we will have for the next six weeks."

"Six weeks!" exclaimed Anne.

"Aye lass, six weeks is optimistic considering the sailing qualities of the *Susan Ganes* and the condition of her hull," stated the captain, indicating that his attention had not been entirely on navigating the channel. "With a little luck though and good weather, we should make it in less than two months." He turned away lifting a long spyglass to check on another vessel rounding the point ahead of them.

Beau Calhoun repeated his invitation. "Come ladies, our feast awaits." With one on each arm, he led them away toward the door of the captain's cabin.

Breakfast indeed proved a sumptuous and elegant meal. As they were finishing, Hattie turned to Calhoun and asked, "Tell me Mr. Calhoun, why would you take the time and effort to come all the way to England to buy machinery when the same items can be purchased from the factories and machine shops located in your own northern states?"

"You are well informed Miss. While what you say is true, the quality is not as good as the parts manufactured in England and I also needed to purchase other goods that are not available to me in the North. I must say I am impressed with your knowledge. Not only concerning the availability of goods in America but also on subjects such as ship design. I overheard you lecturing to your sister. Where did you learn so much about such diverse subjects?"

"I read a lot, both in books and about current events in newspapers." Calhoun looked up in surprise. He was not used to well read women. Southern Belles seemed to pride themselves on a lack of knowledge, especially concerning current affairs.

"We hear much in England these days concerning the issue of slavery in the Colonies. One can hardly have a discussion at my club without the subject coming up," Kirkland interjected, "I am curious why one feels it's permissible to own another?"

"First and foremost, slavery is essential to survival of the South. Without slaves, we cannot produce the cotton and tobacco crops to meet the demands of the industrialized North much less the growing demands here in England and on the continent."

"But, to treat people like cattle or other property seems so cruel and inhuman!" Hattie said, entering the debate.

"Is it any worse than what I have observed here in England? Why on my visits to factories here, I saw people, including women and children in sweat shops toiling longer hours and treated with less dignity and respect than any slave on any southern plantation I have ever visited! I saw small boys stumbling out of mines, dirty and emaciated to the point of starvation."

"At least they have their freedom." Hattie responded. The fire in her eyes indicating she was only warming up for a real debate with this arrogant...man.

"That's a joke! They receive so little pay and live so close to starvation that it is impossible for them to educate themselves or learn a trade that will open up any avenue for advancement. So there they are, toiling away day to day locked into a life of misery bound by their own indebtedness."

Hattie shut up. Calhoun might have a point. She thought about her own escape. The bonds of ignorance and debt were as real and as strong as the chains and whips the plantation owners used to keep the black Africans working in the fields. Without the miraculous opportunities given to her, and her ability to study and learn special skills, she could still be a slave like many of them.

Hattie sat pondering the question as she ate her breakfast. What was the reason for all this pain and suffering, all this debasement of the human soul? Just so a few people could indulge themselves in luxury? Did people really feel they were better than anyone else because they possessed more money and power? Power to control the lives of others and take away their freedom to choose what or who they would become. She vowed to use any wealth that came her way to help others. Never would she grow wealthy on the backs of others. She would search for ways to lift others up not press them down into poverty. She and her family needed to leave England and begin a new life. One of the attractions of going to America was the belief that there, she would find freedom. She wanted the right to choose her own destiny. Even here in this rather plain but relatively spacious dining area reserved for the ship's captain, she saw what a little bit of power and wealth could produce. Was the food she was eating purchased with money accumulated from slave labor? Feeling sick to her stomach, she asked to be excused and left.

Anne also felt sick. She jumped up from the table and in a display of energy seldom seen bolted head long out the door. She bolted like a runaway horse, and made it to the ship's railing before losing her enormous breakfast over the side of the ship. Lifting her head a short time later, she turned to see a concerned Mr. Hapwood approaching. Lifting the back of her hand to her forehead she repeated a performance he had witnessed many times in the past. "Please help me I am dying!" she uttered, as he gently led her to her cabin.

He met Hattie in the passageway outside their cabin. "I think your sister is in for a bad case of sea sickness. Crackers and water for a few days usually does the trick. Try to make her get up and move around as much as possible." He smiled at her then looked again with more attention. "You don't look so good yourself, Miss Hattie. Are you feeling all right? We men of the sea have a saying. 'There are two kinds of people, those that get seasick and liars.' Well if I can be of any help please let me know." Laughing at his own over-used joke, he sauntered off to tend to his many duties.

Hattie admitted she had a bad headache and was feeling tired, even a little sleepy. *Strange, I never feel sleepy during the day. Maybe Mr. Hapwood is right* she thought. She could also be feeling the effects of seasickness. She waited outside the cabin while Anne bumped, frumped, and flopped into bed. Then, she entered and crawled into her own bunk for a short nap.

By noon, Hattie felt better and got back on her feet. Unable to arouse more than a groan from her sister no matter how much she pestered or prodded her, Hattie left their cabin alone. On deck the activity continued, but at a more relaxed pace. Sailors everywhere were busy making things ship shape, jumping to commands from Mr. Hapwood and a large man called Bosun. She made her way to the spot near the rail where the captain had indicated she should stand while on deck.

Mr. Hapwood approached her and asked, "Feeling better, Miss Hattie?"

"Much better thank you. I am interested in the man called Bosun. He seems to be in charge when the captain is not around. Am I correct?"

Hapwood laughed. "No Miss. Bosun is a title given to the most experienced seaman in the forecastle. His position is much like that of a foreman in a shop or head groom on an estate."

Much like Pap she thought. The memory plucked a string in her thoughts. *Here she was on a ship bound for America. She probably would never see Mam and Pap again.* She made a mental note to write to them and let them know she was safe, and inform them of recent events, and her plans for the future. For a brief time yesterday there had been a moment after seeing Bart Janes in that carriage, when she had thought of returning to Janes Manor. Now that opportunity was gone.

"What a strange name Mr. Hapwood, this 'fowksull.' I am fairly familiar with ships terminology, but I fail to recognize it."

"Actually the word is spelled F-O-R-E-C-A-S-T-L-E."

"Oh yes," exclaimed Hattie, "It's the compartment in the forward part of the ship reserved for the crew's quarters. Am I correct?"

"Quite so," sighed Hapwood. "It also refers to the men that reside there as a group. By the time we reach Charlestown you will be talking like a true salt of the sea Miss Hattie. I guarantee," he laughed, "you won't say you learned it all from a book."

"Charlestown! But I thought this ship was bound for Boston?"

"Officially that is true. But the owners of the *Susan Ganes* follow the golden rule. He who has the gold, rules, so to speak. And in this case Mr. Calhoun is paying and he is paying with real gold."

"But why didn't Captain Barnes tell us that before we bought passage? If we had known you were going to a southern port we would have found another ship."

"Exactly, Miss Hattie. Why do you think Captain Barnes and even Mr. Calhoun have been so accommodating? I can say no more, but you think on it and I am sure, a girl as smart as you will come up with the right reason." With this cryptic comment, he turned his back on Hattie and resumed his duties.

Hattie turned and leaned her elbows on the rail. They were leaving the channel headed for the open sea. She watched England slip away over the horizon. She wondered to herself, what mess of porridge have I fallen into this time? What about Kim? He looked so lost, so alone. I failed to realize how much he cared for me. She owed him her life. How could she ever repay him for all the knowledge and fighting skills he had taught her? She learned to read people by watching their eyes and body, but could anyone really read Kim? With tears in her eyes, she said a final farewell to Kim and to Margaret Janes, Peter and all the others that had helped to make her what and who she was. *Oh, stop your blubbering Hattie. Rise above it you are a Kirkland now!*

Chapter 7

Hattie's Journal

19 August 1858: My suspicions concerning Mr. Calhoun and his secret cargo were confirmed today.

By the third day at sea, a routine emerged. Hattie had learned the system of ship's bells and arose to start her day on the first bell of the forenoon watch. By this time, the seamen were busy doing their morning chores and she would have relative freedom to do hers. She checked on Anne as she dressed. Both she and Anne had recovered from seasickness. Anne however, refused to arise under any circumstances before noon. Hattie picked up four covered pots before leaving the cabin. She removed the chamber pot from its place under Anne's bunk. The other three they kept hanging on pegs found about the cabin.

The chamber pot was the largest. It had a space built under Anne's bunk where it could be secured during rough weather, but Anne could never put it back properly. Hattie carried it in one hand and the three smaller pots in the other. She used one for carrying fresh drinking water. Another, she filled with hot water for making tea. She carried food from the ship's galley in the last one. In the morning, this consisted of warm oatmeal porridge made partially with salt water.

Hattie carried the pots topside. She went to the saltwater pump and used salt water to clean the chamber pot and the food pot. After placing these two pots on the drying rack next to the pump she moved to the fresh water cask and under the watchful eye of the quarterdeck crew, filled her fresh water pot. Taking her pots with her, she walked to the ship's galley to "draw a double ration" of porridge, and a pot of boiling hot water from the cook for her and Anne to share. The last thing she did before returning to her cabin was to take a small portion of tea from her pocket and place it in the pot with the hot water. By the time she returned to the cabin, her tea would be ready.

Hattie put the pots in their places and moved to the large hinged box she had lugged to their cabin the night they embarked. This box held a number of tin containers, jars and a set of eating utensils wrapped in a cloth napkin. Tin cups and a small metal bowl completed the items found inside. She spooned half the porridge from the pot into the bowl, and picked up a cylindrical tin with two holes punched in the top. This was one of several "cans" the man in the hotel had given them as they were packing to leave.

"Here, you might as well take this case with you. It is something new an associate of mine is working on back in the Colonies. He calls it evaporated milk. He steams the milk for a time to remove part of the water, hence the term 'evaporated.' He claims this process will keep the milk from spoiling. I tried one can on the crossing. It tastes a little funny. I'm not much of a milk drinker myself, but you ladies may have a use for it."

Anne had wrinkled her nose, and said nothing but Hattie, always the adventuresome sort, had thanked the gentleman and placed it with the growing stack of items assembled in the hotel lobby. She smiled thinking that it had turned out to be one of the more useful items in the box. With a sprinkling of sugar and a little of the evaporated milk the porridge became almost edible. She also found a dollop of the milk in her tea made a nice change.

After she ate her breakfast, she tried once again to get Anne up and moving. "It's such a beautiful day!" she said with all the enthusiasm she could muster. "C'mon Anne give it a go. You are missing so much of our wonderful adventure." In reality, the adventure was fast slipping into a boring, dreary routine, even for Hattie. If only she could get Anne interested in something.

How can anyone function without some kind of a goal? She wondered. Anne didn't even seem to care about survival. Hattie failed to understand how anyone could live with no incentive at all. Anne represented her other half. They should be a team. Hattie cringed at the vision of being harnessed to a dead weight the rest of her life. *Why me?* She uttered to herself.

Emerging from their cabin, she encountered Beau Calhoun. "Oh, Mr. Calhoun, how nice to see you," she said with her best morning smile.

"I see you seem to be your usual chipper self."

"Is my father up?" She said, changing the subject.

"No, he seems to be a little under the weather this morning." He growled, scratching his bearded chin and rubbing his own bleary eyes.

"Is he not well? Maybe I should check on him," she asked, with a note of concern in her voice.

"I fear his problem is one of long standing. He seems to have consumed a vast quantity of my brandy last night as we sat talking with Captain Barnes. Between the two of them, I believe they will exhaust my considerable stores of liquor before our journey is over," he turned and managed to brush against her much longer than should have been necessary. Just short of provoking her, he moved on down the passage and up on deck.

Hattie shuddered as she turned to follow him thinking once again, here was one more reason to avoid being cornered and alone with this rake. Emerging from the passageway, the fresh air lightly tinged with salt spray and the bright sunlight soon revived her naturally high spirits. She glanced around expecting to find Mr. Calhoun. He was nowhere to be seen. She wondered where he could have disappeared so suddenly? She knew many of the crooks and crannies obstructing her view, but he seemed to have found one she hadn't. She worried about her father. His continued drinking would surely ruin his health, and his ability to function in business. Others would echo Mr. Calhoun's assessment that he was a drunken bumbling fool. What would he do when he ran out of the gold coins and the securities he clutched in his precious satchel?

One of the seamen, she thought his name was Sven, was busy working on the railing. He had roped off an area to prevent others from falling overboard. She sat on a nearby coil of rope to watch. He took a long piece of wood that had previously been shaped to match the rounded contours of the ship's rail. He had trimmed the piece by cutting each end at a long angle creating two sharp points. He was trying to place this piece on top of a section of railing that had been crushed and splintered by a blow from some heavy object. *Probably damaged when some of Mr. Calhoun's heavy machinery was hoisted on board* Hattie thought as she continued to watch Sven struggle. He was trying to hold the rail steady on top of the broken section with one hand while he marked the existing piece with a pencil held against the new section.

"May I help?" she asked, moving up to the rope that barred her way. "I could make the mark while you hold the railing with both hands. That would keep it from slipping."

Sven jumped almost dropping the new piece of wooden rail over the side. "Yah, Dat would be good," Sven replied in his strong Danish accent, regaining his composure.

Hattie took the offered pencil and as Sven held the rail in place, she marked a strong diagonal line on the railing next to the damaged wood. After completing her task she asked, "Do you mind if I continue to watch? There are so few diversions."

"No." Was Sven's reply, "Yust stay oudt of the way please. And don't you go scarin me again."

After sawing out the damaged section, Sven used a rasp and chisel to create a perfect fit. He glued the new section of railing into place and tacked it there with a couple of small nails that he removed later. He rummaged around in his toolbox and located several large brass screws. Taking a brace and a small drill bit, he drilled an equal number of pilot holes through the new rail into the existing railing. He then set the screws creating a permanent connection between the old and new sections. After a little sanding and applying a coat of spar varnish, he began cleaning up the scraps and putting his tools away.

After complementing Sven on his work, Hattie left to check on Anne and her father. She peeked in the door of her father's cabin and found him snoring softly. Anne was up bumping about managing to take up all available room in their cabin so Hattie called through the closed door. "Anne, I will be up on deck. Please come up when you are finished."

Emerging from the passageway, Hattie saw Calhoun closing a small hatch in the deck nearby. Curious as ever she waited until he was finished and asked, "What's in there?"

He jumped when he heard her behind him and turned with a surprised, secretive look about him. "Oh, I, was down in the aft hold checking on my cargo," he mumbled as he brushed by her proceeding to his cabin.

Hattie moved off the other way and found her attention diverted by Mr. Hapwood who appeared busy holding a strange instrument in front of his face. He seemed to examine it with intense concentration.

"May I inquire what you are doing that seems so interesting?" she asked.

Hapwood jumped also. "Oh, it's you miss Hattie. Drat, I may have missed my measurement. Please be quiet for a few moments and then I will be glad to answer your questions." He once again placed the instrument to his eye and with a rocking motion began to move a small knob on the bottom.

As she stood observing his actions, Hattie thought to herself, *Well it is sure my day for making men jump.* Soon Mr. Hapwood took the instrument from his eye and reading from a dial wrote down some numbers on a scrap of paper. "Now, Miss Hattie, how may I be of assistance?"

"I simply wondered what it was that you were doing?"

"Navigating." He said, trying to put on a pleasant face and hide his exasperation at being interrupted while performing a highly delicate task.

"Yes, as I watched I began to see what it was that you were doing. Unfortunately the book about navigation that I read did not have any pictures. I was, however, on closer observation, able to deduce from your actions that the instrument in your hands is a sextant, am I correct?"

"Right again, Miss Hattie."

"Were you taking a sun line Mr. Hapwood?"

"Yes. Is there anything you have not read in one of your innumerable books?" He asked trying his best to be polite.

"I am sure I have much to learn Mr. Hapwood. Like today, I may have discerned what you were doing but I have never seen how it is done. I truly appreciate the opportunity to observe an expert in action." She figured a little flattery would help to put him in a better mood.

And it did. He was soon deep into a discussion of the measurements and the timing necessary to take an accurate sun line. He went on to say. "Once you have the sun line you can determine the latitude of the ship at noon each day. Please follow me." He led her down to a small compartment under the captain's cabin where he showed her another mechanism. Opening a door, he examined a dial inside, and wrote some numbers on his scrap of paper. "This is the ship's log. It measures how far we have traveled through the water."

"How does it work? Why is it called a log?"

"It is called a log because originally measurements were taken by tossing a piece of wood tied to a known length of line ahead of the ship. The navigator measured the time it took for the log to drift back to the point where it started. In this manner a crude measurement of speed and distance could be calculated. I am surprised you had not read about such things in your books."

"Why Mr. Hapwood, I am, after all, only human." She replied, thinking to herself that it was easier to get information when she let others believe she was not a complete know it all.

Hapwood continued, "This device is a modern version of that principle. Water enters through this pipe and exits via this second pipe here. The ship's movement causes water to flow through the pipes. This box in the middle, where the dial is located, contains a mechanism much like that found in a clock. It measures the flow and moves the numbers on the dial. In this way I can record the numbers, do a little arithmetic and determine the speed from the distance we have covered since the last noon sun line."

"Why take the sun line at noon?"

"That's easy. The sun reaches its apex precisely at noon each day. This makes the position much more accurate. Did you notice that I was rocking the sextant as I took the measurement? The rocking motion allows one to observe the highest rise or apex of the sun's position."

When they reached the main deck Hattie turned and said, "Thank you so much for the information and the tour. It makes the time pass so much faster when I am entertained by one so knowledgeable as yourself," she cringed inwardly. *Don't lay it on too thick.* "Well I feel a light lunch is in order. Will you be joining us for lunch Mr. Hapwood?"

"I am not sure. I must wait until the captain relieves me. Then we must check the ship's position together. I will probably be late since I have not yet seen the captain this morning."

Hattie left to see if she could find Anne. She found her sitting on the same coil of line she had occupied earlier while watching Sven repair the ship's rail. Anne was dutifully eating cold porridge and drinking a lukewarm cup of tea. Hattie sat down next to her, and munched on the biscuit she picked up as she passed the galley.

Anne turned to her and immediately started complaining. "This trip is so boring. I had anticipated a voyage with lots of other passengers and exciting conversations with strange, handsome young men, with parties and maybe dancing. I still don't understand why we had to sail on this leaky old tub!"

"Anne, how much of father's circumstances are you aware of?"

"Well, I know we had to leave London quite suddenly and he says we can never return. But, I really don't understand it. Why did we have to leave? And why has he been acting so differently since we reached Bristol?"

"Do you know what embezzlement is?"

"Is that when someone uses money from a company for his own use that really belongs to the whole company?"

"That's accurate enough for our discussion. On our first morning in Bristol, father discovered that the Sheriff was making inquiries about him concerning embezzlement charges filed by certain solicitors. Unfortunately, the charges may be true. He made the decision to leave by the first available ship bound for America with room on board for us. I helped him do it. That makes me a criminal too. It's called accessory after the fact. We had to leave on the *Susan Ganes*. We had to take the only ship available."

"That is just not true! We have enough money to buy and sell crooks like those you mention. My father would never be involved in something so, so wrong!" shrieked Anne jumping up and stomping her foot. "I understand he has problems, but they can't be that bad! I just want things to be better. I want, I want, I want!"

"Well," said Hattie, "You can want in one hand, and spit in the other. Then see which fills up first."

"Where did you ever hear such a vulgar thing?" asked Anne with a look of disgust on her face.

"It might seem vulgar to a well brought up, or should I say, pampered young woman. But, that's the way working folks look at a problem. I learned from Pap that it is much better to get to work and start doing something to solve your problems than to sit around whimpering and wailing, waiting for someone else or for the 'Government' to do something about them."

"Owugh!" growled Anne,. Jumping up, she stomped off to her cabin, bent on solving her problem by covering her head and going back to sleep.

Hattie continued to sit on the coil of rope. She too felt a certain frustration about being on this slow moving, leaky old scow. Her father could certainly have paid for accommodations on a faster more modern ship, but time and circumstances did not cooperate. Why couldn't he see that his drinking was ruining the whole family?

Sitting there rocking to the steady, rolling motion of the ship, she could feel her muscles flexing as she naturally kept her head and shoulders steady. She remembered that she had become very lax in doing the exercises Kim insisted she complete every day to keep herself in shape. She got up and began looking for a corner where she could work out in relative privacy. Thinking that the aft hold might have space, she climbed through the hatch where she had observed Mr. Calhoun emerging earlier. She followed the steps down and discovered that there was room but the cargo was placed such that she could not find an open space big enough to meet her needs.

She tried to move one of the crates but couldn't budge it. The long narrow crate had a manufacturer's name printed on it. Someone had tried to cover it with paint but she could still read it *Enfield*. Where had she read or seen that name? Just then she heard a noise and looked up to see Mr. Calhoun on the far side of the hold. If she moved, he would see her! Why not? she decided. She had as much right to be here as he did.

"Oh, Mr. Calhoun," she called, "is there any room over there? I have been taking dance lessons and my teacher wanted me to keep up my routines. I am looking for an open place to practice."

"No, I am afraid not. There is less room here than on the side where you are standing. I really don't think it is safe for you to be down here. You could get hurt by a falling crate...or something." He said with more irritation than concern in his voice.

More likely I'd receive a bash on the skull by a certain scoundrel I know. She thought to herself. As she was climbing the ladder out of the hold, she remembered where she had seen the word Enfield—Rifles! For a moment, she could see them gleaming in the afternoon sun in Mr. Janes' study. She even remembered the smell of the special oil he used when cleaning them. It was one of the few times he had spoken directly to her. She had been dusting the case when he entered. Seeing what she was doing, he had given her strict instructions never to touch the guns inside. He explained that the natural acid on her hands would react with the iron and cause it to rust. Even her cleaning rags were no good. Cleaning and oiling guns was not the work of little serving girls.

Hattie had obeyed his instructions, but later she had found pamphlets in a drawer of the gun case that described the weapons, and how to use them. The pamphlets had contained drawings she found unique and interesting. The artist had drawn each screw, spring and lever used to assemble the gun. They were positioned in such a way that dashed lines illustrated how the pieces went together to assemble the gun. She studied the drawings until she felt confident that she could have assembled them if need be. One of the pamphlets had described an Enfield rifle.

Returning topside she located an area behind the quarterdeck that might work. Seeing Captain Barnes on the quarterdeck, she went up to him. She used the dance practice story, and received permission to practice. As she started to work out, she discovered that there were certain exercises that were difficult to perform all wrapped up in a heavy traveling dress. Smiling to herself, she rushed back to her cabin. Moving quietly so as not to disturb Anne, she changed into her boy clothes. She then ran back to the corner she had so recently vacated.

She worked out on her exercises for over an hour. She was not able to do many of the defensive moves that required a companion, but she was able to exercise her muscles and reflexes, and tone her body. She emphasized the exercises Kim had taught her after her surgery, which strengthened her back and leg injured at birth. She leaned back gasping for breath and happened to look up to see several faces grinning down at her from the rigging overhead. Oh well, she thought might as well brazen it out. So, she smiled and waved as she walked quickly to the saltwater pump and rinsed out her towel and began to rub her face and neck to cool herself off. Then with the airs and dignity of a young woman taking a stroll in a London park, she returned to her cabin.

Exercising became a part of her daily routine. She always had an audience but nothing was ever said. Once or twice she caught Mr. Calhoun glancing her way with what seemed to be more respect than admiring speculation. She felt irritated that his respect should be important to her.

The days passed with monotonous similarity. Anne continued to pout and spend most of the time in her bunk. Hattie saw little of her father. They usually shared the evening meal together and then he would stay late at the captain's table with Mr. Calhoun where they apparently discussed world events and politics into the wee hours. She rarely found him sober enough for any serious conversation with or about his daughters.

Then came the day when he showed that he really cared, and respected her for who she was, and what she had become. An ugly scream interrupted her morning exercise routine. More screaming and the sound of running feet followed a thump. Hattie found herself running toward the screaming. *Is it Anne? Has something happened to Anne to make her scream?*

It was not Anne, but it was awful! One of the sailors had lost his hold in the rigging as the ship was turning on to a new tack. He had fallen to the deck, and lay screaming in a fountain of pulsating blood. Hattie ran forward pushing several sailors out of the way. She reached down, and pressed as hard as she could on the artery above the bleeding leg. "Get a piece of that line around his leg above my hand for a tourniquet!" she shouted. The sailor's leg was bent at an awkward angle and a sharp bone was protruding out of a bloody gash in his pants.

"You," she pointed at the nearest sailor she could see, "run to my cabin and fetch the black case under my pillow. Hurry!"

Just then Captain Barnes arrived shouting, "What's going on around here? You, young lady get away so I can see!"

Hattie looked up and in her sharpest voice replied, "If I get away the man will die! I have medical training, and you are in the way so move back! You go run your ship, and let me try to save this man's life."

"She's right you know, captain," came a strong voice from the back of the crowd. "My daughter has had excellent medical training. In fact she saved my life a little over a month ago." Her father stepped up and with the aristocratic breeding of a lifetime faced the captain full on. Captain Barnes mumbled something about keeping him informed and returned to his quarterdeck.

The sailor arrived with Hattie's case. "Open it," she cried as she crouched down holding the sailor's leg. With the open case was in front of her, she picked up the razor sharp scalpel, and cut the pants away from the injury. After a quick look, she asked for hot water from the galley. She turned and saw Calhoun watching with interest.

"Would you be so kind as to donate some of your strongest spirits to the cause Mr. Calhoun? I will require at least two full bottles."

When the liquor arrived, Hattie doused her hands in it, and ordered the seaman holding the victim's head to start feeding him the other bottle as fast as he would drink it. She poured more of the liquor into the open wound. A thought occurred to her, turning and looking up she asked, "Sven are you here?"

"Ya"

"Go get me that drill, and some of those big screws you used the other day to mend the ship's rail—hurry!"

Hattie looked up and saw the seaman holding her case standing beside her. Turning her head toward him, she ordered, "I don't want to get my hands dirty. If you will reach into that flat covered place inside, you will find a book. In the book, I left a twist of silk thread I use for a bookmark. Get a couple strands and thread one to the smallest needle you see in the case." She pointed with her nose. "See, the needles are there by those things that look like pliers," glancing about she called, "is that boiling water here yet?"

"Here it is." The cook approached balancing a large steaming pot in his hands.

"Good," breathed Hattie as she examined her patient, noting that his breathing was becoming fast and shallow, and that the effects of the alcohol were taking hold.

"Hand me that thing that looks like a loop with a slotted metal band, and a long handle on it."

The sailor who brought her the case touched an instrument, looked at her questioningly.

"Yes, that thing."

Holding the instrument by the handle, Hattie placed as much of it as possible in the hot water for a few moments. She took it out and twisted the end until the metal band popped open. She gently slid the band under and around the sides of the broken bone. She turned to the men holding her patient. "Hold him tight now and gently pull the leg straight as I tighten this clamp." Inserting the band into the slot provided, she began to twist the handle. As the handle turned, the band became smaller bringing the sides of the broken bone together.

When she had it tight, she turned to the man holding the threaded needle. Taking it from him by the end of the thread, she dipped it and her hand into the hot water.

Gasping for breath, she looked up and grimaced. "Would someone be so kind as to quickly pour a little of Mr. Calhoun's finest over my hand?"

She waved her hand and arm in the air to dry and cool them before she reached in and found the severed artery. She began to stitch it back together. Fortunately, she found the artery unsevered but sliced open lengthwise. This allowed her to do the job without putting more dirty hands in the open wound. She prayed that the blood would clot and help stop the bleeding.

With the artery closed up, she directed the man holding the tourniquet to slowly release his hold. She watched to see if the stitches were holding. With a little blood now flowing through the artery she asked without looking up, "Sven, are you here yet?"

"Ya"

"Put the drill and the drill bit in the hot water and tie a string to a screw and put it in there also."

Getting up from her crouch, Hattie rolled her shoulders to relive the cramps, and moved around to the other side of her patient. She checked his breathing and plucked the drill from the hot water. After dousing it in liquor, she moved to the patient and warning the sailors to hold him tight, she placed the drill bit near the edge of the clamp holding the bone, and began to drill a hole in the bone. When she finished, she screwed the bone together, leaving the end of the screw protruding from the bone. She released the clamp and withdrew it from the wound.

After dousing the whole thing with more liquor, she began to close up the wound. When she was done, she had a stitched up leg with a small clean rag at one end and a rather large screw protruding from the center of the wound. She wrapped the area with a clean cloth, and splinted the leg with boards and straps provided by the sailors.

She stood up and noticed Calhoun watching her with admiration and respect in his eyes. She turned to Sven. "Please ask the captain where we can put him. He will need a lot of care for the first few days. We must keep that leg raised higher than his head."

"Vood der carpenter shop vork?" asked Sven. "ve can moof the lumber to the forvard hold und fix a bunk on da lomber rack."

The captain approached and noting the question in her gaze nodded. "That would be a good place. The carpenter shop is near your cabin and you can get there quickly, if needed. Bosun, see that Sven is taken off the watch list. He will stand on and off watches with Miss Kirkland attending to Samuels until he is on the way to recovery, or 'til he dies." These final words simply confirming what all of them knew. That an injury like this at sea had a very low recovery success rate.

For Hattie, the next few days flew by as she struggled to keep Samuels alive. After two weeks, she removed the brass screw from the bone. She taught Sven a series of exercises to keep the leg from getting stiff. Soon Samuels could move the leg by himself, and get around with the crutch, Sven fashioned for him. He was getting so active that Hattie had to lay the law down, and order him to leave the splint on for at least another month.

When not involved in nursing Samuels back to health, Hattie spent time with Mr. Hapwood learning more about navigation. He introduced her to a new book he called, *Bowditch.* The full title was *The American Practical Navigator.* Nathaniel Bowditch only edited the book, which consisted of a compilation of tables used for fixing one's position by using the stars. The front of the book contained a fascinating textbook on the principles of stellar navigation. She and Hapwood would shoot stars on every clear evening, and compete to see who could get the most precise fix in the shortest time. Everyone's spirits began to improve as the navigation fixes showed definite promise of soon sighting land.

Hattie needed to replenish some of her personal food supplies from the boxes they had placed in the ship's hold. She had promised Anne, she would look for her parasol. The days were growing quite hot and humid. Even their strolls on the deck were becoming uncomfortable.

She tried to move a box off one of Mr. Calhoun's crates in order to reach the trunk containing Anne's parasol. As she was moving the heavy box, the lid on the crate came loose. Being ever the curious one, Hattie decided a quick peek wouldn't hurt. After all, she had never seen a cotton gin. Looking through a crack in the lid, she did not see an engine. She saw a cannon! She quickly put the lid back on the crate as best she could, gathered her supplies, and quietly left the hold. *Rifles and cannons and shipped in crates disguised as machinery? What was Mr. Calhoun up to? Was he planning to start a war all by himself?*

All the passengers dined in the captain's cabin that night. A festive mood prevailed. The men had already consumed more than enough liquor. Hattie decided to liven up the conversation, hoping to distract her father from consuming more strong drink. She turned to Calhoun and asked, "What are you really going to do with all those guns and the ammunition you have in the hold? Start a war?"

Immediate silence prevailed around the table. Calhoun answered in a calm arrogant tone. "That is precisely the intention, my little busybody. Maybe not immediately, but sooner or later the inevitable will happen. I intend to see that the South has the arms necessary to fight, if and when peaceful secession fails." Trying to lighten the conversation with a joke, he added, "Should war come I am sure there will be plenty of need for your services as a healer."

"I fail to find much humor in death or human suffering," countered Hattie using the most indignant tone she could muster.

Mr. Hapwood entered the cabin, and interrupted their conversation. "Captain, I think we are in for a blow. Hurricane season does not usually start this early, but I don't like the way things are shaping up. The barometer is dropping fast, and I just have this feeling…"

"Well, Hapwood, I have come to trust your feelings. You folks better go check on all your belongings. Make sure they are securely fastened. Let's go see if we have a blow coming on." With that comment the captain, with Hapwood right behind him, departed for the quarterdeck.

As she and Anne made their way their cabin, Hattie saw Mr. Calhoun open the hatch and scurry down into the aft hold to check on his precious cargo. *There goes the rat down into his lair*, Hattie thought as she ran past.

Thomas Kirkland started to get up and follow the others. He noticed the various amounts of wine left in the glasses. He hesitated, deciding to tarry awhile. *No sense wasting a good year,* he thought to himself.

High winds and the first huge wave struck the *Susan Ganes* shortly after midnight.

Chapter 8

Hattie's Journal

24 October 1858: I have not written in my journal for some time. Many good, but mostly sad things have happened. I am alone again.

t seemed like the wild rocking, swooping, and plunging would separate her from her stomach. Both girls lost their supper hours ago. Hattie discovered how useful the ropes dangling from the overhead could be. For days, she had pushed them out of the way, but they kept falling on her in the night like snakes in a jungle. Now, she welcomed them as a way to tie herself into her bunk, and ride out the storm. The *Susan Ganes* began taking a terrible beating. She had heard crashing timbers earlier, accompanied by worried shouts outside their cabin. Now, she noticed terrible groans, and sounds of splintering wood as if the very hull was being torn apart.

Water rushed in their cabin. It sloshed around for a while, and then drained away only to return refreshed by the onslaught of yet another great wave. She believed they were caught in the danger quadrant of the hurricane as the books she had read described it. Suddenly the screaming from the wind intensified. Then, she realized it was not the wind. It was Anne.

The screams became words. "I'm drowning! I'm drowning! The water is in my bed!"

There were sounds of sloshing and bumping. Then the screaming and bumping sounds seemed to get farther away. It was pitch dark. Hattie could see nothing. She had a chilling thought. "Anne, Anne! Are you there?" She reached down over the edge of her bunk. The bulky body that normally reclined there was gone. All she could touch was water!

Hattie managed to hang on to at least one line as she slid out of her bunk and dropped into the swirling mass below her. She caught hold of the swinging door, hauled herself through and into the passage. She opened her father's door and screamed his name. She detected no answer. Either he was gone or unconscious. She must find help. Moving like a blind person held captive in a tumbling washtub, she crept slowly toward the captain's cabin, praying she could find someone to help her.

Looking in the doorway, she caught a glimpse of a figure outlined by a lightning flash through a porthole. Her father sat slumped in a chair moving in response to the reeling ship like a rag doll riding a bucking horse.

She pulled herself towards him, and began shaking him into awareness. "Anne is gone! We must look for her! Get up and do this for your daughter!" she screamed in his ear. Something must have penetrated. He began to move, shake his alcohol fogged brain, and pull himself up.

Together, they moved to the door leading to the open deck. It was jammed shut tight. It wouldn't budge. The ship corkscrewed. With a sickening drop and a crash, the door flew open and Hattie found herself in a nightmare of moving water and screaming wind. She caught sight of a billowing figure in white frozen for an instant by flashing lightning, climbing into the lifeboat. Hattie grabbed her father's shoulder and pointed. "She's in the lifeboat!"

Her father nodded vaguely at her, held up a hand in a wait a minute gesture and turned away.

Hattie stood, frozen in amazement. Could no calamity penetrate his alcohol fogged brain? In frustration, she turned and sensing a pause in the storm around her, ran the short distance to the lifeboat. Crawling inside, she found a wet whimpering mass wedged between the seats. All her attempts to dislodge Anne's hold on the seats failed. Anne's fear had found a reserve of immense strength that combined with her massive bulk defeated all Hattie's attempts to move her.

Hattie looked outside the flapping lifeboat cover hoping to find help. There caught in the glare of another lightning flash stood her father. He paused at the passageway entrance, looking toward the lifeboat ready to make a move her way. Feelings of love and pride swept over Hattie as she held that image in her mind. He had come back. He really did care.

Closer inspection would have revealed that Thomas Kirkland had returned to his cabin to retrieve his precious briefcase. He wouldn't recognize the crouching determined picture he made. With both arms wrapped around his briefcase, he was prepared to give his all to make that plunge across the deck to reach the lifeboat. Just as he made his move, another huge wave swept the ship, taking all in its path. It pushed the ship over the crest into the full force of the wind. The wave washed Kirkland away like a table scrap down a drain. With hands and arms locked firmly about the briefcase, he could make no effort to even try to grab a line or a stanchion. The water took him deep. The weight of the gold coins in his money belt, and his death grip on the briefcase only hastened his downward dive. Old Jensen the butler would have been surprised to learn that Thomas Kirkland carried the last of his fortune with him to his grave. He had not lost it all before he died.

Hattie's hold on Anne as she worked to move her, saved her during that initial surge from the rogue wave. Both women managed to stay with the lifeboat as it soared far from its nest in the *Susan Ganes*. The light buoyant craft seemed to fly. In the midst of this crazy, crashing, dipping, diving, ride, Hattie caught the end of a rope that whipped about her. Anne had torn it loose from the lifeboat cover when she climbed in. Hattie slipped it under a seat, and tied it there, before she tied it around her waist.

Huddled together in the bottom of the lifeboat, the two sisters clung to one another as the treacherous storm continued to carry them along in its wet, icy, grip. Hattie fought to hang on as the storm continued to wash over them. Consciousness left her as she slid down the side of a long slippery slope to oblivion.

Feeling returned slowly to Hattie. First, she felt something wet slapping at her face. When she tried to brush it aside, she found her hand wouldn't move. It felt like a wooden club attached to her shoulder. When she realized that it was trapped under Anne's leg, she pulled it out, and the sharp needles of returning circulation helped to bring her around.

Why was she upside down? Her feet were jammed under the forward seat, near the bow of the lifeboat while her head rested lower, on Anne's ample thigh.

She looked up. Was she in a tent? No, it was the lifeboat's cover. The sun shining on the outside gave the interior of the lifeboat a golden glow as if she were in a tent. It was hot, she could smell the musty old canvass stretched above her, and she was desperately thirsty. Her mouth and eyes were encrusted with salt crystals. She had to get out or suffocate! Every move brought more pain and agony as muscles and nerves came alive. She found the line wrapped around her waist. After many false starts and fumbling she managed to untie the knot that held her prisoner.

Using her feet and one arm, she kicked loose a section of the cover, and a gust of humid air smelling like wet weeds rushed in. Encouraged by the promise of more fresh air, Hattie continued to struggle until she fell free from the lifeboat and its constraining cover. She landed on her shoulders in cool wet sand. She rested there for a moment trying to catch her breath.

Looking up, she saw the lifeboat's bow caught in the crotch of a tree while the stern rested on the sand near her head. She rolled over on her hands and knees, and looked around. The lifeboat had come to rest on a low hummock of sand in the middle of a swamp or marshy area. The flood of high water from the hurricane must have carried them up some kind of riverbed. Then as the water receded, it left the lifeboat stranded here caught in the tree.

The lower ground around her remained under water. She crawled to the water's edge and tested it. It tasted a little brackish but drinkable. She figured this must be runoff water from the rain that accompanied the hurricane. She scooped up handful after handful drinking some and splashing more on her face and neck. She felt a cooling sensation as the water began to evaporate in the slight breeze swirling around the lifeboat.

Anne! She remembered that Anne was still trapped inside the lifeboat. She crawled back, and checked to see if Anne was alive and breathing. She was—barely—thank goodness! After much pulling and prodding, she managed to free Anne from the lifeboat and drag her onto the sand. She ripped a strip of Anne's dress off. Wetting it in the water, she bathed her face and revived her enough to get her to crawl to the water's edge and drink. They both crawled into the shade produced by the lifeboat and the one tree left standing on their tiny island.

Anne uttered her first words. "What happened to father? I thought I saw him running toward the lifeboat. Is he still in the lifeboat?" She asked as she lifted her head to look inside.

Hattie replied, "I'm sorry Anne. Father never reached the lifeboat. A huge wave washed him over the side of the ship just as he was running to save us. I am afraid he drowned at sea."

Anne simply raised an eyebrow, and shrugged as if Hattie were telling her the time of day. Then she asked, "Is there anything to eat? I'm hungry."

After resting for a little bit, Hattie got up, staggered toward the lifeboat, and began to take everything out that remained inside. She discovered two sealed tins of biscuits and a water keg. She found a set of oars and a mast with a sail attached, lashed in place but the tiller and rudder were missing, probably swept away in the storm. She poked around in a mass a tangled ropes and pulleys. They seemed attached to the sail. One unexpected item turned up. It was her surgical case. *What was it doing here?* Then she remembered that earlier, on the day before the storm, she had checked on Samuels. She was returning to her cabin, but had been hailed by Mr. Hapwood. He invited her to shoot stars. To save time and steps, she had placed the case in the lifeboat rather than return it to her cabin. *Too bad there wasn't something to eat inside,* she thought as she placed it near the other salvaged supplies. Having completed this task she drank some more water, and collapsed on the sand. If Anne wanted a biscuit, she would have to open the tin herself, she needed to rest.

Hattie was up the next day with the sun. Anne was not. She had a slight fever when Hattie checked her. She refused to eat any of the stale biscuits from the tin, but did drink a little water. Hattie didn't blame her for not wanting to eat any of the biscuit. It was stale, hard, and tasteless, probably with little or no food value. But they did fill up the emptiness with something. As she sat chewing on some of the biscuit and washing it down with water, she could feel the intense heat from the sun burning her shoulders.

Hattie decided to see if she could rig the lifeboat cover into a sort of tent for some additional protection from the merciless rays of the hot sun. A cover would help at night, especially if it rained. This task took most of the morning since she was still weak and Anne refused to help. All Anne managed to do was wiggle her body into the deepest shade once Hattie had completed the makeshift tent.

After a rest at noon, Hattie decided to do a little exploring. She was looking for some sign of human habitation, a road or anything that would lead her to civilization. This was a completely different situation from her previous survival ordeal. Here she would welcome being found. She checked the water level surrounding her island and noticed that it continued to recede. The ground nearby should begin to dry up soon.

She returned to camp wet to the waist and discouraged. She discovered no signs of habitation, and she had done enough wading to determine she was caught in some kind of swamp. When she returned, she discovered that Anne's fever was worse. She had passed some bushes that appeared to be willow. She wondered if American willow bark had the same fever and pain reducing qualities as that found in England? Figuring it wouldn't hurt to try, she gathered things for a fire to boil water.

Kim had taught her several ways to make a fire without matches so she didn't have the same problem keeping a fire going that she had last time. Flint and steel proved a poor option since there were very few rocks on her island. She unraveled a piece of light rope from the lifeboat and constructed a fire bow using a nearby stick. Gathering a pile of dry wood and tinder, she began spinning a dry stick with the fire bow. After much effort, she created a small glowing ember, which she brought close to the tinder. Using slow steady breaths, she coaxed forth a blaze.

She emptied the biscuit tin on the canvas, and filled it with some water. She scraped some of the inner bark from the willow branches she had collected while she searched for a piece of flint earlier, and set it to steep in the hot water. Fortunately her medical kit contained a spoon for dispensing medicine. She used the spoon to feed the liquid to Anne. After Anne had consumed all she would take, Hattie drank the rest to ease her own pain sustained in the bruising lifeboat ride, and from her exertions of the day. The pain eased somewhat, only to be replaced by a gnawing ache for some real food. *With all these bushes around there should be something edible,* she thought.

As evening approached, she sat in the sand at the water's edge and tried to plan her next move. *It is so peaceful here right now,* she thought, *with the frogs croaking and all. Frogs!* She jerked upright as a thought entered her head. She could take one of the willow branches she had gathered, and sharpen the end to make a frog harpoon. The stick she selected actually separated into two smaller branches emerging at a junction forming a natural fork. After she had sharpened the stick with her scalpel, she held it over the heat from the fire to harden the points.

Moving away from camp, she tried to spear several large frogs. They would dive deep into the water, frightened by her quick movements. She learned to move slowly behind the frog until the last possible moment. It proved more difficult than she thought it would be. Then her observation skills, and her natural hand eye coordination took over, and she began to have some success. She brought the frogs back to camp, and removed the legs. Impaling the legs on another, smaller, stick, she was soon eating broiled frog legs. Anne rose up to see what she was doing. When Hattie offered her some, she made a face and rolled over saying, "Euwe ugh," and refused to eat.

Hattie sat by the fire as it burned down leaving a small bed of glowing coals. Her thoughts drifted to other lonely fires in the south of England. At least there she had a map in her head, and she knew roughly where she was. If she had a map with her right now, she would still not know which way to go. There were no roads or mountains visible to her. To make a map useful, she would need to know where she was and where she wanted to go. The only guess she could make concerning their present location placed her somewhere on the East Coast of America. Maybe they were in southern Virginia or maybe North Carolina. The wind and currents caused by the hurricane would have carried them in a northwesterly direction. Her last fix with Mr. Hapwood held them off the Carolina coast. If she remembered correctly, the more inhabited regions lay to the north on the Virginia coast. She decided heading north would be best once they recovered their strength, and found something to eat. She would concentrate her search for a way out by heading north and east.

Anne represented her immediate challenge. She had to get Anne well enough to travel, and motivated enough to walk and wade through this swamp. That, beyond a doubt became the heart of her problem.

So solve the problem Hattie. That's what you're good at.

Uttering a half sigh, half grumble, she moved over near Anne. She checked her for fever by placing a hand on her forehead. She rolled up some canvas from the sail using it to make a pillow. She started to fall asleep almost immediately. *Maybe an answer will come to me in a dream,* she thought.

Anne seemed better in the morning, and started eating the biscuits. Existing on an exclusive diet of biscuits, Anne would quickly consume their supply. Hattie decided to explore more of the area to the north. Earlier, she had found a long slim branch of a fallen tree. She had cut off a section about six feet in length. After peeling off the bark, she sharpened one end and hardened it in the fire. She took up this staff as she called it, and told Anne she was off to look for more food.

Anne gave her a sour look and said, "Why won't you stay here and help me? I am a mess. This sand is getting in all my clothes. it's gritty and is giving me a rash. I need you to do something!"

"For two reasons," Hattie replied. "First, I am helping you by finding more to eat. Do you think those mealy old biscuits will last forever? Second, you need to start helping yourself. The sooner you get up and move about the sooner we can start walking out of here."

"I am not walking out of anywhere! Especially if I have to walk in that slimy, muddy, water to get there!" Anne croaked as she gestured at the swamp all around them.

"Oh, yes you are young lady. So you better start getting ready to do just that." With that comment, Hattie set off purposely wading through the creek showing off for Anne's benefit.

She walked for less than an hour before she came to a large patch of reeds growing in the swampy, muddy, ground. She started to fight her way through them, and discovered they were taller than she was. An idea came to her, she took out her scalpel and began to cut the reeds. She would cut for a while, and then bundle the reeds together using two or three as a twist-tie to hold the bundle together. When she had all she could carry and drag, she returned to camp.

She hauled the reeds up next to where Anne sat pouting. "Here," she ordered, "make yourself useful."

"What am I supposed to do with this?" asked Anne, picking up a single reed between her finger and thumb, holding it up for inspection like it was a dirty piece of laundry.

Hattie sighed and asked, "Did you ever learn to weave as a little girl? You know, make little things for your room or for your dollies?"

"No, I had servants that did all that," she muttered, distain darkening her voice.

"Did you watch them?" Hattie asked letting a tone of exasperation creep into her voice.

"Yes." Her tone and the expression on her face seemed to say I'm not stupid.

"Well then, you have the basic idea. Here, I will get you started." Hattie proceeded to show Anne how to use the reeds to weave a large mat.

"Why are we making this?"

"You are the one complaining about getting a rash from the gritty sand, and the dried salt in your clothes. We are going to make mats to sleep on, and to keep the sand out of our clothes."

"How are we going to get the sand out of our clothes to begin with?"

"We are going to take them off, go swimming in the creek, and wash them at the same time."

"But what if someone sees us?"

"We should be so lucky," Hattie replied thinking to herself that her sense of humor was returning. She hoped it was a good sign.

When they had each completed two mats, Hattie got up and started undressing. She took all her clothes off, and holding them in front of her, calmly walked into the creek. A little way downstream, she found a large fallen log that had dammed up a portion of the creek creating a pool and an eddy. The swirling current had cleared the bottom of debris, and dug a hole roughly six feet across. When Hattie stood in the hole the water reached to her neck.

"Hurry Anne," she called, "it's wonderful. The water is so refreshing." After scrubbing the salt and dirt out of her clothes, she placed them on the log, and began to swim about. Soon, a reluctant Anne joined her.

They managed to scrub the worst of the dirt and grit from their clothes amidst laughing, giggling water fights, and some extra well aimed splashing. Hattie kept the game going as long as she could, knowing that the exercise would help build Anne's endurance. Leaving their clothes spread out on the log to dry, they returned to their new mats, and took a nap while the wind dried them off.

Hattie retrieved their clothes from the log. She pulled herself up on to the log, and walked along the log to shore like it was a walk in the park. Anne marveled at her balance and dexterity secretly glad she didn't have to attempt to balance her bulk on the log's slippery surface. To fight the oppressive heat and humidity Hattie opted to wear only her shirtwaist and a single petticoat. She folded her other clothing up, and placed it in the lifeboat. She was amused to see Anne do the same thing. She wondered to herself if the reason was to copy her actions or if Anne simply chose the less arduous task of donning fewer items of clothing.

Having been sidetracked from her exploration to the north, Hattie decided to try again after eating a biscuit for lunch. She still needed to find nourishing food for them to eat. Taking up her walking stick, she set off again. She saw fish swimming in the water as she walked along, and made a note to make some fish traps from the reeds that evening. She found another mound a little larger than the one where they were marooned. This bit of high ground boasted a patch of ripe black berries. She could not determine the exact variety, but who cared. They were sweet and juicy. *Even Anne will enjoy these,* she thought, using a fold in her petticoat to carry away as many as possible. Returning to camp, she found some wild onions along the way. She could only take a few since she had no place to carry them. *I need a basket,* she thought, *another job for this evening.*

As Hattie entered camp, an excited grinning Anne greeted her. She was holding something behind her back. "I have a surprise for you," Anne said as she jumped up and down with excitement.

As Hattie turned from placing the onions and berries on one of the mats, she looked up at the object in Anne's hands.

"It's a sun hat," Anne said with a grin. "I made it just for you. I remembered seeing one like it in a shop before I left London. It was the latest thing, straight from Paris. Oh, Hattie, I hope you like it. I worked all afternoon on it."

"I do, I do like it. This will help keep the sun out of my eyes."

"Yes, and it will help save your skin from those ugly red blotches, and from turning that ugly brown color."

"I have a surprise for you as well, sweet juicy blackberries!"

The girls danced and hopped around. Each showing off their gifts. The thought entered Hattie's head that the two of them might just make it after all.

Just before sunset, Hattie took her harpoon, and returned to the spot in the creek where she had seen the fish. There were several, and they seemed to be trapped by the receding floodwaters. She speared two and left the others for another day. Returning to camp she cleaned the fish, and broiled them over the campfire. A different Anne greedily devoured her share of fish and onions. They ended their feast with the last of the blackberries and a drink from the creek.

In the evening firelight, Hattie made fish traps while Anne wove a basket under Hattie's direction. These tasks completed, both girls unfolded their heavier dresses, and using them for a cover, settled down for the night. Just as she was nodding off Hattie heard Anne say, "What is this glorious feeling I have right now? I have never had this feeling in my life before."

"They call that feeling self worth. It hits us when we work out our own problems or reach out and do something for someone else without being asked." Hattie smiled as she added, "Be careful, it can become very powerful and addictive."

"It sure makes one feel like living again," Anne said as she drifted off for a well-earned night's sleep.

Anne was the first one up for a change. She ran naked into the creek screaming and splashing. The thought passed through Hattie's head to caution her about dashing about without carefully inspecting the area, but she forgot in the excitement of the ensuing water fight that left both girls wet and exhausted.

Hattie prepared to leave camp. A few minutes later, she stood dressed in a tattered shirtwaist and grimy slip, bare feet supporting a lean whip of a body. Her sunburned face now smiled out from under a sun hat, made in the latest London fashion. In one hand, she held a six-foot spear, while the other held a basket. Holding the spear aloft, she declared in a deep thundering voice. "Behold, Hattie, Queen of the Swamp!"

"Well Queenie, giggled Anne, "fetch the princess a fine repast for supper." She gave Hattie a limp-wrist wave in her best high society London manner.

Hattie set off as usual combining her search for food with an exploration of the area around their camp. She started out in a northeasterly direction this time. She began to notice that there appeared to be fewer pools of brackish water, and more solid ground in this direction as she moved farther away from camp. She had tried this direction earlier, but floodwater from the hurricane had covered a lot of the ground where she was now walking. As the water receded and the land began to revert to the normal water level, she felt this direction might lead them out of the swamp.

She focused her attention on watching the trail, and noted changes in the type of grass and bushes around her. She did not immediately hear the grunting, squealing, and thrashing ahead of her. When the noise penetrated her senses, she froze. *Fight or flight,* that primitive decision flashed through her subconscious. A brief assessment of the noise revealed that it was not coming toward her. In fact, it seemed to diminish, becoming less frequent. She dropped her basket, and grasped hold of the long surgeon's lancet she carried in her bodice. She began to move ahead quietly.

The huge pig gave a final dying lunge as she peeked through the grass and looked into its eyes. From what she could see, it appeared that a falling tree had trapped the pig during the hurricane. The churned earth and musky odor bore evidence of its struggle for survival. The animal had either heard or smelled Hattie as she moved up the trail. Its final struggle had left it exhausted and dying. Hattie moved around to approach the animal from behind, not wanting to have an argument with the flashing forelegs or toothy snout. Taking careful aim, she buried the lancet behind the pig's ear, penetrating the brain, and putting the animal out of its misery.

Hattie worked as quickly as possible. She butchered as much of the pig as she could possibly carry. Leaving her staff stuck in the mud, with the basket on top, to mark the location, she carried a large load of meat back to camp.

She snapped a quick command at Anne. "Cover this with canvas." She immediately ran back for another trip. She expected to have to fight off the carrion birds but none had yet appeared. As she was cutting up a second load of meat, she happened to think, the hurricane had probably left so many dead critters around that the carrion population was overfed already. She was able to make four trips before the first buzzard showed up. She wrapped the last load in as big a piece of hide as she could salvage.

On one of her trips back to camp, she had instructed Anne to take the empty water cask, and go east on a trail she showed her. She described the brine filled pool she had discovered earlier, and told Anne to fill the water cask with the brine left in the pool. She described to Anne how she could tell it was the right pool by the salt encrusted logs surrounding it. She also had her scrape up as much salt as she could find on the logs, and bring it back to camp.

After returning with her final load, Hattie went off to locate a large number of green sticks she could use to build a drying rack. Giving Anne a sharp knife from her surgical case, she showed her how to cut thin strips of bark from the smaller green branches and to use the strips to tie the bigger sticks together to make the rack.

They took a break, cut off pieces of pig meat, and broiled it over the fire for a late lunch. Hattie set off in search of firewood while Anne, began to cut the meat into long strips. She placed them in the brine for a short while, and then hung them on the rack, over the smoking fire.

Hattie made trip after trip, each one taking longer as she searched for the right kind of firewood to create a smoking fragrant fire. The hurricane had left a great deal of wood about. However, much of it was too large for Hattie to break into small enough sticks to carry back to camp. On her last trip to camp, Hattie brought several larger branches that could be placed in the fire one end at a time. She intended to use these to keep the fire going through the night.

After placing the meat on the drying rack, Anne had taken the second biscuit tin, and placed some water in it along with pieces of meat, onions and some greens that Hattie had found. She kept this simmering on the edge of the fire as she continued to dry the meat according to Hattie's directions. Hattie was amazed at the amount of work Anne accomplished. It was as if a long dead lamp had come back on burning brightly inside her.

They took shifts through the night tending the drying fire. The butchering, carrying the meat, and then hauling all that firewood had totally tasked Hattie's strength. Without Anne's help the drying meat would have spoiled. She heaped as much praise on Anne as she possibly could.

They gorged themselves on the fresh hog meat for the next few days until it started to go bad. Hattie located a larger selection of edible plants to eat with the meat. She even found some random corn stalks and a pumpkin. She startled a flock of ducks, and found several fresh eggs. She located and harpooned several fish caught in the fast drying pools.

They couldn't have arrived at a better time of year. Autumn was fast approaching, and many plants and food crops in the surrounding area were ready for harvest. At first, Hattie marveled that they were able to discover so many different domesticated food plants. She wondered why they would exist in the swamp. In the days that followed she found random patches of melons and squash, more corn, and other grains. These plants were never in large orderly fields ready to harvest but grew in mixed plots in little glades in the swamp. Then it hit her. The wild pigs and birds would rob the farmer's fields, eat the plants, and carry the seeds back to the swamp. Had her goal been to hide out this would have been a perfect place. But the swamp also had a dark and steamy side, which was about to devastate her.

Chapter 9

Hattie's Journal

20 November 1858: I encountered more bad men. I am
rescued by a good one.

Hattie stayed close to camp for several days. She tried to think up games and exercises to build Anne's strength and endurance necessary for the impending journey. They had plenty of fresh vegetables and meat to eat. They also had a good supply of dried meat and did not need to worry about starvation for a while. They made a couple more baskets to hold the dried meat and began making plans to leave the camp. Hattie told Anne about the trail she had been following when she discovered the pig. They discussed the availability of the squash and corn. They could eat the squash with the last of the fresh pig meat. It was starting to go bad and wouldn't last much longer. The corn, they could eat fresh or dried for future use. The squash and pumpkin seeds could be roasted and stored. They planned to carry the dried corn, seeds, and dried meat with them as they traveled.

Much to Hattie's delight, Anne agreed that the time had come. They would leave as soon as they had prepared as much of the dried food items as they could carry in their baskets.

Later that day, they took a swim and for the first time just lounged around. They talked like sisters should. Hattie told Anne about some of her previous adventures. Anne related how lonely and bleak her life had been. She had received every thing she asked for—all except love.

She told Hattie. "I realize now what I had missed growing up in a house without love. I lived in an empty shell made of wood where no one cared what happened to anyone else. I began to feel just as empty myself."

"I think father cared," Hattie said, trying to console her. "He just couldn't get past the guilt."

"Tillie cared. As I look back, I see the little ways she tried to make me see and help me feel love. I was so mean to her. I feel so bad for the way I treated her. She would try to tell me stories about our mother, but I was too wrapped up in my own selfish desires to listen. She told me that our mother came from a very prominent family with close ties to French and Spanish royalty. I think Tillie said that some of them were Moors who crossed over from North Africa."

"I feel sure wherever she is now that she understands and forgives you."

"I hope you're right Hattie. I so hope you're right. I want to make amends, but what can you do when someone is dead and gone? Will God help you reach out to those that are gone so you can say, 'I'm sorry?' Do you ever wish there was a way to visit with our mother again? I so want to put my arms around her, say I am sorry for the mess I've made of my life, and thank her for what she went through to give us life."

The next morning, Hattie set out early to locate and harvest the last of the isolated plots of corn and squash she had located earlier. She took two baskets hoping to fill both. Conditions created tough going. She waded through swamp water and mud. She had trouble locating a couple of plots, and she found others instead. It was late afternoon before she stumbled back to camp.

The area around camp was real quiet—too quiet. No smoke drifted up from the fire. She had asked Anne to keep it going. She began to get a really bad feeling.

"Anne! Anne, where are you?" she called. No one answered. Dropping her baskets, she ran the last few yards. She checked under their canvas awning. Anne was not there. She spotted Anne's clothes piled on the bank, and for a moment, she felt relief. Anne had gone swimming. She looked around the bend into the pool by the log. It was empty. Anne was gone. She had simply vanished.

Hattie didn't remember much of the next few hours. Like a robot, she mechanically went through the motions of searching for Anne. She wept until her heart and eyes were dry. Then, she fell to the ground and cried some more until sleep claimed her tired body. For the next three days, Hattie searched for some sign of Anne. If some wild creature had carried her off maybe she would at least find something left to bury. She had read stories in books about alligators and crocodiles. She wondered if such creatures roamed this swamp? Had Anne been captured by pirates or indians? Maybe a band of runaway black slaves had found her. If so, why had they left the boat and all their things? Strong men, capable of carrying Anne off could easily dislodge the lifeboat and float it away. It would bring some money in any seaport even if they didn't have a use for it themselves.

To make things worse, it rained steadily for the next two days obliterating any hope of finding tracks or signs of a struggle. Hattie sat under the flap tied to the lifeboat nursing a smoking, stubborn fire. She just wanted to keep something alive. It was good to have the lifeboat there. She wondered if she could find a way to get it out of the tree and launch it. It was hopeless. She remembered how they struggled when she and Anne tried to move it. It was stuck deeper in the sand now. The boat must remain, lodged firmly where it was. She would have to stick with her original plan to walk out of the swamp.

Walk away from the last of her family?

Once again, Hattie felt the soul wrenching pain of losing another family. Would she ever see them again? Would heaven be a place where families could be together? Would Anne be there with the positive spirit Hattie observed during the last few days? Would God know her heart had changed from a selfish brat to a loving caring person? Questions without answers plagued Hattie as she sat crying in the rain.

The rain stopped on the third day replaced by a fresh wind from the northwest bringing crisp cooling relief from the hot muggy weather that had covered the swamp in a steaming cloak since they landed. Hattie felt renewed, and her good-natured high spirits started to return. She spent the day parching corn and pumpkin seeds. She baked squash and corn in the coals. She ate until she felt she would burst. She speared one of the strange ugly fish with the whiskers, and baked it in the coals to eat with her vegetables. She had eaten enough pork for a while, and figured she would get plenty more in the days ahead.

She took ropes and canvas from the lifeboat sail and using a needle and thread from her instrument case, she made a backpack to carry her case and food supplies. She placed a freshly sharpened scalpel in her bodice. With her staff in her hand and the backpack loaded and on her back, she stopped for one last hopeful look near the swimming pool—nothing. She turned, straightened her shoulders, and waded off through the swamp.

It took Hattie three days filled with mud, mosquitoes, and misery to reach civilization. When that happened, it came in the form of a farm wagon driven by the blackest man Hattie had ever seen. His name was Matt, and he was hauling a load of what he called "sweet taters" to market in Suffolk, which he thought was in Virginia.

He offered to give Hattie a ride, but indicated she would have to jump off if someone came along, because it wouldn't be right for him to be seen carrying some white girl in his wagon. He could never seem to explain the reasoning to Hattie. She remained glad for the ride. Hattie tried to find out what living in America was like. He didn't seem to want to talk about it.

As they drew close to town, Hattie jumped off the wagon and took a different road. Matt had indicated that the road he was taking led through the town to the open market. She wanted to skirt around the town and avoid meeting too many people. She intended to keep going until she came to a bigger city, where she might find work as a clerk in a store or possibly even teaching.

It was getting on toward dark a day later when Hattie reached a larger town called Portsmouth. She walked through the railroad yard, heading toward a number of large warehouses. They were all built with freight doors and loading docks that opened onto a railroad siding. Some had freight cars waiting to be loaded. She found one with an open door, and decided to spend the night inside since it was starting to cloud up and could rain.

The crunching of gravel and the whispering voices awakened her. It was dark inside the railroad car. She hoped no one could see her. She quietly moved to one of the defensive positions Kim had taught her and waited, hoping they would pass on by.

The crunching noise stopped, and she heard a whispered voice say, "Here's one that's open. Wanna stay here?"

"Check it out first," said another voice.

A scratching noise preceded a flickering light from a match. The light revealed a hand, arm, and face of a bearded man and the crouching figure of Hattie, prepared to defend herself and her territory.

The man with the beard chortled, "Hey, Pete, we done found ourselves a woman!"

"Lemmie see," the one called Pete growled. "Sure would be nice to cuddle up with a woman on a wet stormy night. It's been a long time."

"I wonder if she's got any money on her?"

A second match flared, revealing two grinning men placing their hands on the floor of the boxcar, preparing to hoist themselves up and in.

They never made it. One took the butt end of Hattie's staff in the face, and the other was swept off his feet by a fast moving backpack. He landed on his back in the gravel hitting his head on a railroad tie. In the silence that followed, Hattie jumped out of the boxcar, and ran full speed down the side of the track before they could figure out what hit them.

Hattie ran as fast and far as she could until a pain in her side forced her to slow down. *Now it was time for stealth not speed,* she reasoned. Seeing a long line of warehouses ahead, she moved toward them. She checked a couple of doors but found them locked. She noticed a passage or alley between two warehouses but passed it by. Then, she saw a corner with a slight opening. She walked up to inspect it. She knew she couldn't fit inside let alone get through that opening, but an idea came to her.

She took the food basket and extra clothing from her pack. She tied the straps from her pack to the staff and let it hang down. Next, she placed the spare clothing over the pack. With her straw sun hat on top of the pole it looked like a woman standing in the corner. When she had the figure set up the way she wanted, she backtracked to the larger alley, squeezed through the opening, and reached the other side of the line of warehouses. She hoped that the figure would delay the men. *They should be a little more cautious the second time.* She smiled to herself as she walked away.

Hattie's subterfuge created a severe dent in her possessions. She had her instrument case in her hand and the scalpel in a pigskin case tucked in her bodice. She had practiced in camp drawing and throwing the scalpel the way Kim had taught her. The balance wasn't quite right, but she could stick a squash at ten feet nine out of ten times. She considered this a last ditch move. She didn't really want to kill anyone, even in self-defense. Plus, she might lose a perfectly good scalpel.

She heard yelling and cursing behind her. Those men were not going to give up. It also seemed like there were more than two. They must have found some more recruits. She moved as quickly as possible while still trying to remain quiet, toward the next set of tracks, where she found a long line of loaded boxcars. She tried several doors. All were locked and sealed up tight. She was climbing over a coupling between two of the cars when she heard the sound of men running.

She froze.

They were arguing about whether to go into town or to search this set of cars. They had her trapped if they came looking over here.

She suddenly realized that the convenient handle she was grasping was not a handle but a step, part of a ladder up the end of the car. She slowly and quietly climbed up and flattened out on the top. The clouds from the earlier shower began drifting away, and more moonlight filtered through. At first, she tried to keep her head down but the smell of cinders and smoke imbedded in the boxcar made her want to sneeze. Hattie raised her head and looked up. She realized that she had made a mistake. One man looking along the top of the cars was all it would take to spot her. She would stick out like a bump on a log. She spied a boxy hatch looking thing on the end of the car and inched along to get a closer look. She found some kind of a cover. If she could get it loose, she might be able to climb down inside the boxcar. The first one she tried was bolted on tight. But, she could see a lot of covers ahead on other cars. One of them might be loose. She began to inch her way down the line of boxcars.

The third one she tried wiggled under her hands. The bolts were only on finger tight. Either a lazy worker or a previous entrant had helped her out. Silently taking the bolts out and removing the cover seemed to take forever, but it was a job that could not be rushed. The wrong noise would bring searching men faster than a dinner bell at lunchtime. Finally, she worked all the bolts loose. Lifting the cover revealed a black space below. Unwilling to take a leap of faith into the black hole, Hattie reached as far down inside as she could. She touched only air.

What now?

She tried taking the instrument case and lowering it down. It touched a firm surface. She estimated that there must be almost three feet of open space above the cargo. Letting go of the case, she slid head first through the hole.

Hattie touched a soft but firm surface, and lowered herself down. She stood up and pulled the cover back in place. With some adjusting she was able to secure two of the bolts and push some of the others through their holes.

It should be good enough to fool the drunken bums chasing me.

None of the moonlight she had feared earlier, managed to filter inside. She could see nothing. She moved away from the opening in case someone should try to look inside. She could hear the men shouting as they looked for her. The door rattled once as someone tried to open it, but the lock convinced him to move on. The noises from the search party drifted away. Lack of further movement soon dulled her senses. Eventually, she rolled over on the mattress-like surface and fell asleep.

Hattie awoke to a rumbling crash that rocked the bed beneath her. She looked up in panic only to discover the car was moving! Long thin beams of sunlight dancing on dust motes flashed from cracks in the boxcar sides. There was enough light to recognize that her bed was a cotton bale. The whole boxcar was full of them. There was another rattling crash as the train reversed direction and began to pick up speed. There was no hope of escape now. The train was moving too fast. She would be exposed in broad daylight if she tried to climb out of the hatch she had entered the night before. Even if she could get out and jump, she would be spotted. She decided the best thing to do was sit back, enjoy the ride, and plan her next move.

It proved hot and dusty riding on the top of the cotton bales. Hattie moved to the center of the car. She noticed that the stacks of bales sloped down to form a sort of valley in front of the car doors. She slid down and moved to the door with the largest crack. She could feel some fresh air coming through, and the moving air helped to cool her off. She found a comfortable spot with her shoulders against one bale, her feet propped up on another, and her nose close to the crack in the door. It was not nearly as uncomfortable as it sounded. She relaxed to the rhythm of the rocking car and dozed off once or twice.

Soon a rattling deceleration announced that the train was slowing down. Just as she began planning to climb up to the top of the car, the train came to a stop, and the door in front of her slid open with a crash!

She found herself staring at a grinning sandy haired older gentleman. His twinkling gray eyes sat beneath bushy eyebrows and peeked over rosy cheeks. The dimple extending from his crooked little smile gave him a crafty, but friendly appearance that helped Hattie relax. "Well, young lady, have you had enough time to rest and think up a good story to tell me? I'm anxious to hear why you hopped aboard my train last night. You really raised a ruckus. It's a good thing I'm the only one who saw you climb through the top hatch of this car," sticking his head inside he looked concerned, "hot in here. You better come on out."

"Your train?" Hattie asked, employing the question for a question strategy.

"Yep, my train, all forty boxcars worth, and no one ever said Eli Wiggins was inhospitable. I got a club car hooked on the back with some nice cold water. What say you to havin' a drink with me while we discuss the fare for your ride?"

"But sir, I have no money." Hattie said batting her dark brown eyes at him in an attempt at matching his jocular banter.

"No need miss, the pleasure of your company will suffice. Please pardon my poor attempt at humor." He said, his manner becoming serious.

Eli Wiggins was as good as his word. He helped Hattie down from the boxcar, and they moved towards the rear of the train. "We need to hurry," he said. "They put us on this siding to let the scheduled passenger train by. We will have a clear track all the way to Richmond if we hurry."

They had barely found comfortable seats in his club-car when the train gave a lurch and began to pull out onto the main track. "This is a beautiful car. Is it yours?" Hattie asked as she looked around at the walnut paneling and brass fixtures, and ran her hands over the plush velvet upholstered seats. "It rivals our study at home in Janes Manor."

"Where is Janes Manor may I ask?"

"Why it's in Sherbourne, England," answered Hattie with a look of haughty innocence. She had decided to put on a front, a term she had read about in a modern novel. The hero had been a dandy with little or no capital, but he managed to keep people guessing while he worked his way into their good graces and out of their money. Hattie had no intention of trying to manipulate Eli out of any money, but she did hope to create an impression that she was a well-bred young lady who found herself in unfortunate circumstances. All of which was true of course.

Hattie related the part of her story concerning the voyage to America, the hurricane and the loss of her father and sister. She also explained how happy she was to meet a real gentleman and find sanctuary on his train. Mr.

Wiggins, or Eli as he insisted Hattie call him, appeared fascinated by her story. He was also impressed with her claim to English aristocracy. "Hattie, now that doesn't seem to be a name an English lady such as yourself would have. Is it an old family name or what?"

"Oh, it's what you Americans call a nickname. My full name is Helen Marie Kirkland."

"I like Hattie better. Do you mind if I call you that? Americans are not much on formalities."

"That would be fine, Ah, Eli. I do so like your carriage, or what ever you call this car we are riding in. Do all Americans ride in such cars?" asked Hattie trying to change the subject

"Oh, no, Hattie," grinned Eli. "This car belongs to the B & O Railroad. Mr. John W. Barrett, President of the railroad loaned it to me for this trip," he leaned forward and took a posture of confidentiality. "You see, he and I are in a little business venture. We both feel that sooner or later war will break out between the North and the South. We plan to stockpile cotton in warehouses owned by the railroad and leased to me. We will store the cotton in Baltimore until southern cotton is no longer available, and when the price goes up we will make a huge profit. This load will fill all my warehouses."

"So Eli, do you live in Baltimore?"

"Oh no. I live in Hagerstown, Maryland."

"Does buying and selling cotton comprise all your business activities?"

"No. I buy bulk goods in the East or from overseas, some even from England, and ship them to my place of business in Hagerstown. From there, I receive orders from out West, places like Pittsburgh, Chicago and many smaller cities that are growing up in the West. I trade or buy farm produce and other commodities and sell them to buyers in the East."

"What a marvelous idea!" exclaimed Hattie, "But why would they pay someone in the middle? Why don't people just deal directly with each other?"

"I get lower prices and lower shipping rates because of my volume buying power. Besides, I own a lot of stock in the B & O." said Eli proudly, "And I can hold inventory in my warehouses to cut down on delivery times to the small buyers out West."

"You mentioned earlier that you intend to place this cotton you have on this train in a warehouse and just sit on it until the price goes up. Have you

ever given any thought to selling the cotton to the eastern mills and returning to Virginia for another load as long as the supply route remains open?"

"Yes, I have, but it costs too much to bring the boxcars down here
empty and tie them up when I could be using them to transfer materials
east and west."

Hattie leaned forward with her chin in her fist and asked, "Have you
ever considered a triangle route? Start with this cotton. Place it in the
warehouse until you find a buyer at a profit. While that is happening, load
the boxcars with goods for your warehouses in Hagerstown. After unloading, take selected goods out west to Pittsburgh, for example, and sell them.
Load the boxcars with manufactured goods needed in the South and send
the boxcars to a southern city to be emptied. You could load them with
more cotton to replenish the warehouse in Baltimore." Hattie leaned back
and asked, "Wouldn't that work?"

"Well, young lady, I like the way you think," mumbled Eli as he
rubbed the dimple in his chin and pondered Hattie's idea. "There are
definitely some things to work out like moving the boxcars from one
railroad line to another. Some have different gauge tracks and the boxcars can't ride on them." He squinted through his bushy eyebrows. "The
main problem as I see it is I would need to use other railroads and B &
O wouldn't like it."

"But, couldn't one have the right size cars waiting and transfer the
cargo?" asked Hattie. "What do you mean, B & O wouldn't like it? I
thought that you were a large stockholder in B & O?"

"I am."

"You say you own B & O stock, but you act like B & O owns you? I
thought you fought a war with England so you would be free to choose?
Sounds to me like you traded a king for a corporation."

"Lots of people might agree with you. In fact that's the beauty of our
political system. People argue about subjects like that, and politicians use
the arguments to line up votes. If the situation gets too bad, and enough
people get worked up over the issue then laws get written to rectify the
problem. But, there is always somebody who doesn't like the law. They
want it changed their way so the whole process starts all over again. It is
far from a perfect system, but it has worked well for over fifty years. I want
to get back to this triangle trade thing. I guess I have been fixated on running goods east and west. I never gave much thought to taking a trainload

of freight south through the mountains. It might just be a possibility." Eli eyed Hattie with added respect. "How did you come up with that idea?"

"I read a book one time describing the triangle trade route used by ships. It stuck in my mind because one leg involved transporting slaves from Africa. I hate the very idea of anyone owning another human being. The thought makes me sick."

They continued their discussion of trade until, a man in a black cap labeled *conductor* entered the front of the compartment, and interrupted them. "I'm sorry Mr. Wiggins, but we need to let another train go by. We will be delayed in Richmond for a few hours."

"Tell you what Ed, why don't we just telegraph Mr. Barrett and let him know we will be delayed a whole day in Richmond. My niece, Miss Kirkland, is in need of a new wardrobe. She has lost all her luggage and we need to go shopping."

"Very good, sir," smirked the conductor giving Hattie a knowing look as he departed.

Hattie felt like giving him something to make him smile out of the other side of his mouth. She looked over at Eli and said, "I can't let you do that."

"Oh, yes you can young lady, and it's not a gift. You earned it. When I take action on some of your suggestions, I will profit much more than the cost of a new wardrobe."

Eli bought Hattie all the clothes a young American woman of means would need. They found her a room in the best hotel in Richmond. Eli promised to return in the morning to pick her up so they could continue their journey to Baltimore. Hattie hardly got any sleep that night. She soaked so long in the bathtub that she used up all the soap that made bubbles.

Eli hardly recognized the tall elegant young woman who greeted him in the lobby the next morning. Dressed in her new clothes and mimicking the regal manner she had observed so often on Margaret Janes; she created a look that stopped several of the people passing through the hotel lobby. Even a trio of young southern belles stopped and stared, wondering who she was.

Eli appeared nervous and fidgety all the way back to the train. Hattie asked, "Eli, what's the matter? Have I done something wrong? Do you want me to leave?"

"No, Hattie, it's just the opposite. I want you to stay. I gather from what you have told me that you have a problem. Namely, you have no place to go. Is that correct?"

"Yes"

"Well, I too have a problem. I was married once, and I loved my wife very much. We made a vow to live together for eternity even though our Pastor only blessed our union 'til death do us part. I believe that if we want it, God will honor an eternal marriage covenant. But, there are these well-meaning people back in Hagerstown who insist on trying to hitch me up with women I don't want to be with. If I were to marry, I would feel unfaithful to my first love, my first wife.

"I can understand why you would not want, or even be able to be with a man after the way you were treated. I don't want that with another woman either. I guess what I am trying to say is; what do you think about us getting married in Baltimore, making a vow to *not* be intimate? Could we just be good friends? This could solve problems for both of us. I am excited about implementing some of your ideas, and I want you as a partner, helping to make them work."

Hattie looked at him for a long time. He seemed honest and sincere, and she was in a difficult situation. Should she take a chance, or should she decline his offer and try to make it on her own? Maybe it was the merry twinkle in his blue eyes looking apprehensively through those bushy blond eyebrows or maybe her need to feel a sense of security for a change. Something in what she saw or felt caused her to smile and say, "It sounds like a good plan to me. I don't like the idea of using the sacred vows of marriage as a business arrangement, but I have read about royal marriages that have done well with less going for them than we seem to have."

They decided a simple ceremony by a Justice of the Peace would do just fine. After the wedding, they saw to the unloading of the cotton, and the loading of supplies Eli knew he could sell out West. Eli took Hattie to visit several of his business associates. They visited a lawyer and signed documents authorizing Hattie to conduct certain business affairs on behalf of Eli's trading company. Eli's lawyers weren't too excited about doing this since involving women in business affairs was still considered a rare and risky endeavor.

Hattie asked Eli to recommend a man familiar with European finances. He found someone at one of his financial institutions and arranged for

Hattie to meet with a Mr. Josiah Wilkins. He represented several European financial organizations doing business in America. She showed him the securities her father had given her and asked him to check on them for her. She signed an authorization for him to take any necessary steps to set up an overseas account for her. Based on his recommendation, she established a Swiss account in a Zurich bank. The whole idea might be a waste of time. She believed the securities were worthless. Mr. Wilkins was not so sure. He felt that she had nothing to lose so why not see how it worked out.

Six days after meeting for the first time, Eli and Helen Wiggins arrived in Hagerstown ready to begin a new life together. Neither one wanted to jump into Hagerstown high society, what there was of it, so they just quietly went to work on the ideas they had discussed on the train. The one thing they did do was to find a house they both liked. They both felt uncomfortable living in the house Eli had built for his first wife.

They found a place on the edge of town. The front was faced with locally available Stonehenge Limestone renown in the local area. The stone had weathered revealing the unique wavy laminate that made it so beautiful. An arch made from the same stone held an iron gate wide enough for their carriage. Matching pillars placed between wrought iron fence panels bordered the street. They shared a stable with a small pasture and larger woodlot with the neighbors where they could run their horse. Someone had put in a garden at one time, but the plot had gone to weeds. The warehouses and the railroad station were close enough so they could walk. Because of their proximity to the train station a streetcar ran by the house that would drop them at the store. Hattie liked the large number of rooms and the tree lined drive that led from the street. The new house was cleaned and ready in time for Christmas.

Eli had a piano in his original house and asked Hattie if they should keep it. His first wife had not played, but he had picked it up on a trade for farming equipment. A man coming through town heading west had finally talked his wife into seeing the error of her ways. Eli, thinking it would add class to their parlor, had brought it home. Hattie was thrilled to have a piano to play. One of the first things she did in her new home was to get the instrument tuned.

Over the holidays, Hattie met most of the women that had tried to marry Eli off. Most had good intentions, wanting only to see him happy.

Hattie's gracious charm and fine English manners soon eliminated many of the bad feelings that remained. Hattie heard a few comments like "twice her age" and "what about children" but these dwindled away with the passing days.

By the time she turned twenty-one in late February, she was deeply involved in helping Eli manage his business. Her ability to understand the nature of business came from her studies and from conversations overheard at Janes Manor. Her natural nosey curiosity caused her to listen in as Mr. Janes discussed his affairs with his wife, and also when he invited friends and associates to his home to discuss business matters. Hattie was especially cognizant concerning the implementation of railroads in commerce—thanks to Mr. Janes' interest in railroads.

As Eli's faith in her abilities grew, he began to make more trips to set up the triangle trade routes. Relationships with other people needed to be built to facilitate staging points. He needed to locate buyers and agents who could provide bulk orders at various locations.

Hattie soon gained the confidence of Jim Tanner who managed the warehouses and Andy Dawson the local store manager. Jim's job was to keep the warehouses organized and the loaded boxcars moving. Andy ran the store where they sold goods at retail to people in Hagerstown. He also managed the bookkeepers that kept track of company accounts and inventory levels. Hattie was impressed with their diligence and honesty. If they had a weakness it was a shared dependence on Eli to make any and all key decisions. She could see ways to improve efficiency, but for the immediate future those changes would have to come from Eli.

When Eli was home, Hattie would discuss ways to improve operations, and Eli would issue orders to Jim and Andy. It wasn't long before the two managers caught on to what was happening. Hattie would come around and ask questions about how a certain thing was done. Then, a few days later, Eli would show up and give them orders to change the way they had been doing business for years.

A day arrived when Hattie was checking some accounts in what had come to be known as her office. After a polite knock on the door, the two men entered.

Jim said, "We need to talk to you Mrs. Wiggins."

"How can I help you gentlemen?"

"Well," Jim replied, "we got it figured that all these changes Eli's been coming up with lately are really coming from you."

"Mostly, things are happening faster, better or cheaper, and we see that as a good thing," Andy added. "But, we got us a couple of problems."

"Anything I can do to help?" asked Hattie.

"We feel many of these changes could be put in place faster if we was to get going on them, sort of try them out before Eli told us to do it."

"The problem with that is Eli might get sore at all three of us. But he is more apt to take it out on us," said Jim. "The other thing is, it wouldn't be right for you to be seen ordering us around in front of the men."

Hattie thought about this for a few minutes. Then she said, "What if you men were to come here every morning for a short meeting. We would call it a status meeting for the benefit of the other workers. We would discuss any changes among the three of us. Those that we felt would need Eli's blessing; we could put on hold until he could meet here with all of us. If that sounds good to you, I will talk to Eli about it when he gets back tomorrow. What do you say?" Both men nodded and left smiling, anxious to get back to work.

Hattie sat at her desk. Her thoughts drifted to the future. Jim, Andy, and even Eli were centered on their own jobs, their own place in the business. But there was a big country out there. A country poised on the brink of greatness. She was only now beginning to realize how big America was, and how big it could become.

Why you could drop ten or more countries the size of England in here and have room for more left over.

Such a vast country would need people. They would come. They would come from all nations bringing their ideas, their cultures, and their problems. Those people would need the goods and services she and Eli and others like them were providing.

Right now, at this time, a man could buy himself a wagon, a team, and travel into the wilderness. He could create a home, a dream, a life for himself, and his family. He could still provide the basics of life pretty much by himself. He could build his own house. He could raise his own crops or hunt his own food. He could defend himself and his family. Still, he needed tools and a wagon to carry them. He needed things made by others to survive. To get these things, he needed to produce something from his labor that others wanted. He needed to produce crops, grow animals for food, or harvest the natural resources he discovered. He needed to change his labor or his goods into money in order to buy the things he couldn't make or grow for himself. That's where Eli and Hattie came in. They provided the means that made it possible for the people and the nation to grow.

Her vision began to expand beyond the present day to day business of shipping goods from place to place. Of course it was an important part, a necessary part to be played in the growing of this great land. But, she also saw how every year new methods and new machinery created changes. On a very small scale it was happening right here in their own business. Jim and Andy, focused on their day-to-day work had not been able to see how simple changes, or installing a new machine would improve their efficiency. She, an outsider, had seen the improvements that could help them become a better business. But, what did the future hold in store for all of them?

Right now the B & O railroad looked like the solution to moving goods from the developed cities along the eastern seaboard to the expanding western markets. Her idea to move south had opened Eli's mind. It had made him think off the track so to speak. What would happen in the future when people filled the whole country? Society would become as integrated and complex here in America as it now was in England and Europe. A much greater transportation network would be required to meet the demands of the people settling all over this huge country. Would trains be enough? They could only run where tracks could be laid. They could only haul so many cars. They could only go so fast.

Men, and women, were by nature impatient beasts. They wanted it all, and they wanted it now. That drive would create a demand for more goods delivered better and faster. It would generate better ideas, better services, better tools, and better machines. Progress could only come from people working smarter. Skilled, educated people attacking each problem with new, innovative solutions.

Would the American people dig in and find solutions? Or would they sit back and wait for a king, a congress, or a corporation to do it for them? Right now plenty of pioneers were ready and willing to work out solutions. Would that always be the case? Or would America become complacent, just another civilization, a nation full of Annes with too much time on their hands doing too little to help themselves?

She could feel that complacency nagging at her right now. Eli seemed perfectly willing to give her everything she asked for. She could just sit back and relax for a change. She didn't have to get up and get going every morning. She was no longer driven by starvation, bad weather, or fear of bodily harm. She had transitioned from surviving to living a comfortable life.

Hattie jumped out of her chair. No way was she going to let that happen to her. She would continue to remain useful and be of service to others even if she had to sweep the cobwebs out of every house in Hagerstown!

Chapter 10

Hattie's Journal

8 April 1860: *My soft life has been turned upside down again. I have a new responsibility.*

Eli arrived home late looking excited and flustered. At first, Hattie thought it involved the negotiations he had just completed with a group of railroad companies who ran tracks south and west of the B & O. The agreement they reached formed the final link in Eli's plans to move manufactured goods south in exchange for cotton and tobacco. Hattie sensed that Eli had something else troubling him. He had that same look she remembered seeing the day he proposed on the train headed for Baltimore.

"Well Eli, are you going to tell me what else you have been up to, or must I guess?"

"I have a surprise for you," he admitted, using that crooked little grin she had come to know so well.

"Where is it?" *This man is trying to spoil me rotten,* she thought. All this attention makes me nervous.

"Down in the cellar," he mumbled, as he opened the cellar door, and indicated she should follow him down.

When Hattie reached the bottom step, she turned to Eli and said, "I don't see anything."

"Lift up your lantern and look over in the far corner behind the furnace."

When Hattie did as she was directed, all she could see were nine pair of wide-open white eyes looking at her. "Who are they?" she whispered." Then recognition hit her. "Eli, I told you I would not have slaves or servants in this house!" Many of their friends in Hagerstown owned slaves, and Hattie had told Eli what she thought of the practice. She thought he had understood her. *Be calm Hattie, be calm,* she told herself.

"They are runaways." He replied, "I found them in among the cotton bales just like I found you. They were lucky. The route the train followed was the new route we will be using to haul goods from the South. The patrols have not yet caught on to the fact that we will be hauling freight north across connecting railroads."

'What do you intend to do with them? How did you get them in here without my knowing?"

"I slid them down the coal chute." He answered and then added, "I plan to move them out of here as soon as I can."

"How?" Her nosey neighbors were active proponents of slavery. What will they think? Or worse yet, what will they do?

"Have you heard of the Underground Railroad?"

"Yes, I heard some of the women talking about it in the store the other day. The subject creates a lot of strong feelings both ways around here. We can get in a lot of trouble if the wrong people find out we are harboring slaves in our cellar."

"I know. That's why we will have to be very careful who we talk to, and what we do to help these poor folks go north to freedom."

"What do you mean *we?*"

"Well, us then," he replied still tying to elicit her support.

"Well, *us* ain't doin' nuttin," she caught herself. In her irritation she had started to talk like Jim. "Excuse me. I've been ordering Jim around too much lately. You didn't deserve that. But, we need to discuss this calmly. I am going to go upstairs and make a pile of sandwiches while I think about this. You my friend, go get that crock of buttermilk from the back porch. We will feed these folks before I let you know what I think *us* should do." With that being said, she turned and stomped up the steps.

Good thing I baked bread today, thought Hattie as she slapped butter on the bread and made thick roast beef sandwiches. *There are those apples in the barrel in the cellar. We might as well use them up before they go bad. Winter is about over anyway*, she thought as she put the sandwiches on a big platter. While she maneuvered the heavy platter down the steps, she thought of Connie Austin. *She would be the one to see about taking care of these people. Connie's voice had been the loudest in favor of helping the runaways. The problem was, the woman liked to talk too much.*

When she arrived at the bottom of the steps, she put the heavy platter on the table by the stairs. Picking up the lantern, she turned it up and hung it on the nail already placed in a beam overhead. She had just filled her apron with apples from the bin when Eli showed up with the crock of buttermilk and a stack of tin cups. She mentioned Connie and he smiled that crooked little smile and winked at her.

"One step at a time old man. I'm not jumping all the way in on this project yet. I just want to know if you think she can keep her mouth shut." She muttered out of the corner of her mouth.

After everyone had eaten, Hattie brought down spare quilts. After all, it was still March and the cellar was cold. She began to load the cups on the empty platter. "Can I help you ma'am?" came a quiet, baritone voice from the corner.

She thought for a minute. There was no way to look in the kitchen windows from the street. The view showed their back yard now filled with wind blown leaves, an overgrown hedge, and dead or dormant flower stalks. The back of the yard bordered on the wall of the stable where they kept the horse and buggy. "Yes, I guess I could use the help." Hattie said as she turned and walked up the stairs followed by a skinny boy maybe fourteen year's old, threatening to sprout right out of the bib overalls he was wearing. The first thing she noticed were the long graceful fingers holding the buttermilk crock.

"Where you want this crock?" He asked, looking at her with intelligent dark eyes set in a thin chocolate colored face.

"Put it over there on the table. Mr. Wiggins can put it back when he returns. He went to find some people that can help you go north." Hattie said as she busied herself with cleaning the platter and the cups. She tensed a little when he moved toward her, but he just picked up a towel and began to dry the cups.

"No need to be afraid of me ma'am," He said, grinning at her.

Hattie smiled thinking how close he had come to eating the platter she held in her hands. "I have a good friend named Matt. He's meaner and blacker than you are. I figure I could just bring him over here to protect me if you were to try anything. What's your name?" she asked.

"Sam"

"Sam what?"

"Just Sam, never had no other name."

"Why do you want to go north Sam?" Hattie asked as she cleaned the kitchen table, and motioned for him to sit and join her.

"I wants to be free. Free to do what I wants to do, not what some man with a whip tells me to do. I wants to have a family some day, and know we can stay together without one of us getin' sold off."

Hattie just sat and looked at Sam. She had to think this out. Going north would be rough. The work, if he could find it, would be hard. Probably harder than what he had endured on the plantation down south. She remembered Mr. Calhoun saying that most slaves were treated better than she had been treated as a servant in England. It would be a big price to pay just to say, "I am free."

She thought of her own struggles alone in the hills of England and later in the Carolina swamp. Many times, she would have traded her situation for a hot meal, a bath, and never mind the price. In fact, was she guilty of doing just that when Eli asked her to marry him? She hoped that was not her reason, but it did add weight to her decision. She looked at Sam. He sort of slouched in the chair with one elbow on the table. He seemed to be staring at the table as if lost in thought. His fingers tapped out a rhythm on the top of the crock. What was he thinking? She didn't ask. She didn't want to know. She just didn't want to get involved—or did she?

Eli came in blowing on his hands. "Cold out there,"

Hattie didn't ask where he had been. "What took you so long?"

"I was checking a couple of different routes. You wanna get these people out of here, so it's best we do it tonight. There is always somebody looking around during daylight. There's a wagon leaving in a couple of hours. I don't know how much room they have. I will need to take them one at a time 'til we fill it up. It'll be easier to move through the alleys with only one or two with me." He paused looking around. "Did you save me something to eat?"

"You go on down and pick out the first one. Sam and I'll scare you up something to eat."

"Sam is it? Eli chuckled over his shoulder as he headed for the cellar with a little gleam in his eye.

"Any buttermilk left?" Hattie asked looking at Sam.

"Yas'm" Sam said, shaking the crock to prove his answer.

She moved her head in the direction of a cupboard door. "There's some glasses in that cupboard. Get one down and fill it for Mr. Wiggins while I see if there is enough meat left on what I hoped would be a good soup bone for a couple more sandwiches."

Eli entered the kitchen followed by two frightened young girls. "These two want to stay together. Sisters, I would guess," he said, looking at Sam who nodded in the affirmative. "They don't say much but they follow orders real good. I'm going to take the two of them first." He picked up one of the sandwiches and the three of them headed out into the night.

Hattie turned to Sam. "Why don't you go get the next one ready. Make sure they understand to be quiet and obey Mr. Wiggins."

"They unnerstan'. They jus' scared." Sam said as he moved to the cellar stairs.

Before making the next trip, Eli paused to warm himself by the kitchen stove.

"Cold out there?" asked Hattie.

"Yes, and it's starting to rain"

Hattie moved to the back porch and returned with two slickers. "Here put your slicker on and use mine for whoever goes with you. It will keep the rain out and the black color and shapeless form will make it easier to keep you from being spotted."

"You talk like you have had some experience at this sort of thing." Eli noted with a knowing grin.

"I've had a lot of practice playing sparrow in the barnyard." Smiling at Eli's questioning look, she turned away, a stray thought entering her head. *I wonder how Kim is doing? I miss that silly grin. He would reach out and help these people without a second thought.*

Thinking of Kim reminded her that she had been avoiding her exercises. *I better stay in shape if I'm going to help these people… Whoa!*

Well there's my answer, she thought to herself. She made a pot of tea and sat down at the kitchen table to review in her mind what she had read and heard about the Underground Railroad. How they helped move escaped slaves to freedom, north from here into Canada.

She sat at the table reviewing her strengths and weaknesses. Her strongest attribute rested in her ability to move about in plain sight without arousing suspicion. Her weak point was a lack of knowledge concerning the local geography and the customs and feelings of her friends and neighbors. Work, study, and attention to detail should help solve those problems. Think! What was it Kim had taught her? Learn to read people's eyes and body.

"Many times people tell more with body than with words."

She needed to get out of the office, and spend more time chatting with the ladies that came into the store. Invite them over for tea. What American social climber could resist a fashionable English Tea? She could make afternoon tea a routine social event. Women see and hear a lot of things, and they love to talk about them. She would just need to judiciously lead the conversation in the right direction to fill in the blank spots in her knowledge.

Eli appeared and interrupted her planning. "One more is all they can take," he said, shaking the rain off the extra slicker.

Sam approached with another boy his size. "This be the las' one down there," he said indicating the cellar. "He be goin' and I be stayin'."

Hattie figured he overheard their earlier conversation. "Let's get this last one over to the wagon and then the three of us will set down and talk about this." Her tone and posture indicated the indecision she still felt.

While she and Sam waited for Eli to return, Hattie went into the parlor and sat down at the piano and began to play. Sam stood by the door and listened. "You sure play good Miz Wiggins. I wish I could learn to play like that."

"You can. All it takes is practice."

"No, ma'am, you gots to have a piano, a nice home to put it in, and time to play and.."

"I guess you're right Sam it does take a lot. There were times not too long ago when I was sure I would never have a chance to play music again. Don't ever give up Sam, and you will always come out on top."

"Dat be easy fo' you to say."

"Say what?" Eli asked coming into the room.

"Sam was just telling me he would like to play the piano."

"Well, I for one think we should leave that for another day. Sam can you make a place down in the cellar for the rest of the night so we can all get some sleep?" Eli asked as he headed up the stairs to his bedroom.

"Sure can."

"Well then let's hit the hay. I don't know about you two but making that trip in the cold rain has worn me out, I'm going to bed."

Hattie and Eli discussed the situation while preparing for bed. They agreed to keep Sam around for the immediate future until another way was found to send him north.

The next morning Eli turned to Sam and explained that he would have to stay out of sight. He would be able to move about the house when they were home, but he could go outside to visit the privy only when it was dark. Eli and Hattie left for their morning meeting with Andy and Jim.

When they were alone in the office Hattie turned to Eli and said, "I have been giving this problem a great deal of thought while you were out playing *Eli to the rescue* last night and I have some ideas I would like to share with you."

He gave her his little sidewise grin. "Go ahead."

"My original inclination was to reject any thought of further involvement in helping these people run away. On further thought, I find I can't do that. Too many people have reached a hand out to me when I needed it. I just can't refuse to help. Why, the first stranger I met in America was an African named Matt. He gave me a ride even though getting caught with me in his wagon would have meant a beating, or worse. Here are some ideas I came up with. First, Sam stays with us, but only if he agrees. Can you arrange some kind of paper to make him a legal free man?"

Eli nodded.

"But, we must tell people that you purchased him on your trip south because I needed some help around the house while you are gone. If people think he is a slave that will create an impression that we are with the slaveholders. It will give us more credibility to move around and help the Underground Railroad. Which by the way, I think you have been more involved in than you have led me to believe?"

Eli nodded—again.

Hattie continued, "I will only agree to this if I can help Sam. It's time I started to pay back something for all the help that has come my way. I want him to feel free—that there is something in this for him. I want to educate him and teach him to play the piano. He will then have the same start I had. Hopefully, he will make something of himself. What do you think?"

"My only question is where did this sudden interest in Sam come from?"

"He stepped up and volunteered to help last night. He didn't sit around expecting someone to wait on him. When he helped me in the kitchen, I saw intelligence and self-determination in his face and in his actions. He is one of the good ones Eli. I want to see him make it. I guess you could say, it's a way for me to pay back the opportunities given to me earlier in my life."

"I agree."

"You seem to be a man of few words today?"

"I said I agree. If I didn't then I would have something to say," said Eli grinning that crooked little smile. "Oh, yes there is something I can say. I think the paperwork will be an easy problem to solve. There, are you happy I added my two cents worth?"

"Yes, I feel a lot better now." She laughed, "How can I resist that crooked little grin?"

"What's the matter girl? Going gaga over some guy just because he grins at you?" Hattie stifled a rebuttal wondering if Eli had any idea how close he came to the truth.

When Eli and Hattie got home that evening, they presented the plan to Sam. He also agreed but didn't say too much. He too just grinned.

It took over a week to get the proper papers fixed up for Sam. In the meantime, he stayed in the house or in the barn. Hattie picked up a McGuffey reader and suitable clothes from the store. She started in teaching Sam to read and to play the piano. He would practice while she was out running errands or working with Eli on business matters. Hattie delayed setting up the tea parties until she could present Sam as her new "servant."

Once they had the proper papers, they moved ahead with their plans. Hattie soon felt comfortable moving the runaways Eli would bring home. They settled into a routine. Sam would get the buggy ready and drive Hattie wherever she needed to go unless it was not considered appropriate.

When Hattie was working at the store, Sam would sit on a stool and watch the customers and clerks as they went about their business. It wasn't long before his presence went unnoticed. Sometimes Hattie would have time at work to help him with his lessons. In the evening, he would do lessons or play the piano.

One day, Sam noticed that more people than usual were climbing the stairs to Hattie's office. A lull in the flow presented him with the opportunity to walk up, and ask Hattie if she needed any help. Walking into her office, he noticed a ball of scrap paper on the floor in front of Hattie's desk. Picking it up, he asked, "Should I throw this away?"

Hattie had her head down reading some form and when she looked up she said, "Oh hi Sam, yes I am finished with it now. You can throw it in the trash."

"Was it important?" asked Sam looking at the paper. "It seems to be just some pen scratching."

"That's all it was, but I was using it as an evaluator."

"Did it work?" He asked turning the ball of paper around with his fingers trying to figure out how or what an evaluator was.

"Sure did. It solved my problem."

"How?"

"Andy needed to hire a new man. He had five good applicants and couldn't decide which one to hire. He asked me to help him. Actually, that ball of scrap paper helped him. I just watched.

"Firs one put da ball in da can get da job?" Sam asked as he deftly tossed the paper ball across the room arcing it into the trashcan.

I should have let Sam do these interviews, thought Hattie.

She enlightened him. "You get the idea. But, it was a little more complicated than that. I placed the trash ball on the floor where each applicant could see it when they came in. Two of them ignored it. One asked if they should put it in the trash for me. One simply leaned over and picked it up and tossed it toward the can. He missed. One picked up the ball asked if it was important. When I said no then he walked over and placed the ball in the trash. So, Sam, which one would you hire?"

"Not the one who missed the shot that's for sure. And not the two that ignored it. I would probably go with the las' man. He know if it not important it go in da trash. Shouldn't have to ask fo' permission to put it there. But, Miz Hattie what if dat man don't know nutin' bout da job?"

"Remember, Andy already told me all were qualified. I didn't have to worry about that."

Later that evening, as they were shelling peas for supper, Sam asked Hattie, "What's profit and overhead?"

Hattie continued to work on the peas. When they had them all shelled, she picked up the whole bowl and placed it on the table. "You see this bowl full of peas?"

"Yes," Sam said, rolling his eyes as if to say, *I'm not blind, after all there it is right in front of me.*

"Can you count far enough yet to tell me how many peas are in this bowl?"

"Yes, you want I should show you?"

"No. I wanted to make sure you had the idea of counting clear in your head. I want you to go out to the barn, and get a handful of that corn we have been feeding to Blackie."

"Yas'm," Sam said as he left wondering if she was going to mix that old feed corn with them peas. He shook his head, peas mixed with that feed corn wouldn't taste too good!

When Sam returned Hattie ordered, "Put the corn on the table here by me, and we will continue. Now you pretend you are a farmer over near Fiddlersburg, and you grew these peas in your field." She handed Sam the pan of peas. "I want to buy your peas so I give you this much money." She took some of the corn kernels from the pile Sam had placed on the table.

"That's not money that's corn."

"Right, but remember I said to pretend. So you need to pretend each corn kernel is a gold piece. Now how many gold pieces did you get for your peas?"

"Twenty-six," said Sam, pushing the corn into small groups and counting quickly. "That don't seem like much ifn' it's a big field."

"Pretend it's a bad year. Now I have all the peas and I load them on Eli's train with all the peas from other farmers, and I take them to Baltimore where they don't have any peas. A man pays me forty kernels of corn for them," said Hattie taking forty kernels from the pile on the table.

"Who gets the leftover corn?"

"That belongs to the Bank."

"I think I wanna be a Banker," said Sam his smile showing strong white teeth.

"Don't we all," grumbled Hattie. "Back to pretending. Now, I received forty kernels for my peas. I paid you Twenty-six," she said taking twenty-six corn kernels and putting them back in the bank.

"Why did you put the corn back in da bank's pile?"

"Because I took it from my bank account to pay you for the peas, and I want my investment back. Now, how many kernels do I have left here in front of me?"

Sam made a quick count. "Fourteen?"

"Correct," agreed Hattie. "Now, I take two kernels and pay the railroad for hauling the peas. I take two more and pay the men who loaded the peas on and off the train. I take one kernel and pay Jim for doing the bookwork." Each time Hattie moved the corresponding kernels away from her pile, and placed them in a separate pile.

"How many kernels do I have left?"

"Nine, but what's those in that other pile?"

"That's the overhead you asked about. I paid five kernels or gold pieces for service from others to do this business transaction. The nine kernels are my profit. Does the lesson answer your original question about profit and overhead?"

"Yes. But why don't dat farmer in Fiddlersburg jus' sell the peas in Baltimore?"

"Because he didn't know where or when to sell them. He would have paid a lot more to the railroad to ship the peas, because he had such a small shipment. Eli made a profit, because he combines all the crops he buys into a single trainload and conducts a single transaction on the other end. He receives a reward because he performs a needful service for others."

"We still got a pile of corn in da bank. Who get dat?"

"That's a lesson for another night. Right now we need to cook your peas for supper."

"Dats good, 'cause countin makes me hungry."

The next day Hattie came home early from a temperance meeting. As she opened the door, she heard the piano. The music being played was like nothing Hattie had ever heard before. The melody in the background reminded her of Bach. But it was overshadowed by lilting, syncopated rhythms that dominated the piece. Where had such a song come from? She knew she had never bought any sheet music that sounded like this. Rushing into the parlor, she discovered Sam playing, and there was no sheet music on the piano.

"Where did you learn that song?" she cried rushing up to Sam. He got up from the piano with a guilty look on his face. "I'm sorry miz Hattie; I thought you wuz gone for da day to that women's temperance party. I wuz jus playin around. Did I hurt the piano?"

"No, the piano needs to be played. I left the meeting because those women are just too radical for me. They want to eliminate strong drink from the planet! I don't believe in drinking. I saw what it did to my father. But, I still believe that everyone has a right to choose what he or she takes into his or her body. There need to be laws to prevent those under the influence from hurting others, but…Sam you got me off the track! That music where did it come from?"

"It come from inside me. I jus play what I feel."

"It's strange but wonderful. It makes me feel all wiggly inside. It makes me want to tap my toes and dance around." Hattie said as she spun around the parlor. "Sam you need to get it down on paper. You could start a whole new era in music!"

"Can't, ma'am. I don't know that much about music. You needs to teach me some more."

"I wish I could, Sam, but my music lessons were terminated in a rather abrupt manner and I never learned enough about writing music." Hattie sighed remembering Eliza's failing health and the decision she made to return to her family just before she died.

"Well, I can tell playing the piano is coming along fine. How about the reading, writing, and arithmetic?" Hattie asked, changing the subject before she became totally morbid.

"I keep thinkin' bout those corn kernels we pretended was gold da other night. Can I have another lesson bout dat?"

"Very well, why don't you fetch a handful of 'Gold' from the stable before we start while I get my thoughts in order," Hattie said as she moved to the kitchen table.

Sam returned with a double handful of corn from the sack in the stable.

"I hope you left Blackie something to eat."

"If we goin' to turn it into gold I want a lot!"

"We will get to wanting a lot in a minute, but first let's look at the basic reason that gold seems so important in our lives."

Hattie continued with a question. "What do you know about the red Indians that live out west?"

"They be dangerous folks, takin' scalps and such."

"Yes, they do that. Let's go back to a time before the white man came. The Indians lived in small tribes. They made their own shelter and hunted or raised their own food. They made their own weapons for hunting and for protection. A small tribe could and did exist without any outside influence. But even in the tribe some were better hunters, others better tent builders, and some made better robes and clothing. The Indians in the tribe would trade or barter among each other because it was more efficient to do so."

"Then came da white man."

"Exactly," said Hattie. "The white man introduced pots and pans, knives and guns, glass beads, and other pretty things. The Indian's lifestyle changed. They grew to depend on items they couldn't grow or make for themselves. Soon they were trading with the white man to get them."

"When do we get to the gold?"

"Soon," answered Hattie.

"Then a different kind of white man comes into Indian lands. He builds a home and settles on the land. He has needs that are supplied by folks back east or even across the ocean in England for instance. He can't or doesn't want to live off the land like the Indians. To meet his needs, he has to trade something he has produced for corn-gold like I showed you the other night. Sometime back in history, people established a gold-based economy. That means they would trade the gold they earned by providing a product or service to someone for products or services they needed or just wanted," she paused as a picture of Anne flashed through her mind.

She continued, "Gold is heavy and hard to pack around so a system of money emerged. Smaller coins from less precious metals and notes on paper promising to pay gold on demand began to appear, and most of the real gold went into the banks where it could be protected from thieves."

"What happen' if da thief run' da bank?"

"Sometimes that happens. There are people who do not trust banks, so they must protect their own gold. But, we are getting off the subject. The point I want to make is that something: gold, silver, salt, wampum, paper or even corn becomes a means of exchanging the work we do to produce a service or product into a common commodity recognized and traded by everyone."

"I think I see what you getin' at. I works fo' you and I earn lessons and my pay by doin' work. I trades my work fo' money!"

"Very good," beamed Hattie. "And with your pay, you can buy clothes or that stick candy you like at the store. I could pay you more money, but then you would have to pay it back to me for the food you eat, the bed you sleep in, and the lessons I give you." Hattie giggled at the look of consternation on Sam's face.

"I likes it better da way 'tis."

"That's the way families operate. They work together on the barter system, and if someone can't do their share, love makes up the difference." Hattie said as her former families flashed through her mind. Mam and Pap, Margaret Janes, Kim, Anne and Father, and now Eli and Sam filled that part of her life.

"Sam, see if you can sum up what I have been talking about. Speak English properly the way I have been teaching it to you."

"Gold is the commodity we use to form the base for our money system. Money represents the work we do, like providing service, building something, or growing food. The harder we work and the better we do things the more money we make. Then, we take our money and buy goods or services we cannot produce for ourselves. That's how we live." Sam said smiling.

"Very good. I want to make one correction. Doing something better does not always guarantee higher pay for that service. It does increase the chance that you will be asked to do the service again. Sometimes the customer wants faster service or something made from cheaper materials, because it is good enough for his needs. The customer is always right, is a good motto most of the time, but you also have to learn to read your customer and provide the best service. Also, it is important to recognize that the more complex society becomes the more difficult it is to find a way to change your work or talent into the money needed to buy the goods and services you want. Society is changing. America is growing. It is filling up with people. New inventions appear every day. Our lives will change and so will the way we work. We will need to change to meet new, complex demands if we are to be successful in this world."

"I see. Be da mos' successful we can be. Dat be our goal."

"No Sam. The ultimate goal is serving others to the best of our ability. We may not achieve the most money or success in this life, but in the long run we will feel better, and leave this life happier if we can say, 'I have done something good for someone today."

"Dat why you helpin' me miz Hattie?"

"Could be Sam, could be. Only time, or the good Lord can answer that."

Chapter 11

Hattie's Journal

18 November 1860: They elected Abraham Lincoln
President. I think we might have a war soon.

---

ummer came to Hagerstown, but the Wiggins household didn't pay
much attention to the weather. Hattie followed the national election for
President of the United States with great interest. She avidly read the
newspaper articles and generally favored Abraham Lincoln. She just liked
the way he talked. Not being allowed to vote dampened her interest. In
fact it really irritated her. Eli, convinced that Lincoln would win, continued
to secure trade routes and materials that would prove profitable when war
broke out between the North and the South. He would vote for Lincoln, a
strong abolitionist, even though his vote in the state of Maryland would be
drowned out by the strong support for the Southern Democratic candidate,
John C. Breckinridge.

One night that summer after they had finished eating and Sam had left
to go study, Eli mentioned that he was taking an extended trip to Chicago.
Several of his friends wanted him to look over the prospects of investing in
a new railroad line that would extend from Chicago through the northwest
portion of the country meeting up with the Columbia river in the Oregon

territory. Other financial interests had grabbed up the routes through the central plains and in the southwest. This time, he had an opportunity to get in on the ground floor with his friend James J. Hill.

Hattie felt ambivalent. She believed they had enough to do for the present time. But it was his money. He had earned it. She felt she should support him. It would be a long trip since he wanted to visit some of the present outlets for commerce in the Northwest and evaluate the possibility of expanding his business interests in that direction.

He also wanted to visit an old school chum from his days growing up in Georgetown, Ohio who now lived in Galena, Illinois. They had done business when he lived in St. Louis. Galena could be a good location for a business hub. He might be gone as long as a month.

More buyers were moving into cotton and the price was rising with the competition. Eli had backed off since the profit margins were now lower. This pleased Hattie since she would have fewer shipments to deal with while he was gone. She could focus on just managing the local east-west trade and the store here in Hagerstown. This would give her more time to spend with her personal reading and helping Sam with his schoolwork and piano. She had been reading about Elizabeth Blackwell, the first woman in America to obtain a medical degree, she wanted to write a letter to her, and learn more about obtaining her own medical degree.

The following morning, Eli left for work early. He had a lot of things to go over with Jim and Andy. He wanted to be sure they had all the delivery schedules and prices for the various goods that would be coming in to Hagerstown while he was gone. He was concerned that they would depend on Hattie for the information. He wanted her to be free to entertain the local ladies and to gain information that might help any runaways that might show up.

Hattie spent the morning housecleaning. There are times she thought when having a couple of girls to help out would be nice, but she planned to stick to her guns and not have any servants. She had Sam helping out because she wanted everything special for the afternoon tea. Plus Eli was bringing home a special guest for dinner that evening. If she could get her hands on him she would shake him till his teeth rattled. Here he was going on a long trip. He needed his clothes washed and pressed from the last trip and he brings home a guest. Men! She grumbled to herself.

Sam silently agreed since she kept him going non-stop all day helping her with "women chores."

The tea went off great. The main topic of discussion was the coming election. That opened up a genteel debate on the slavery issue. Hattie identified at least two ladies that were firmly opposed to slavery that until now had not expressed a definite opinion. The discussion then turned to voting rights for women. There was little debate but a lot of discussion. Everyone felt slighted that half the adult population of the country went unheard on Election Day.

The women continued to express common opinions on the right to vote longer than Hattie had planned. Some of them were in heated debate shouting the same arguments back and forth at one another as they left in their carriages. Hattie listening from the steps was unable to discern any difference of opinion between sides. An outsider listening would hear angry comments on similar points. Hattie just had time to check on the meal and give Sam his serving instructions when Eli and his guest appeared.

"Dr. Fairchild, I want to introduce you to my wife Helen. She is the person we discussed on our trip from Baltimore to Boston last week."

Hattie thought to herself, *do I feel anger, pride or humility that I was the subject that kept two perfect strangers entertained on an all day journey?*

"Helen, this is Dr. James H. Fairchild, President of Oberlin College. I almost went to school there. It is one of the most progressive schools in the country. If I had made the decision to attend school in Oberlin, I would have missed the opportunity to meet and marry my first wife. Oh how little decisions can change our lives." Both Hattie and Dr. Fairchild nodded in agreement.

Hattie moved back and forth between kitchen and dining room as she finished the meal preparations. On one of her trips to the dining room Dr. Fairchild said, "I understand from your husband that you are self educated and quite well read Mrs. Wiggins."

"I do read a lot and seem to have an above average ability to retain what I read. I am also an inquisitive person by nature. Others may require the assistance and aid that comes from having a good teacher. I seem to do well on my own."

"Do you feel that a formal classroom education has merit?"

"Oh, yes, I received medical training from a man with a real gift for healing. I could never have gotten that level of training from a book. So I recognize the value of having a good teacher. I'm sorry if I may have sounded pompous or arrogant. However, I have met people that cannot learn anything from personal reading. I feel frustrated at times when such individuals fail to give me credit for what I know. I have deep respect for the institutions of higher learning. But, sometimes more credence is placed on the diploma than on the individual's ability."

"We recognize that problem at Oberlin. We are trying to create a way in which individuals like yourself can take a battery of tests, and be granted a degree without having to attend certain courses. We have been able to cut the time required to obtain a degree in half in many cases."

"That is fantastic!" exclaimed Hattie. "Do you have a medical program? I would like to become recognized as a Doctor of Medicine."

"Well, that's a pretty big step, Mrs. Wiggins," chuckled Fairchild in a depreciating manner. "But we might be able to give you a head start with a preliminary degree."

"What would I have to do?"

"Our students take a break during Christmas each year. If you were to arrive in Oberlin on the 17th of December, we could do some testing at that time."

"When would the testing be complete?"

"That would depend on the level you achieved. We would start with basic courses, and continue to test you until you reached the level where additional studies would be required." Dr. Fairchild said.

"Oh Eli, what do you think? Should I try it?" asked Hattie turning to him with an expectant look in her eyes.

"Yes, dear, most definitely. The invitation for you to participate in this program was the primary reason Dr. Fairchild came here tonight. I plan to arrange my affairs so that I can be here to manage the business during that time."

"No, Eli, I want you with me. I will need the moral support!" exclaimed Hattie.

"Well, we'll see what December brings," said Eli in a noncommittal manner.

After this bit of news, Hattie's meal, while excellent, seemed anti-climatic. They spent the remainder of the evening discussing the value education can play in improving and opening new opportunities for people. They agreed in principle but Hattie was not able to convince Dr. Fairchild that a person could gain an education without attending school.

In answer to Hattie's remark that a diploma was simply a piece of paper, Dr. Fairchild asked, "Hattie, why did you pour that brandy from a new bottle into the decanter without tasting it?"

"Well, first, I don't particularly care for brandy or for any strong spirits, but I recognized from the bottle and the label that the brandy was Eli's favorite, so I just opened it and poured it in." As soon as she had spoken Hattie realized why Dr. Fairchild was smiling.

The label on the bottle and a diploma were similar. The label represented a promise to the user that the contents were a certain quality and consistency. A diploma also represented a promise. A recognized school of higher learning guaranteed, through the diploma, that the recipient met certain standards of knowledge and training. Both the diploma and the label established a level of trust in the bottle's contents or in a person's competence.

Dr. Fairchild continued his argument. "Teachers also play an important part in the education process as mentors. They can offer an opinion contrary to that expressed by an author. A person reading a single book may fail to grasp this different point of view. He or she may not find the other side of the issue due to a limitation in their library or inability to recognize that another answer to the question exists. Also studies conducted in a classroom environment promote questions that a single student might not think to ask. A synergy emerges from group activity that can bring about solutions to problems that one or even two people may not consider. Great advancements in knowledge could well be lost without an open group discussion. Open minded people looking for solutions can always achieve more than individuals restricted to a rigid mindset."

This argument caused Hattie to think of all the people that had helped her. She considered how shallow her training would have been without people like Eliza, Margaret, Kim, Mr. Hapwood and Eli. Dr. Fairchild left to catch the late night train to Oberlin and life in the Wiggins home returned to normal. Well, not quite normal.

Hattie returned to her habit of reading late into the night. Dr. Fairchild had recommended several books she might want to study before the tests. She soon exhausted the local libraries. She placed orders with Eli's buyers in Washington D.C. and in Baltimore giving them special instructions to scour the bookstores for any books related to advancements in medicine, science, mathematics or philosophy. She checked the mail coming to the store after every train arriving from the East. The mail clerk received strict instructions to meet each train and bring her mail to her at once.

Sam sat on his usual stool waiting for Hattie. It had been two weeks since Eli left. Hattie, consumed with her own studies, encouraged Sam to pick his own subjects to study. She still held progress reviews, made suggestions, and helped Sam decide what to study next. At the present time he was studying the shoppers in the store. He thought he might want to have his own store some day. In a few years he would need to earn his own pile of corn. He smiled thinking of the lessons involving corn as a substitute for gold. They had recently talked about money lending, debt and interest. Hattie had encouraged him to stay out of debt. It could put him in chains that would turn him right back into a slave, forcing him to work at some job he didn't like in order to pay off debts incurred for things he didn't really need. He liked her comment that interest never sleeps or takes a day off.

He liked to watch the shoppers in the store as they went about selecting different things they needed or just wanted. He had asked Hattie one day why she had moved the staples like flour and sugar to the back of the store. She had told him there were two reasons. First, they could be loaded from the rear faster with less mess in the store. Second, almost every customer came to the store because they needed staples. That's why they were called staples—everyone needed them. If the customers had to walk through the store to get them they would pick up other products on impulse. Hattie even called it "Impulsive Buying." Sam smiled. He liked the way she did things. Other folks might be impulsive but not Hattie.

Sam's gaze continued to scan the crowd. One of the jobs he had acquired was to spot people trying to put something in their pockets without paying. They would look around to see if a clerk was watching. They never noticed Sam. He was just part of the furniture. He had learned that there were certain signs or movements people made before being dishonest. Hattie had mentioned a few and he had picked up some on his own. The store paid him a penny or a penny's worth of candy each time he was successful. He usually took the penny, but not always. He did have a sweet tooth.

He sat across the store in direct view of the clerk operating the cash register. They had worked out a signal. He would raise both arms over his head as if to stretch out the kinks from sitting on the stool too long. Once he gained eye contact with the clerk, he would make a subtle movement with his head and eye to point out the suspect. When the suspect wasn't looking or had moved on, Sam would indicate the location of the stolen merchandise by placing a hand inside his shirt, a pocket or rubbing his arm to indicate a purse or bag.

Sam slumped on his stool watching the shoppers. He had stayed up late the night before reading a book about hunting tigers in India. It had been interesting to study and learn that there were two kinds of Indians in the world. He noticed that hunting tigers was much like hunting men. Many of the techniques mentioned in the book were similar to the way southern plantation owners hunted runaway slaves.

Then the one person in the world he didn't want to meet walked in. Seth Rankin wore the same slouch hat he had on the day Sam slipped away from him in Jackson, Mississippi. His dirty buckskin hunting shirt covered massive shoulders and a protruding belly. He stomped through the store, his jeans stuffed into mud-crusted boots. Sam, hoping he was unseen, slipped through the door concealing the stairs leading to the upper offices.

Hattie looked up irritated by the knock at the door. She was deep into a book she had received in the morning mail called, *The Federalist*. The author had compiled a series of newspaper articles written by someone called Publius. It turned out this was a pen name used by some of America's founding fathers when they wrote a series of articles to the newspaper to help people understand the American Constitution. The articles had been written more than sixty years earlier, and Hattie was having difficulty following the arguments.

She was fascinated by the depth of understanding these men had into human nature. Reading between the lines, she was able to comprehend just how much these men valued personal liberty and at the same time how they recognized the need to come together for the common good. Could people really put the lust for power and prestige aside and work together? Sighing at the interruption, she put a smile in her voice and called, "come in."

Sam slipped through the door. Fear caused a wide-eyed look to dominate his normally cheerful face. Hattie asked, "Sam, what's wrong? Is someone trying to rob the store?"

"Worse than that miz Wiggins," Sam replied glancing at the door. Hattie got up and moved from behind her desk. At that moment the door crashed open! Sam leaped to the side as the large red-faced man Sam had seen downstairs stepped into the room. After one look at Sam, he took a step to grab him by the shoulder. Suddenly his wrist was locked up behind his back and a hand was slamming his face into the wall beside Sam. A finger and thumb pressed something in his neck, and he slumped forward falling down a long dark tunnel.

He awoke to find himself bound securely to a heavy wooden armchair. Sam was gone. A slim woman with dark brown eyebrows that slanted up like bow waves from a fast moving ship was sitting behind the desk reading a book.

"What's goin' on here?" he demanded.

The woman looked up from her reading. "That's supposed to be my question. After all this *is* my office."

Straining his muscles against the ropes, he found them tight. "Why you got me tied up like this? Wipe my nose. I'm bleedin'. Blood's getin' all over my huntin' jacket," he ordered.

"What's the matter don't you like mixing your blood with that of the slaves you've tortured?" Hattie murmured keeping her nose in her book. She figured ignoring him would irritate him and keep him off balance. The tactic seemed to be working.

"Are you one of them crazy abolitionists?" he growled, trying to wipe his face on his shoulder.

"No, as a matter of fact I am a slave owner." *At least on paper,* Hattie thought to herself. "Now, if you will calm down and ask nicely I will wash the blood off your face and bandage the cut over your eye. You might start by telling me your name, why you broke into my office hollering like a wild man, and attacked my boy."

"Name's Seth Rankin. I come from Mississippi. I was up here lookin' for another runaway and come in this store to get some chawin' tobacco. Then I sees *my* boy a settin on a stool big as you please. I knowed right off it was Sam. I turned to talk to the clerk, and when I looked back he was gone! Only one place he could go, up the stairs to this office. I heard him talking, and walked in to get him. The next thing I know you got me tied up in this chair, bleedin' all over myself."

"You keep referring to your slave. Are you really the owner?" asked Hattie.

She moved over and began to clean the blood from Seth's face. She rinsed out the rag in a basin that had been sitting on a bookcase behind him.

"Well, that's a questionable matter." He said, trying a disarming grin. He winced when the grin caused the cut over his eye to start hurting. He also discovered a loose tooth and a cut inside his mouth. What had he run into?

"Can you explain what you mean by that remark?" asked Hattie moving back to sit behind the desk taking a position of power.

"Well the owner done give up on findin' Sam. Besides it was the third time he run off so we figgered he jus' keep runnin' anyway. Boy's too smart for his britches." Hattie was forced to agree with this disagreeable excuse of a man. But then she'd met up with worse.

"Well, Mr. Rankin, while you were resting, I did some checking. Slave market is down right now what with the elections and war cries being heard across the nation. Plantation owners are cashing in their assets. Many feel this is not the time to expand by purchasing new slaves. A boy like Sam, hmmm, might bring two hundred on a good day." Hattie said as she reached inside a locked drawer in her desk and pulled out a small bag that clinked when she placed it on the desk. She opened the center knee drawer and withdrew two documents. She took five twenty dollar gold pieces out of the bag. She played with them a while, watching Seth's face as she did so. Then she stacked them neatly on the desk.

"I have here two documents. One is a release for all claims against the slave named Sam along with his description. I think it would be in your best interest to sign the document and take the money and leave before I charge you with assault against me. And oh by the way, a fee for administering to your wounds, since I am recognized in this community as a healer."

"That's robbery! I can get closer to four hundred back in Mississippi!" roared Seth.

"Robbery would probably be the charge if your boss were to find out, now wouldn't it?"

Seth just glared at her in frustration. Then his shoulders slumped, but his good eye looked from her to the coins. There were more coins in the bag. "What's the other document, sworn complaint or something?"

"No. That's just to show you I am a nice person."

"Nice is not a word I would use lady, but I do admire your grit." Seth interrupted with a grimace.

"To continue," said Hattie pointing to the second document, "I will sweeten the pot a little with this voucher for any goods we have for sale in the store below to the tune of, say, twenty dollars?"

"Make it a hundred," said Seth. They haggled for a while and settled at forty-five dollars in trade.

Hattie cut Seth loose, signed the voucher and gave him the gold after he signed the release. Seth grimly touched his face, gave the knife still near Hattie's hand a forlourn look, and left the office.

Later that night after they had eaten and cleaned up, Hattie asked Sam to tell her the story of his escape. "Mr. Rankin be takin me to town with him ever week fo' 'bout a month. We loads up with supplies den he stop at the tavern fo' a few 'Warm me ups,' befo' we heads home. Only he stay in dat tavern a long time. It be cold out in dat wagon. I tried scrunchin' down 'tween the bags and such, but it don't work too good. I 'bout froze dat firs' trip. Nex time we go, I took the old quilt Mr. Rankin sits on to drive dat wagon. I curls up in it and sleeps all the way home. He so drunk he don't know no better. The las' time when I 'scapes I took the quilt and bunched it over a couple of sacks. Dat make it look like I be sleepin'. I hope I's long gone befo' he gets home and tries to kick me 'wake to unload dat wagon. Jus' wish I coulda seen his face. He'ee." Sam giggled as he ended.

"Sam I'm glad to know the story about your escape. It shows great courage and intelligence," Hattie said, with a frown, "but I am disappointed in your speaking and grammar. We have been working so hard to improve your opportunities in life, and you continue to use this slave talk. The way you speak, and what you say reveals your education and intelligence. You are not being uppity when you speak well. You are telling the world I am smart, and I know what I am talking about. Others will respect your abilities more, and you will find more opportunities for success. If you want to be a field hand or serve others at some menial job all your life then talk any way that suits you. If you want to be a business man and run your own store then you need to convince people to have confidence in you and to respect your abilities."

"Yes ma'am. I know you are right and I promise to do better."

The train Eli was riding moved at a slow and uncomfortable pace. Eli didn't care. He was elated with what he had heard at the meeting in

Chicago. He had succeeded in buying in on the ground floor of the rail-road venture to send tracks to the Columbia River and even into Canada. There was talk of land allocations in the Dakota and Montana Territories. It would take a few years for that to happen but the potential was enormous.

His train was headed for Minneapolis and St. Paul. He wanted to evaluate the markets for shipping products to that area before the railroad went beyond that point. Eli planned to make a side trip to Galena, Illinois. He wanted to see about a shipment of lead. Lead meant bullets and if war broke out lots of bullets would be sold to the government.

He had an old boyhood friend that had moved to Galena. He wasn't in the lead business, but he might know some folks that were. Eli was also looking for an agent to handle his affairs in this area. Hiram had lived in St. Louis before moving up to Galena. Eli had tried to help him in business when he worked in St. Louis but things had never worked out. Hiram took too much bad advice from too many stupid or self-serving men. Eli would just get him moving in the right direction, and then he would have to go back to Hagerstown. The durn fool should have stayed in the Army. The business of fighting was the only business he was really good at, and he had learned that at West Point. Eli remembered hearing something about him preferring to be called Ulysses now, but to him he would always be good old Hiram, his next-door playmate. Boy they really got into some jams back there in Germantown. Eli was the idea man and stubborn Hiram would get it done. Eli wondered if the old fighting spirit was still there.

Eli stepped down from the carriage. He stood looking at the sign on the false front of the store. The sign read "Hides, Harness and Saddles." *Well, I guess it could be worse,* he thought to himself. He put on his trademark salesman's smile and walked in. The place was crowded with merchandise hanging everywhere. It smelled good though. Eli liked the smell of freshly tanned leather and oil. He asked the clerk for Hiram and received a blank look. He asked if Mr. Grant was in. The clerk nodded and pointed to an office up a flight of stairs at the side of the store.

The two men met at the top of the stairs in a backslapping handshaking embrace. After the initial "How ya beens" and "Good ta seeyas," the two old friends sat down in comfortable leather chairs in Grant's office. He brought a bottle out from his desk and raised an eyebrow at Eli.

"I don't think so, I just had my breakfast. Little early in the day for me," said Eli. Grant put the bottle away but Eli thought he saw reluctance in the movement.

"So what brings you to the fair city of Galena, Eli?"

"I didn't really need to have an excuse to visit an old friend, but I am interested in picking up a load of lead bars. I would like to get at least five rail cars loaded up and out of here in less than a week. Do you have any pull with folks in that business that might cut me an honest deal?"

"Not right now, Eli. The total production for the next month was just contracted to a Mr. William Callahan. He says he's from St. Louis, but I ran into him the other night. If he's from St. Louis then he and I sure ran in different social circles. He got a little drunk later in the evening and started talking with a southern accent. May have called himself Calhoun once or twice. I can't be sure, but a man by the name of Calhoun has been picking up all kinds of military stores all over this region. He floats 'em down the Mississippi on barges as fast as he can get 'em loaded.

"What's your feelings on the possibility of war with the South?" asked Eli.

"It'll happen if Lincoln gets elected. Some friends of mine are already making noises in Washington to get me back on active duty. I may even take a commission in a state militia if the right offer comes along. What about you?"

"I'm not much of a fightin' man. You know that from our old school days, remember? I preferred dancin' with the girls to fighting."

"But, Eli you are one sharp man when it comes to moving the right goods to the right place. A man like that is valuable. An army runs on beans and bullets, and you are the man that can make that happen."

Eli rubbed his chin the motion emphasizing the dimple in his cheek as he considered his answer. "My new wife and I are strongly opposed to slavery in America. We want to see it stopped. If you get called up, and war is declared get in touch with me. I will consider working with you. Maybe we could work out some kind of position where I could help out without actually being in the army."

"You sneaky son of a gun, when did you get married again? I remember that story you fed me about eternal marriage and loving Sarah forever. So what happened to change your mind?"

"A very special girl came into my life. We are soulmates, the best of friends. Our relationship is totally platonic. I know it's hard to believe. Wipe that silly grin out of your whiskers. It started off as a business arrangement believe it or not, but I am beginning to feel different about it. Our relationship seems different now than when we were married, but we haven't had time to discuss how we feel now."

"Old Eli the lover boy from Georgetown, Ohio. She must be old and uuugly!" Grant laughed till tears came out his eyes.

"Not on your life Hiram. I watched her walk through a hotel lobby in Richmond. I saw men dropping like flies, mouths hanging open. Some of the most beautiful women in Virginia stopped in their tracks in obvious envy. She is definitely no ugly old hag! On top of that, she's got a brain sharp as a needle, and she can put your head through a wall with some kind of Chinese fightin' moves."

"Too bad we can't put her in uniform. Sounds like she could win the war single handed," was Grant's reply. They continued to discuss the possibility of war and the "remember when" stories started to repeat.

Eli looked at his watch. "Well, if there is no lead to be had, I better get on the afternoon train to Minneapolis. Look, if cooler heads prevail and war is averted I want to talk to you about being my agent here in this neck of the woods. Think it over and send me a letter detailing the products that will be needed as the country grows toward the northwest. I need to know what kinds of crops, produce, or minerals I could expect to buy and transport back east. I will sit down with my wife, and we will evaluate the possibility of turning a profit. It would be like old times. You and I work well together when other folks mind their own business. I want you in on this, but only if you want it."

"Eli you need to understand that my first love is serving my country. If I can't get back in the army, I will sure give your offer serious consideration."

On that note they parted with the usual "good to see you again" and "keep in touch" comments.

Two weeks after leaving Galena, Eli returned to Hagerstown. He was just in time to cast his vote for Lincoln. Hattie and Sam were full of stories to tell him concerning Seth Rankin's visit. Eli told them about his visits with Grant and the Hill consortium. He failed to mention what Grant wanted him to do if war broke out.

Business was picking up as the demand for food in the east was answered by the need for manufactured items out west. Hattie and Eli added extra carloads of goods going both ways in order to keep up with the demand. The scheduling problems compounded with the addition of each carload kept them working late into the evening. They needed to hire more men, but good workers were hard to find since many were looking toward fighting in one army or the other. They were not interested in long-term employment.

They all left work early one day in order to get cleaned up and dress for a dinner engagement later in the evening. Sam put the buggy in the stable, fed Blackie, but left him harnessed for the later trip to the party. He put a handful of corn in his pocket hoping that after they returned later that night, he and Hattie could discuss the finer points of handling money. Sam was coming from the stable when he heard a carriage stop out front. Ducking around the side of the house he took a quick look. He recognized the carriage folks hired when they got off the train. He thought for a moment, and figured it must be the train from Washington, D.C. The timing was right. He watched as two strangers got down and started up the walk to the front entrance.

Hattie answered the door. The taller of the two asked to speak to Eli Wiggins. Both men appeared nervous and apprehensive about remaining outside. Sam ducked back and moved quietly to the kitchen door.

Hattie sensed their anxiety. "Won't you gentlemen come in? I will tell Eli you are here. Whom shall I say is calling?"

"We would prefer not to say ma'am," replied the shorter, stockier man.

Hattie directed them to chairs in the parlor and went to fetch Eli. When she returned a few minutes later she announced, "Mr. Wiggins is changing just now. We have been working at the store, and we have a party to attend later this evening. Is your business such that we should consider canceling our engagement?"

"No ma'am, we shouldn't be too long. We want to catch the connecting train to Chicago. It leaves in an hour, so our visit will be brief."

His explanation was interrupted by Eli's appearance. Both men rose as he entered the room. Hattie said, "I will leave you gentlemen to your business." She walked out to the kitchen closing the parlor door.

Hattie hurried immediately to the pantry. It was possible to hear a conversation in the parlor from in there. Some time in the past, a hole had been punched in the plaster. Hattie had hung a sampler with a picture of a house over the hole. The house windows were not cross-stitched and the base fabric had a loose weave. She could see and hear what was going on in the parlor from there. She was surprised to find Sam sitting on the stool kept in the pantry. He looked up with a guilty "I'm sorry" expression on his face. She motioned him off the stool but did not indicate he had to leave. They both watched and listened to the scene playing out in the parlor.

The taller man handed Eli a document. "We understand that you are a supporter of Mr. Lincoln for president?"

"That's correct. If this is some kind of an inquisition, I remind you gentlemen that this is a free country, and I can vote for whomever I choose…"

"No, no Mr. Wiggins. You have us all wrong," said the shorter man. "We are here to ask for your support. We have discovered a plot to assassinate Mr. Lincoln as he makes the trip from his home in Illinois to Washington. We are looking for people loyal to Mr. Lincoln to help us set up decoy trains and other maneuvers, designed to ensure his safe arrival in Washington in time for the Inauguration. We are asking for your assistance. Our sources tell us that you travel to various places as a part of your work, and that you are a supporter of Mr. Lincoln. It would be easy to generate a cover story for your appearance in different locations. Will you help us?"

"Of course." Eli responded after a slight hesitation as he considered the implications.

The shorter man took a small book from his pocket. "This is a code book. It contains a series of codes you will use to decript letters or telegraph messages we will be sending you in the future. Please keep it in a very safe place and let no one know what you are doing. The front pages of the book contain instructions needed to read the codes. Do you have any questions?"

"No. I guess the less I know the less someone can wiggle out of me," he grinned trying to ease his nervousness with a little humor.

"That's correct. We hope nothing will come of this. It may all be a hoax or false alarm. The President or President Elect should have a dedicated force of professionals assigned to protect him. Right now such an organization does not exist. It is up to a few of us who support the idea that the President, regardless of his politics represents the will of the majority of the American people. And as such, he deserves protection from anarchists and others that would destroy him and the principles contained in our Constitution," said the shorter of the two men.

The other man looked at his companion as if he wanted to tell him to save the speeches for another day, but instead he said, "Mr. Wiggins, thank you for your willingness to help. Now, we must be on our way. We don't want any spies to wonder why we missed our train connection. That could put you in danger and ruin your usefulness to our cause. Good by and good luck." With that they left as quietly as they came.

"You can come out now," said Eli looking right at the sampler. "Send Sam over to Tom and Nancy's with a note explaining that we may be late. We need to discuss this."

Sam fed Blackie the corn from his pocket when he reached the barn realizing that tonight was not the time for a corn lesson.

Chapter 12

Hattie's Journal

24 Jan 1861: *I just received a letter from Dr. Fairchild at Oberlin College. I have been awarded a real B. A. Degree.*

Eli looked at Hattie as she entered the parlor and asked if she recognized either of the gentlemen. Hattie shook her head and Eli said, "I think the taller one was Allan Pinkerton. He does a lot of private police work for the railroad. I think I saw him once in Chicago. He was pointed out to me one day as we passed going in different directions. I was on my way to sign some freight contracts and he was just leaving the same office. I don't think he saw or remembered me. Our mutual business acquaintances probably let him know about my political preferences, and the traveling I do. That connection could have brought him here today."

"Pinkerton Detectives are always in the newspaper," said Hattie. "They have been mentioned in several articles about train robberies. Their record for bringing criminals to justice and recovering stolen property shows real inside knowledge. If any one would know about a conspiracy to kill Lincoln it would be them."

Eli nodded in agreement. "I would be curious to know if they were involved in the John Brown incident at Harper's Ferry. That disaster sure interfered with our delivery schedules to and from Washington, but I don't recall anyone at B & O headquarters saying anything specific to me. I think I will make some discrete inquiries without letting anyone know my real motives."

Hattie jumped up and exclaimed, "I forgot all about the dinner party! I need to get dressed. Why don't we discuss this some more tomorrow?"

As it turned out two days passed before the subject came up again. Hattie brought it up on the way home by asking, "Were you ever able to contact anyone about the plot to assassinate Mr. Lincoln?

"I received one of those coded messages the two gentlemen mentioned."

"Anything I should know?"

Eli didn't answer right away using the time it took to put the buggy in the barn as an excuse. He was torn between telling Hattie everything and following the instructions in the coded message. The instructions involved a plan that might place him in danger, and he didn't want to frighten her. When they entered the kitchen, he changed the subject by asking, "Is that roast pork I smell?"

"Yes, it is. Tom Jamison from next door borrowed a bag of salt today. He was butchering a couple of hogs and ran short. I had Sam take the salt out to that farm he has outside of town. He helped out for a bit, and Tom sent a nice big loin roast home with him. We have some baked sweet potatoes and a pot of greens to go with it," said Hattie. "Oh yes, and the fall apple crop is starting to come in. We will have baked apples and fresh cream for desert so don't go stuffing yourself with meat."

"She got a wagon load of dem Winesap apples you like. We probably be makin' applesauce all week long," added Sam looking at Eli for a reprieve from "women's work."

Eli continued to avoid a conversation about Lincoln by heading for his study to do accounts. Sam turned to Hattie and asked, "Will you teach me some more about handling money?"

She thought for a moment wondering why Eli was being so evasive. She felt the urge to pin him down on the subject. She shook it off knowing Sam's lessons were important. Taking down some teacups, she placed them on the table. "This one with the red flowers we will call ready cash. The one with blue flowers will be insurance. Yellow will be lifestyle, and pink represents charity, or the Lord's Money. Pretend the corn represents your profit for the year above the amount it takes for living expenses and to run your business, or provide whatever service you have been giving to the community. I want you to take the corn and put what you think is a responsible amount in each cup."

Sam put all the corn in the cup with red flowers. "Why did you do that?"

"It's my money and I want to spend it now!"

"What happens if you get sick and can't work?"

Sam thought for a minute and put some corn in the blue flowered cup.

"One day, you will be too old to work and you don't want to live in the poor house."

Sam sighed, made a face, and put more corn in the blue cup.

Hattie continued. "There is a positive side to the money you put in the blue cup. The bank will use your savings to invest in business ventures and pay you interest to use your money. That way your money is growing while you are not using it. Remember the farmer selling peas? Well, he may need to borrow some of your money the next year to raise more peas. He pays the bank a fee, called interest, to borrow the money, and the Bank pays that interest to you.

"So borrowin' be a good way to grow your business?"

"It is if you pay it back soon. Interest can be a heavy load if you let it get away from you. Some people spend the money they borrow on foolish things called *liabilities* instead of using the money to grow *assets. Liabilities* cost money while *assets* create money. If you get out on the limb like you said before, the Bank will cut you off, and you have to pay them with your *collateral.* That *collateral* could be your farm. Then you would not be able to make any money at all. But, enough of that for now let's get back to the tea cups.

"You decide you want your own horse to ride. Remember, you will have to rent a stable and feed him. A horse can be a liability or an asset. If you use him for pleasure, which provides little or no service to others, he becomes a liability. If you use him to increase your ability to perform a better service, you receive more money. That makes the horse an asset."

Sam put some corn in the yellow cup.

"The Bible says to give unto the poor and the needy."

"Hattie, that isn't fair! I'm the one who is poor and needy!"

"Well, you think it isn't fair? Have you tried to help someone who is in need?"

"Sure I have, but why not jus' help them? It doesn't take any corn to do that."

"Sam, what does the corn represent?" Hattie asked patiently.

"Money."

"What does money represent?"

"It represents my reward for the service or the products I produce for the community."

"Could you say that money replaces your service? You worked for it and earned it, so if you gave money wouldn't that be the same as giving of your time and labor to help someone?" Sam nodded in affirmative, took some of the corn, and put it in the cup with pink flowers.

"I still think it is more personal and shows more charity if we give directly of ourselves. Just giving money to the poor be a easy way out." Sam muttered.

"I agree," said Hattie. "But we can't always be there at the moment someone happens to need us. People will go to their Church or a charity organization to ask for help. The organization will make sure there is a legitimate need and then help those people. When the good Lord blesses us with an abundance we need to share. People who don't share can easily get caught up in the power of controlling others with their wealth. That can create a situation a lot like slavery."

"Sounds to me like lots of opportunity for folks to say they be the charity and just run off with the money, but I don't cottin to the slavery idea either."

"Sam, where is all this distrust for people coming from?"

"I got eyes. I watched people like Seth Rankin and others takin' a little here and a little there from the Master. Then you set me to watchin' at the store, and I see lots of folks that look like they be honest, a reaching in the candy jar when they think they can get away with it."

Hattie thought for a moment. "Not all people are bad. There are many who build their lives and businesses on honesty and integrity. They have found that the rewards will come to those who can be trusted."

"How do you find the ones you can trust?" asked Sam. "I sees so many I can't trust, it makes me fearful to trust anyone."

"Well Sam, I don't have a real good answer. I can only tell you how I look for people I can trust. You can start by trusting someone on little things, and slowly build a relationship with them one step at a time. Each step up increases the level of trust. Sometimes, I use what Kim taught me about watching the eyes and body for indications of deceit. Another way is through the application of logic. Let's say you trust one person and they trust someone else. It makes sense that you can trust their friend also. The fallacy with this logic is in the situation. In one instance, the three of you may share a common goal. At some future time this friend of a friend may come to you with a completely different motive. Can you still trust him? Where is the friend you do trust? Now you must decide. Maybe the risk is low so you agree. At this point you are building a relationship similar to the one I first described."

Sam thought for a moment "I can see where someone could get you out on a tree branch and then cut it off behind you. Where is your protection?"

"Your protection rests in how well you read people and in your core beliefs."

Sam sat back in his chair and smiled. "I sees where you headin' talking about apple cores now. You getin' ready to set me to peelin' them apples to get to the cores before you tells me the answer."

Hattie smiled and said, "Not yet. How does an apple grow? It grows from the stem connected to the tree forming the core first. Then the fruit forms around the core. My reference was not to an apple, but to each of us as human beings. Each person has a core of beliefs. That core defines the way a person lives his or her life. Let the apple represent what that person really is or wants to become. The fruit that grows around the core is what other people see. You could even say when they see the color, shape, and even taste the apple, they know what variety of fruit it is. Does your *apple* represent the same qualities? Always remember. It may take a lifetime to build up a high level of trust with someone. You can destroy that trust in an instant with one foolish act. An apple may look delicious but when you bite into it you find out it is rotten. The building process must start all over again. Learn to trust your core values but take small bites at first. Establish your own core values early before you need to make a decision and stick by them. It makes it harder for people to entice you away and cause you to eventually violate what you truly believe."

Sam sat thinking about what Hattie had said. Then he smiled. "Sort of what happened to Adam and Eve. They got talked into eating the wrong apple, and look what a mess we all in now."

Hattie looked at Sam with a serious expression on her face. "It might have been part of the plan all along."

She thought about Anne. Her inability to progress as a productive person had lain dormant until she was forced to work, and use her knowledge and talents to survive. The whole human race would have lain dormant in the Garden of Eden. They would not have progressed. Would they have had enough knowledge or initiative to even have children? They would have failed to keep the commandment God had given them to multiply and replenish the earth. She decided to think and study a little bit about that dilemma before broaching it with Sam.

"Let's get back to our corn and cups," she said, picking up a cup painted with stalks of grain. "Let's say this cup represents investments."

"I don't need no 'vest.' I be lookin' good enough!" He strutted around the kitchen to prove it to Hattie.

After he sat back down, Hattie continued, "What do you know about the long trip Eli took recently?"

"All I know's he went to Chicago."

"Yes that's true. He went to Chicago to see about an *investment* in a new railroad being planned for the northwestern corner of the country."

"Why would any one want to build a railroad through that country? It be full of wild savages. I heard talk about them Sioux. They be the baddest of the bad!"

"There is that *risk*, but the *rewards* could be great. They represent parts of what we call investments. Eli and I both believe that the country will grow. The dream of owning land and having the freedom to live life on your own terms without interference or following the dictates of others is a strong attraction to people living under a repressive government. People will come to America. They will need the goods we sell. We have to get the goods to them. Does it make sense then to help build a railroad?"

"I guess so, but you can't do that." "I know you be quick. You gots dem moves of yours and all, but you not gwine hammer them big spikes all day long."

"That's right and," Hattie smiled, "I'm not going to make you do it either. We have better things to do with our time. We both need to *invest* in our education right now. But, we can pay someone else to go do the work. And when the job is finished, we will be able to charge people to use the railroad and that way we recover our *investment* and even make a *profit*.

I want you to think over what we have talked about and write me a paper with your definitions of investment, risk, reward, and profit. Think you can do that?"

Sam nodded.

Hattie kept busy at her office. A pile of newspapers dumped on her desk held her attention at the moment. Somehow the buyers she had asked to send her books thought she wanted to keep up to date on the rapidly evolving political situation sweeping across the country in the wake of Lincoln's election. The rhetoric of politics filled every newspaper. Editors had added pages devoted to arguments for and against slavery and secession.

Instead of writing articles that would bring people together for the common good they printed arguments that built higher and stronger walls between the different viewpoints.

Probably to sell more papers, thought Hattie.

The will of the majority fractured and began to waiver. Southern aristocrats demanding the right to rule their plantations independent of the laws imposed by the United States Congress presented a tower of strength and a rallying point for abandoning the Union. Heated cries from radical New England abolitionists shouting "good riddance" helped to dominate or demoralize the majority. Lincoln, still months away from inauguration, held to his message. "A house divided cannot stand."

Hattie, disgusted and dismayed by the turmoil in her adopted country, buried her head and mind into preparing for her examination at Oberlin College.

The day finally arrived for her to depart. As it turned out, Eli became much too involved in frantic business deals and the intrigue of transporting Lincoln to Washington. He was unable to go to Oberlin with Hattie. *Probably just as well,* she thought to herself, *this way I can concentrate on my studies and not keep him up at night.* According to Dr. Fairchild, Hattie would get little sleep over the next few days.

Dr. Fairchild met Hattie at the train station, and took her to a rooming house near campus where she would stay during the testing. She began the tests the day after she arrived. The morning series tested her knowledge of reading, literature, history, geography, government and philosophy. The afternoon tests centered on science, mathematics and engineering. Each session involved a written test with a two-hour time limit followed by an hour-long oral examination. She wrote two papers each evening on subjects assigned after the oral examinations. She used the college library for reference and as a place to write her essays. No time limit was imposed other than the need to attend her next test session the following morning. The subject matter became more difficult each day, and the process took six days.

Dr. Fairchild escorted a tired Hattie to the train on Sunday. He smiled and said, "I think you did well. I will be sending you a letter notifying you of the results."

Hattie thanked him, crawled to her seat, and slept the entire way home.

As Hattie awaited the results of her examinations, the talk of war and rebellion boiled around her. She had come late to this party. She felt Mr. Lincoln was right. The people should respect the vote of the majority and search for a solution. What she failed to recognize was that the search for a compromise had been going on for many years and tensions had built like steam in a kettle. Compromise was not the answer. There were no winners only losers. The goal of building something new and better, suffered defeat at the hands of power and pride.

She began to rationalize that it was not her problem. Her love for the ideals expressed in the Constitution and the spirit she felt in America began to falter. Maybe she should return to England and live a quiet life on her savings. Her share of Eli's business amounted to enough money to keep her comfortable the rest of her days. The securities her father had given her had proved to be quite valuable. Was she above the issues? Was she an Englishwoman or an American?

Where were all these negative thoughts coming from? Her feelings for Eli grew stronger every day. Sam was quickly becoming a younger brother with a spirit that matched her own. She reveled in the spirit of liberty that was America. To slink away and feast on the success she had achieved here would be a sacrilege. She was fighting the day she entered this world, and she would continue to fight for what she believed until they put her in a grave! Now was the time for her to get busy and go to work.

What book contained the expression, "It's better to be part of the solution than a part of the problem?"

The letter from Oberlin College arrived on a wet cold day in late January. Dr. Fairchild had appended a short personal note stating that her test results and the school's actions were so unique he doubted a permanent record would exist of her achievement. She should keep the enclosed letter and diploma in a safe and secure place and not lose or destroy them.

Mrs. Helen Wiggins

Hagerstown, Maryland

Dear Mrs. Wiggins,
It is with great joy and enthusiasm that I take this opportunity to congratulate you on the remarkable achievement of passing all our qualifying level examinations with the highest scores ever achieved at this institution. We are pleased to award you the enclosed Batchelor of Arts Diploma from Oberlin College. This is the first time a diploma has been awarded without a requirement for at least some additional classes.

I would also like to inform you that we are prepared to award you a Batchelor of Science Degree upon completion of two consecutive laboratory classes in a scientific discipline. It is our opinion that such laboratory work will satisfy the necessary graduation requirements. This work would be necessary if you are to pursue your objectives in the field of medicine.

Once again my warmest regards on a job well done.

Sincerely,

James H. Fairchild, PhD
President, Oberlin College

Hattie was ecstatic. All her hard work had paid off. She was a recognized scholar. She now had the credentials to educate others. She knew she would continue to help those who needed her medical skills. Why should she conduct experiments in a laboratory? The whole world was her laboratory. Men were calling themselves doctors that had no training at all. She had received training from the finest medical man on the continent of

Europe. If her patients wouldn't accept that, she would just find other people who needed her care. She seldom charged for her medical help anyway.
Eli provided for her needs and then some. She couldn't wait to tell Eli the
good news.

The month of February passed quickly. Plans to bring Mr. Lincoln to
Washington changed many times. More and more it appeared that Eli,
Hattie, and a man named Joshua Oliphant would function as decoys. On
February 20th Eli and Hattie set out for Harrisburg, Pennsylvania. Not
wanting to be recognized they traveled separately.

Hattie, dressed all in black carried a large hatbox. Upon arrival in
Harrisburg, they took separate carriages to the hotel. Hattie worked on
Mr. Oliphant's disguise as they waited for Eli to arrive. The Pinkertons
believed that word may have leaked out that Eli was helping them. He took
a much more devious route to the hotel and entered through the employee's
entrance disguised as a janitor. Hattie opened the hatbox, took out her
theatrical supplies, and worked on Eli, so he would appear to look like Mr.
Lamon, Lincoln's bodyguard.

Filled with tension and nervous energy they spent the next day in the
hotel waiting for word to move. They had to stay hidden and in disguise,
since Lincoln might leave at any moment.

The timing needed to be precise. Lincoln would depart the hotel by
a side door at the same time that Eli, disguised as Lamon and Oliphant,
disguised as Lincoln left via the main lobby. Hattie was to follow them and
take a separate carriage to the train station.

Hattie disguised as a man, entered the lobby first. She moved quietly
to a corner and watched as Eli and Oliphant passed by. She paused for a few
seconds and observed a man following them out. At the curb, he got in a
carriage with two others, and they followed Oliphant and Eli. Hattie stayed
right behind them.

Their carriage stopped a block from the train station and one man got
out. He moved quickly down a side alley with one hand in his coat. On
impulse, Hattie called to her driver and had the carriage stopped. She got
out and followed the man. The man walked with a heavy step and moved
with short quick movements, as if looking for something. Hattie used these
clues to keep him in sight while staying concealed.

As they approached the train station, the man moved to a position where
he could board the slowly moving train. Under cover of the noisy engine

and shouting crowd Hattie moved closer matching the train's movements. They both began to walk along the path paralleling the track. Suddenly, Hattie noticed that they had left all the other people and were alone! Her quarry came to the same conclusion. He turned with a gun in his hand and a wicked grin on his face. As he lifted the gun to take aim at her, she disappeared in a blur of black movement. The gun flew from his hand. He landed on his back seemingly paralyzed. A moment later Hattie dragged the unconscious man behind a stack of boxes near some trash containers.

Moments later, a black figure seemed to float into the space between two of the passenger cars now gaining speed as they left the station. Eli and Oliphant, oblivious to Hattie's action, visited together as the train out of Harrisburg reached Hagerstown on schedule.

In the confusion generated by their activities, Mr. Lincoln embarked on a train headed for Baltimore without incident. He passed through that hotbed of southern sympathizers undetected during the early morning hours of February 23rd arriving in Washington unscathed.

Hattie and Eli continued on from Hagerstown to Washington where they had been invited to observe the inauguration. They did not get very good seats due to the crush of soldiers sent to protect the President. Later they were escorted to the White House in secret and received a personal thank you from President Lincoln for their support. He expressed regret that he had to make such a clandestine entry. Hattie paraphrased one of Kim's homilies, "Sometimes deception is the better part of valor."

From that time on Hattie, Sam, and Eli would step carefully. They were living in a State that claimed neutrality but had strong southern sympathies in the brewing conflict. Talking in private, Hattie and Eli agreed that Maryland may profess neutrality, but it's location and political position placed it right in the middle should open rebellion break out. They must tread carefully to avoid being shot by either side. By the middle of May, an uneasy peace settled over the countryside as Union troops descended on Washington to defend the Capital. They controlled Washington but the Rebels controlled the countryside of Virginia and Maryland.

Eli in a move designed to reconcile his business affairs with his politics, sold all his interest in the B & O Railroad. He proceeded to sell all his stockpiled war materials to the Union. He had advanced a large sum of credit to southern planters leaving him cash poor. He took what cash he could collect and instructed Hattie to place it in her account in Switzerland. They would continue to run their business in Hagerstown, but all grandiose schemes were cast aside as they prepared for the coming struggle.

By late April, the situation had deteriorated to the point that Eli believed the people of Maryland and Virginia would rise up and march on Washington. Governor Hicks of Maryland was hard pressed to maintain his neutral stance and fully recognized his folly. Neutral ground could quickly become a battleground.

Battle brewed south of Washington as well. Fort Sumter fell to the South Carolina militia on April 15th.

Hagerstown became a city divided. The counties to the east and cities like Baltimore were heavily in favor of supporting the South. The counties west of Hagerstown possessed family and financial interests closely connected to Pennsylvania and Ohio, both solid environs of the North. Hattie and Eli spent many late nights working on ways to maintain business interests within both camps. By mid-July it became obvious that open conflict and a shooting war could envelop Hagerstown.

Hattie purchased a new wagon. It was considerably bigger than the buggy pulled by the aging Blackie. Eli purchased a pair of young Missouri mules capable of pulling it all day and night if necessary. She began to modify the wagon to carry medical supplies, and had a cushioned bench installed lengthwise on one side. Many of the doctors living in Hagerstown had made their choice to join either the Union or Rebel forces. Their departure had severely restricted the availability of medical aid within the community. Hattie believed she would need the new wagon in the days ahead.

A few days' later Confederate forces defeated the Union army at Bull Run, a creek near Manassas, Virginia. Southern supporters in Hagerstown went wild shooting guns and dancing in the streets. Northern sympathizers ducked for cover, ashamed of the reports of incompetence being reported in the newspapers. It appeared that a southern aristocracy led by the plantation owners would emerge crushing Hattie's hopes for a life of freedom for all men. The constitution she had grown to love began to crumble around her.

Eli entered Hattie's office holding a letter. "General Grant has asked me to come to Tennessee and join up with him. He claims the war is far from over, and he needs my help. He sees a long struggle ahead. Victory will depend on superior numbers and logistics. He wants me working behind the scenes to expedite the transfer of supplies. We talked back in Galena about ways to move goods through the western states. My ideas appealed to him, but he cannot find army personnel with the knowledge or skill to move materiel and keep his army supplied. He's one of my oldest dearest friends. He needs me, Hattie. I need to go."

"You have no other choice Eli. We both agree the Union must be preserved and I won't see people like Sam sent back to slavery."

"What will you do while I'm gone?" asked Eli. "The business we have built together will disappear, either to fire or fraud. Without my constant juggling and conniving, the jackals waiting to feed on the defenseless will tear it apart."

"Eli, I have been on my own before. I am a survivor. Besides, I have recognized medical skills. All the doctors in town have chosen sides and many have already left. I will be busy keeping folks alive and well. Sam and I will rig a special white flag for the new wagon. Word will spread concerning my neutrality, and my English accent will help. I fear more for you than for myself."

Chapter 13

Hattie's Journal

9 August 1861: *Eli has left and I fear Sam will follow. I'm to be alone again.*

Just as Eli predicted, supplies began to disappear from the warehouses. Jim hired additional watchmen at night. Making spot checks didn't seem to help. The thieves always seemed to know when he would be gone. Andy had his problems at the store as well. His clerks were running off to fight for one cause or the other. The new people he hired proved unreliable. More merchandise was disappearing out the back than was being sold over the counter.

Hattie purchased her neighbor's barn when they moved back to Boston to live with her parents The new barn had room for Blackie and the buggy as well as the mules and wagon presently being modified to meet her medical needs. She converted the old stable into a warehouse. Under the pretext of working the mules, and making them feel comfortable with the medical wagon, she and Sam moved food and other merchandise from the store and warehouses into the old stable.

She also converted the dining room into a medical examination room and had additional cots placed in the spare bedrooms. Her reading had taught her that during a war there was never enough room for patients to receive treatment during recovery. She didn't plan on treating wounded soldiers, but the military would commandeer all available hospital space. She wanted a place to help people just trying to exist while the battles raged around them.

Hattie and Sam were eating a cold supper after a day of preparing for the coming emergency. Everyone they met expected bullets to start flying in the streets of Hagerstown at any moment. Lifetime friends and even family members ceased communicating lest they become violent. As they worked to make changes to the house, she noticed Sam acting strangely. His usual sunny disposition remained hidden behind a grim faced frown. During supper, she looked over at Sam. "Is something bothering you?"

He squirmed in his chair and played with the food on his plate. *You'd think he was trying to ask me to marry him,* thought Hattie.

He finally blurted out. "I wants to go fight for my freedom."

"But Sam, you have your freedom. You have the paper I gave you and a copy of the one Seth Rankin signed."

As her gaze dwelt on Sam's eyes, her hopes fell. The look of determination she saw there would override all her arguments."

"I know, but I want to fight for all the slaves left in the South that can't fight for themselves. I be good at fightin' what with those moves you teachin' me. Me'n Andy went shootin' a few weeks ago. He say I gots a natural eye."

"You're too young Sam. No army will take you. Why you are only sixteen." Hattie paced the room with her arms folded and head bowed as she tried to think of arguments that would convince him to stay.

"I be seventeen soon and they be getin' up a regiment of colored soldiers in Pennsylvania. I already checked it out. They take me right away. The sergeant I talked to at the store the other day; he say I might even get in as a corporal, since I can read and write. I wants to go miz Hattie. I needs to help my people be free!" Sam said, with a look of fierce determination in his face.

Hattie sat looking at this young idealistic man that had grown up right before her eyes. Sam was right, he was a man, and should have the freedom to make his own decisions. "Sam, I want you here and I surely need you. But, if this is what you must do then you have my blessing." She placed her empty teacup on the table, and left so Sam wouldn't see the tears running down her cheeks. She slowly stumbled up the stairs to her room knowing he would be gone in the morning.

Hattie needed a task to take her mind off Sam's leaving. She had to fight these blues and cure herself, or she wouldn't be able to help anyone else. The fast disappearing supplies from the store and warehouse would soon force her to close the store and implement her plan to provide medical aid to the local residents. Skirmishers attacking the railroad had succeeded in destroying several shipments meant to replenish her lost supplies.

She decided to release all the workers before someone got hurt defending the store. In a final meeting with Jim and Andy, she encouraged them to take what they could in merchandise as a severance payment before everything disappeared. She then reduced the prices on all remaining merchandise and advertised the sale in the Hagerstown newspapers. She wanted everyone to have a fair chance at purchasing what would likely be stolen anyway. What she couldn't sell, she moved to the old stable or into her house.

After the sale was over and the shelves stood bare, Hattie composed another, final advertisement for the newspapers. She informed everyone that Wiggins Merchandise was out of business for the duration of the war. She stated her intentions of remaining in Hagerstown and offered her services as a healer and medical practitioner to any and all in need. Accident, injury, and illness would continue to strike those left at home while the conflict raged around them.

It was to these poor souls that she would reach out. Soldiers wounded in combat would be treated and sent on their way without regard for the color of their uniform. She would not harbor any soldier in her home. All must leave after receiving treatment.

She described how her English heritage and short time in America made it difficult for her to judge the rightness of either side in the conflict. The medical needs of those not engaged in open warfare would command her highest priority She described her medical wagon and the white flag that would fly any time the wagon was engaged in an errand of mercy. She asked all to honor her neutrality. In a final reminder she added, "After all, one day it may be you riding in the wagon under that flag."

Loud knocking awakened her one night a few days later. *Why can't people ever get sick during the day?* She wondered as she stumbled down the stairs. The knocking came again, not from the front door but from the kitchen. She stumbled in that direction. "Who is it?" She called, lighting a lamp.

No one answered, so she moved cautiously to the door. Had someone missed her advertisement in the paper and decided to rob or harm her?

What moves would Kim make?

She slowly opened the door revealing a skinny, underfed young girl holding up an older woman about Hattie's age.

"Please help us!" cried a tear stained dirty face looking up through straggly brown hair. Hattie placed the lamp on the kitchen table, and reached down for the older woman just as the child collapsed. The woman was surprisingly light. Hattie was able to carry her to the bed in the converted dining room.

"What's wrong with her?" Hattie asked the girl.

"She's just plumb tuckered out. We bin without food for three days, hiding from sojers and ruffians. Ma kept tellin' me she was eating while all the time she bin givin' it to me."

Hattie moved back to the kitchen and opened her icebox. She took the soup left over from her supper and placed it back on the still warm stove. She looked at the girl and asked, "Did you see that pile of firewood out back when you came through the back yard?"

"Yas'm."

"Run fetch me a few sticks. No, better yet bring all you can carry. We better heat some water. A hot bath will help both of you."

As the girl turned and left, Hattie took out a loaf of bread and began slicing. She looked in the icebox and removed the remains of a pat of butter. *Not much left and I don't know how long it will be before I see any more*, she thought as she began to spread butter on the bread. The soup was only lukewarm when she poured some in a bowl and went back into the dining room now converted into an examination room. She turned up the lamp and began to examine the woman. Outside of heat exposure and malnutrition, she seemed to be in reasonably good health. Hearing a load of wood being dumped in the wood box, she reentered the kitchen. Looking at the girl she asked, "What's your name?"

"Mandy."

"Is that short for Amanda?"

"Yas'm."

"You don't talk a lot do you?" she said, and then smiling added, "What is your full name and what is your mother's name and why did you come to me?"

In a frustrated monotone voice, Mandy began to recite, "My name is Amanda Coulson. My mother is called June Coulson. We asked people for food, but ma is in such a bad way they think she is sick or something. They sent us to you. Everybody else had too many of their own problems to help. How about you? Are you too busy to help us?"

Hattie smiled and said, "Of course I can help you. I hope I didn't scare you or offend you with my lack of good manners. I get a little nervous when people come here in the middle of the night. Look Mandy, I want you to sit here and eat some bread and butter while I take care of your mother. There is a bowl in that cupboard and some soup left in the pot on the stove. Help yourself."

Hattie turned to the sink and pumped some water on to a clean cloth and went back into the dining room. *I guess I need to start thinking of it as my examination room now that I have examined a patient here,* she thought.

She bathed the woman's face and neck, and spooned the broth into her. Soon the woman began to respond. "That's so good. Thank you. You are an angel of mercy."

Hattie liked the sound of that expression. She decided to find some bright red paint and letter a sign on each side of the wagon. She would call it the *Mercy Wagon.* She wondered if someone with a talent for sewing could make her a flag with the words "Angel of Mercy" on it. That might grab everyone's attention more than just a plain white flag.

The soup began to revive the woman. Hattie asked her. "Do you feel a little better now that you have some food in you?"

"Yes," June replied. "I think I can get up and we will…"

"You will not leave here until I am satisfied that you are well enough to travel," Hattie said with a stern tone to her voice. "I want you to come with me to the kitchen. I have a tub behind the stove and hot water heating. You and your daughter will bathe and get a good night's sleep. We will talk more about you leaving in the morning."

"But we have no clean clothes. We lost our packs when we had to jump from the train."

"Don't you worry about clothes. I have some things that will do for tonight, and we will fix up something for you in the morning." Hattie turned and moved to climb the stairs to her room saying over her shoulder, "I hope Mandy left you some bread in the kitchen. Why don't you get ready for that bath while I fetch you something to wear. There is soap on the table next to the empty soup bowl. You might as well take both of them to the kitchen and get started."

Upon returning to the kitchen, Hattie placed two night dresses over a chair and moved to the examination room. She had set in her mind that it must be cleaned and made ready for the next patient after every use. She decided to start a good habit pattern right away.

It had been a long time since she had practiced healing on a fulltime basis. She had helped out from time to time and delivered a few babies when called upon or in an emergency, but most of her time had been taken up with helping Eli and teaching Sam. Until recently, resident physicians satisfied the medical needs in Hagerstown. Now her needs and the needs of the community had changed. She must adapt and meet changing challenges—again.

By the time Hattie returned to the kitchen, June and Mandy had cleaned themselves and the kitchen and were ready for bed. Hattie showed them to a guest room with two single beds and all three retired for the remainder of the night.

A huge old oak tree grew just outside Hattie's window. She liked the way it screened the afternoon sun in the summer. Many varieties of birds and a family of gray squirrels called it home. Normally she slept with her window open, and the birds would wake her each morning. Lately, she had been keeping the window closed and locked. Strangers and even friends up to no good prowled the night streets of Hagerstown. Sam and Eli had been afraid for her safety, and had rigged a series of bells attached to various doors and windows in the house. Hattie had disconnected the bell for the kitchen door since it was the one the family used the most. Last night's visitors reminded her of the need for an alert system, so she had reattached the cord. When the bell to the kitchen door began ringing, it awakened her immediately.

She remembered that she was not alone in the house. She had guests and needed to get up and prepare breakfast. The bell for the kitchen door tinkled again as she was dressing. She wondered how many times it had rang before it penetrated her sleepy brain?

She stepped into the kitchen and discovered her guests, still in the night-clothes she had given them, busy washing the clothes they had on when they arrived. Glancing out the window she saw the rest of their clothing gently flapping in the breeze on the clothesline in the back yard. Next to them, she saw the sheets and cloths that she had used the previous evening.

June looked up from her work and asked, "Anything you need washed while the water is still hot?"

Hattie stood speechless. She could only shake her head and stare in amazement. All the little housecleaning jobs she had scheduled to accomplish that day were already done. "It looks to me like a couple of elves have been up early this morning, and they have been pretty quiet about their work until they went outside."

"Is that what woke you? I told Mandy not to slam that door," said June, wringing the rinse water from the final garment.

"Miz Wiggins, I found some eggs out in the henhouse. Is it all right if I fry them up for breakfast?" Mandy asked as she entered the kitchen with the eggs in a fold of her oversize nightdress.

"Why don't you give me the eggs and go down into the cellar through that door over there and slice off a little side meat to go with these eggs." Hattie said as she took the eggs from Mandy.

"I was hopin' you would say that. I saw it hanging there when I went lookin' for the washboard."

As Mandy disappeared into the cellar, Hattie asked June, "How old is she?"

"She'll be fourteen in October. I don't know what I would have done the last few weeks without her. She is small for her age like her grandma, but she's got spunk. She gets her size and determination from her Pa's family. His ma had to wear heel shoes to clear five foot."

"Where is he now?" asked Hattie as she got out the water pot to make tea and the heavy cast iron skillet to fry the side meat and eggs.

"He's with the good Lord in the Celestial Kingdom. He was killed by a mob when I was pregnant with Mandy. We bin living with my brother out in Missouri. That's where Tom and I met. We moved up north to Illinois after we were married, but when Tom died I moved back home. My brother, Luke, was the only kin that would have me.

We had to leave there when the fighting started. Skirmishers killed Luke, and his wife and kids went to live with her parents. They wouldn't have me, so Mandy and I left for St. Louis. We are headed for New England. I figured to get a position there and wait out the war. Then I plan to go west."

Celestial Kingdom? That's a strange name for Heaven, thought Hattie. "Why wouldn't your brother's family want you?"

"I guess they thought I was tainted or touched or something. They weren't the worst. There were folks around where we lived that would have killed me if they thought I was practisin' my religion. Luke made me promise not to go preachin' or readin' in the "Gold Bible" as he called it, or he would kick me out. I held to my beliefs, but I been holdin' it in. Not lettin' on to anyone." Tears began to form, and June's mouth twisted up as she muttered, "not even Mandy."

"Not even Mandy what?" asked Mandy, coming up from the cellar with a plate full of side meat.

Hattie could tell that June didn't want to discuss the subject in front of Mandy, but she wanted to learn more about this "Gold Bible." Talk of a book made of gold piqued her incessant curiosity.

They all worked together to make breakfast. Hattie was amazed at how smoothly everything worked. Their movements around the kitchen seemed to mesh like the gears in a clock. They ate in silence, the sign of good food, and hungry mouths. Hattie's mind was spinning over the things June had talked about. It was as if some force was pressing on her to find out more.

That force ebbed under the need to organize her life and create some way to survive in the days ahead. She had the knowledge and the skills. The incentive was real. After all no one wanted to starve when they could do something about it.

An idea came to Hattie as she was drying the dishes and putting them away. She was using a dishtowel with intricate embroidery. She turned to June and said, "Do you happen to know anything about embroidery or piecework?"

"Why yes I do. Missouri women are famous for their piecework quilts. I especially enjoy creating my own designs. I call it making pictures from cloth."

Hattie beckoned June to follow her into the examination room. She pulled out a piece of heavy linen fabric. The piece she held in her hands was bleached to a dazzling white. It measured about a yard wide and a little longer the other way. She held up the material giving it a thoughtful look. Then she dashed upstairs to her room returning in a moment with an assortment of silk undergarments in various pastel colors and one that was bright red. "Eli was always buying me these. I wore them to please him. He is off helping General Grant, so I don't think he will notice them being gone."

"What do you plan on making?" June asked picking up a piece of the beautiful material.

"I don't plan on making anything. I want to pay you to make me a flag with an Angel on it and the words 'Angel of Mercy' in red."

June looked up at her with agony on her face. "Oh, Mrs. Wiggins, it would be a crime to make a quilt out of such beautiful things!"

Hattie replied, "I read a book once and it said, 'let the punishment fit the crime.' If there is any law and order left in this community, I am sure they have more to worry about than me cutting up my underwear."

"Why would you want to get rid of these?" asked Mandy as she gently caressed the silken fabric.

"My husband is a great business man. He always says 'it pays to advertise.' So that's what I am going to do! I will advertise and avoid being shot at the same time."

"I still don't understand," said June.

Hattie looked at June and said, "Actually, you are the one that gave me the idea. Last night you called me an *Angel of Mercy*."

Holding up the fabric in both hands Hattie looked at June and asked, "Will you make me a flag? I want a figure of an Angel and the words 'Angel of Mercy' on each side of this piece of white cloth."

Different thoughts seemed to pass across June's face. A look of concentration followed an initial gaze of deep thought. Then a smile of revelation and a frown of concern caused her to shake her head. "I can do it, but the angel can't have no wings."

This remark set Hattie back for a moment. She thought about the angels she had seen in paintings or book illustrations. She realized that they had all represented dead people or spirits. She didn't want to fall into either one of those categories so she readily agreed.

Hattie moved over to her desk, picked up several sheets of paper, and handed some colored pencils to June. "Why don't you sit here at the desk and use these while Mandy and I go out in the stable and see to my animals." It was doubtful that June noticed them leaving. She was so deep into her design.

As they walked out the kitchen door into the back yard, Mandy began to follow the path to the old stable now used for storage. Hattie called to her, "Not that way, we need to go through here." She indicated a new gate cut in the fence.

"I bought this larger stable, barn actually, from a couple who moved back to Boston a few weeks ago. We were already sharing the back paddock with them, so it seemed like the thing to do, especially after I purchased the mules. I really need to get someone over to cut some of these bushes out of the way and clear the path. I was going to have Sam…" She stopped walking for a moment blinded by the rush of tears and sense of loss that burst upon her.

"Who's Sam?" asked Mandy walking up to her and peering through the gate Hattie held open. "Did you lose a dog? Or was he your favorite horse? I know how rough that can be. I had to leave my horse back in Missouri. He was a Walker. Smoothest horse at coverin' ground in the whole Ozarks."

Hattie blindly followed Mandy through the gate guided by the poles of the small corral wedged between her old fence, and the barn she had purchased from the Abernathys.

As they approached the door, she said, "Sam was a runaway slave that worked for me for a while. He was more than a servant, but less than a son, too old for that, more like a younger brother."

Mandy turned in amazement. She couldn't imagine this refined English lady with a colored ex-slave for a brother!

Hattie smiled at her and said, "Better close your mouth before you open that door. There are lots of flies inside."

They both went to work. Hattie quickly observed that Mandy had a natural love for the animals, and they responded to her touch and soft murmuring voice. Hattie said, "I can see that you have a lot of experience working with animals. They seem to almost understand you. What else do you like to do to keep busy?"

"Mostly I spent all my time with the animals or doin' outside chores. Helpin' Uncle Luke was what I liked to do. I didn't feel right workin' inside the house. Oh, I can cook and clean as good as my cousins, but they always seemed to get the easy jobs. Uncle Luke and Marnie didn't have no boys so I sorta moved on to helpin' outside more and more."

"What about school? Can you read and write?" asked Hattie.

"I can get by with the writin'. Readin' is what I like best. I would get a book from the town library or from our neighbors and find me a nice shade tree. I would read while my horse chomped up all the grass."

Hattie turned and started for the door saying, "Why don't you finish up here. I will be back in a moment." She went out the door and walked over to the old stable. She picked up an old feed sack from the back of the stable door and entered the tack room. She selected several books off the shelves in the tack room and placed them in the sack. Next, she climbed up in the hayloft and located some paintbrushes and a can of red paint left over from the last time Sam had painted the stable. Picking up the sack of books on her way out the door, she returned to the barn.

As she walked in the barn, Mandy had just finished mucking out the stalls. She said, "Them is a fine set of mules you got there if'n I didn't know better I woulda said they come from Missouri."

"You have a sharp eye Mandy. They were bred, born, and trained in Missouri. My husband Eli took them in on trade. We used to buy, sell, and ship merchandise from the Atlantic Ocean to the Mississippi River."

"I heard you tell Ma that he is off fightin' with General Grant. We heard talk of him building an army up around Cairo. That's why we took the train here when we left St. Louis. We didn't miss the fightin' though. A bunch of sojers raided our train. We heard a bunch of yellin' and screamin' from the passenger car behind ours, so we jumped off and hid. We left all our stuff on the train."

Hattie handed Mandy the sack full of books. "Here, these are for you to read. As you finish one we will talk about it together. Speaking of talking, I think it would be wise if you would use proper grammar as you speak. Reading these books will help. Every time you speak, people judge what you say by the language you use. When we speak, we usually wish to convey an idea or thought to our listener. When you use proper English and good grammar they are more apt to listen to what you say. I have observed you long enough to know that you are not an imbecile. You could well have a better solution to a problem than I do but to whom would someone listen? A Missouri farm girl or an English lady?"

"I never thought about it that way before." Mandy said with a thoughtful expression on her face. Then brightening, she asked, "What's the paint for?"

"I want to brighten up the wagon. What I have in mind is painting the wheels and spokes with this red paint and doing some lettering on the side. Do you feel up to helping me?"

"Sure, but not in this nightdress and my only other clothes are hanging on the line."

Hattie bounced the heel of her hand on her head. "I'm so sorry. That problem is so easily solved that it completely slipped my mind. Here, follow me." She waked briskly back to the old stable.

Hattie stepped into the stable and walked to the back corner stall. There on a rod were a number of women's dresses in various sizes. "These were left over from the sale we had a few days ago. I brought them home thinking I could make them over to fit me if I got desperate. Let's see if we can find anything to fit you and your mother without a lot of rework."

They were able to find two dresses and some petticoats that would fit. Hattie picked up a number of shirtwaists and other garments to complete the wardrobes. Both left the stable loaded down with a large armful as they made their way back to the house.

Mandy changed while Hattie entered the examination room. June was deeply involved in her artwork and hardly looked up. A quick glance showed Hattie the right person was on the right task. She went to a recently installed cabinet and took down two old smocks to cover their clothes while they painted. She returned to the kitchen just as Mandy appeared dressed for work.

Returning to the barn they began to paint the wagon. Hattie began sketching out letters on one side while Mandy started to paint the spokes and wheels on the other. "We might need some more paint," said Mandy as she completed the front wheel.

Hattie told Mandy where additional paint could be found and asked her to look around for a smaller brush. She was having problems doing the edges of the letters with the one she had. Mandy returned with the items they needed to finish the job. After finishing one side each they agreed to take a break for lunch and let the paint dry.

Having finished before them, June was busy preparing lunch when they returned. There was a pan of cornbread in the oven and a pot of beans with a ham bone on the stove for supper. She had bread and jam with fresh buttermilk ready for lunch. Hattie sent Mandy to the cellar to bring up an apple for each of them as she cut slices from a block of cheese in the icebox. After lunch, they all went into the exam room to look at June's drawings.

"Oh, June, They're wonderful!" exclaimed Hattie. "I think I like this one. What do you think Mandy?" Hattie lifted one of the drawings depicting a running woman with a Rod of Asclepius clutched in her hand. "How did you come up with the idea to use the Rod of Asclepius?"

"I found it on the cover of one of your medical books. I didn't know it was the rod of...whoever. I thought it might look like a sword but not the killing kind. It sort of reminded me of the Bible story when Moses holds aloft a staff with a serpent on top. He tells the people they will be healed if they will look to the serpent and not to the danger on the ground. I wanted to show the angel using a healing symbol."

"What is that thing?" asked Mandy picking up the paper for a closer look.

"It's the symbol associated with medicine and healing. Asclepius was the son of Apollo. He was a practitioner of medicine in ancient Greek mythology," Hattie explained to Mandy.

"How do you know so much stuff? Who was Apollo and this Ascelpiece fellow?" asked Mandy.

"I read a lot of books when I was your age. I first learned about them when I studied Greek mythology. I will be glad to teach you if you are willing to study."

"What's all this about reading and studying? We aren't going to be here long enough for any of that," grumbled June as she began to gather her other drawings into a neat stack.

Hattie looked at June and said, "June, I wanted to talk to you about that. You need to stay for a few days and recover your strength. I need you to make the flag, and I can use Mandy's help with my animals. Will you think over the idea of staying here longer? Maybe even stay until this war comes to an end? After that I can make no promises. I may be moving on myself depending on what happens. You said you intend to go out West after the war is over. If you continue east you will just have to cover this ground again. Who knows what the situation will be like when and if things settle down."

June looked at Hattie and said, "We will stay for a week and see how it works out. We really have no place to go, but I need to be sure you really need us. I won't take no charity." She snapped with a firm set to her jaw.

Loud banging on the front door interrupted their conversation. Hattie moved in that direction while June, still in her nightdress, scurried up the stairs to change. A dusty sweaty man stood on the porch breathing heavily.

"We need you to come to the train station Mrs. Wiggins, the train from Baltimore was fired on by rebel troops and several of the passengers were injured. The only other doctor available says they are northern merchants on their way to sell goods to the Union Army and he won't help them! Please hurry one of them is bleeding bad."

Hattie turned to Mandy and asked, "Will you hitch Blackie to the buggy? The paint is still wet on the wagon. I will get some things I need together, and meet you around front. Hurry!" Hattie nodded to the man and said, "I will be there as fast as I can." She closed the door and began to assemble what she might need by the front door.

When June returned, Hattie asked, "Will you and Mandy finish painting the wagon and get started on my angel flag as soon as you can? Events are moving faster than I anticipated. You will have to clear all the papers and flag making material out of the examination room. I may need to bring home one or more patients for follow-up treatments.

A glance out the window showed Mandy pulling up with the buggy. "Now do you see why I need help?" she asked as she hurried down the steps with her arms full of supplies.

None of the injuries proved fatal. Some wounds from flying glass and splinters required stitches. One bullet wound needed cauterizing. A small child had fallen from her seat and landed on her nose. It bled a lot but a cold compress took care of that.

Thank goodness the weather is turning cooler, thought Hattie. Next winter she would have to locate an icehouse. She could always boil water for hot compresses but cold ones were effective in many situations. If this madness extended into next summer, she would need a supply of ice. Maybe she could convert one of her now empty warehouses. That would work unless some crazy fool decided to burn them all down.

Hattie was climbing into the buggy to return home when the train conductor approached with a signal for her to hold up. He turned out to be an old friend of Eli's. He motioned her toward one of the freight cars. Sliding open the door he revealed several boxes. "I took up a collection from the passengers you helped tonight," he muttered quietly. "I have the money if you want it, but I know the railroad would also like to chip in and contribute. I think there are some things here you may need." He loaded seven boxes into the back of Hattie's buggy, and presented her with the money he had collected.

Hattie started to take the money, but changed her mind. She smiled at the conductor and said, "Why don't you keep the money and when you come through here just leave a box or two of items on the loading dock for me. I will let the station agent know what I need and you can try to fill any of my needs on your trips through town. I wouldn't expect that you could find everything I need so I will put together a long list with priority items on top. Do you know a Mr. Josiah Wilkins of Baltimore?"

"I've heard the name, ma'am."

"I will send him a letter and see that he contacts you. He is my financial manager and can guarantee payment in gold for any items on my list. If you feel you can help me, then we need to discuss our arrangement in detail. Do you ever remain over in Hagerstown?"

"Yes, ma'am. I have a layover here when I transfer to the Chicago train on Thursday. I pull in here at 3:00 pm. And I leave for Chicago at 7:00"

"My buggy will be parked in back of our old store. We are no longer in business, but the building still belongs to us. If you will meet me there, we can establish a system whereby you could deliver food and medical supplies to me. Mr. Wilkins could pay for them when you return to Baltimore.

Mr. Murphy, I know you are a good friend of Eli's but business is business. I would expect you to turn a reasonable profit on our arrangement. What do you say? Will you do it?"

"Ma'am, it would be a pleasure. I read the article you wrote in the paper. It was me that asked for you to help us this afternoon. I know a couple of other conductors that feel the same way. We have family and friends here in Hagerstown and we want them to have some type of medical help if they need it. You can depend on our support." With a slap on Blackie's rump and a wave to Hattie he jogged over to the already moving train and jumped aboard.

Hattie drove straight to the barn to park the buggy and unhitch Blackie. The lettering on the wagon caught her eye. The wagon had a permanent top like a surrey with roll down panels for bad weather. The letters on the box spelled out "Mercy Wagon" in bright red paint. The lettering was better than she could have done. June was a real artist. She hurried to the house anxious to see how the flag was coming along.

Chapter 14

Hattie's Journal

24 December 1861: Three lonely ladies make
do for Christmas.

The wonderful smell of home cooked food met Hattie as she entered the
kitchen door. June had managed to find all the ingredients for an apple
pie and it smelled heavenly. The beans and ham hocks were bubbling
on the back of the stove. Mandy was just setting the table. She turned to
Hattie with a grin and asked, "How did things go? Must not have been
as bad as you were led to believe. Mom has been checking the street. We
figured if you had patients you would stop out front. I kept a watch on the
barn. When I saw you turn in, I started to set the table. Mom is working
like crazy on that flag you want. What did you think of the wagon?"

"I love how the wagon turned out you did an excellent job! I am so
exhausted, but happy that I didn't have to come home to an empty house,
and try to find something to eat on my own. You both are so good for me.
You have been here less than a day and already it feels like we are family."
Hattie said as she flopped into a chair and began to rub the kinks out of
her neck trying not to let Mandy see the tears welling up in her eyes at
thoughts of family.

June walked into the kitchen. "I have the first side of the flag pinned on the white background would you like to see it?" Both Hattie and Mandy moved quickly to Eli's study. June had moved her things out of the examination room to prepare for injured patients. She had draped the flag over Eli's desk to show her work.

The letters cut from red silk were trimmed with black giving them a shadowed effect. They surrounded a figure of a running girl carrying the Rod of Asclepius made from fragments of hemp rope. The figure wore a dress made from thin strips of different colored blue silk. The different shades produced a shadowed effect that outlined the legs giving the figure a look of movement. Pieces of pale tan silk simulated exposed skin. The loose black hair seemed to fly with the wind.

"What did you use for the hair? It looks almost real," Hattie exclaimed in amazement, reaching out to lightly stroke the figure.

"That was Blackie's contribution. I felt he should be present somehow even though he wouldn't be pulling the wagon," said Mandy.

"I had to use blue for the dress. It was the only color that was available in several shades to create the shadows I wanted," said June.

"The whole thing is simply stunning!" exclaimed Hattie, "now, Mandy if you will come with me I also have a surprise." With a final loving stroke on the flag, Hattie moved to the kitchen and out the door with Mandy on her heels.

Hattie led the way to the barn where she showed Mandy the boxes Mr. Murphy the conductor had given her. Three of the boxes each contained twelve of the new Mason canning jars. Another contained a number of odd shaped containers filled with various spices. There was a box of fragrant bar soap straight off the ship from Paris. A case of tins filled with Vermont maple syrup and another of tea completed the load. Hattie was surprised when Mandy's smile turned into a frown when she saw the last box.

"What's the matter?' Hattie asked as she saw the look on Mandy's face.

"Mom don't take with tea drinking."

"Why is that?" asked Hattie. *No tea? That's like no life!* She thought to herself.

"I don't rightly know. All I know is that she won't drink it and won't let me drink it. Same goes for coffee and liquor."

A subdued Hattie and Mandy stacked the load in the barn for the night and returned to the house ready for supper. Hattie needed to ask June some serious questions about her beliefs. But, every time she tried to ask a question something would come up or June would change the subject. It seemed that something kept getting in the way. June had the table set in the kitchen. She turned to Hattie and asked, "Is this all right? I figured with it just being the three of us and all, why carry everything into the dining room?"

"I much prefer to eat in here. With Eli and Sam gone I didn't think I would use the dining room. That's why I turned it into my medical examination room." Hattie said as she moved to the cupboard to get a cup and saucer. She would fix herself some tea and see what kind of reaction it raised with June. If Mandy was right they might as well have it out now before the bond growing between them became any stronger. Mandy looked at Hattie with raised eyebrows. Hattie winked at her and continued to make her tea.

Nothing was said about the tea while they ate. The conversation centered on June's design for the angel and on loading supplies in the wagon. Hattie began to relax and feel comfortable for the first time since Sam left. She hadn't realized how much she missed having company and someone to talk to. Her afternoon teas had ended before Sam left. Women with so much to talk about before the election, now started to hide behind the same walls that were growing across the nation. Her disappearing tea party guests represented on a small scale how stubborn factions and selfish ideals were ripping apart the whole fabric that made America great.

After the meal they cleared and cleaned the kitchen. Once again Hattie was amazed at how well they worked together. The task was completed in record time. Hattie wandered into what was now her examination room and looked around. She moved to the parlor, walked over to the piano, sat down, and began to play some of the old church hymns Eliza had taught her. The memories of happy times with Margaret and Eliza entered her thoughts. She began to hear June humming along as she finished her chores in the kitchen. Mandy picked up one of the books Hattie had given her to read.

Hattie transitioned to a Chopin piece unwilling to break the feeling of contentment that had settled over her home. A warm spirit seemed to fill the house. It was like nothing else she had ever felt. She wanted that spirit to stay forever. June wandered into the room, sat down, and picked up her sewing. Hattie looked over her shoulder and asked, "Do you feel the peace and warmth that is here tonight?"

June looked up from her hand sewing and absently remarked, "I think the Holy Ghost is here with us."

Hattie stopped playing and stood up saying, "Angels, Golden Bibles, Celestial Kingdoms, and now ghosts; what is going on here? Where is all this coming from?"

"It's all part of the Restored Gospel of Jesus Christ," said June, looking up at Hattie with a smile on her face and eyes that seemed to glow with a fire from within.

Hattie's mind flashed back to a day on a dock in Bristol. "I suppose you will be telling me there is a Prophet on the earth?"

"There was until a mob killed him in Carthage, Illinois. Now I am not sure. I believe the Lord has called another but when I was forced to leave that had not happened. I have been cut off and isolated by my brother. I have only heard rumors and tales. My beliefs are sacred to me. I would love to share them if you are interested, but I don't want to destroy the friendship building between us. I just won't argue about religion. I would love to have an open-minded discussion. I would rather wait..." June squirmed a little on the stool and looked up at Hattie again. She said, "I have done some thinking while you were gone. If the offer to stay here is still open I would like to stay. Mandy and I can find work and pay for our room and board..."

"You will do no such thing!" interrupted Hattie. "I won't take a red cent from either of you. Why you have done more around here today than I could accomplish in a week. I really do need help. My services may be required on a moments notice. You can't imagine how good it feels to know that a warm meal will be waiting in a clean house with good company to share it. In fact I am willing to pay you, not charge you for staying here!"

"Does that mean I have to clean that stable every day?" asked Mandy from the doorway with a grin on her face.

"Mandy, you can do anything you want outside the walls of this house and inside the boundaries of my property," replied Hattie. "Just promise to stay—please."

After breakfast the next morning, Hattie and Mandy loaded the medical supplies they had sorted the night before into the special compartments in the mercy wagon while June cleaned up in the kitchen and went back to her sewing.

After lunch Hattie took the mercy wagon out to give the mules a run and to show off the new paint. The flag was not ready, so she stayed in town where she felt relatively safe. She stopped at the post office to mail a letter to Eli and one to Josiah Wilkins. She intended to send similar letters the next day just in case the train didn't get through. She received many comments and smiles from people on the street when they saw her wagon. It pays to advertise, she thought. I only hope I can handle the business when it comes.

And come it did. Later that evening she made a call to set a broken arm. A boy left at home when his father went off to join the army had gotten between a cow and her newborn calf and failed to get out of her way when it was dinnertime for the calf. After forcibly lifting him out of the way, the cow flipped him across the pen and his arm caught in the fence. The rest of him kept going. Hattie's payment for setting the arm consisted of a box of twelve baby chicks, two-dozen ears of sweet corn, and a three-gallon can of fresh cream. She promised to return the cream can when she returned to check on the arm later that week.

Upon her return home, Hattie asked June if she knew how to churn butter. June replied, "Mandy does." Both women heard a groan from a figure in the next room with her face buried in a book.

"Why, Mandy, you can churn and read a book at the same time. I know, I did it lots of times back at the manor."

"You lived in a manor and had to work?" asked Mandy. "I thought all great ladies had servants to do the work?"

"I was …a special kind of servant. My mistress sort of adopted me. She lost a baby girl about the time I was born. I guess that's when she began to care about me as a person. At first helping me was a way to overcome feeling sorry for herself. Later, when I went to work at the manor, I was allowed certain privileges. Reading books from the manor library, and learning to play the piano being the most important to me. I guess I picked up my ladylike manners as well, but that was due to my ability to mimic those around me as much as any formal training. I always felt that good manners consisted of treating people with respect, in tune with the customs of their own culture, not expecting them to figure out my customs or culture."

"Will you teach me how to act like a lady?" asked Mandy

"Show me how well you can churn butter first. Then we will talk about it," laughed Hattie.

Word spread quickly concerning Hattie's skill as a healer. With June and Mandy to help, they made the changes in the rooms on the main level.

The dining room became the examination room. The hardwood floor polished to a high gloss made it easy to keep clean. The linen cabinet and china hutch functioned well as storage for medical supplies, instruments, and clean bandages. The parlor served as a waiting room for patients, or as a room to relax when the three residents had a break. Eli's study became Hattie's office where she kept records on each patient and conducted private discussions. She tried to see ambulatory patients on a morning schedule. June's domain consisted of the kitchen, laundry room with its special boiler for hot water and the cellar.

Mandy ruled outside. With help from the mules and the two older women she was clearing out the fence and much of the overgrown shrubbery and constructing stone paths between the barn, stable and outhouse. She had plans to enlarge the chicken house and build a new corral in the spring. Every time Hattie returned from an out of town visit it seemed as if something new had been added.

The beautiful fall foliage turned a rusty brown and leaves flew from the trees. The weather became colder as the three women prepared for winter's siege of mud, snow, and the maladies that always seemed to come with the season. More of Hattie's patients showed up with colds and fevers brought on by the deteriorating weather. Soldiers bivouacked in tents on open fields suffered the worst. There was little Hattie could do to help them. Tempers and differences seemed to subside as everyone fought sickness and the winter weather.

Hattie received a tom turkey from one of her patients so they had turkey and all the trimmings on Christmas day. June made pumpkin pie with whipped cream for dessert. She made over a new wool dress for Mandy and a winter cape for Hattie to wear when she drove the wagon. Hattie gave June and Mandy perfume from stock she saved when the store went out of business.

Someone left a large box on the front porch on Christmas Eve. When they opened the box, they found a new Singer sewing machine. Hattie suspected Mr. Murphy and the other conductors of being the mystery gift givers. Mandy had carved rosebuds from the cakes of soap stored in the barn. She had saved the shavings to sweeten the laundry when they washed nightgowns and other undergarments. Another unexpected guest showed up on Christmas day—a half-starved puppy. They named him Mike.

Eli showed up for a surprise visit between Christmas and New Year's Eve. He wanted to be home for Christmas but had difficulty getting through. Raiders destroyed sections of railroad track as fast as they could be repaired. He was disgusted with the greed and bureaucracy that delayed and manipulated the procurement and movement of supplies to the armies that needed them.

His visit was short. He needed to get certain messages to Grant and deliver the supplies or the spring offensive would bog down and the war would go on longer than necessary.

His trip to Washington produced promises of added guards for his supply trains. Now, he must wait and see if the politicians would hold to their promises or revert to filling their own pockets at the expense of suffering soldiers. The merry twinkle in his eyes had dulled to an icy glitter, and the ready smile had become a grimace. He praised June's cooking and approved the changes made by Hattie and Mandy. Secretly, he wished he could stay.

News of Sam's decision to join the fight caused a shake from bowed head and an even grimmer smile. Hattie could read the fear in his eyes that they might never see Sam again. On the morning he left, they embraced for a long time. Neither one wanted to be first to let go. Their future together might not exist. The reality of that thought caused both to grasp on to every second together that time would allow. They walked to the train station together.

Whatever the cause, be it soot, steam, or sadness Hattie wept all the way home. Wondering once more, could she rise above this madness? *I've done it before,* she thought but it doesn't get any easier. Maybe it's a sign of old age, things get harder to change as we get older and more set in our ways.

The mercy wagon with flag flying became a common sight on the streets and roads around Hagerstown. Hattie began to notice people pulling over or even stopping at intersections to let her pass. At first she thought it was just common courtesy, but soon she realized they treated her like the fire department wagons. She wondered if she should add a bell? *Probably just scare the mules,* she thought.

Hagerstown received a scare in early January when word came that General Stonewall Jackson was bombarding Hancock some thirty miles to the west. For two days Rebel cannons rained steel shot and explosives on the town. It made many of Hagerstown's residents realize how impersonal war could become. Such a bombardment on Hagerstown, currently occupied by federal troops, could even result in injuries to those who favored the southern cause. Everyone breathed a sigh of relief when Jackson withdrew and moved west, away from Hagerstown. Distance and bitter cold forced Hattie to change the plans she made to offer relief to the residents of Hancock. She was only able to help the few who arrived by rail after the bombardment ceased.

A huge snowstorm in late January curtailed Hattie's trips in the Mercy Wagon. Many of the roads out of Hagerstown were little more than winding trails leading to isolated communities and single farms tucked into mountain hollows. Hattie knew there were people out there who could use her help, but if they couldn't get out to fetch her, she couldn't get in. With her work restricted to helping those in town, she found more time to help Mandy with her schoolwork. Mandy's main excuse that there was outside work to do failed as the cold drove her indoors. Mandy loved to read but when left on her own she would pick novels involving romance and adventure. Hattie wanted to try and broaden her education.

She asked Mandy if she had ever studied Shakespeare? Mandy's negative headshake and look of horror described her feelings. "Some people may say that man knows something but he writes so funny I can't make heads or tails of what he is saying," said Mandy.

"But I thought you enjoyed good romance novels?" Hattie inquired.

"Did Shakespeare write about romance? "asked Mandy, suddenly more interested, "I thought all his stories were about kings, wars, and boring stuff like that."

Hattie reached over and opened a book and found the story *Romeo and Juliet*. "Here Mandy, I want you to read the first part of this story."

After reading for a little while Mandy turned to Hattie and said, "This fellow Romeo sounds like he is in love with a girl he can never have."

Hattie said, "It happens to be one of the most famous love stories in English Literature. But notice line six. What does it say?"

"From what I can figure out they both die in the end. It must not be much of a love story if they don't live happily ever after."

"Mandy, what happens to you, your mother, your father, me, all of us? We all die eventually. Life, and love, is about the journey. It's about the struggles, the good times, and the bad. It's about getting up when you are down. It's about giving a helping hand to others to lift them up. It's about living together, learning what works and what doesn't. It's about…"

"I think I get the picture. And this Shakespeare knows something about all this?"

"He says some pretty intuitive things especially about human nature and how to live and work together. Once you get used to his style of writing it really begins to make sense. You need to give him a try."

"How about horse sense? Does he know anything about horses?" Mandy asked with a grin.

Hattie took the easy way out as she said, "Why don't you read and find out for yourself."

The cold weather reminded Hattie of her previous desire to store ice for medical and personal use. With no equipment and no one available to hire, she wondered how she could get the ice she needed. While visiting a family in Williamsport near Lemon's Ferry she noticed that the ferry was icebound. There was smoke coming from the chimney of the operator's hut, so she stopped to inquire about obtaining ice from the river. With his ferry frozen in the river, the operator was more than willing to contract for the delivery of all the ice she wanted. He would organize the work and deliver the ice to her warehouse. He indicated that the sawmill located on a nearby creek was also shut down for the winter but could deliver the sawdust needed to insulate the ice. Returning to town she made arrangements for Matt Tanner, Jim's oldest boy to open the warehouse she selected. He agreed to be there when the deliveries started. She smiled as she thought to herself, *that's one warehouse that won't burn very well if Stonewall Jackson or J.E.B. Stuart decide to come calling.*

One night after supper June and Hattie were cleaning the kitchen. Hattie asked, "Tell me what you know about Joe Smith and the Gold Bible?"

June replied, "I need to give you some background, so you can understand the whole thing. As a young boy of fourteen, Joseph Smith was curious about religion. He kept getting different answers from different preachers, so he decided to pray to God for an answer. He just wanted to join the right Church. He wasn't looking to write a book or start his own Church or anything like that."

"Did he really think God would answer a fourteen year old boy?" asked Hattie.

"Well the Bible says that if you ask with enough faith, God will answer you. So he went off into a grove of trees and prayed. God and Jesus Christ appeared to him. They told him not to join any of the churches he was looking into but to wait for more information. I guess they wanted him to grow up a little and maybe test him to see if he had the faith to be a real prophet."

"So what happened next?"

"Well, he was tested. Many of the preachers he visited tried to tell him he was wrong. They said God didn't talk to us any more. We have the Bible and that's enough. Joseph knew what he saw and heard when he had his vision. It was real and the preachers couldn't talk him out of it. Interesting thing was they really tried. They didn't just leave him alone. They could have shrugged off the story as a fantasy dream of a young boy."

"So far this sounds like a whopper of a tale. Somebody should write a book about it. I've read some novels with worse plots." Hattie remarked.

Just then they were interrupted by Mandy as she came in from feeding the chickens and animals. "No eggs again, I guess even the chickens have given up," she said, "I thought moving them into the barn with the animals would warm them up but it hasn't worked yet."

June turned to Mandy and said, "Please join us when you get your coat off. I think it's time you heard this too."

"Heard what?" asked Mandy as she flopped into her favorite chair.

"I have been telling Hattie about Joseph Smith. I promised your Uncle Luke I wouldn't talk about it while I was living with him. I honored that request and never said a word not even to you, Mandy. But, it burns within me, and it's such a powerful part of my life that I just can't keep still any longer. It's like I have just discovered the greatest cookie recipe in the world, and I just want to share it with my friends."

Hattie turned to Mandy and said, "Your mom has been telling me about a young boy who was about your age when he prayed to God and saw a vision." Hattie looked at June and said, "Please, will you continue with the story?"

"When Joseph got a little older he was visited by an angel. His name was Moroni."

Hattie smiled and said, "I bet he was Italian with a name like that."

June smiled and continued, "Actually, he was a prophet that lived here in America a long time ago. His father, a prophet named Mormon, compiled a book written on gold plates. The plates contained writings, like your journal Hattie, from many prophets that lived here. He gave the plates to his son Moroni to hide because a people called Lamanites were hunting them down to kill them. These Lamanites were the ancestors of the natives that still live here in America. When the white settlers first started coming here they chased them out west. The book he wrote we call *The Book of Mormon*. It contains a record of God's dealings with the people that lived here far back in time, even before Jesus was born in Bethlehem."

"So Joseph Smith didn't actually write this Gold Bible," mused Hattie. "How did he get it then?"

"Moroni told Joseph where he buried it. After a number of visits and trials Joseph was permitted to dig it up, and with the help of the Lord, he translated it into English. It has since been published as The Book of Mormon."

Hattie jumped up from her chair. "This is one book I must read! I'm going down to the library and check it out right now."

June smiled and said, "I don't think the library is open right now. Besides, I don't think they will have a copy. It is extremely hard to find because so many churches have had it banned."

"I can see why," said Hattie. "If the book is true then Joseph Smith was truly a prophet, and that would put them all out of business. No wonder they had the Mormons chased all the way out in the desert.

"I can see that we have only touched on the problem. The Constitution protects everybody's right to worship as they please, but there are a lot of people who won't want a new religion starting up as it's in our nature to resist change. And not everyone is going to believe it's real any way. There will be all kinds of arguments raised to sway people's opinions. Who and what can you trust?

"Right now this nation is polarized and people are choosing sides over slavery and secession. Open warfare has been declared. I can see another war raging at the same time. A war for men's souls. One where good and better religious convictions could separate families and friends. How can we make the right choice? Where is the truth? What do we lose if we make the wrong choice? Does it really matter that much? So many questions, so few answers."

June leaned forward a benevolent smile on her face and shining convic-tion in her eyes. She said, "There is one thing you can do. You can pray to God for an answer like Joseph Smith did."

Hattie gave a little chuckle and replied, "Only if you believe God really answers prayers anymore. Some folks have a long way to go June."

Their discussion was interrupted by a knock on the door. Someone had slipped on the icy street and knocked themselves unconscious would Hattie come and check them out? By the time Hattie returned June and Mandy had gone to bed. Hattie wearily trudged up the stairs to do the same. Before drifting off to sleep the discussion with June entered her mind. She fell asleep with a prayer in her heart asking God to give her an answer.

Chapter 15

Hattie's Journal

10 April 1862: Gen. Grant has fought a major battle.
No word from Eli.

Mud came to Hagerstown in the form of spring. Streets turned to mud. Rivers overflowed and produced more mud. Mandy and Mike rode the mercy wagon with Hattie to help navigate the mud holes. At times both Hattie and Mandy would get down to push. Mike learned to drive the mules. He would bark and nip at the mule's legs. No one knew what breed Mike was, but he sure liked to herd those mules. When they returned to solid ground, he would stop them, so Hattie and Mandy could climb back onto the wagon.

Mandy began to help Hattie treat the patients. At first all she did was hand Hattie things and fetch things from the wagon. As she learned the routine, she would anticipate Hattie's needs and have everything ready in advance. As the workload picked up at the house, she would take charge of preliminary clean up and patient preparation. Examination room cleanup became her responsibility when she was available. Both June and Mandy were capable of providing basic nursing for patients. Several times, Hattie kept patients overnight or for a couple of days for observation. When this happened, all three of them would take a part of the night shift.

Hattie received a letter from Sam. His unit was assigned to cleaning stables and latrines, driving wagons, and cleaning up after meals. He was not issued a gun and no one taught him how to use one. It looked like he would go through the war and see no action. He thanked Hattie for teaching him to read, write, and figure. These skills kept him away from most of the really dirty work, since someone had to keep records and write reports. He figured that if the army would do more fighting and less writing the war would be over a whole lot sooner. His latest job was helping the commissary officer keep track of supplies. He said many of the supplies were spoiled and that tools and equipment arrived broken or with missing parts. The commissary officer wrote letters to complain, but no one ever bothered to answer.

Life settled into a routine. Hattie would see patients at home in the mornings, make visits in the afternoons, and on most evenings. When she was home, there was usually at least one patient in the house requiring care all night. June and Mandy tried to take as many night shifts as Hattie would allow. Many of her patients were unable to pay and Hattie found it necessary to send letters more often to Josiah Wilkins asking him to purchase more medical supplies. Many patients paid in commodities so they always had plenty to eat.

An evening occurred without patients in the house. It had been a fairly easy day and all three women were grateful for the opportunity to relax. Mandy was reading in Shakespeare. No one needed to ask her what she was reading, the frown of concentration revealed all. June had mentioned earlier that Jesus Christ had visited the Americans and that He had made mention of that visit in the Bible. Hattie decided to find the passage where He said, "other sheep I have, which are not of this fold." After finding this verse in John, she continued reading. When she reached verse 30 in Chapter 10, she stopped. Hattie grew confused as she read, "I and my Father are one." There it was again. Hattie remembered reading several passages even singing songs as a little girl, which referred to God the Father and Jesus Christ being one.

"June, I have a question," said Hattie. "The last time we talked about religion you said Joseph Smith saw God *and* Jesus Christ at the same time."

"That's correct. He went into the grove of trees to pray and they both appeared to him." June answered looking up from her needlework.

"How can that be? This Bible is full of verses that say there is only one God. This verse I just read quotes Jesus as saying he is one with the Father." Hattie said holding the Bible she had been reading aloft like a torch as if to shed additional light on the subject they were discussing.

June said, "I can answer that in two ways. One way would involve a long discussion about the Apostasy of the Early Christian Church. I think that discussion should be reserved for another day." June closed her eyes and turned her face upward as if looking at the ceiling. Oh I wish I had a Book of Mormon! She offered a quick, silent prayer, *please send me the right answer*. Lowering her eyes she looked at Hattie. "Do you remember the first morning after we arrived?"

Hattie nodded her head and said, "Yes. You and Mandy were up early and completed a number of household chores I was dreading."

"I was referring to the way we worked together to prepare and clean up after breakfast. And, how we naturally worked together following one plan and accomplishing one goal."

"That's right," exclaimed Hattie. "I remember thinking to myself how we seemed to mesh together like cogs in a machine."

"I believe that is what Jesus means when He says 'I am one with the Father. The verse means they are one in plan and purpose. They don't need to think about what the other one is doing or wait for direction because they have already established and agreed to a plan. If you think about it, the example I mentioned about our working together in the kitchen is probably not unique. How did you and Eli run your business? Didn't he take off to buy and sell and grow the business leaving you here to run the store, move the merchandise, and make sure the books balanced? Jesus knew that the bond he had with Heavenly Father was much closer than mere mortals could ever hope to attain or understand. The only way he had to describe that bond to his disciples involved the concept of being one. Remember, the Bible passed through many edits and translations. The words used to describe that concept took on subtle changes in meaning."

Hattie said, "I think you are right June. I like your reference to Eli and I working together for a common purpose. The Bible also says 'shall a man...cleave unto his wife: and they shall be one.' The Bible says one flesh, but I like the idea that they need to have one plan and one purpose also. They need to show that oneness to others, especially to their children."

June smiled mournfully at Hattie and sighed, "Here we are a couple of lonely women solving the world's marriage problems. It seems so easy to solve problems when you are on the outside looking in."

"I agree," said Hattie, "if one person dominates the discussion and forces their will on the other then the plan will fail. Both must be in agreement that the plan is not a compromise but something better than either could originate on their own. It can't be my plan or your plan it must be our plan. We wouldn't be in the middle of this crazy war if people would just take that approach. Why doesn't God step in and make it right?"

June slowly shook her head. "It can't be that way. We are here on earth to learn for ourselves. We must have the ability to choose. Unfortunately, most people choose to only look out for themselves."

Hattie thought back to the day she tumbled from the lifeboat onto the sand. She had crawled out to drink first, before she thought of Anne. She said, "Sometimes we need to take care of ourselves before we can help others."

"I agree," said June. "But, making ourselves rich and powerful at the *expense* of others is not right either. I have heard you say that society rewards us for our service. That reward must not come from the power or influence we gain over others. The only acceptable reward should be what we earn with our own knowledge, skill, and work."

Hattie could only nod her head in agreement. "Well, now that we agree that the world's problems cannot be solved by a few lonely women lost in the middle of a battleground, I think I will try and get a full night's sleep." She rose from her chair, turned down the lamp, and climbed the stairs to her bedroom wondering if she was doomed to always be one or would she be able to find an eternal partner some day.

The birds chirping outside Hattie's window woke her early. She put on one of the plain muslin gowns June had made using the new sewing machine. They were easy to wash and the material was available from the bolts stored in the old stable. All three had agreed that fashion would have to take a back seat to practicality. It was like wearing a uniform of sorts, what with all three of them dressed in the same style. June made them in several pastel colors so it was always a surprise to see which color each of them chose to wear on any given day. This morning, Hattie picked a pale lavender. If the sun wouldn't cooperate she could at least feel like a spring flower.

Entering the kitchen, she noted that Mandy had on an old gray dress and her work boots. That meant she planned to spend the day outside or in the barn. The new walk they had worked on together helped keep their feet out of the mud but the animals seldom cooperated.

After breakfast Hattie and June worked together to take care of the morning appointments. Barring any surprises, it should be a quiet morning. In the afternoon, Hattie visited the Laughlin farm north of town. Several of their children had a croup. During a midmorning break, she made a trip to the privy and stopped to remind Mandy to have the mercy wagon ready after lunch. She looked in the barn and in the old stable but couldn't find Mandy. She started to get worried before she saw her coming back from a copse of trees across the field behind their house. Mandy waved indicating she was all right. Hattie noticed that the wagon was already loaded for the afternoon trip, so she returned to the house. Entering the house, she asked June. "Have you noticed Mandy acting strange lately? I went out to talk to her, and watched her come out of that copse of trees by the Simpson place. She waved and smiled, but I still feel concerned."

June turned and smiled at Hattie. "Maybe she thinks she's in love. She has been a little evasive lately and has made several excuses to run errands uptown. I want to give her a chance to tell me when she is ready. Life can feel strange to a girl her age. I need to trust her to make good decisions based on what she has been taught. Let's give her a chance to come to me when she's ready."

"I agree, said Hattie, "life can get real emotional for a young woman her age. I remember how I fantasized about Peter Janes before I had to leave the manor. I had us married and pushing baby buggies. He probably didn't know I was even there."

The trip to the Laughlin farm took Hattie over two hours. After examining the children, she instructed their mother on how to care for them and started for home. She found it peaceful driving the Mercy Wagon on a spring afternoon with the trees beginning to bud and the grass turning green in the meadows along the river. The songbirds had returned from their southern journey and added their voices to the steady clop-clop of the mule's hooves.

She remembered similar trips with Kim. He would point out different herbs and plants with medicinal value. They would play the observation game where each would try to find more kinds of birds or flowers over a given distance. She wondered how he was doing. He had told her stories about India and Tibet where bandits would hide in the trees and waylay unsuspecting travelers. The shape just off the road would probably have remained hidden had she not been thinking about bandits and picked it out of the foliage. She had Mike with her and he was attentive but didn't bark or growl. After stopping the wagon, she and Mike hopped down to take a look.

She found a badly beaten Union officer lying unconscious in the bushes. His flowing, golden hair and blond goatee would have created a regal look if he were not bruised and bloody. His hands were still tied behind his back. Hattie cut him loose and propped him up against a tree and ran to the wagon to get her bag and a canteen of water. She was able to revive him enough so he could walk to the wagon with her help. Loading him into the wagon was a struggle, but they finally made it. After giving him another drink, she covered him and instructed him not to uncover until she told him it was safe. Hattie kept the mules moving at a fast pace until she reached the edge of town. She slowed them to the patient walk she used when returning from a visit.

Once safely in the barn, she checked on her patient and found him unconscious again. She couldn't help but notice that his uniform was tailored, and under his scrapes and bruises, he cut quite a dashing figure. *Probably looks good on the back of a horse,* she thought. I hope he can fight as good as he looks. She unhitched the team and turned them into the pasture. Lighting a lantern she cleaned his wounds as best she could. The harsh alcohol revived him making him jerk. He asked, "Where am I?"

"You are in my barn. You have some nasty cuts. Please lie still while I clean you up."

"Who are you?"

"If you will stop asking silly questions I will get you fixed up and then we can talk." She said continuing to clean the dried blood from his cuts and scratches.

She was about to stitch up a nasty cut on his knee when the barn door began to open. It was Mandy. Peeking in the back of the wagon she asked, "Is everything all right?"

Hattie looked up from her work. "Yes, but this gentleman needs something to eat. Will you go in the house and get something easy to swallow? His mouth is in no condition to chew tough food right now."

After fixing the cut on his knee, she looked up and said, "I made a vow not to harbor any soldiers in my home during the war. I am going to bend those rules and let you stay here in the barn until you are well enough to travel. I would prefer not to know your name. Will you agree to remain hidden and leave as soon as you are able?" the man nodded. "As soon as Mandy returns and you have something to eat, we will help you climb into the hayloft."

They laid some loose boards against the wall of the barn creating a lean-to, which they covered with hay. An old horse blanket became a cover over additional loose hay placed on the floor of the hayloft. As Mandy and Hattie walked toward the house, Hattie asked, "Did your mother say anything?"

Mandy replied, "No, as a matter of fact she was in the cellar trying to find a few potatoes for our supper. I filled that bowl with bread and warm milk and left before she returned."

"Good, let's pretend that everything is normal. If she asks any questions, we tell her, but the fewer people that know what we have in the hayloft the better I like it. Be careful in the morning when you go out to feed the animals. We will make an extra large amount of porridge in the morning. You will need to take it to him when you go out."

"Ughew, I hate that stuff." Mandy said with a grimace.

"I know, but it is soft and gooey enough for him to eat. His mouth is cut up pretty bad."

"What happened to him?

"He wandered away from his unit and was captured by a Rebel patrol. He took a terrible beating. I guess they wanted some kind of military information," said Hattie, opening the kitchen door. "Remember now, not a word to your ma unless she asks."

The soldier stayed in the hayloft for two days and then he was gone. They never saw or heard anything about him. Hattie breathed a sigh of relief. Little did she know that in the days and years to follow she would help many soldiers. They never entered her house, but many men wearing blue or gray received food and medical care in that hayloft.

Hattie worried about Eli. Rumors and newspapers mentioned a large battle being fought by Grant's army. He lost a lot of men on the first day. Eli had not sent word to her since the battle, and she was worried that he was there when the Union troops were overrun. The dull ache that always sat inside her grew with each passing day. A knock on the door usually meant her medical services were needed, but it could bring good news or bad concerning Eli.

It wasn't a knock on the door that delivered the news. Hattie and Mandy were at the warehouse loading supplies delivered by Murphy the night before when a man approached and handed Hattie a letter. "From Murphy," was all he said before he was gone, running to catch the train to Washington.

The letter was short. Eli was safe! He had been in Pittsburgh during the battle, locating supplies. He indicated that he was involved in a shouting match with some of Gen. Buell's people who wanted to wait for additional supplies to arrive before releasing the train. He had bypassed them and bribed the engineer and conductor to take the load of troops and supplies through early. It was lucky he did. The arrival of his train turned the tide of battle. He mentioned that Grant was extremely frustrated. He spent more time and energy trying to train his troops and motivate his officers than fighting the enemy.

The next morning turned hot. It seemed spring was gone overnight and summer was upon them. Hattie's last patient for the morning needed an icepack. She asked June if she knew where Mandy was. They looked but couldn't locate her anywhere. Frustrated by the delay Hattie hitched Blackie to the buggy threw an empty burlap bag in the back and headed for the ice warehouse. As she entered the street where the warehouse was located. She thought she saw someone duck around the corner. She pulled up in front and reached for her key to the padlock. She noticed that the padlock was hanging loose. Someone was in the ice warehouse. She approached the door slowly. Just as she was about to open the door, it swung open and a figure stepped out.

Hattie had Matt Tanner pinned to the warehouse wall before she recognized him. He was screaming, "Lemmie go, lemmie go!"

Hattie paused recognizing the voice. She asked, "Matt, what are you doing here? Did your mom send you for some ice? Is there a problem at home? Do I need to go see if I can help?"

"No, no, no, I, I, I…was just taking a nap where it was cool." He stammered out of the left side of his mouth, the right side still pressed against the wall.

Hattie realized she still had Matt pinned to the wall and released him. He staggered back, and looked as if he wanted to run away. Hattie smiled, there was so much guilt on his face anyone would know he wasn't "taking a nap." Things began to click in Hattie's mind. She thought she knew what was going on. She only hoped things had not gone too far. "I'm sorry if I hurt you Matt. But I wasn't sure who was in the icehouse, and I didn't want to take any chances. It could have been a thief or some foragers from one army or another. Please forgive me if I hurt you."

Matt reached up and rubbed his face. "That's all right. I deserved it. I should have let you know. I come here every day…for that reason. Did you come for some ice? I can get it for you."

"Will you? That would be nice," said Hattie, as she turned toward the buggy trying hard not to burst out laughing.

When Hattie returned to the barn Mandy was waiting for her. With more time to compose herself, Mandy's guilt was not so obvious. But, now that Hattie knew, Mandy's movements confirmed Hattie's suspicions. As they were lifting Blackie's harness on the hooks in the tack room Hattie asked, "How long have you and Matt been meeting in the icehouse?"

Mandy's shoulders slumped. She paused before turning to Hattie with a pleading look in her eyes. "Please, don't tell ma. We were only talking."

Hattie made an exasperated face. "Do you know how old that, 'we were only talking' line is? Now, what is really going on? If you tell me the truth, I might not tell your mother."

"Matt wants to go fight for the Union. I want him to stay here. I love him and want to marry him. I was just trying to talk him out of joining up."

Hattie pressed her fists into her sides and gave Mandy an exasperated look. "Mandy, you just turned fifteen! You don't need to get married so young! You have your whole life ahead of you. I will pay for you to go to Oberlin College and get a good education…" Hattie stopped. She realized that her words were as old and worn as the ones Mandy had used on her.

She decided to try another tactic. "You say Matt's too young to go fight. I say you are too young to get married. I happen to believe that both arguments are true. What if you invite Matt to come to the house and talk this over with your mother and me? I promise not to say anything to your mother until you have a chance to set up the meeting. Let your mother and I have a chance to point out some things you may not have considered. Will you agree to that?" Mandy nodded.

Between Mandy's delaying tactics and sick patients it was four days before they finally met in Hattie's parlor. The delay and maneuvering added another member to the meeting. Matt's mother, Edith Tanner, also attended. Hattie felt like a fifth wheel, but realized someone would need to arbitrate this discussion. June asked if she could give prayer before they started. No one objected.

Hattie led off by filling the mother's in on what happened at the ice-house. Mrs. Tanner said, "You should've knocked some sense into the boy while you had him pinned to the wall."

Hattie asked, "Matt, how old are you?"

"I'll be eighteen next month," Matt said trying to sit a little straighter and look more mature.

"What skills do you have?" asked June. "Do you have a trade? Have you gone to school? How can you support a family?"

"He has been doing a good job helping out around the house, but I doubt if he has the experience to get a good job and support a family," said Edith. "I really think we need to send one of them off somewhere until this blows over and they are a little older."

"You send him off, and he will end up in the army getting himself killed," wailed Mandy jumping up and running out the kitchen door with June right behind her. Matt sat on a stool brought in from the kitchen with his hands clenched between his knees. His eyes moved from Hattie to his mother as if it was his fault Mandy had run off.

June, with a tear stained Mandy in tow, returned a few minutes later. As they entered the room, Mandy released her mother's hand and standing straight and erect said, "I apologize for acting like a child. I guess my real problem is I don't want Matt going away to fight in this war that doesn't make any sense."

Hattie said, "No war makes sense if you aren't committed to the argument that causes it. Many people are fighting for a cause they feel is just. They fight for a way of life that is precious to them.

Unfortunately, the actual fighting starts when powerful men want more power. They get other men committed enough to do the fighting for them. Leaders become so caught up in their belief in the rightness of their own goals that their pride won't let them back away and find a peaceful solution," Hattie shook herself mentally, realizing she was preaching again. "But, we need to get back to discussing the reason we are here tonight.

Everyone here needs to agree to a plan that works for all of us. How do we do that?"

Mandy raised her hand and said, "I would like to propose that a part of that plan be a goal that Matt and I get married but not until I am eighteen."

"Does anyone object to that part of our goal?" asked Hattie. There were no objections.

Matt spoke up, "I would like to say something. I have been thinking about what Hattie said earlier. I realize that I am not committed to any of the arguments that started this war. I really don't know enough to choose a side. I have friends that are fighting on both sides. I like and respect all of them for what they are doing but my commitment is not there. I should remain out of the fighting. It's just...everyone else is doing it why not me? If I stay here two things will happen. I will be branded a coward for not joining the fight, and I will not be able to control myself around Mandy. Call it love or call it lust the pull is too much for me to control when we can be together every day. Mom's right I need to leave town."

Hattie thought for a moment and then said, "Matt do you know Mr. Murphy?"

"Sure, he's the man that drops off the packages that I give to Mandy," he dropped his head, ashamed, "That's how the whole thing started, Mandy and I being alone waiting for those packages to come and all," he looked at Hattie. "What can he do?"

Hattie smiled and said, "It looks like I am a larger part of the problem than I thought. Matt, how would you like to become one of the packages Mr. Murphy delivers?"

Matt looked at Hattie and gave her a tentative nod.

She continued, "I will write a letter to Mr. Josiah Wilkins, ask him to meet with you, and find you some suitable position. He is a very intelligent man with a lot of personal contacts. I am sure he will be able to come up with something. How does that sound?"

"What will he have me doing?" asked Matt.

"You and Mr. Wilkins will have to decide once he talks with you. He may find you a school or place you as an apprentice. It will depend on your ability and interests."

"What about me?" Mandy asked.

"You are more than welcome to remain here as long as you and your mother wish. I want it to last forever but I realize that people must live their own lives and make their own decisions. Your eighteenth birthday is a long way away. Why don't you strive to live this one a day at a time, at least until you turn eighteen. With this war, who knows what or where any of us will be when it ends."

"Who will pay for Matt's trip to talk to this Mr. Wilkins?" Edith asked.

"I'm sorry," said Hattie, "I thought I made it clear that Matt's expenses would be paid by me. I have a personal account with Mr. Wilkins. I will make it clear in my letter that Matt's expenses are my responsibility." Hattie thought to herself, *I hope this is one of those times where throwing money at a problem can create a solution.*

June had made shortcake and Hattie had been paid for a recent visit with strawberries so they sealed the solution to the problem with strawberry shortcake with whipped cream. At times Hattie worried about all the rich creamy deserts they ate but cream was plentiful on the farms around Hagerstown and many patients paid with dairy products. Hattie's thoughts went to Sam and how much he liked this desert. She hoped he felt like he was helping to free his people.

Hattie met with Murphy the next day and explained the situation. She gave him a letter for Mr. Wilkins and arranged for Matt's younger brother to be his contact for all future packages.

Murphy also gave her a letter from Eli. Good news, Grant was finally getting his troops trained and things were going better with the war out west. He hinted that future letters would have to travel part way by steamship, whatever that meant.

Chapter 16

Hattie's Journal

17 September 1862: *We are in the middle of the war that touches all our lives.*

Hattie wrote her letter to Josiah Wilkins containing two requests. The first was to find a position for young Matt Tanner. The second was to try and locate a copy of The Book of Mormon for her. She indicated that two copies would be preferred but one would do.

It had been such a beautiful morning when she set out for the train station. She had decided to walk. Now as she returned home she wished she could go back and change her mind. The wait at the station had been longer than she anticipated. Murphy's train had been delayed. She should have expected that to happen. There had been an unusual amount of activity lately that few were willing to talk about. Just more saber rattling she thought to herself. Even Murphy had been grimmer faced than usual. His final comment about Rebels occupying Hagerstown set her to wondering if this was a safe place to be?

A breeze came up offering a refreshing breath of air. Then a carriage drove by creating a cloud of dust enveloping her and causing a sneeze. She took a handkerchief from her pocket to clear the dust from her face. Later, looking up she saw an unusual sight.

Three men were leaving the hotel located in the next block. She recognized two of the men as prominent local businessmen. Both were strong, vocal, southern sympathizers. The third man had his back to her. As he walked quickly away, turning down an alley, she recognized something familiar about his walk. As she tried to place where she had seen that particular way of walking, she heard sounds of a horse leaving the back of the alley at a gallop. Whoever he was he was not hanging around to be reintroduced.

Hattie crossed the street not wanting to talk to the two men. Both were loud, boisterous, and condescending to her. They failed to recognize her medical skills or claim to neutrality. When she met them they would pump her for information on Eli's whereabouts. They reminded her of the vultures she saw circling over that old dead cow back in England. She remembered that cow with gratitude for saving her feet. Without those leather insoles for her boots she would have never made it. Looking down the street deliberately avoiding eye contact with the two men on the other side, she saw the mercy wagon approaching.

There is mercy left in the world now I have a reason not to talk to those two blowhards.

As it turned out, Mandy had a message. She was needed at the Horner farm. The Horner boys had been racing to see which one could harvest the most wheat with their scythes. The younger one had sliced a large gash in his older brother's leg. Hattie figured she would need to hurry if she wanted to save the leg. After a quick check to make sure the proper supplies were in the wagon, Hattie and Mandy took off as fast as the mules would go.

Arriving at the Horner farm, Hattie went to work on the boy. Fortunately the shinbone had stopped the scythe and no tendons had been cut. She cleaned the wound, and stitched it closed. She left instructions on bed rest and elevating the leg. She was concerned about infection since it had taken time to come to town and for Mandy to find her. She cautioned Mrs. Horner to look for signs of infection or a spreading redness up the leg. Meg Horner paid Hattie with several sacks of recently harvested wheat. Having done all she could to help they turned the mercy wagon around and began the long trip home.

Mandy turned to Hattie and asked, "Do you think I am doing the right thing staying here while Matt goes off to Baltimore?"

"Yes, Mandy, I do. Baltimore isn't that far. The mail service is fairly reliable and if your hearts are true then distance and time will only forge a stronger bond."

She thought of her first love, of Peter with the golden hair and bright blue eyes. Time and distance had paled that memory. A purely physical attraction could not stand up to time and distance, there had to be more. Matt and Mandy would have to work at building a lasting relationship. The extra effort would either strengthen or break the bond. Both would profit either way. But, explaining that to a headstrong girl in love for the first time was not Hattie's job. She was grateful someone else had that responsibility. For a young woman without any children of her own, she seemed to get involved in being a mother a lot.

"Where are we going?" Mandy asked as Hattie turned the mules down a crossroad.

Hattie got the mules moving in the right direction and then replied. "I thought I would check on Ben Doyle while we are out this way. If he has the grain mill operating we may be able to trade this load of wheat in the back of the wagon for flour."

"I thought he shut down for the summer when he crushed his thumb?"

"He did but I saw him in town the other day and he said he was going to try and get set for this years grain crop. His hand is still in bad shape. It will take a long time to heal, but he says his boy can do a lot. I don't think the boy is strong enough. That's one of the things I want to check out. He needs to start up again, or he will miss this year's crop. That will mean no income this year. The Bank may carry him but Ben would just as soon stay out of debt if possible. If he is up and running, I want to give him our business. With the grain harvest starting, I will be taking a lot of grain in on trade for medical services, and I sure don't want to grind it by hand. How about you?"

Mandy nodded in agreement. The road they were on was rough and treacherous with several turns and steep grades. Both Hattie and Mandy had all they could do to just hang on in places. It was a beautiful location with the falls tumbling down the granite cliff to the millpond below. There were even geese on or near the pond. *Probably flying in from Canada*, thought Hattie. As they approached the mill Hattie could see water falling off the turning wheel. It was indeed in operation.

Ben Doyle walked out to meet them. Hattie could see Frank, Ben's oldest, moving a sack with a two-wheeled dolly. A ramp had been constructed so that the loaded sack of processed flour could be moved to a staging area ready for loading into a wagon. Hattie commented to Ben on the efficiency of the concept. Ben replied, "Necessity is the mother of invention they always say. We had to rig up something Frank could move. It's working so well, I think I will leave it set up after I am able to move the sacks. It sure saves on the back. I should have thought of it a long time ago. So, Miz Wiggins, what brings you all the way out here? I just had my checkup and didn't expect to see you for a few weeks."

"We have five sacks of wheat from the Horner's. The boys were playing with tools too big for them and one took a scythe in the leg. I think I got there in time to save the leg. We will just have to wait and see. I was hoping I could trade this wheat for flour if you were up and running."

"Sure thing, said Ben, looking over at Frank, he yelled, "Hey, Frank don't start another sack yet. Bring that dolly down here to the wagon." Frank and Mandy each trying to outdo the other soon had the wheat out of the wagon and five sacks of flour in their place. Ben in the meantime had gone up the hill to another storage building and was pushing a wheelbarrow full of apples down the hill.

Walking up to Hattie, Ben said, "Frank, you and Mandy get up there to that springhouse and fetch down a couple of those jugs full of sweet cider for Miz Wiggins. Now, Hattie, that cider will turn quick in this heat so don't wait too long, or you will have every drunk in Hagerstown sniffin' at your door."

Hattie laughed and said, "I thank you, Ben, we can use the apples and the cider will be a welcome change. I can guarantee with Mandy around it won't last long. But, you don't have to do…"

"Yes, I do. I don't think there is another doc in Maryland or Virginia that could have saved this thumb. A man don't know the value of a thumb till he don't have one."

"That's true. I read in a book one time that having a thumb and a brain is what separates man from all the other creatures. I guess we should appreciate being special more than we do."

Hattie and Mandy waved goodbye to the Doyles, and they started the long pull up the side of the mountain. Mandy looked at Hattie and said, "You sure have a lot of good friends."

Hattie nodded and replied, "I'll take friendship over wealth or power any day." They smiled at each other and were silent, each thinking their own thoughts for the rest of the trip home.

Hattie's day was far from over. June had sent several patients living in town home but the waiting room was full of people from the outskirts who preferred to wait. During lulls in her workload, Mandy managed to get the mercy wagon unhitched and to take care of the animals. She enlisted people waiting to take patients home to help her unload the wagon. Hattie finally sent the last person home close to midnight. All three fell into bed exhausted.

The next morning Hattie slept in. She felt she deserved it. Therefore, it was late in the day before she heard the news. Lee's army had crossed the river near Sharpsburg, only fifteen miles to the south. The streets of Hagerstown filled with families from south of town who were trying to avoid being caught in the middle of the battle that was sure to erupt. General McClellan with a huge army was preparing to stop Lee's advance. If McClellan could defeat Lee the war might end right here in their back yard.

The threat of impending battle created a lull in Hattie's workload. It seemed that everyone's illnesses were forgotten in the face of real devastation. All three women became busy restocking supplies in the examination room and in the mercy wagon. From past experience Hattie knew that casualties could spill over to her care. Hattie's biggest fear was that one army or the other would commandeer her medical supplies. She would just have to trust the honor and integrity of the officers in command.

The battle raged south of Hagerstown for three days with both sides taking heavy losses. General Lee finally was able to stall the Union army long enough to retreat south across the Potomac River into the Shenandoah Valley. The badly mauled Union army did not press forward to attack. The people living in and around Hagerstown breathed a sigh of relief and went about the task of rebuilding their lives. Hattie treated burns and other injuries as people tried to salvage possessions from burned and destroyed homes and farms.

Hattie received a call to help with five children that had been trapped in a root cellar during the battle. Both parents became lost during the fighting. The children only needed nourishment and treatment for minor cuts and bruises. The real suffering resulted from the loss of their parents. The father's brother owned the farm next door. He volunteered to take the children and raise them.

Tired and heartsick Hattie turned her mules homeward remembering her own family and how their loss had pushed her to the point of almost giving up. She didn't have an uncle to lean on. All she had was brains, a stout stick, and the determination to rise up and meet life head on.

The mules stopped. Shaking her head from a doze; she realized she had been daydreaming depending on the mules to take her home on this familiar stretch of road. When she looked up she discovered three dirty unshaven men on excellent horses in the middle of the road. The smallest one spit tobacco juice in the dust. "I think she's the one, Sarge."

Hattie figured the one in the middle must be Sarge when he said, "Yup, she fits the description. He said we couldn't miss the eyebrows and he was right." He gestured with a pistol held in his hand and continued, "If y'all just follow me ma'am nobody will git hurt. Snooker and Johnny will be right behind the wagon on each side. They be at least two guns on you at all times so don't try any fancy tricks and we'uns will all get home safe tonight. Y'all jus keep them mules a follerin' me."

He slapped the mules to get them started and led them off at a fast trot. They held to that pace for the next two to three hours. Hattie noticed more men riding out on either side scouting the road. They must have had some type of signaling system because on several occasions they all stopped and pulled off the road to hide and let other vehicles pass. During these times, Snooker and Johnny would be close and both held loaded pistols on her.

At the last stop, Snooker asked, "We goin' ta blindfold her, Sarge or what?"

Sarge replied, "We will need to move camp anyway, so it don't make no difference. Let's jus' keep goin while we still got daylight." He looked at Hattie and directed her to drive the wagon behind a line of bushes that had been tied to a fence. The soldiers replaced them after they passed. The road became increasingly rough. Soon it was no more than a trail through the dense undergrowth. Hattie could hear water running but couldn't see a stream or river. Rounding a cluster of boulders, they came to a clearing near a small waterfall. A group of men dressed like the three that had taken Hattie stood near a campfire. A man lay on a pallet under a tree.

He looked up and called to her, "Do I call you Mrs. Wiggins, or Angel? Or do you still prefer the name Hattie?"

Hattie got down from the wagon and walked toward the figure. When she was about ten feet away she stopped and said in her best rendition of a southern belle accent. "Why Mr. Beauregard Calhoun as I live and breathe. What in the world have you gone and done now? Did you go and shoot yourself with one of them there Enfield rifles you smuggled out of England?"

Calhoun looked up at her. "You don't seem as surprised to see me as I thought you would. Did you get a look at me last week as I rode out of town or have your powers of deduction improved?"

"A little of both," said Hattie as she approached, "Yes, I did see you leaving town the other day, but I failed to make the connection at that time. Knowing the scoundrels you were keeping company with, I figured it might be you," she continued, "I heard from my husband that a man answering your description was buying lead for bullets in Galena a while back so I suspected you were alive. I can't imagine the *Susan Ganes* surviving that storm. You need to tell me that story. I was sure she went down. I have contacts in the South that searched for a record of her making port. When I heard nothing, I even mourned for you."

"We made it to an island off the coast of South Carolina. The guns were offloaded onto a barge and the ship scuttled. You will be glad to know that your friend Hapwood survived. Captain Barnes did not. We were sure you were lost when we watched the lifeboat go over the side."

He winced as she pulled at the dressing saying, "I caught a Yankee minnie ball in the thigh while harassing the blue devils chasing after our wounded the other day. The bullet passed clean through the thigh, but I broke the bone..."

"Killed the fastest horse in the regiment afore it stopped," said Snooker as he spit part of his chaw into the fire.

"Yes, old Blue Boy was fast but it's hard to outrun a minnie ball. He fell on the leg as he died. I've had two surgeons look at it, both wanted to amputate. Then I remembered the job you did for that sailor on the *Susan Ganes*. Will you try to save my leg for old times sake?"

Hattie looked around her and said, "If I say no, it looks like I might get a minnie ball for breakfast, so I better say yes. I need to get a better look. Snooker, bring me the two lanterns located in compartments on either side of the wagon under the seat. Open the little doors near the front corners of the wagon and you will see them in there. Bring them over here and get them ready. Johnny, will you get me the big black case in the compartment located on the right side of the wagon. You get to it by opening the door on the outside between the wheels. One of you other men lower the tailgate and bring me the box you see under the bed in the back of the wagon. You might as well bring the bed while you're at it. Loosen the straps and then grab the two handles and pull. It will slide right out."

Calhoun lifted himself up to watch the men working around the wagon. He said, "That's some outfit you got there. I really like the flag. *Angel of Mercy*, how did you ever come up with that?"

"Pays to advertise." Hattie replied, then turning to the men, she barked, "Let's get a couple of tripods put together over here. I want to hang those lanterns about six feet off the ground." She smiled thinking to herself *it's fun to see men jump when I speak. I wonder how long It will last if Calhoun dies?*

Hattie's examination confirmed Calhoun's diagnosis. The horse had broken the leg not the minnie ball. *The doctors that looked at this must be idiots,* she thought to herself. It was a clean flesh wound that had been well cared for by someone. The break was clean and did not appear badly splintered. She looked up and asked, "Who has been taking care of this wound?"

Calhoun said, "I have. So far it has cost us a gallon of moonshine. I remembered how you dumped my finest rum on that sailor's leg."

"Well Mr. Calhoun…"

"Major Calhoun please, I must maintain some authority around here even if it does appear that you have taken over."

"If you have any of that moonshine left you better take a big swallow, no, make it several swallows since I am out of chloroform. Then we will see about setting this leg."

Once Major Calhoun was under the influence, the repair of the broken bone and the gunshot wound went quickly. Hattie remained awake most of the night to ensure the dressing and splint remained in place. She fell into an exhausted slumber in the early morning hours and awoke to a steamy pungent smell. It was Johnny holding a cup of some sort of liquid. He said, "heard you was a tea drinking English Lady but all's we got is this here chicory coffee." Hattie smiled and declined hoping she would be allowed to return home for a decent cup.

Hattie stretched to get the kink out of her back and neck. She got up to check on her patient. He was still sleeping, so she moved over to the fire looking for Sarge. She found him sitting on a rock near the fire. He looked up and said, "Ya'll ready to head on back now?"

Hattie answered, "Not quite yet. I need to talk to the Major. His condition is critical right now," quickly adding at his concerned look. "Oh, he will live, but how he lives is the question."

"Well we better go wake him and get things settled because I be getin' a little nervous. We bin' settin' here too long as it is."

When they returned, Major Calhoun was awake. Hattie explained to him that he could ride a litter back to the southern lines, but the jostling would keep the bone from healing properly. He would spend the rest of his life with a limp far worse than hers. The second option was for him to return with her and stay under her care for at least two weeks. She explained her policy of neutrality. He would need to stay in her barn with the leg immobile. His chances of recovering full use of the leg would be good. She would leave him to discuss the options with his men. She turned away and walked toward her wagon.

While they talked the men had loaded all of her equipment except the bed. Hattie checked on the mules. Seeing that all was well, she climbed up on the mercy wagon seat. Rubbing the sleep from her eyes, she awaited their decision. Soon she saw the men carrying the bed back to the wagon with Major Calhoun still on it. She crawled over the seat and clamped special iron brackets to the bed and anchored the damaged leg in a sling to minimize jostling.

The return trip took a while. They traveled slowly due to the patient and the caution the rebels took in what was now enemy territory. Hattie admitted that they were very good at moving about undetected. She even picked up a couple of tricks that might help her in the future. When they reached town, she waved the soldiers off and finished the trip on her own. June and Mandy helped move Calhoun to the hidden lean-to in the hayloft.

Calhoun spent two weeks in the barn. For some reason Hattie was feeling better about helping the soldiers. In many cases they were men fighting for what they believed to be a just cause. In the case of Major Calhoun, he had friends in the local community. If he were discovered Hattie could go to them for help even though she didn't particularly care for them as individuals.

It was business as usual except with more tension. The Major as Mandy called him healed rapidly, and one morning when they went to check on him, he was gone. Mike hadn't even barked during the night. When Hattie went to feed him his breakfast he wouldn't eat. *Must have fed him something good last night,* she thought to herself. She sniffed at the dish. Moonshine! Walking back toward the house she saw the jug sitting under the porch. She retrieved it, and giving it a shake discovered it was almost full. They must think I need it for medicinal purposes and they would be correct. She fully intended to use it outside not inside the body.

Mark Tanner dropped off a package from Josiah Wilkins marked personal and a letter from Matt. Matt's letter wanted to know if everyone was all right. Everyone probably meant Mandy thought Hattie. Josiah had pulled strings and got him accepted at the U. S. Naval Academy at Annapolis. He was already enrolled for the fall term. Hattie's concerns that he would end up fighting in the war diminished as she reasoned that with any luck the war would be over before he graduated. She wondered how Josiah had managed that trick. She knew those appointments didn't come easy or cheap. It would give him an excellent education and career, and it surely met his goals. Hattie wondered how Mandy would take it. Mrs. Tanner and June would have nothing to fear. The Academy was very strict about midshipmen not being married.

The package also contained a note with the comment, "Enjoy the reading." Opening the package Hattie found two almost new copies of The Book of Mormon. She wondered if June had a birthday soon. Christmas was too long to wait. Maybe, she would just leave it on the sewing machine for June to find and wonder how it got there. That seemed like fun. Might as well enjoy life while we can. One never knew when the next disaster would come along and change her life again.

Chapter 17

Hattie's Journal

1 Jan 1863: Lincoln signed the Emancipation Proclamation.
The slaves are free

The Civil War continued to dominate daily living. Hattie spent more and more time treating war related injuries. Women and young children tasking their bodies to perform work normally left to grown men filed into her home with injured bodies. Hattie and Mandy had one and sometimes two occupants in the hayloft. June spent her evenings rereading her Book of Mormon. Her smile and gentle caring attitude added a healing spirit to the home. Hattie sensed that her patients felt better just by being in her home when June was there. Hattie seemed guided by an unseen hand, making decisions and trying techniques that had never entered her mind before. Hattie's workload kept her from reading anything except schedules or looking up procedures necessary to help her patients. Promises to start reading the Book of Mormon with June would break under pressure from patients with challenging problems.

A cold day in early December brought a problem Hattie could not cure. She found Blackie dead in the pasture. Hattie figured it was old age.

He had been with Eli before Hattie arrived. She had no idea how old he was. The ground was frozen hard so they doused him with kerosene, and burned him in the pit they used to burn bandages and linens from victims of the smallpox epidemic sweeping through Hagerstown. The black oily smoke rose straight up into an overcast windless sky. As Hattie watched the smoke, she hoped heaven had a place for horses. Blackie earned the right to be there.

Eli's latest letter described his frustration with the Union army. He had been expecting a large shipment of supplies that had taken him months to assemble. Nathan Bedford Forrest with his southern cavalry destroyed the railroad tracks north and south of Jackson, Tennessee. Both Eli and Grant were furious with the Union officers who claimed they had stopped Forrest, when all they had done was chase him around while two columns of southern soldiers smashed the railroad lines creating a huge hole in Eli's supply route. Other than that he was well. He hoped Hattie had a Merry Christmas.

Christmas for Hattie was not what you could call merry. Sickness and injury knew no calendar. Mandy caught a bad head cold and needed to be isolated from patients and could not work outside, so Hattie and June added Mandy's workload to their own. In addition to the additional work a huge snowstorm hit Hagerstown making travel difficult. Fortunately frozen armies don't move about much, so there were fewer man-induced casualties.

The continued bad weather gave Hattie a few free evenings to read a little in the Book of Mormon. June and Hattie discussed some stories and passages but Hattie found it difficult to find enough time for serious study. Hattie read enough to realize a book this complex and detailed could not have been conceived and written by a young man with a limited education. She considered herself a quick and avid reader with an ability to comprehend complex writings. Speed reading this book was difficult for her. She did read enough to marvel at the constant struggles between good and evil that happened over and over again. She recognized that the same pride and lust for power that drove men to do violence and evil that she found in the book, also existed in present day America.

As she read the stories, she recognized a cycle that kept repeating. People blessed with wealth and power would begin to believe they held the power not God. Destruction would occur when the people began to take pride in their own accomplishments, and failed to recognize God's hand in their success. Their own pride would bring them down. Once they were humbled and returned to God, the blessings would return. She began to recognize that pattern in her own life. Catastrophe would strike and she would rise up by using her knowledge and skills. However, she seemed to recover quicker and do better when she used her talents to help others. She remembered a song that Eliza had taught her to play on the piano, "Praise God, from Whom All Blessings Flow." She decided that real wealth came from God, not from man.

With Mandy down in bed with her cold and fever, feeding the animals fell to Hattie. She enjoyed the chance to get out and do something physical. She always felt better when she did the exercises Kim had taught her. After feeding the mules she would work out in the barn. June had fashioned her a loose fitting top and men's pants. She would wear a long coat to and from the barn, so anyone passing by would not see her wearing pants. She was surprised one morning to hear a knock at the barn door. Quickly throwing on her coat she opened the door and looked outside.

Frank Doyle from the mill was standing there holding a lead rope in his hand. On the other end of the rope was a beautiful bay mare with a large white blaze on her nose. Frank said, "When we got up this morning this horse was in the barn with ours. She had this note tied to the halter." He handed Hattie an envelope.

On the outside it said, "*Please deliver to Mrs. Helen Wiggins, Hagerstown.*" Hattie opened the envelope. The note inside was unsigned.

I heard about your loss. A buggy is no good without a horse to pull it. This little mare will go all day in harness but has the worst riding gait in the world. We call her Blaze. She needs a loving home.

Merry Christmas.

Hattie looked at Frank and asked, "Do you have any idea who did this? Who they were?"

"No Ma'am, except someone spit a wad of chawin' tobacco in the snow by the pond where the tracks ended."

"Well, thank you for bringing her to us Frank. Let's get her into the stall and then go in and see if June has lunch ready. I don't want to send you home without something to eat."

"Sounds good to me," said Frank, as he led Blaze to her new stall and fed her a measure of corn.

As they were walking to the house, she asked Frank. "How is your father doing?"

"Just fine. He's getin' his grip back from doing the exercises you give him. Of course we got the mill shut down right now, but he is able to hold a hammer and saw, so we are busy building a new grain bin for next year."

As they entered the kitchen Hattie saw Mandy in her nightgown making a mad dash for the stairs. She called out, "If you can run that fast you better get dressed and get out to the barn and see what Frank brought you for Christmas!"

"Oh Hattie!" screamed Mandy, when she came back from the barn, "Where did you get her? She's lovely. Can I ride her?"

"The note said her gait is pretty rough for riding. You can try her if you want, but it will cost you. No more moping around this house using that cold as an excuse for not doing your chores." Hattie believed half of Mandy's sickness centered on a lack of letters from Matt Tanner.

"You dress warm young lady. I don't want you back in bed. You hear?" added her mother. "You might as well eat something to keep up your strength. The mail train from Baltimore won't be in for another hour." They all laughed at this remark. It felt good to have Mandy back in high spirits again.

Mandy returned sooner than expected. She looked at Hattie with a worried expression on her face and said, "You need to come out to the barn with me quick. I was out giving Blaze a good workout, getting her used to the buggy, when this man staggered out of the woods."

She turned and left. Hattie jumped up and grabbed her coat to cover the pants she was still wearing and ran out after her. In the barn she found Mandy helping a half frozen figure out of the buggy. Hattie arrived just in time to help Mandy as the figure began to topple over. Hattie looked at Mandy and said, "We need to get him in the house right now!"

"Hattie we can't do that. What if he's a soldier?" Mandy said looking up with a worried expression on her face.

Hattie felt caught in a trap of her own design. If she moved the soldier into the house, she was in violation of her neutrality pledge. If she didn't, this one would surely die from the cold. The barn was just not warm enough for him to stay there and recover.

They laid him on the filled grain sacks leaning against the wall. A quick examination revealed that he had been shot just above the belt on the left side. The wound needed immediate attention. It had been left unattended too long. Hattie's concern increased as she listened to his hoarse congested breathing.

The examination revealed one additional fact. He might be a soldier, but he was not dressed in any military clothing just rough homespun trousers and a shirt covered by a long, black, wool coat.

"We will worry about neutrality if and when the time comes Mandy. From the looks of his clothes we might be able to convince people that we took him for a civilian."

They needed to enlist June's help to carry their latest guest into the house. Hattie cleaned and sutured the bullet wound and made a poultice for the cough. She brewed a large pot of tea made with her own recipe of herbs. Hattie turned and said, "All we can do now is pray and let the good Lord do the hard work. We need to get a cup of this herb tea down him every four hours. So, it looks like we will be back to night shifts for awhile."

The tension eased a few days later when Hattie found out that their guest was a photographer working with Mathew Brady. They had been taking pictures of battle scenes for the eastern newspapers. In an attempt to get a good shot of one particularly grisly scene, her patient had himself been shot. The bullet had hit his camera and glanced off catching him in the side. The camera had saved his life but was left in ruins.

Because he had positioned himself in an isolated spot, he had not been discovered until long after the battle was over. Captured by rebel soldiers, he had been taken to the outskirts of Hagerstown. They seemed to recognize the horse and buggy. When they saw it approaching, they dropped him in the snow and rode away.

The next day Hattie was able to find him a train headed for Washington. She never did learn his name. They had agreed that the less said about their encounter the better. Hattie did not appreciate the need to glorify the death scenes with casualties littering the earth that these men were capturing on film. Such pictures sickened her and were in direct contradiction to her efforts to glorify life not death. She hoped the "reality of war" displayed in these photographs would motivate future leaders to seek out alternatives prior to open conflict. She feared that only when the leaders at the top of the chain of command felt that their own lives were threatened would alternative solutions become possible.

As the weather warmed, Hattie prepared for another killing season. The mercy wagon with its flag flying was always granted passage. She saw Union and Rebel cavalry units on different days and different roads. They would wave as she passed but her wagon was never stopped or inspected. It was as if she existed in a bubble, isolated from the war. Hattie was too much a student of human nature to grow careless. It would only take one arrogant "by the book" officer catching her with the wrong colored uniform on her patient riding in back to upset all her good works.

She began to notice that wounded from both sides were being given safe passage. Both armies seemed to recognize the need to care for fallen comrades. Violent bloody battles lasting only days were often followed by long periods of calm while opposing forces regrouped and cared for the wounded. Hattie's hayloft was always occupied during these periods of calm. Hattie continued to wonder if the killing would stop? It was becoming more obvious that the South was destined to lose the war if it dragged on for a long time.

She wasn't surprised to learn that the southern armies under Gen. Lee were becoming more aggressive. If they were to succeed they would need to gain the upper hand quickly. The Union forces gained strength and experience with time. Unfortunately at this time in the war, Lee was sending his forces right through her area. Raids, skirmishes, and battles raged around, but never in Hagerstown. She constantly saw spies and small patrols from both sides. But, she was a sparrow in a forest full of hawks and eagles, just a part of the scenery. She prayed it would stay that way.

The three women might just as well have been lost on a desert island. June never received mail. Hattie heard from Eli about once a month. His letters were short and full of sad news concerning people he knew or business associates that had been killed or wounded in the war. Sam sent one letter rejoicing over the Emancipation Proclamation, but dismayed over how long the war was going on. He was still helping his commissary officer.

Both Sam and Eli mentioned their disgust with dishonest supply agents getting rich at the expense of soldier's lives. Matt wrote few letters and they seemed to get farther apart with time. Hattie was not surprised. Mandy retaliated by writing only when she received a letter. The local townspeople were friendly but not sociable. No one had time for social events. Invite the "wrong" person and you became a part of the "wrong" side.

It was difficult to tell who was winning the war. From Hattie's viewpoint it was the grim reaper. She was reading in The Book of Mormon one evening about how the length of their war had hardened many hearts but had softened others. Many had become more teachable and been baptized. She wondered if she would need to be baptized again. She figured once was enough.

When she brought it up with June, it turned into a discussion about authority. Had God authorized the preacher who baptized her? Would God recognize her baptism? In the same passage, she read about a prophet named Helaman who went forth and preached the word of God. He called people to repent and be baptized. Why did she have to repent? She followed the teachings of Jesus that she read about in the Bible. That seemed good enough for her. Maybe after this war was over God would send men out to preach the word of God. She would pray to God and see what happened. Maybe she would receive an answer.

Hattie began to run low on critical medical supplies. Josiah Wilkins and Murphy were not able to fill her orders. Murphy indicated that he had not heard from Josiah directly for the last month. He had been buying what supplies he could with money previously given to him by Hattie. She decided to take the train to Baltimore and speak with Josiah directly. Upon her arrival, she discovered that he had moved his offices. No one knew where he was. A cold feeling crept into Hattie's stomach. She checked with all known associates only to discover that Josiah had departed on a steamship headed for Europe. He had been gone for two months. The local bank in Baltimore still had her working capital and Eli's funds. He used the account from time to time to expedite delivery of supplies to Grant's army. Unfortunately, the majority of their wealth resided in Switzerland. Josiah had set up those accounts and they were closed to her. She was not broke or bankrupt, but she was no longer a wealthy woman.

She boarded the train to return to Hagerstown. As the train pulled out, she recognized a familiar face sitting in the row ahead of her. Getting up she approached the man.

"Mr. Pinkerton? I don't know if you remember me. We met briefly at our home in Hagerstown. I am Helen Wiggins, the wife of Eli Wiggins."

Allan Pinkerton looked up and smiled. "Of course I recognize Hagerstown's Angel of Mercy. What can I do for you?"

Hattie explained her problem with Josiah Wilkins and asked, "I was wondering if there is any way to find out what happened to Mr. Wilkins. It's hard to believe the stories I have been told."

Pinkerton replied, "I do have some contacts that may be able to shed some light on your problem. Let me see what I can do to find out what happened or where he is. Are you doing all right? Is there anything I can do to help you right away? I know with Eli working for General Grant you are pretty much on your own."

"I'm fine right now, financially anyway," replied Hattie. "It's just that I had plans to help some people that have helped me and without those funds I won't be able to do that."

They discussed Eli and what he was doing. Pinkerton had visited with Eli a few months ago and reported to Hattie that while a little thinner, he seemed to be in good health. Then he leaned back and looked at her with a contemplative smile. "I seem to remember that you had some bit of involvement with the feint we pulled in Harrisburg. A man named Oliphant and Eli helped us out on that? Were you involved?"

"Well, I was there. I helped them with their makeup and costumes but I stayed pretty much in the background."

Pinkerton folded his arms across his chest and looked at her with a knowing smile on his face. "We found a gentleman tied up behind some trash barrels at the railroad station after your train pulled out. You wouldn't happen to know how he got there would you? He claimed we had a shadow on him or he would have killed Lincoln. Of course we let him believe that

Oliphant was Lincoln because at that point, we were not done with the deception. I often wondered how he was waylaid?"

Hattie gave Pinkerton a wide-eyed innocent look. "All I did was ride back home in another car, so I wouldn't interfere with the deception." Then she smiled and said, "I did have to run to catch the train. I was, shall we say, delayed for a bit?"

"Catching that particular man was a coup we did not expect. He would have tried again to assassinate the President. Someone did our country a great service Mrs. Wiggins. I only hope I can find out some good news for you about this Wilkins fellow."

Their conversation was interrupted as Murphy came through announcing the next stop would be Hagerstown. Hattie got up and returned to her original seat. Allan Pinkerton wondered to himself how such a quiet, refined lady could have disabled one of the most adept agents he had ever encountered.

Maybe, in the future he could...Nah. Use a woman? One like her? It couldn't have been her.

Hattie kept the bad news to herself after returning to Hagerstown. She had purchased some supplies from the account in Eli's bank. She didn't want him to come up short so she quickly sent a letter letting him know about the problem. She mailed it from the station before going home. Murphy helped her load the supplies into the buggy when Mandy drove up. She was really getting good at driving the buggy with Blaze in harness. The little mare had quickly become a part of the team. Even Mike seemed glad to see her. After sniffing the packages and finding no food smells, he went off to mark his territory at the edge of the train platform. Hattie thought to herself that some days a dog's life seemed better than hers. At least it was less complicated.

June and Mandy were thrilled with the new outfits Hattie had found in Baltimore. She had been lucky. She happened to be in the store when a shipment fresh from Paris arrived. She used the positive balance remaining from Eli's cotton sales account. That was before she found out her money was gone. They all dressed up to make sure everything fit. They had a mock fashion show as they took turns parading down the stairs. Then the irony of the moment sunk in. Here they were all dressed up with no one to please and nowhere to go.

The following morning Hattie decided to start an inventory of medical supplies. She would have to keep close track of what she had left, especially her limited supply of chloroform and laudanum. She used a safe located in the cellar for these and certain other drugs and herbs that she needed to dispense in careful and accurate dosages. Without Josiah's help and contacts, she wasn't sure if she could obtain any more.

She felt grateful that the weather was getting warmer when she checked her coal supply. She had a source that delivered directly from West Virginia but his deliveries were undependable due to poor roads during wet weather and the constant army patrols. She used coal from the railroad but only in emergencies.

The decision to buy more coal now or later was not the problem. Buying anything required money. A month ago that was not a problem, now it was. She was developing this dull pounding in the back of her head. The need for money began to influence everything she did or wanted to do. How could she think, plan, or help others without the proper supplies? She had grown to depend on Josiah and his ability to provide anything she needed from her overseas accounts. Now she didn't have that resource. What could she do?

She sat on an empty keg in that cold dark cellar with her elbows on her knees and hands over her face. Think, plan, and do Hattie! She demanded of herself, but no answers came. Her problems had grown beyond solving with her own skills and knowledge. How could she rise up to meet this challenge when there was nothing left? She had exhausted her physical and emotional reserves. She had grown dependent on Josiah Wilkins, and he had literally taken her props out from under her!

> Beware the trap of trust,
> for human beings are prone to lust.
> Trust only God whose love is true.
> He alone can guide you through.

She thought she must have read those one-liners somewhere. Her feel-bad moment was interrupted by June calling down the cellar stars, "Hattie, there are two gentlemen here to see you." Hattie recognized from her tone that they were not patients and they were not friendly. What more could go wrong?

Mr. Samuel Pollack and Mr. Ralph Burns sat on the sofa in the waiting room. With backs straight, collars starched, knees together, and hats perched on knees they looked like a couple of vultures on a dead oak tree waiting for her to keel over and give it up. Hattie smiled politely and asked, "How may I help you gentlemen?"

Neither bothered to get up when she entered. Pollack leaned forward and presented her a business card. Burns said, "We are from the Department of State in Washington." He paused as if this statement was supposed to elicit some form of response.

Hattie simply sat and smiled.

Burns continued, "It has come to our attention through official channels that you are in possession of considerable wealth that belongs to certain English and European banks. These financial institutions require immediate repayment of their assets. Your failure to pay will create an international incident with foreign governments that could result in you being deported from the United States and returned to stand trial for embezzlement."

Hattie looked at the two men in total disbelief. "But I am a citizen of the United States. Why would you not defend my right to stay here?"

Pollack shuffled his feet and leaned back in his seat. He said, "There is some question about your citizenship…"

"But I'm married to a free born American. I have the proper papers signed by your Government indicating my citizenship." Hattie replied.

"We are afraid that there are discrepancies in your papers. For instance we have no record of you entering this country through any port of entry or seaport."

Hattie began to realize the enormity of the problem. Eli had worked with certain lawyers in Baltimore to insure all her papers would be in order. Unfortunately, those lawyers possessed strong southern sympathies and as such any documents they prepared, would be viewed with suspicion by members of the Federal Government. Plus those lawyers wouldn't fight to protect Eli's interests since they knew he was helping General Grant. She decided to try another argument. She said, "Well, I am sorry to inform you but there is no money. It just doesn't exist."

Pollack simply smiled through thin lips and said, "It doesn't matter to us Mrs. Wiggins. You will have to prove your case to the English courts. The United States must turn you over to them or risk an international incident that could affect English neutrality in the present conflict."

"So that's what this is about!" exclaimed Hattie. "You people won't support me because it will alter relations with England? Well I think that stinks! You will leave my house at once! I will not listen to such self-serving drivel. Gentlemen, you are no longer welcome in my home." She stood up, pointed at the door and barked, "Show yourselves out!"

Neither man moved. Then Pollack spoke, "You leave us no alternative Mrs. Wiggins but to call in the U. S. Marshall and have you forcibly arrested."

"What did you just call me? *Mrs. Wiggins?* Then you admit, I am married to an American citizen! Oh by the way before you return with the U.S. Marshall, have an order in your possession *personally signed* by President Lincoln. Then and only then will I leave my home."

After Pollack and Burns left, Hattie sent telegrams to Eli and to Allan Pinkerton explaining the situation. She continued to see patients and waited for something to happen. She really didn't fear the outcome. For some reason she felt confident the situation would resolve itself. She put her pending extradition and loss of capital behind her. She tried to concentrate on helping others while she was still able to do so. As days passed she began to relax. The problems she feared never materialized. She did keep a bag packed in the barn fully prepared to run if necessary. She was *not* going back to England! America had become her home.

She received a telegram from Allan Pinkerton. He was coming to visit her. She was not to worry. A few days later, he arrived with Mr. Pollack and a third gentleman with a familiar bearing but she couldn't remember ever meeting him. After they were seated Pinkerton opened the discussion saying, "Mr. Pollack has a few words to say and then he is leaving."

Pollack arose and said, "On behalf of Mr. Burns and myself please accept our heartfelt apologies for any trouble we may have caused you. The United States of America, Umrumph...Deeply appreciates your service to our nation and I humbly apologize for doubting your integrity or loyalty to the United States." Having made his speech, Pollack turned and left.

Pinkerton turned to Hattie and gave her a wink. "Well I guess if you can accept his apology, I will report that portion of my duty was concluded satisfactorily. Now, on to other items, Lord Miles is here representing the English government and he has some questions for you. Lord Miles the floor is yours."

Lord Miles looked at Hattie over the top of his spectacles and began. "Mrs. Wiggins may I ask you to tell us what your relationship is to a Thomas Kirkland?"

"Thomas Kirkland *was* my father. He was lost at sea in a hurricane off the coast of North Carolina."

Lord Miles continued, "Well aahurmph, do you have any way to verify that fact?"

"Yes, although you may find it difficult to find them. There is a war in progress you know. A Mr. Beauregard Calhoun currently serving as a Major in the Confederate Cavalry was also a passenger on the ship, The *Susan Ganes*, at the time. He can confirm that my father was swept overboard during the hurricane. He also indicated to me that Mr. Hapwood the first officer survived the voyage and can confirm his testimony. I have no knowledge of Mr. Hapwood's present whereabouts, but perhaps Mr. Pinkerton could locate him for you, for a fee." *Might as well throw a little business Pinkerton's way*, thought Hattie.

Miles continued, "Aahurmph, there is the matter of a number of negotiable securities that Mr. Kirkland had in his possession when he left England. Certain securities liquidated by a Mr. Josiah Wilkins seem to match those that are, aahumrph, missing. I understand that you are acquainted with this gentleman and that he was functioning in your behalf when he cashed these securities?"

"I received some securities from my father just before we left England. He had taken a folder from a satchel he carried with him at all times. He removed roughly one third of the papers and presented them to me indicating they were my inheritance."

"Do you know what happened to the other ones?"

"I think they may have gone to the bottom of the ocean with him when he was swept over the side of the *Susan Ganes*. The last time I saw him he was trying to reach me and he had the satchel clutched in his arms. If they were not found in his cabin on the *Susan Ganes* then they indeed went to the bottom with him. Major Calhoun was his cabin mate, and may be able to shed additional light on their whereabouts. I believe that I read in a book on English Law that securities of this type can be proven lost if two or more witnesses can verify that they were indeed lost or destroyed. Should you be able to locate Mr. Hapwood or Major Calhoun then you would have your two witnesses. A recovery of two thirds may go a long way towards satisfying your English moneylenders."

"Aaharumph, such may be the case." Lord Miles conceded, "That only leaves a discussion of the remaining third, which aahrumph, are in your possession. Mrs. Wiggins?" He gave Hattie a questioning but belligerent look over his glasses.

"But, they are not in my possession," smiled Hattie, "Mr. Wilkins has absconded with all our assets. I repeat our, assets, my husband Eli's and mine. The money obtained from those securities would only represent a small percentage of the total amount we lost."

"May I interrupt," said Pinkerton, "Mrs. Wiggins would you return the base amount of the securities to the English government if it could be found?"

"Of course, I really didn't want my father's money in the first place."

"Lord Miles, my lawyers in New York are prepared to negotiate a settlement for the value of Mrs. Wiggins' securities. I feel that we can reach a monetary settlement without bothering Mrs. Wiggins any further. Do you have any additional questions for her at this time?"

Lord Miles looked over his glasses at Hattie one last time and said, "No, I think that concludes our business. Oh, one last thing Mrs. Wiggins, would you have any way to contact this Major Calhoun?"

"Why Lord Miles, I would think with your English neutrality that you would stand a much better chance of finding him than I would." Hattie said blinking her eyes from under those prominent eyebrows of hers, as she thought to herself. *And I hope he puts an English made gun in your face when you do catch up to him.* Hattie remained seated as the two men rose to depart. Pinkerton pantomimed that he would return alone later. Hattie wondered what else could he want to discuss?

Chapter 18

Hattie's Journal

9 April 1865: *Lee surrenders to Grant at Appomattox. The war is over!*

Pinkerton returned the next afternoon. Hattie had just returned from a house call. Josie McCall delivered twins the previous week and Hattie had driven out to check on their condition. Hattie instructed Josie to place them in the sunlight as much as possible to counteract the jaundice. She had just finished putting the mules out to pasture when she saw Pinkerton coming up the drive in a rented carriage. As she walked toward the house, she wondered if he would tell her to flee or fight.

As it turned out neither alternative proved necessary. She entered the kitchen to find June preparing tea for their guest. Hattie's eyebrows went up. For June the very act of boiling water for tea was a sin. Hattie asked, "Would you like me to finish with that June? I really don't want you to do something that violates your beliefs."

June looked up from filling the teapot with boiling water and said, "It's no bother. If it's bad news I want you to feel we are here to support you."

Hattie smiled her thanks and proceeded to the waiting room. Pinkerton was alone.

At least we will have a chance to talk without interruption. "Good morning sir," Hattie said cheerfully, "should I sit down for the bad news?"

"Please sit, but the news isn't that bad. We have located Josiah Wilkins and he maintains that your assets are intact. He heard about the plot by the English to put pressure on the State Department to separate you from your money.

He claims that he took an unplanned vacation to a cottage he has near Saratoga, in upstate New York. He says he needed time to wrestle with some problems he was having. He contends that he had no intention of embezzling any of your funds. I feel he is telling the truth. He made very little effort to hide his trail. My people were able to easily track him down.

I have taken him to New York City where he has promised to work with my lawyers to settle the issue with Lord Miles. The bad news is that it will cost you a large percentage of your personal account. My lawyers and accountants feel they can salvage some of the profit you gained from investing your principal. Wilkins actually did a credible job of making money with your money."

"What about Eli's investments?" Hattie asked.

"His investments are safe for the time being pending reconciliation of certain claims against the account by his creditors."

"What do you mean his creditors?" Hattie inquired with astonishment.

"Apparently, Eli has contributed a great deal of his personal fortune toward helping General Grant. I doubt if there will be much left when all is said and done. I'm sorry Mrs. Wiggins but we may have saved your fortune from embezzlement only to pay it to Eli's creditors."

Hattie looked up at Pinkerton and smiled. "I guess it's for the best. I was getting too soft living the easy life anyway. Will you have some tea Mr. Pinkerton?"

As Hattie poured the tea Pinkerton looked at her with a glint of humor in his face. "Mrs. Wiggins, you haven't asked what happened. Would you like to know a little of the background to the story? Why Mr. Pollack delivered such a heartfelt apology?"

Hattie continued to pour as she replied, "I always love hearing a good story."

Pinkerton began. "After I received your telegram, I contacted several friends to find out the facts. One of those friends set up a meeting with Mr. Edward Bates, the Attorney General."

Hattie interrupted, "I'm sorry Mr. Pinkerton but I am not terribly familiar with your political system. Why would the Attorney General be so important in this matter?"

"He is the head of all law enforcement in the country. The U.S. Marshalls work for him. Remember, the people who were supposed to magically appear and cart you off to jail? Well as you know they failed to appear. The reason why makes quite a story."

Pinkerton settled back his teacup on his knee and began. "So, I have my meeting with Secretary Bates, who happens to be my employer by the way. I gave him some background on your participation in our deception in Harrisburg. He immediately ordered his Marshalls, who had already left Washington, to return and await further instructions. The next day, he attended a cabinet meeting and discussed the situation with Secretary Seward."

"Who is he?" Hattie asked as she refreshed his tea.

"Secretary of State, and through a couple layers of bureaucracy, the boss of the two scoundrels Pollack and Burns that were here throwing their weight around. Well, the conversation between the two started out on a friendly basis but soon escalated into a heated debate. President Lincoln walked in and caught enough of the argument to silence the two and request a private meeting after the scheduled cabinet meeting. Each was to bring someone who could shed light on the facts. Secretary Bates invited me to accompany him and Secretary Seward selected Pollack. Pollack presented a convincing argument to have you thrown out of the country. I told what I knew about your background and the good works you were doing here. Then the President asked the critical question, 'were you the young lady involved in the deception at Harrisburg?' I explained your involvement as best I knew it and, ahrumph, I may have embellished the story with what I suspected."

"So what happened next?" Hattie asked, leaning forward and indicating her escalating interest.

"President Lincoln turns to Pollack and says, 'Young man I will not have this nation involved in such low-life skullduggery no matter what the price! You are to cease and desist with this approach. Find another way to solve the problem or lose your job! You will personally deliver an apology to Mrs. Wiggins, and you,' he said, pointing at me, 'will witness said apology and report back to me on a satisfactory conclusion to this situation.'

With that he stood and we were all dismissed from his office." Pinkerton chuckled remembering the story. Hattie just smiled. They said their good-byes and Pinkerton departed giving Hattie a wave and a smile.

It took several months for the accountants and lawyers to reach a set-tlement. When the last account had been settled, Hattie realized that there might be just enough left to send Mandy to college, but she and June must find a way to remain self-sustaining after the war. She could maintain her medical practice but the physicians returning from the war would reopen their practices and her patient base would decline. Her lack of credentials could become a problem. She intended to tell all her patients to return to their previous doctors. In fact she had gone to the newspaper and asked them to print a batch of leaflets stating her desire for them to return to the care of their original physician once the war ended. She intended to give each patient a copy. She loved helping people but not at the expense of starting another war, this one between herself and the Hagerstown medical profession.

She thought about teaching, either in a classroom or piano lessons. When Sam and Eli returned she would need to consider their plans. Would she have enough money to help Sam with his education? Recent corre-spondence with Oberlin College indicated they would take him as a stu-dent. Would he want to attend? All of them had changed. Would they be able to find a common plan or would they be at odds? She could not hope to settle anything until they were all together again.

Would this stupid war never end!

Earlier there had been a terrible battle at Gettysburg where Lee had lost many men. She had been busy for a time. She had parked the mercy wagon alongside Lee's retreating column for a week. She used up all the supplies that were on the wagon and all her energy. When she had no more to give Mandy had placed her on the couch in the back of the wagon and they had returned home. By the time she recovered and restocked the wagon, the column had disappeared into Virginia. President Lincoln had given a speech at the Gettysburg Battlefield. He talked about enduring. She didn't know about the men but the women that talked to her believed they had endured enough.

A gentle knocking on the kitchen door interrupted her thoughts. June opened the door as Hattie entered the kitchen. The open door revealed a disheveled woman in riding clothes. Spying Hattie walking across the kitchen she removed her bonnet and tried to comb her hair with her fingers. She was obviously aware that she was a good-looking woman and used her beauty as a shield. A faint wisp of recognition passed through Hattie's mind as she spoke.

"Mrs. Wiggins, my name is Mary Ann Yingling, I visited you here at a tea party several years ago with my sister-in-law, Candice Caple, perhaps you remember me?"

Hattie smiled in recognition. "I know Candice quite well and I seem to remember you attending one of my afternoon teas. How is Candice? I have lost track of her since she moved to Baltimore to sit out the war with her parents?" Hattie remembered Candice as a loud, boisterous, beautiful, woman very much in favor of slavery.

"She is well. We visit from time to time the war permitting." Mary Ann said her tone implying that the war was seriously interrupting her social calendar. "I am living on my parent's estate in Eastview, that's in Carroll County. My husband William joined the Union army." Her mouth curled up like she had tasted something nasty, "I felt it best to live at home until things are resolved."

Hattie wondered what she meant by things? But, she asked cheerfully. "What brings you to Hagerstown on a night like this?"

"I am searching for my husband. I have checked at the Franklin Hotel, Washington House, Lyceum and at Key-Mar College. No one seems to recognize the name or want to tell me anything. I feel they would have some recollection of the name since he has several relatives living in the vicinity. Either they disagree with his convictions to fight for the Union or they fear the spread of Smallpox, which I understand represents a very real threat at this time. I have come to you for two reasons, first to ask if you know of his whereabouts and second, I am in need of a place to stay. I understand that you sometimes have spare rooms suitable for gentlewomen?"

Hattie's stomach had flipped over at the name William Yingling. She knew exactly where he, a Union soldier, was. How could she respond to this woman, possessing obvious sympathies for the southern cause and continue her claim to neutrality? She looked over at Mandy who had entered the room as Mary Ann was talking.

The question passing through both sets of eyes tensioned the air between them. Finally Hattie said, "Mandy why don't you put Mrs. Yingling's horse up in the barn, be sure to give it a good rubdown with hay from the *loft* while we continue our visit in the parlor." Mandy left but not before giving Hattie a look of understanding.

Hattie looked over her shoulder at Mary Ann as she led the way into the parlor. "How do you feel about your husband fighting for the Union?"

Mary Ann began taking off her hat, gloves, and riding coat. She proceeded to toss them towards June. As she flopped tiredly on the settee in the parlor, she said, "I think the man is a fool! He has this idea in his head that preserving the Union is more important than the right to own slaves. He maintains that his grandfather fought for freedom during the Revolutionary War and his daddy fought the War of 1812 against England to preserve freedom for *all* men. He has created such hard feelings with my daddy that I doubt if he will be allowed back to visit, *ever*! I just don't know if I can live without being close to mommy and daddy, but I really do love him, and want to stay with him too. I'm so mixed up. I had hoped to find him and take him home, dead or alive so we can settle the fight, and I can live a happy life!" she began to sob quietly, a tactic she had apparently used so often, in Hattie's opinion, that it had become habit. Would it work this time? Hattie didn't think so.

Mandy appeared in the doorway with a strange look on her face. She said, "Hattie, can I speak to you for a minute?"

Hattie turned to June and said, "June why don't you show Mary Ann to the room next to my office while I help Mandy." June nodded but her expression indicated that she didn't understand why Hattie wanted to put Mary Ann in the small room with the single, rather uncomfortable iron cot when there was a more comfortable bed located in an empty room upstairs. With a mental shrug, she handed Mary Ann her coat, and led the way toward the room Hattie had chosen.

Hattie moved into the kitchen to converse with Mandy who said in an excited whisper. "I did what you told me and then talked to Corporal Yingling. He said he was indeed married to Mary Ann but he wasn't sure he wanted to see her, at least not before he felt better. He wants to sleep on it. He will talk to her in the barn in the morning, and see how it goes from there."

Hattie nodded. "I agree. It is not going to be a pleasant conversation, but I feel that they need to talk. In the morning, I want you to take Mary Ann out to the barn, and promise me you will leave. This is their problem not ours. Oh, one more thing. Go back out to the barn and ask Corporal Yingling not to reveal his hiding place. Ask him to think up some reason for being in our barn that doesn't involve our caring for him there. I really don't trust Mary Ann. She may have good intentions and may say nothing, but she is the type of person that could let something slip without thinking." Mandy nodded and crept out the kitchen door.

Hattie walked through her office and knocked on the door to the small bedroom beyond. She found a weary Mary Ann already preparing for bed. Hattie indicated the iron cot. "I'm sorry we can't provide a more comfortable bed, but this is all that we have at the moment. I have heard some rumors that wounded soldiers may be receiving medical care in this area so you may want to continue your search in the morning. Mandy will not be available in the morning so you will have to saddle your own horse. Does that present a problem?"

A weary Mary Ann looked up from her seat on the edge of the cot. "No, in fact it will be better if I saddle her. She gets fractious around strangers, and I have done that chore many times. I so appreciate your help. I will plan on an early start, so if you are not up, I will just see myself out. Thank you for your help."

Later the next morning Mandy made her report to Hattie and June. She had found a hiding place in the old stable, but was only able to hear the end of the argument. Mary Ann had stomped out of the barn leading her mare and had vaulted into the saddle. She had shouted, "Go fight your silly old war then! I hope when it's over you will be ready to come crawling home!" She had lashed the horse with a quirt and galloped off turning onto the road east out of town. Corporal Yingling had followed her with his eyes until she rode out of sight. Then he had slowly shook his head, clutched his wounded side, and staggered back into the barn.

General Grant had been placed in command of the Army and he was slowly driving Lee southward toward the wall of devastation created by Sherman's march to the sea. At least the raiding and pillaging had stopped in and around Hagerstown. It looked like President Lincoln had preserved the nation but could the people rebuild? Each day brought news of new attacks on southern strongholds. Sherman had taken Atlanta. Sam had been transferred to the troops that were helping the recently freed slaves. She prayed for his safety.

After one especially taxing day, Hattie came into the kitchen to find June singing. Maybe I was wrong thought Hattie. It seemed there was at least one woman that had not endured enough.

She said, "June what is wrong with you? Every other woman and child in Hagerstown has had enough. We are saddened by lost loved ones and tired of struggling to stay alive while our fathers and husbands and even our sons are gone, and are no longer here to ease our burdens."

June looked at Hattie and said, "I just trust God. He tells us that our trials will be great, but we can rise above them if we but trust in Him. I just do what I can, and turn the rest over to Him."

"I wish I had your faith June. I have always had to depend on myself for everything. No one ever..." Hattie stopped talking. Her mind began to rewind scene after scene from her earliest memories with Mam and Margaret to her recent trials with Mr. Pinkerton. People had been there when she needed them. Sure her life was full of trials. Wasn't everyone's? But where would she be without the help and opportunities given to her by others? Of course she had worked hard. She was blessed with an incredible memory and ability to assimilate knowledge. Her physical dexterity resulted from her early need to control her body in order to make it function. Someone had always been there to place opportunity in her path. Even the books she had borrowed from the Janes' library. Someone had to write them and someone else had to buy them and place them there, so she could read them. She had simply taken advantage of the opportunities presented to her by others.

She had learned to push herself physically from early childhood. Her endurance, dexterity, stamina, and quickness had all resulted from hard work and practice coupled with dogged determination to succeed stemming from her birth problems. Then Kim had entered her life and raised opportunity to succeed physically to the next level. She could just as well have turned out like Anne, unwilling to work or even save herself. Maybe June had the right idea. Maybe there was someone that cared enough to want her tested to the limit of her capability. Someone wanted her to rise up and reach as high as she could. Life was the ultimate learning experience. Trials were not stumbling blocks they were springboards to opportunity. Someone else had always made the springboard all she needed was the faith to jump on it.

It was a bright spring day in early April when Hattie answered a knock at the front door. Two Union soldiers stood there. Hattie's first thought was I've been turned in for harboring the enemy. These soldiers are here to arrest me. Her second thought, seeing a missing arm on the Major, was that he needed help. The war had just ended so she felt free to help if he needed it.

The Major's grim faced message concerned Eli. He had been shot and killed in the last hours of the war. He had been riding with a train of supply wagons when they were attacked by a troop of Rebel cavalry.

The soldiers left her a letter from General Grant. He expressed his own personal sorrow at losing a dear friend. The letter contained an account of what happened and Grant's gratitude for the sacrifices Eli made to help him and the nation. He promised to visit Hattie when he could. Hattie thanked the soldiers and then started in on the hardest, dirtiest jobs she could find. She wanted to keep herself occupied. Her grief would have to wait. Could she stand to lose another family member? Where was the joy she was supposed to find in living if everyone she loved ended up dead?

She paused in her work. She felt a warm comforting feeling. She realized that for the first time she knew that she had indeed loved Eli. Their marriage of convenience had grown into something more. With this realization came an outpouring of grief. Great sobs released pent up emotions she never knew were there. "Oh Eli," she cried out, "What have I done? I let you think I didn't really care for you. I truly do and always will."

War weary soldiers began to return home. They went through town in small groups or as lone riders. Trains began to run on time as tracks were repaired, bridges rebuilt, and roads reopened. Many soldiers stopped by with injuries that needed tending. She wondered how so many of them knew she would help them. On many days her waiting room would not empty until close to midnight. Hattie didn't mind helping them but she was painfully aware that being able to see the back of the shelves and the bottom of chests indicated the end of her medical supplies. There were little or no funds left to restock. She began to wonder if she could make bandages from the confederate money many forced upon her. It wasn't good for anything else.

A cold drizzling rain descended on her, turning the backs of the mules a deep brown color as they plodded through the mud. Hattie and Mike were returning from a visit to the Humphries. The oldest boy, now looking like an old man had returned from the war with an infected wound in his neck. Hattie was able to clean the wound and leave a little supply of herbs for hot soaks that she hoped would be enough to help his body heal itself. The only other thing she could prescribe was good food and cleanliness. She was out of everything else that might help. Her shoulders slumped and she pulled her collar tighter trying in vain to keep the rain from trickling down her back.

She was tired. The mules were tired. Even Mike had lost his perkiness. The canvas on the wagon drooped. Wear and tear and weather had faded the signs painted on the wagon. She had retired the banner the day the armistice was announced. June had washed it and placed it on the shelf in her closet. Some day she would be able to take it out and remember the good times. Right now all she could think about were the bad and the sad.

Mandy was not in the barn when she pulled in. She didn't know whether to feel irritated or uncomfortable. She shrugged realizing to increase either of those emotions would be impossible. Both were sitting on maximum as it was. Once in the shelter of the barn, she shed her coat. Shaking the rainwater off of it as much as possible, she hung it on a nail to drip dry in the barn. She fed the mules a well-deserved ration of corn and rubbed them down before wearily turning to the door leading to the house. As she was walking up the path trying to stay on the stones Mandy had so carefully placed there seemingly a lifetime ago, she began to hear the piano. First the base notes thumping through the walls and as she got closer the whole rollicking sound of the music. Her shoes seemed to tap along on the rock path with a will of their own. There was only one person she knew that played that kind of music.

Sam? Sam was home!

She ran the rest of the way, crashed through the kitchen door, and buried her head in his chest.

Her head was resting in his chest? This wasn't Sam. The Sam she knew was her height. What was going on? This man was tall and strong, built like a rock. What had happened to her skinny little helper in the flapping bib overalls? Yet, the laugh was the same and the smile was the same. Sam had returned from the war, but he had returned as a man not as the skinny boy that had left her.

All Hattie's weariness and irritation vanished in a flood of joy. She looked around the room. June smiled at her over her shoulder as she went about fixing food for supper. Mandy beamed, happy the surprise had worked so well. Hattie leaned back and asked, "Sam, what have you been eating? I could make a million if we could bottle it and feed it to every skinny kid in America. Oh, it is so good to have you home!"

"I missed you too Hattie. Looks to me like these folks been takin' good care of you while I bin gone. Seems like I knowed them all my life the way you scribed 'em in your letters. It feel right good to be home wichu."

The four of them laughed and talked, exchanging stories. All of them paused momentarily when Hattie told Sam about Eli. Sam nodded to himself, full of understanding of how such a thing could happen. He remembered back to that night long ago when the man with the bushy eyebrows and crooked smile had helped him down the coal chute and changed his life.

Sam wanted to sleep in the barn so a happy but weary bunch trudged off to sleep. Dreams for the future passed through each person that night. Not all the dreams could become reality. The freedom to choose one's own destiny many times foiled the dreams of others. Had they known the future that night, the morning smiles would not have been so bright.

The morning blazed bright, clear, and beautiful, as only May in Maryland can be. After breakfast, the four settled in the parlor to discuss the future. All agreed that the immediate future required a plan simply based on survival. Hattie's medical business, while still demanding, would soon taper off. They needed to look for alternatives. Hattie was surprised to discover that the other three refused to feel dependent on her for their support. All wanted to be self-sufficient and provide a service, which would generate income for them. After some discussion they all agreed to keep their eyes and ears open and to look for areas of service within the community. The discussion broke up as Hattie's patients began arriving. Mandy and Sam disappeared as Hattie and June became involved in treating patients.

Sam went out to the barn with Mandy. He looked at all the work she had done, nodded his head and said, "Y'all been busy out here while I bin' gone. Place looks nice." He walked over to check out the animals. He rubbed the mules ears and fed them some hay. Then he said, "Be all right wich you ifn I takes the buggy and checks out this new horse?"

Mandy shrugged and said, "It's all right with me. I suppose if Miz Hattie needs to make a run she would want to take the mules. Don't be gone too long. There is some heavy work to be done here and I can use your help. It'll be good to have a man around here. We bin' lettin' some things go because they's no one to do the heavy lifting."

Sam smiled and said, "I be your man. I'll be back by noon. I jus wants to drive around and see what's goin' on. I might be able to come up with some ideas to hep get things started again." He opened Blaze's stall and led her out. With Mandy's help they soon had the buggy ready to go.

After Sam left, Mandy just sighed and began the never-ending job of cleaning out the stalls. Must have a regular mountain of manure out back. Too bad there is no way to use it. When the stalls were clean, she moved over to check the chicken coop. She had expanded the hen house twice over the last two years. She was taking care of over two hundred chickens. She loved training good setting hens and seeing how many chicks she could hatch. They were getting more eggs than they could eat. Hattie was always getting paid with chickens and Mandy had developed some crossbreeds for eggs and others for meat. She had one bunch in a separate pen that produced roasters running close to ten pounds of dressed weight. Maybe she needed to talk to Hattie about the possibility of raising chickens for sale. The problem was everyone around here had their own chicken yard and more eggs than they could eat. Well it was just an idea.

Sam liked the way Blaze worked. She was faster than Blackie had been and easier to control. He kept her to a steady trot for a while and then dropped her down to a walk. He had no destination in mind. He just wanted to look over the town and some of the surrounding areas to see what was happening. There were still a few soldiers walking or riding through the area and when he went past the train station he saw twenty or thirty more sitting around waiting for trains. He decided to explore some of the roads leading out of town. He spotted old Mrs. Macon trying to dig up a garden patch and stopped to visit.

Sam pulled up alongside the road and asked, "Mrs. Macon what you doin' out here in this hot sun? You aught to be settin' up there on the porch in the shade drinkin' sweet tea or sippin lemonade."

Mrs. Macon waved and replied, "Sam when did you get back in town? It's been a while since I saw you last a settin' on that stool in the store. I ain't got no tea, no lemons, and no sugar. When's Hattie going to open that store? She was the only one that could get them big lemons. All's I got is a jug of cold water. You're welcome to get down and have a drink. Y'all got a cup?"

Sam sighed, thinking to himself, *some things be emancipated some ain't.*

"You going to help Mrs. Wiggins open her store now that you're back?"

Sam got down from the buggy and walked over to the fence and leaned on the rail. He said, "I'm fine right now Miz Macon. Don't know about the store. What with the war and all I ain't sure what Miz Wiggins gona' do. Why don't you work up this here garden patch with a horse and plow? Seems to me you wastin' time and effort wif' dat shovel."

"Sam, I don't have no horse, I don't have no plow, and I don't have no man. He was killed at Gettysburg. I'm just trying to get in a little garden to try and stay alive."

Sam reached up and scratched his chin. "I seem to remember Mr. Macon he kept over eighty acres plowed up and in crop of a year?"

"That's true Sam, I got the land but no horse and no man to work it." She said as she jumped on the shovel. Sam could see that the conversation was over for the time being. He waved goodbye and climbed back in the buggy and headed off for home. As he rode along a thought started buzzing around in his head.

Hattie could see her workload dropping off as her patients returned to the doctor they had used before the war started. She was done seeing patients by ten o'clock. She decided to go out and give Mandy and Sam a hand in the barn. When she got there, she found Mandy staring at her chicken coop. Sam was nowhere around.

She walked up to Mandy and asked, "Where's Sam? I thought he was out here helping you?"

"He went to give Blaze a workout and to get reacquainted with the town. He said he would be back by noon. After lunch we are going to work in the barn. I thought you might want us to fix up the wagon too. It is really starting to look shabby."

Hattie shook her head. "I think fixing up the wagon is a good idea. But, I don't want to repaint the signs. Let's see what color paint we have available and just do a regular paint job on it. I also want to talk to Sam, and see if he can remove the panels and compartments and turn it back into a regular wagon. I think the mercy wagon needs to go away. I really don't want to create a situation where the returning doctors can accuse me of stealing patients. If people need me they know where I live and the buggy should do nicely for any future house calls I might make. I really feel it is time for the Angel of Mercy to retire." She sighed. With sad faces and heavy hearts Hattie and Mandy left the barn and started for the kitchen.

Just then Sam pulled up in the buggy. His smiling face lifted both their spirits. All three worked together to unhook Blaze and put the buggy away. Sam kept humming to himself as they worked. Hattie wondered if he had found a girl friend or something. She shrugged it off as just his high spirits at being back home. As they were finishing, June called from the kitchen door that lunch was ready.

As they were eating lunch Sam said, "Miz Haye whuka doomools?"

Hattie looked at Sam her irritation showing. "Sam please don't talk with your mouth full! I know I taught you better than that. Now swallow, take a drink of water and say again all after 'Miz.'"

"I'm sorry Miz Hattie, I guess I picked up some bad habits talking with the other soldiers. What I was trying to say is, what are you going to do with the mules if you retire from chasin' after sick folks?" Sam said, taking a giant bite of his sandwich to make up for lost eating time.

Hattie looked over at June and using her expressive eyes seemed to say, what should I do? June smiled back. Hattie turned to Sam and said, "Have you any ideas? I was thinking we better sell them. Mules like that would bring a good price in today's market. Everyone needs good stock for farming or for their business."

"That be...I mean that is my point." Sam interrupted, "What would you think if I was to make a deal with some of the folks that gots...I mean have no mules to plow their fields, I could work their land on shares."

Mandy looked at Hattie and said, "I've got an idea too. I was thinking about all the chickens I've got out back. They make more eggs than we can eat. With men coming back from the wars and all, more people need eggs. Maybe we could set up a stand and sell eggs? We could also sell the roasters and fryers I bin'...have been breeding."

Hattie looked at June and asked, "I suppose you have some ideas? What would you like to do?"

June looked at Hattie for a long time and then began, "I want to go out west to The Great Salt Lake Valley. I feel that is where I belong. I want you and Mandy to come with me, but I realize that you have your own lives to live. I don't want to lose you. I really want us to stay together as a family. I know that I will need to save enough money to pay for my trip. I will also need a little extra to live on until I can find something out there. I thought maybe I would take in sewing and create fashionable dresses and hats for women."

Hattie was stunned. It never entered her mind that June would want to leave. At first she just stared in open-mouthed amazement. Then she said, "I like all your ideas. But, before we get too far along we need to do a little more research. Sam, I want you to sit down and do some figuring. Remember if you farm land on shares you need to pay a portion of the crop to the landowner. You will need to figure upkeep for the mules and buy the equipment necessary to work the land. What crops will you plant? You need to ask around and find out what is needed. Is it something you can sell locally or will you need to sell your crop to a buyer from a large city? Remember we talked about the cost of transporting crops to market. Then you need to be sure you know how to raise the crop you intend to sell. What variety of seed do you need? Just buying the seed becomes an expense when you don't have seed from the previous year."

Sam was following Hattie's remarks and as she talked his shoulders slumped lower and lower. Mandy was also listening. She too realized that much of what Hattie was saying applied to her as well. The slumped shoulders and downcast faces finally penetrated Hattie's brain. She stopped talking for a minute. Then she smiled and said, "Please, forgive me. My mind was focusing on all the uncertainties. What you have all done is much more productive than my own self-centered depressed attitude. I thought I was done with starting over. I may have sounded negative but I really think you have hit on things that will work. Let's explore a little more and talk about this tomorrow. Why don't each of you look deeper into your idea. I promise to start thinking positive! We can do this. I know we can. I have done it before."

Chapter 19

Hattie's Journal

9 August 1865: *We are all hot and tired but well.*
Someone is watching over us.

With fewer night and evening calls those living in the Wiggins house were able to establish a stable routine. They would discuss the day's events and plan follow-up activities. A portion of time was always set aside to discuss any inputs or adjustments to long-range goals. If these changed immediate plans, they discussed and agreed to new assignments. Hattie and June insisted on time for studies. Mandy and Sam preferred the times when they would gather around the piano. Hattie would play and they would sing together or Sam would play and the women would dance about making up foolish steps to his syncopated music.

That first Christmas after the war proved bittersweet. They all gathered to sing songs and have a big dinner but there were empty seats. Hattie missed Eli's crooked grin across the table. June and Mandy remembered past times with their families. Sam seemed the happiest, but he showed a pensive expression. When Hattie asked him what he was thinking about he answered, "I just rememberin' all the boys that won't be home this Christmas and all the love they families be missin' with them gone."

That night, they all sang songs and drank apple cider punch. June made cookies decorated with frosting. Sam said, "Miss June I sure do love these cookies, especially the ginger ones. When I gets married I wants you to learn…I mean teach my wife how to make 'em."

Later that evening, they read about the birth of Jesus from the Bible. When they finished June said, "The Book of Mormon also tells the story of Jesus' birth. A prophet named Alma wrote this over eighty years before Christ was born. She opened her Book of Mormon and began to read. "And behold, he shall be born of Mary, at Jerusalem which is the land of our forefathers, she being a virgin, a precious and chosen vessel, who shall be overshadowed and conceive by the power of the Holy Ghost, and bring forth a son, yea, even the Son of God."

Hattie looked up with a startled expression on her face and said, "June that's wrong! Jesus wasn't born at Jerusalem. Everyone knows He was born in Bethlehem! We just finished singing the song, *Oh Little Town of Bethlehem*. That proves that Joseph Smith made a mistake writing the Book of Mormon, and it must mean he wasn't a prophet!"

June looked up from her reading. "Hattie, Joseph Smith did not write the Book of Mormon, he *translated* the words of ancient American prophets inscribed on golden plates. Do you remember the other day when we were talking about Janes Manor? I asked you where it was located and you said Sherborne, England. How far was Sherborne from Janes Manor?"

Hattie glanced down as she did the calculation. "I would say that the Manor was about seven miles from the city itself, but you would have no idea where the village was located in England. That's why I just used the nearest large town as a reference."

June smiled at Hattie. "When Alma said these words to the people of Gideon they had been living in America for over 500 years. They knew about Jerusalem but had never heard of Bethlehem. By the way do you have any idea how far Bethlehem is from Jerusalem?"

Hattie shook her head and said, "No."

"Seven miles."

Over the winter, Hattie reestablished contact with some of Eli's eastern buyers. She found a market for Mandy's eggs and live chickens. When it began to warm up, they expanded their own garden. Sam practiced working the mules by spreading the manure and plowing a larger area back of the house. They planned to grow more than they needed and sell the surplus. June took the lead and directed the others as they planted a huge garden with a large variety of vegetables. Mandy's chicken business showed so much promise that they decided to clean out the old stable and move the chickens in there.

Hattie was surprised at the supply of tools and hardware that had been stored in the old stable. They discussed the possibility of opening a hardware store. Further investigation revealed that the tools left over from the sale were not common items that would sell quickly. It would take a while to sell the tools. A one-day sale would not work. June suggested that they use the old store. It still belonged to Hattie. She also owned a few warehouses near the train station as well as the icehouse. Their business meeting as they called it was interrupted by a knock at the door. It was Andy and Sue Dawson.

Chairs were found for everyone, and June brought in the cookies she had prepared as a treat for later. They discussed pleasantries for a while then Andy looked at Hattie and asked, "Hattie what do you plan to do with the store? I have been looking for work but there isn't much going for a man with my background. Running that store and taking care of Eli's books was all I ever did. I don't have any savings. Sue had to live while I was off fighting and things are tough for us right now. I was hoping you might want to open the store again."

Hattie caught several small smiles. "We have been discussing ways we can earn a living Andy. You are not the only one needing to start over. One of the things I considered was selling the store."

Andy's expression showed his anxiety. He started to say, "Well I was hoping…"

"Did you want to buy the store?"

Andy looked aghast at this suggestion. "No ma'am I don't have the money to buy the boardwalk in front let alone buy the building and then try to stock it. I went to the bank and they think opening the store is a good idea but they want something as collateral. All I got is what's in my head. They don't seem to think that's worth a whole lot."

"Well I do," said Hattie. "The problem is I don't have the capital either. We would have to start small and only service local needs. We could not hope to deal in long distance contracts, or moving whole trainloads of merchandise. In fact the type of store we can afford would have to be totally

different from the previous one. Especially now that the Tanners have all
moved to Baltimore. Andy, why don't you meet with Sam and I at the store
tomorrow and let's discuss this further."

Sam looked up with a startled expression on his face. He could see the
look in Andy's eyes.

*He sure don't want to work with no ex-slave, somebody he remembers as a kid
sittin' on a stool. All I want to do is work those mules, and maybe start me a little
farm. I think Hattie has gone off her rocker. I sure hope she doesn't trade those mules
in for a load of women's dresses!*

After Andy and Sue left, Sam turned to Hattie. "Why do you want me
to go down to the store with you?"

"Sam, you know as much about the store business as Andy. He spent
most of his time in the office. You sat on that stool for days at a time
watching what was going on. You know how to set up the merchandise and
market the products. For example, June will need a section of the store for
her hats and dresses. Where would you put them? What window display
would be more apt to attract a buyer? One that's full of hats and dresses or
a row of dressed chickens hanging on a rack? When we start, that might be
all there is to sell in the store."

"But the mules, Miz Hattie what you going to do with my mules?"
Sam failed to see the look of surprise and consternation on Mandy's face.

"Sam, the store will only take a little of your time at first. After all,
Andy will want to do his share of the work. June will need to be there to
take orders and talk to her customers. I have been thinking about the mules
a lot. What do you think if you and Mandy work out a schedule where both
of you use the mules and the wagon on a hire out basis? We might even be
able to trade mule services for products we could sell in the store. For example Mrs. Macon may want to hire the mules and a driver to plow some land
and help her get in a crop. We take a share of the crop as payment for our
services. Then we sell the produce through the store. That cuts our risk. You
don't have to nurse the crop. You only show up when she needs mule labor."

Sam's face lit up in a big smile. "Hey then I can line up other work for
the mules. I can keep them busy all the time."

Mandy stood up and said, "What do you mean *I*? *We* can keep them
busy. I am as good a mule skinner as you are any day!"

"That's right," said Hattie. "Mandy has been driving those mules for
years. She needs to earn money for school. I had planned to pay for her

education, but it looks like she will have to earn at least part of the money herself. Maybe if this scheme works out we can get another team or put Blaze to work. Hauling loads will make up a large part of the job. We need to get that wagon worked over, so it will have more carrying capacity. We might want to look around for a buckboard or other light wagon for smaller loads for Blaze or for one-mule trips. Remember, most of the plowing will be done with one animal. You both might be busy at the same time."

Now, Hattie thought, *I've got everyone else busy, what am I going to do?*

The next morning, all four of them went to the store to meet Andy. It had survived in better condition than Hattie expected. Of course, she had anticipated total destruction on several occasions as opposing armies had moved through the area.

After looking over the property, they agreed that Andy was to have a one third partnership in the store. In return he would provide his labor and expertise. They would all pitch in and fix the leaky roof and make other repairs. Partitions and shelves needed to be moved to best display the merchandise they would have available when the store opened.

Once the painting was done, Andy and Sam were assigned to load up all the remaining goods stored in the old stable. Mandy helped her mother set up her corner of the store to display the hats and dresses she had made for the three of them as samples. June needed a space partitioned off as a dressing and fitting room, plus another to be used as a workroom. The bolts of cloth left in the barn provided her with an initial inventory.

The cleanup and renovation kept them all busy for weeks. They finally decided to open the store on a Monday morning in late summer.

Hattie still felt ill at ease. What was she going to do with her life? Eli was gone. Memories of Eli crowded out new ideas. She was constantly thinking, what would Eli do? She had plenty of work to keep her busy, but the work reminded her of the good times with Eli. She realized how much she had depended upon his knowledge and support. People were still approaching her for medical treatment and there was plenty of work needed to set up the store. She found herself going through the motions but not living a full and happy life.

She was busy cleaning windows when she saw Murphy walking up the street. He waved and asked, "Are you getting ready to open the store again?"

Hattie, thankful for a break from her chores, sat down on the bench she had been using to reach the top of the windows. She replied, "Yes, we plan to reopen on Monday. I don't know how much business we will get. We are dreadfully short on merchandise. We have very few men's work clothes and only a few useful hardware items. We do have some things that didn't sell when we had the closeout sale, but I would guess they didn't sell for a reason. If people didn't buy them at the time, they probably won't need them now. Fortunately, the dress material that didn't sell came from the more expensive bolts. June will be able to use much of this fabric for her hats and dresses. There is considerable rebuilding and repairing going on around town, and I could sell all the hammers, saws, nails, and screws I could get. June is going to open a dress shop but we have none of the latest materials or fashions in stock. And there you have it. All my problems laid out in a neat row."

Murphy smiled as she was speaking then he said, "I see young Mandy down at the station with crates of chickens and boxes of eggs. I know the buyer. He wants more if he can get them. So, if you take any chickens in on trade I think he would take them off your hands. Well, I got me a train to catch. See you next Thursday," he waved and continued on to the station to catch his next train. Hattie failed to see the big grin spread across his face.

Big gruff old Murphy, Hattie thought to herself, that man has done more for me than I can ever repay. I hope some day to make things right with him. He seemed to spend more time in Hagerstown now than he did before the war. He mentioned one time having family here. Maybe she could do something for his family and help him out for a change.

Sam and Mandy were running down the street toward her. She was immediately on alert. Sam had a piece of board in his hand and he was waving it at her like a sword. As they approached, they both slowed down to catch their breath.

Mandy said, "We were cleaning out the barn and decided to take out the hidey hole where we kept all the soldiers. Sam was ripping out the boards and he found this." She pointed to the board Sam was carrying.

Sam held it out to her. "There was another piece with more names on it, but I split it in two before I realized what it was. We thought you would like to have this one as a remembrance. I could varnish it up so the names wouldn't fade. We could put it in the examination room. You know like other doctors hang up their certificates? Seems to me you helpin' all these folks would be like proof you good at healin' and such."

He handed Hattie the board. On it was the following inscription. It was obvious that different hands held different writing instruments from knife points to lead pencils:

Ultimatum

To those poor souls who lay their head upon this pallet and owe life or limb to the Angel of Mercy, let it be known any man who betrays the neutrality of this bed shall suffer far worse at the hands of the undersigned.

G. A. Custer, Cpt, USA

B. C. Calhoun, Maj, CSA

G.R. Smedly, Sgt, 5th Maine, USA

A.J. Wallingard, Cpt, 3rd Georgia, CSA

H.C. Hastings, 2nd Mass, Arty, USA

Abe Graft, Pvt, 26th Ohio, USA

J.B. Ryder, Lt, 27th Louisiana, CSA

A.S. Mattingly, Pvt. 22nd New York, USA

Jesse Keith, Pvt, CCR, Louisiana, CSA

P.O. Stegal, Pvt. 3rd Alabama, CSA

F.J. Greene, Scout, 1st Vermont, USA

D. Ferree, Sgt, 6th Pennsylvania, USA

G.A. Arnold, Cpt, 3rd Virginia, CSA

W.A. Pottinger, Pvt, 14th Ohio, USA

J.B. Lortree, 5th Mississippi, CSA

W.J. Sackett, Cpt, 4th Tennessee, USA

L.J. DeRose, Cpl, 5th New Jersey, USA

G.A. Smith, Pvt, 6th Indiana, USA
W.H. Yingling, Cpl, Patomac Home Brigade, USA
J.R. Hadley, Pvt, 12th Georgia, CSA
J.K. Fry, Sgt, 14th Indiana, USA

Hattie looked at the names. Some she remembered. Others she didn't, but she remembered each suture, each broken bone, and the bullet-shattered tissue she repaired. Bloody bandages that she changed by lamplight. Infections fought, some won, some lost. Letters written to family left at home, from Maine to Louisiana. She knew that in some cases that letter represented the only contact made during the entire war. Yes, she would keep this dirty old board with its message of trust and support. Not just names scratched on a board, but men bonded by common pain and illness sending forth a message of protective solidarity transcending lofty ideals and enemy colors to support the more basic need for simple decency and survival.

She looked up at Sam and Mandy and gathered both of them in her arms holding on as tightly as she could. She said, "I never suspected this. Sometimes we can't spend the rewards for service in this life and then sometimes we are surprised by a bonus." She dropped her arms took a deep breath and sigh, and turned back to the windows. "Come on you two. Pick a window and let's get back to work. We need to earn enough to eat unless you want to try eating that board for breakfast."

They opened the store on Monday. At first sales were good. June had several orders for new dresses. Hattie collected partial payment to ensure a commitment from the buyer. She used the money to send an order to Baltimore for the necessary fabric, thread, and trim. Fortunately, the styles were such that most of the orders could be completed with a limited number of colors and types of material much of which was left over from the previous store. June had been successful in limiting her customer's tastes to simple styles in the beginning.

Then sales at the store began to taper off, and a strange thing began to happen. People began to deliver goods to the store in payment for medical services Hattie had supplied during the war.

The stories were similar. "Here is a hundred pounds of flour for helping my son when he had pneumonia last winter." Said one man as he pulled up to the loading dock. The next day customers appeared, ready to exchange their produce for different items in the store. All insisted that Hattie take a generous portion as payment for some service rendered by her over the past few years.

Items accumulated in sufficient quantity that Andy was able to negotiate for a railroad car loaded with produce to be delivered to the East Coast. Then Murphy walked in and wanted to know which warehouse Hattie wanted to use for the goods he had brought on the train. When she went to pay him Hattie discovered that much of the merchandise had been donated. Murphy explained that the Angel of Mercy story had spread across the eastern seaboard. When folks she had helped heard she intended to reopen her shipping business they sent "samples" to "test the market." Murphy brought bales of men's trousers and shirts. One Company in Fall River, Massachusetts sent three bales of men's red woolen long john's with a note attached. "Pete Nattick sends his best. His wounds have healed and he has returned to work in his father's factory." There were crates of hand tools from a company in Utica, New York—supposedly left over from production before shifting to gun barrels.

He handed her a large folder filled with manufacturing companies from New England to Charleston eager to reopen trade with the western markets. Then he handed her another one from St. Louis and Chicago filled with requests for different items needed on the frontier. Hattie looked at Murphy and said, "We need to talk about this. Who is responsible for all this merchandise and orders? Who is behind it?"

Murphy smiled and said, "People liked the idea of helping you for a change. Folks who sent sons into the war run a lot of the businesses listed here. They want to repay you in some way for your service."

"That's fine Murphy. But, I can't afford to rebuild a shipping business like Eli had before the war. That type of operation takes capital. There are cash flow problems that could send us into bankruptcy. Besides Eli is gone. I have no one that has the contacts or expertise to set up a network... Murphy? How would you like a new job?"

The words just seemed to pop out of Hattie's mouth of their own volition. Could she really make it work? Would Murphy go along? Did he have the ability to make it happen? Well what did they have to lose? She was starting from nothing now. If that's where they ended up, what's to lose? Why not give it a go?

Murphy's smile was her answer. He said, "I thought you would never ask. It would be a pleasure to throw in with you."

Hattie and Murphy visited with June and Andy that afternoon. They agreed that a new business arrangement was needed. Murphy would work on a commission basis for six months. If at the end of that time he had generated enough business they would see the lawyers in Baltimore and organize a new business with Hattie owning forty percent. Each of the other three would own twenty percent.

Mandy's chicken business made good money until she decided to go to school in the fall. She sold out to a local farmer for enough to pay for her tuition and expenses. Sam gave up his rent-a-mule idea because they needed the mules to haul loads from the warehouses to the store and for delivery and pickup of merchandise in and around Hagerstown. He began to take more interest in running the store and helping Hattie by coordinating distribution of products to the western markets.

June developed a thriving dress making business. Word reached Washington concerning the quality and style of her clothing. She finally had to open a shop in Washington to fill all the orders from the wives of government workers and politicians. She was especially pleased when the wife of the French Ambassador ordered a gown from her Washington store.

June set up a network of talented seamstresses working in their homes but following her patterns and fabric choices. She carefully hand picked each worker. She paid each one based on the quality and quantity of completed work, not for hours marked on a time card. She found talented sales ladies capable of running the store in Hagerstown and in Washington, D.C. The demand for new designs and high quality consumed all her time.

Hattie began to look for someone to help her. She was unable to locate anyone with the background in finance or business. Andy had never liked the distribution business. He preferred to just manage the store in town. Keeping the books for a rapidly growing organization continued to demand all her time. It never occurred to her to even wonder how two women, a young girl, an ex-slave barely old enough to be called a man, and an itinerant Irish immigrant could build a business empire out of the dust and blood of a terrible Civil War. But, they were making it happen in spite of the turmoil of reconstruction taking place around them.

Hattie learned of President Lincoln's assassination while sitting at her desk balancing the month's receipts against expenses and cash on hand. They were making financial progress, but it was still slow. She was deliberately keeping profit margins small by putting most of their profits into growing inventory. People were moving west. Eli had been right. With the end of the war came growing pressure to build railroads across the country. The gold rush to California called many to the West Coast even before the war. Now those people wanted the products necessary to build and develop a land rich in natural resources. Others held in check by the war now felt a need to build a new life on new land. With a tide of immigrants at their backs they pushed west.

Hattie's thoughts moved in two directions. She could stay here and develop a supply network to support this growing migration or she could move with it. Was her destiny tied to Hagerstown or would she follow the flow? She rebelled at the idea of being tied to anything or following anybody.

Hattie shook off the thought. She wanted to stay with June, Mandy, and Sam. Their home was here in Hagerstown. They were her family. Why sould she want to break free from them to jump into the unknown again? Sam and Mandy both needed more education.

Sam fixated on working with those mules, but what would happen if someone invented a small enough engine to put in a wagon? Driving mules could become a skill without a need. Many mule drivers would have to learn a new trade. It would be easier for Sam to learn a new trade if he had a good education as a foundation.

Mandy would be leaving for school soon. Even if she married Matt Tanner they would probably settle here eventually. June had an established business. She was building a name as one of the leading designers of women's fashions in America.

There was talk of a Constitutional Amendment that would give Sam the right to vote. They were about to turn the corner financially. It wouldn't be too many years and they would become a part of Maryland society. The emphasis on reconstruction might make Sam a candidate for congress or even the senate.

A noise down in the store interrupted her wool gathering. Walking quietly to the head of the stairs, she looked down on two men with drawn guns.

Who would hold up a store in broad daylight in downtown Hagerstown?

Hattie decided to take a direct approach. As she started down the stairs, she called out. "No need to get excited gentlemen, what is it you need? We are a little short on some items. Especially cash money in the register, we depend a lot on the barter system around here, but if you will let us help you, I am sure we can work something out before someone gets hurt." By this time she was on the main floor and walking toward the two gunmen.

The taller of the two had turned and backed up to cover her descent. He held his gun on her. "We came in here looking for the mercy lady. We got a friend outside of town. He's shot up pretty bad. Your boy here and the clerk at the counter don't wanna cooperate. They won't even give up any medicine"

Hattie continued to slowly approach the gunman. "That's correct. All the medicine I have is at the house or in my medical bag in the buggy out front. I am a healer, perhaps you have heard of me? I am known as the 'Angel of Mercy'. If you will put those guns away, I will go with you to see if I can..."

The storeroom door opened and Andy walked in with a sack of coffee beans completely unaware of what was happening. When he saw the man at the counter turn toward him with his gun raised, he threw the sack of coffee beans at him, and made a dive for the floor.

Sam scooped up a can of peaches and hit the gunman in the head as he tried to avoid the coffee beans. Then he ducked for cover expecting the other man near Hattie to start shooting. As he looked around from his position on the floor, he saw both gunmen on the floor unconscious. His target was bleeding from a scalp wound and the other man had seemingly collided with a keg of nails.

Hattie kicked his gun toward Sam and said, "Cover them Sam. I'm going to get my medical kit out of the buggy. Andy, you run get the Marshall."

As she moved toward the door, a third man entered the store gun in hand. As he moved to cover Sam and Andy, Hattie stepped up beside him and grabbed his gun arm. He let go like it was a hot poker. As he moved to jerk his arm loose, he suddenly found himself on his knees looking at the gun in Sam's fist. Hattie was the first to speak. "If you gentlemen will be so kind as to lay quiet until the Marshall gets here we will straighten this all out."

The kneeling man whined, "All we want is something to fix up our partner. He's laid up in the woods outside of town and needs help. He's bleedin' real bad. At least he was when we left him. We heard about the mercy woman and came to fetch her."

Hattie leaned over and looking him in the eye growled, "Well you found her. However, most people have the courtesy to ask for help not run around pointing guns at helpless citizens."

"Look lady if you're helpless, I'm a monkey's uncle!"

Sam moved to where he could cover all three. He smiled at the man. "Hee, hee, y'all bit off a chaw biggern' y'all can handle. Now if'n I was you, I'd do as the lady says, else she fix you good, one way or t'other.

Just then, Andy arrived with the Marshall. Hattie stood up and said, "Marshall, I need to go and check on the one out of town. This fellow here says he's bleeding, and seems to know where he is. Why don't you get him in my buggy, and we will go find the other one. With the Marshall holding him at gunpoint the third man got in the back of the buggy and the three of them set off. By the time they found the man, he was dead from a gunshot wound to the stomach. Hattie later found out that the four men were wanted for a bank robbery in Waynesboro.

Word started to get around that robbing Hattie's store was probably a bad idea. Hattie viewed the news as good and bad. Fewer robberies would be good, but some of the more timid customers might not do business with them. She was surprised when June reported later that her business picked up as many women curious to find out what happened made appointments for dress fittings. It seemed that more females than expected felt that women could be as vicious as men.

Hattie was working the counter while Andy and Sam helped Murphy unload a boxcar of merchandise. A couple entered the store looking for Sam.

"My name is George Ruffin and this is my wife Josephine. I am looking for Sam Wiggins. I was told he worked here."

"That's correct," Hattie answered. "He isn't here right now, but I can get him for you. What is the nature of your business?"

"Sam served in the war in a regiment I formed. We are on our way to Washington, D.C. and thought we would stop by for a visit. I was impressed with his knowledge and education. I am looking for fellows of our race to help us build support for the Fifteenth Amendment giving us the right to vote."

Hattie's interest perked up. "Isn't that amendment supposed to give women the right to vote also?"

Josephine Ruffin chimed in. "Why yes it is. Are you interested in supporting women's suffrage?"

At Hattie's nod Josephine continued, "We are planning a convention in Boston in November why don't you join us there. We will be organizing the American Women's Suffrage Association at the convention. Are you the lady they call the Angel of Mercy?"

Hattie nodded.

"I will be working with Lucy Stone and Elizabeth Cady Stanton. Our goal will be to promote the right for women to vote as a part of the Fifteenth Amendment."

Hattie wanted to talk more, but Sam entered the store, and she decided to wait for a better time. Sam obviously knew Mr. Ruffin. The Ruffins pulled Sam away from her and out the door anxious to renew their friendship. Customers wanting service occupied her attention, and she was unable to follow the remainder of their conversation. She still wanted to find out more information about the convention that Mrs. Ruffin had mentioned. It was several months away. Maybe she would be able to attend.

Chapter 20

Hattie's Journal

16 March 1869: General Grant is now President. I went to the Ball.

Mandy decided Oberlin College was too far away from Matt. She applied and passed the admissions examination at The University of Maryland in Baltimore. June and Hattie were happy for her since it was close enough for her to visit them on a regular basis. Mandy was happy since she would be able to see Matt. He had graduated from the Naval Academy and was stationed at the Washington Naval Yard. Matt was anxious for a seagoing assignment, but with peace declared, he would have to wait a while. There was talk of reducing the size of the Navy. Hattie and June laughed together over the idea that he might have to find a real job. Hattie reminded June that there were a lot of commercial vessels looking for qualified officers. Leaving the Navy might not be the end of his seagoing career.

Sam received a letter from George Ruffin with an invitation to join him on a tour promoting the Fifteenth Amendment. Hattie encouraged him to accept. She felt it would be good exposure for him. He would be required to act and speak as a proper gentleman. She felt more confident in his ability than he did. With June and Murphy helping, Hattie outfitted Sam with a "front" or new wardrobe. He looked so mature and confident when he boarded the train for Washington that Hattie knew her job of raising a man from a "boy" was a success. A cold blade seemed to pass through her at the thought that he might not return. Were her tears those of pride or pending loneliness?

As she turned to make the long lonely walk back to the house, Murphy appeared at her side. He had come in on the Western Express and the excitement in his walk and face drew her attention.

"We need to go to Abeline, Kansas. The railroad has pushed that far and Texas cattlemen are expected to bring herds of cattle to the railhead. If we can get there first and hire us the right man to buy for us, we can make a fortune bringing that beef to the eastern markets. I need you to help me in this. Hiring the right man for the job can make all the difference. We may have to agree to a contract with bonuses and incentives that I don't know anything about. Also with you along we will have a majority ownership position and won't need to wait for approval. That delay could be crucial in our hiring the right man for the job."

Hattie looked at him and thought of all the other projects she had going. *Could Andy take over the bookkeeping while she was gone?*

"We better go talk to June and Andy right away it sounds like any delay could eliminate us from the competition."

They both moved quickly to the store to confer with the other two owners. All agreed that time was of the essence and that Murphy should leave on the morning train. Hattie would have two days to clear her desk and brief Andy on things that might come up. Then she would leave on the next westbound train.

Hattie felt challenged and invigorated. The trip would give her an opportunity to see some new country and dust off her negotiating and people reading skills. She wasn't as concerned about making money as she was in providing opportunities for others to receive a reward for their labor. She would also be able to view first hand the Wild West that was being talked about everywhere she went. Maybe it would help settle her mind about moving there herself.

When Hattie boarded the train, she was surprised to see a large number of women on board. As she settled in her seat, the lady next to her asked, "Are you with the movement?"

Hattie wasn't sure how to answer, so she asked, "I'm sorry but I am not certain I understand the question. To what movement are you referring?"

"We are all going to Topeka to march for Women's Suffrage. There will be an election and it includes giving women the right to vote. There will be speeches by leaders of our movement and marches. We plan to go door to door and cover the entire city of Topeka."

Hattie listened intently to her as she thought about the opportunity to listen to some of the speeches and learn more about the movement. She felt a strong desire to participate, but she would have to see how her participation might affect her business in Abilene.

"When is the election?"

"They say it will happen in early April."

"I may be able to get back to Topeka in time. I will have to check with my business associate. He is in Abilene now on business."

They had considerable time to discuss the movement over the next few days as the train made its way west. Hattie met many of the leaders. Some of them knew Josephine Ruffin. They were uncertain if she would be there or not. Some of the women she met expressed concern over combining the women's right to vote issue with the rights of the former slaves. Feelings in Kansas still ran high even though the war was over.

Hattie waved goodbye to her new friends and continued on to Abilene. The crowd of people on the train changed. She noticed more laborers on their way to the end of the tracks looking to find work. Businessmen, farmers, and ranchers helped to fill the car. All had a gleam in their eye. Some were there to take what they could get from the land and then move on. Others had a look of permanence to them indicating that they were builders preparing the way for the flood that would soon fill the whole land.

She had a thought. *What would happen when they ran out of space and started to wash back filling the country. Would people still have a desire to build a better life or would they stagnate in a tide pool of humanity unable to find a way to rise up to the surface and climb out of complacency? Had she grown complacent with time and easy living? Could she rise up again or would she find some excuse to fall into the muddy backwash of life?*

One of the gentlemen with a gleam in his eye managed to maneuver himself into the seat next to her. He introduced himself as Roger Winston from Croyden, a place near London. He opened the conversation by asking, "Are you English by any chance?"

"Why yes, I am." Hattie replied giving him a small polite smile. She hesitated to give him too much information before finding out more about him, but it felt good to hear a British accent again. He, on the other hand, seemed to want to tell her his whole life's history.

She soon discovered that Roger was a graduate mining engineer heading west to make his fortune in the mineral rich land of California. When he discovered that Hattie would be leaving the train in Abilene his ardor waned. It seemed that his intention had been to establish a longer lasting and more amorous relationship to the end of the tracks and possibly all the way to California.

Hattie breathed a quiet sigh of relief when the conductor announced. "Abilene in ten minutes."

Murphy was at the train station with another man. Hattie realized that she was the lone woman leaving the train. She was surprised and grateful for the consideration shown to her. All the men were polite and helpful even though only minutes before they had been pushing and shoving each other in order to be the first off the train. Would such deference last when women received equal rights?

As Murphy approached he said, "Hattie let me introduce you to Joe McCoy. He is the one who built the stockyards and put Abilene on the map. Joe this is Mrs. Helen Wiggins but we all call her Hattie."

Joseph McCoy was a man of medium height with prominent cheekbones and eyebrows as black as Hattie's. His eyebrows curved around his eyes like two caterpillars perched on walnuts while hers curved up and out. His neatly trimmed beard and moustache hid a firm mouth showing more resolve than good spirits. Hattie liked his serious manner. She felt he would stand behind his word. She reached out her hand and said, "I'm pleased to meet you Mr. McCoy. I understand that you built this town almost by yourself?"

McCoy gave a small smile and replied, "That was true at the start, but folks have been coming in lately to give me a hand. Why we must have close to a hundred citizens by now. It's still too early in the season to expect any trail herds, but I predict that by summer, this town will be booming. Why don't we go over to my hotel? I have set aside a nice room for you on the second floor overlooking the street. We will give you a chance to clean off the travel dust and then have dinner at my place. Have you ever eaten food cooked the Mexican way?"

Hattie shook her head.

"Then you will be in for a special treat. I have this cook that will tingle your taste buds just before they catch on fire."

Hattie took a short nap in her room. She had agreed to meet with Murphy and Mr. McCoy at six o'clock in the hotel lobby. She awoke in plenty of time to prepare. Taking liberal advantage of the pitcher of water in her room and the basin placed on the dresser she was able to rid herself of most of the dirt and grime picked up on the train. Deciding to change dresses she took her traveling dress and shook it to get the dust and dirt off. Then she brushed it and hung it in the closet in her room.

She debated about wearing her harness.

The harness, as she called it, was a gift from June. It contained a number of narrow pockets sewn to a belt of cloth that fit over her ribs like a second skin. It could be worn inside or outside her corset using the small flat buttons and buttonholes June had placed there. She had several. The one she liked best was made from a silk fabric making it comfortable to wear next to her skin. The pockets held a special set of surgical instruments Josiah Wilkins had purchased years earlier from a German company as a Christmas present for her. In retrospect, she figured he probably purchased them with her money. In addition to the surgical instruments, it held a flat compact sewing packet.

June had used some of her first profits to assemble portable sewing kits for all her workers. The kit, about the size of a man's leather wallet, contained pins, needles, thread, a few buttons and some of the new, recently invented safety pins. Hattie's kit was modified to hold surgical thread and sutures.

The final item in Hattie's harness was a special knife. It operated much like a man's straight razor except it had a double-edged point. A brass knob on the side locked the knife to the handle, which could only be released by pressing on a spring-loaded catch. The knife had arrived in the mail shortly after the war ended with no return address just a note saying, "Thank you for saving my life." She wore it in its special sheath-pocket just behind her left breast. All of her dresses designed by June contained a slit flap in the fabric under her left arm giving her access to the knife while dressed. She had never been forced to use it but Kim had taught her what to do should an emergency arise. She remembered all the rough looking men that had been on the train and decided to wear her harness.

Dinner that evening was indeed a fiery experience, but one she enjoyed. Mr. McCoy turned out to be a great storyteller. He regaled them with his adventures before settling in Abilene. Murphy had previously discussed the purpose of their visit so after the meal as the men lit up their cigars they began discussing possible candidates to fill the cattle buyer position. As it turned out, McCoy had no one in mind at the moment. Hattie figured that he was either trying to corner the market himself or his standards were difficult to meet. She stifled a yawn and excused herself deciding to walk back to her hotel before it became too dark. Her real reason was to get away from the cigar smoke and retire early.

After politely refusing an escort back to the hotel, she left to walk the two blocks alone. Her route led her past the livery stable. She decided to inquire about the availability of a horse and buggy. She thought it would be a pleasant diversion to ride out and see some of the country the next day while she waited for Mr. McCoy to locate the right man for them.

Entering the livery stable, she called out, "Is anybody here? I wish to inquire about renting a rig for tomorrow."

"No one here but us chickens," came a voice from the hayloft. Soon a set of scuffed, trail worn boots followed by jean-encased legs began to descend the ladder at the side of the stable. "The hostler has gone home for the night. I can let him know in the morning you want to rent a rig. I'm sure he can oblige you. What time would you be wanting to leave...Miss?"

"The name is Wiggins, Mrs. Helen Wiggins. I would like to leave at eight o'clock in order to see some of the surrounding country before it gets too warm. I plan to return the rig about noon...Mr.?

"The name's Jaimison Miles ma'am. Most folks call me Jim. I was wondering if you would need the services of a guide. I been riding over this country for a few years now and I could probably show you the interesting parts. Although one prairie dog hole looks pretty much like the next." He said, through a disarming grin.

"I thank you for your kind offer Mr. Miles. I may have misled you. I really am not too concerned about what sights I see. My objective is simply a diversion while I wait for my associates to complete their business."

"Is Mr. Wiggins with you?"

"No, unfortunately Mr. Wiggins died the day before Lee surrendered to Grant at Appomattox."

"Would that be Eli Wiggins? Why I drove a herd of horses from North Texas to the Mississippi River above Vicksburg and sold them to him. He was one sharp trader, knew his animals real well he did." Miles thought to himself, *Eli knew his women real well too. This is one beautiful and smart woman. I wonder how an old codger like Eli ever managed to lash her into double harness?*

"You sound like you know animals yourself?" Hattie inquired, looking him over again but still seeing only a down at heel cowboy with hay still stuck in his hair.

"Ma'am I've been buying and selling animals all my life. My Ma was kin to a bunch of Irish horse traders. We roamed all over making our living trading animals, usually horses and mules. In fact I sold Eli a set of the best mules that ever pulled in harness together."

Hattie smiled and said, "They are still pulling in harness together whenever I can get them away from my...kids. They pulled me through the war. I have probably counted every hair on the backside of those same mules. Right now we are using them to haul loads to and from our store in Hagerstown."

"So Mrs. Wiggins who are these business associates you keep referring to?"

"Mr. Dan Murphy is my business partner and we are here discussing business with Mr. McCoy. Do you happen to know them?"

Jim Miles got a little grim around the mouth as he said. "Now that's a pair to draw to."

"I guess that's an expression with which I am not totally familiar. What does it mean?"

"It's used to describe two of a kind or two similar personalities. It comes from the game of poker where a player has a pair of like cards such as two kings or two of the same number. A player uses them to build a hand by drawing cards to match the pair. Thus the term, 'A pair to draw to.'"

"You seem quite familiar with this game called poker?"

"Yes ma'am, that game is the reason I am sleeping in this hayloft instead of in the hotel with y...Excuse me please ma'am I didn't mean I would be sleeping with you. I meant in another room nearby." Jim stuttered and stammered his ears truning red while he tried to get out of his embarrassing situation.

"Well, Mr. Miles, I don't wish to take up any more of your time, so I will be on my way to *my* hotel room for the evening. Thank you for the pleasant conversation. Perhaps we shall meet again before I leave town."

Hattie's drive outside of town was as boring as Jim Miles said it would be. One prairie dog hole did indeed look just like the others. She cut her drive short and met Murphy for lunch. He indicated that the right man had yet to be found. She said nothing about meeting Miles.

After lunch, she took a book and found a comfortable chair in the hotel lobby. She became interested in the game of cards being played at a table nearby. She deduced that the game was poker. At least it was similar in nature to the game Mr. Miles had described the previous evening. She continued to watch the game over the top of her book. She noticed several things about the game. First, a lot of colored chips passed from player to player as different gentlemen were successful at winning the "pot."

Soon she noticed that the game involved a certain amount of lying and cheating. All the players from time to time would do the former and two individuals working together seemed involved in the latter. They also seemed to be winning more than their fair share of pots and thus were accumulating most of the chips used in the game. It wasn't until one of the other players ran out of chips and actually paid money to another player that she realized that the game had real life consequences. She began to understand how Mr. Miles could end up sleeping in the hayloft without any money. *He must not be a very good player,* she thought to herself.

Because of boredom or curiosity Hattie continued watching the game, her book forgotten. She was surprised when she realized it was time for the evening meal. She opted to eat in the hotel dining room before receiving another invitation to eat with Mr. McCoy. She didn't think she was ready to eat such spicy food two nights in a row.

After eating she asked the waiter if he could find her a deck of playing cards like the ones being used by the gentlemen in the lobby. He brought her a new deck indicating that they were a courtesy from the hotel. Apparently Mr. McCoy wanted her to have anything she desired.

She practiced shuffling and dealing the cards in her room. She then began dealing random hands, counting the cards, and suits in the deck. Working the mathematics in her head, she began to gain an appreciation for the probabilities associated with the various winning hands she had observed the night before. She realized that this was a game easily learned but difficult to master. One could play the probabilities or hope for a lucky break. One could also cheat as she had observed the two men doing the night before.

She had learned that the lying she observed was called bluffing. A good bluff in poker was similar to tactics many used in business. She could see how playing poker would be an excellent way to practice her observation skills. It was always good to know when someone was lying to you or was about to back out of a contract. Succumbing to the temptation to "bluff" however would quickly result in lowering one's moral standards.

While Murphy and McCoy continued their search, Hattie continued to watch the poker game. Later, at lunch the next day, she was surprised to see a different Mr. Miles approach her table. This one was clean, shaven, and dressed in a black suit with polished boots. At her look of surprise, he explained that his uncle had wired him funds and he was about ready to leave on the train heading east for Kansas City where a possible business opportunity awaited. He asked if he could join her for lunch. At her nod, he seated himself across from her.

As they finished eating gunfire erupted in the lobby! People were turning over tables and trying to get out through the kitchen. Miles tried to pull Hattie under the table but true to her nature, she ran toward the gunfire to see if she could help.

As she entered the lobby, she could see one of the gamblers that had been cheating the night before standing behind the table with a smoking gun in his hand. He was saying, "The man pulled a gun on me and accused me of cheating! It was a fair fight. Look you can see his gun there on the floor."

Hattie moved to the man on the floor and checked his pulse. She was just in time to catch one beat before it stopped. The man was dead.

She looked up at the crooked card player. "I don't think you will need to worry about him accusing you of cheating any more this man is dead." She got to her feet and asked, "Isn't anyone going to call the Marshall or Sheriff or whatever passes for law enforcement around here?"

Someone in the crowd answered her, "It was a fair shooting ma'am. The man pulled a gun and this fella just defended himself. No reason to call the law, besides we ain't got no law around here anyways."

Hattie stood with her hands on her hips. "Well, the least you could do is take him somewhere and notify his people so they could see him properly buried!" Shamed by the fiery look blazing from her eyes some of the men helped a shamefaced Jim Miles carry the corpse to the livery stable where they could lay him out. Hattie thought she heard someone say that he had no people and would probably stay in the stable until McCoy buried him— or paid someone to do it for him.

Hattie walked around town for a while after the shooting. She needed to calm her nerves. She realized that almost every man she met was carrying a gun in a holster on his hip. She began to realize that her guardian training was of little use against a gun. Her moves were mainly defensive and she needed to be close to her assailant.

She decided if she were to move West on a permanent basis she must learn to shoot or depend on others for protection. She located Murphy down at the train station. She told him about her encounter at the gunfight and also about meeting Jim Miles. Murphy agreed to locate Miles and discuss the possibility of hiring him as their buyer. He indicated to Hattie that he didn't hold out much hope of hiring him since the Irish traders were an independent bunch that liked to travel around a lot.

Hattie returned to the hotel. She had just sat down with her book when Murphy and Miles walked in. Jim Miles had agreed to a six-month contract as their representative in Abilene.

That would get them through this season. He also agreed to locate a buyer to take his place should he desire to leave after the six months. He wanted a minimum wage of one hundred dollars a month for the six months in advance. Hattie and Murphy agreed provided the money was an advance against the ten percent he would receive for any cattle purchased by him and sold in the eastern markets. They discussed contract details and established a line of credit on their Kansas City Bank. Hattie was surprised that the men simply shook hands on the deal. Another western way of doing business that was unfamiliar to her.

They were too late to catch the east bound train, so they purchased tickets for a train leaving in two days. The men went up the street to seal the deal with a drink at the saloon. Hattie settled down in her chair to watch the poker game. As she watched, she practiced the observation skills Kim had taught her. She had figured out the rather sloppy technique used by the two gamblers to cheat the others. She was also able to read the player's movements and predict when they had good hands and when they were bluffing. One of the gamblers approached her and invited her to play in the game. She declined, thinking to herself that she wasn't ready to get shot at this point in her life.

Later that evening, Jim Miles showed up and sat in the game for a while. Hattie studied his style and quickly noted the manner in which he would tell his opponents what he was doing. She got up from her chair and motioned for him to join her in the café for a moment.

When they were settled, Hattie ordered tea and Jim had coffee. After they were served she said, "Jim I don't want to interfere but those two crooks in there are going to end up with your advance, and you will not be any good to me. I want you to stop playing. If you won't stop then you need to watch me and only play the hands I signal are good. I also notice you doing certain things that tell the other players when you have a good hand and when you are bluffing. You need to change or they will clean you out!"

"I'm sorry Hattie. I was hoping my luck would change and I could win back the money those two won from me the other night."

"Luck has nothing to do with it! Those two are cheating! The man that was killed this afternoon was correct when he accused them of it. That's the other reason I want you out of the game. I spent a lot of time and money coming out here. I didn't do it for the fresh air. If you really want to fix these men go find someone good with a gun. They can protect us after you get us both in this game. I will expose them as the cheats they are."

"Do you really think you can do it? I can find just the men for the job. I am sure everyone would be grateful to catch these two red-handed." Hattie just smiled and nodded. Jim left to find his friends.

When Jim returned, Hattie had settled back in her chair and was reading her book. She looked up to see two men with Jim. One was an older man dressed all in buckskins with a weathered roadmap for a face. Hattie sized him up with concern showing on her face. He looked more able to bounce grandkids on his knee than shoot a gun. He took a seat in the lobby where he could cover the poker players with a clear line of fire. The other man was younger. He looked a little familiar to Hattie, but she couldn't place him at first. Then she made the connection. He resembled one of the wounded soldiers she had helped during the war. Maybe he was a brother or cousin. He looked like he had been born smelling gunsmoke with those cold gray eyes and black untrimmed beard. Unfortunately this was not the time or place to discuss "do you know so and so?" Seeing him gave her a sense of confidence that all would be well.

Within two hours after they started playing Hattie had the crooks sweating. She was not aware of the western code about protecting women. She would have been safe from these two even if there were no guns at their backs. The other players had stopped but were hanging around. Only Hattie, Jim, and the two crooks were playing in the game. Hattie knew how much Jim had lost and when his pile of chips reached that level she began to apply pressure with every hand. Soon the crooks knew they were in trouble. One made a sloppy move to cheat and everyone in the room saw it.

Hattie pushed her chair away from the table and stood up with her hands far apart. "Gentlemen, you can see that I have no gun, but I am calling you both cheats. That last sloppy attempt to build a good hand on the bottom of the deck, was so obvious that everyone here saw it. Here are your choices. You may draw a gun on an unarmed woman and face certain death from the guns behind me. Or you will be stripped to your long johns in the morning, loaded in a wagon, driven south into Comanche Territory, and left to fend for yourself. Which shall it be?"

After a long pause and a careful look around the one who killed the man earlier said, "We'll take our chances with the Comanche in the morning." Then with his hands in plain sight he got up and slowly walked toward his room in the hotel.

Hattie turned and walked up the stairs to her room. She was barely able to get ready for bed her fingers shook so much. What was she thinking? Those men could easily kill her while she was sleeping! She decided to sleep with her harness on under her nightshift.

Hattie arose well before dawn the next morning and decided to go through her exercise routines before she was due downstairs. She had just finished dressing in her exercise suit when her door crashed open! The two crooks rushed inside. One held a gun on her while the other twisted her arms behind her back and pushed her through the door.

"Now we will see who takes a ride in Comanche Territory. Do as I say and you might live a little longer."

The three of them moved as one to the back stairs where Hattie saw a man slumped over in the corner bleeding from a head wound. *He must have been their guard,* she thought. She decided to wait for an opening where she had more room to maneuver.

The stairs led down to an alley that ran behind the hotel. The man behind her began to push her down the alley toward three horses tied to a post at the corner of the hotel. Hattie decided she'd had enough. She grabbed the man's hand, and with a twisting motion drove him into his partner. They bounced apart like balls on a pool table.

The two rushed at Hattie from opposite sides. Hattie caught one by the wrist and threw him into the other. The collision sent both men rolling in the alley. One came up and tried to tackle her. She grabbed the back of his head and smashed it into her rising knee. She turned in time to send the other flying through the air and into the side of the hotel. As he made a feeble effort to get up, She flipped his companion on top of him. Both came up spitting blood and charged together. Hattie let them close in. She smacked one on the nose with the heel of her hand and using him for leverage, kicked the other one in the knee sending him down writhing in pain. The one with the broken nose took one last swing at her. She dislocated his shoulder and drove him head first into his companion. She took away their guns and loaded the two unconscious crooks on their horses and mounting the third horse led them to an empty boxcar she found on a siding and managed to dump them inside.

After turning the horses loose, Hattie washed the blood from her shirt-sleeves in a nearby water trough, turned, and calmly climbed the steps into the hotel. She kept her pace slow and sedate until she was in her room where she broke down gasping for breath. She had never tried to counter two people at one time before. She knew she had been lucky. The men were overconfident and unprepared for her style of fighting. She hoped that she would never have to do that again!

She never saw the man with the cold gray eyes looking out of the livery stable hayloft. He chuckled to himself and uncocked the Winchester he had been holding on the two crooks during the fight. He settled back down in the hay and turned to his companion. "Now that's a woman to ride the river with. I suppose we better go on down to that there rail car later on, and read out of the good book to those two gents." The old man next to him just continued to snore softly his hand lightly resting on the pistol nestled underneath him.

She kept out of sight as much as possible that day as she waited for the train heading east. Several people approached her asking what had happened to the two men. She gave them a blank stare, shrugged, and shook her head.

The consensus was that they had simply rode away unwilling to face the Comanches. One man remarked that they would be better off if the

Comanches had killed them. They would never play another hand of poker west of the Mississippi.

As the train passed through Topeka, Hattie bought a paper and discovered that the vote for women's suffrage had failed. *I suppose the time is not yet right for women to take on a man's responsibilities,* she thought with a sense of wry sarcasm.

Jim Miles proved to be as good a trader and businessman as he claimed. The cattle shipping business boomed. Demand was high and the prices were good. Hattie was pleased that the ranchers had found a market, and she felt good about supplying needed beef to the people on the East Coast. Their business expanded and they talked about moving to one of the larger cities but no one really wanted to leave Hagerstown.

Shortly after Christmas that year, Hattie found a letter waiting for her at work. It was an invitation to attend President Grant's Inauguration Ball in Washington. June, as excited as Hattie, worked for weeks to finish a gown for her. Inauguration Week finally arrived. They went to Washington together since June had business to discuss with her shop manager.

At the ball, President Grant singled her out for a waltz. As they danced, he thanked her profusely for Eli's service to him and to the country. He wished there was some way he could publicly proclaim the great service Eli had performed in helping him preserve the nation. He mentioned that Allan Pinkerton was a close personal friend and if he could ever do anything for her, she was to contact him through Pinkerton. A routine message was sure to get lost in the maze of bureaucracy already insulating him from those he trusted. He wished Eli were here to help him through the confusion and infighting already building around him.

On the trip home, Hattie noticed that June was extremely quiet and pensive, even for her. She turned to her and asked, "June, is something wrong? Have you received some bad news about Mandy?"

June shook her head. She looked at Hattie with tears in her eyes. "Mandy's fine, in fact, she just joined the Church. I'm leaving. I just sold my business here in Washington to Myra. I have enough money to take the new train route west to Great Salt Lake City and join up with those I left behind many years ago."

"But June, what about Mandy? What about our business in Hagerstown?"

"I sold out my share to Murphy and Andy. I knew you would make a fuss so I took the easy way out. I hope you understand. I placed the down payment in a trust fund for Mandy. She can draw money when she needs it for school. Murphy and Andy will continue to make payments to the fund for the next five years to cover her living expenses. I'm sorry I didn't let you know sooner. I knew you would try to talk me out of it, and I didn't want to argue with you. That would just breed conflict between us and create hard feelings. I love you like a sister. I wish you were my sister. Please understand that I am not leaving you or Mandy. I am just moving on with my life in the only way I know that will bring me eternal peace."

Chapter 21

Hattie's Journal

5 May 1870: *I start a new life. I feel like a new person!*

attie helped June pack and select the items she would need to open her own store in Great Salt Lake City. It turned into a special time for both of them. It wasn't quick and it wasn't easy. Every little item had some memory attached. June obviously could only take a few of the things with her. They both began to realize that the things were not the important part—only the memories they represented. In order to keep their emotions in check, they got down to the business of business. Unfortunately, the day for parting came much too soon. Hattie knew that with the railroad making trips across country and running close to Great Salt Lake they would be able to visit and to communicate on a regular basis. This helped to make the parting seem like a vacation or business trip. As long as Hattie could keep this idea in mind, she would manage to get through the ordeal—a day at a time.

Sam's letters and visits arrived at longer intervals as he moved on with his life. To use his new way of talking he began feeling "large and in charge." Hattie still hoped he would come back, take over the store, and help her. But, she began to realize it would never happen. Events were pumping his ego right now, and that was one thing he didn't need.

She prayed for a delay before the day she felt would surely come. The power pendulum could soon swing in the other direction and white men with influence, education, and power could again control government and business in the South.

The struggle for total equality would continue for Sam's race and for women, but for now there were too many voters comfortable with their own lives, unwilling to create any lasting changes. Education would help but without motivation it might not prove effective. Generations would need to grow up, slowly adapting, and accepting the idea of total equality. She doubted that she would see a total transformation in her lifetime.

With June and Sam gone, Hattie began to spend more time at the store. Andy was good at his job, but he couldn't be there all the time. Today, she sent him to help out in the warehouse. They needed more help, but both Hattie and Andy were cautious about hiring any one. The shelves needed stocking. The goods in the warehouse were not organized in a manner that allowed for quick and easy access or rapid distribution. They needed some type of mechanical conveyor to move and distribute loads to assigned locations. She sat writing a want ad for the local paper when two young men entered the store.

"May I help you gentlemen find what you are looking for?"

The shorter of the two said, "We are traveling across country without funds and need to find work for a few days. Do you know any place where we might help someone and find a place to stay?"

Hattie slid her draft advertisement across the counter. "Will you read this for me please? I would like your opinion."

The taller of the two picked up the paper and began to read. A smile blossomed on his face. "This sounds like you need a little extra help around here. How does one go about applying?"

"I guess, besides being able to read, you need to lift heavy loads, drive a mule team, and take directions from a woman. Do you have any problems with those qualifications?"

"No ma'am. We both grew up on farms. Our parents taught us how to work."

"Report here tomorrow morning. Ask for Andy. He will be back by then and he will assign your work for the day. We will take it a day at a time. You will receive your pay of one dollar a day as long as there is work and you are willing to do it."

The taller one asked, "Do you know of a place around here that might have a room where we can stay?"

"No, not off hand. Why don't you look around and see what you can find. If nothing turns up before six o'clock, be here and I will take you to my place. I have a hayloft that has harbored some pretty important people in the past. You can sleep there until something better turns up."

Both men uttered a polite thank you, turned, and walked out. Hattie wondered if they would show up that evening, the next morning, or not at all. She sighed, and decided to run the advertisement in the paper anyway. While these young men appeared trustworthy they did not seem to be looking for permanent positions.

When Hattie closed the store at six, the two men were standing in the shade of the oak tree at the end of the block. She smiled and waved to them indicating they should follow her home. She went around to the back of the house and opened the barn doors. Blaze and the mules were in the pasture but Mike was there to welcome her home. She let Mike get a good sniff at her guests so that he would know they were not strangers. The next time they entered the barn she might not be with them.

She pointed at the hen house. "Why don't you fellows go gather the eggs and come to the kitchen door. I will need a minute to straighten up and see what I can find for supper."

Hattie opened the door a few minutes later and ushered her guests into her kitchen. "I think some introductions might be in order. My name is Helen Wiggins. I run the store you stopped at earlier. Since you showed up this evening, you must have been unsuccessful in finding any other lodging. My barn is open as long as you need it. I will serve breakfast and supper each day. If you want lunch, you need to make do on your own. Now, you are..."

The taller man spoke. "I am Elder Groves and this is my companion Elder Jones..."

Hattie interrupted, "Strange, you both have Elder as a first name..." Then she laughed. "Did June Coulson send you here? The only men named Elder that I know of are Mormon Missionaries. The only way you could be here is if June sent you."

Elder Jones said, "I'm sorry but we don't know any June Coulson. Is she a friend? She may have sent us but the message came from the Holy Spirit not from her directly."

Elder Groves added. "We happened to run out of money and train ticket at the same time. We must not be the first members of The Church of Jesus Christ of Latter-day Saints you have known?"

"That's correct. I have a very special friend that just recently left for Great Salt Lake City. She lived here with me for almost ten years. She is a member of your church. We had many discussions about Jesus Christ and The Book of Mormon. In fact I have a copy, and I read from it almost every night. I almost feel like I am a member of your church."

Elder Jones said, "It's not our church it is The Church of Jesus Christ. It is His true church restored to the earth at this time by a prophet of God."

"You are beginning to grasp my problem. I have these mixed-up ideas and partial understandings. I have read The Book of Mormon and have prayed for an answer. I don't know if I have received an answer or not. It all sounds so logical and complete, but I know my faith is less than June's. She just seems to glow when she reads or talks about the Gospel of Jesus Christ. How do I find that glow?"

"Maybe we can help," quipped Elder Groves giving Elder Jones a nudge and a knowing look.

Hattie set about cracking eggs into a bowl and slicing bread. She soon had scrambled eggs and toast with fresh butter and jam for supper.

"I apologize for the meal. I am afraid I am not much of a cook. June did most of our cooking. Now that I am alone, it just doesn't seem worth the effort to prepare a meal. I have been debating with myself about hiring someone to cook and keep house for me."

Elder Jones asked, "Why are you so busy? What is it you do? It seems to me if you own the store you could hire a clerk and spend more time at home."

"You're right of course. But, the store is not all of my business. In fact, you observed an unusual day. My partner Andy Dawson had to help out in the warehouse. I normally spend my time juggling our shipping schedules and accounting for our finances. We ship goods east that are raised out west and we ship manufactured products west that are made in the east or overseas. You will get a taste of what I do tomorrow when you start moving things in the warehouse. Well gentlemen, our simple supper is ready if you would care to join me."

Elder Groves asked if he could offer a prayer. After the prayer they ate and all retired for the evening. Hattie sat in her reconverted parlor for a long time. She opened her Book of Mormon and read several passages. They all seemed to mention the need to be baptized.

She wondered if it was necessary for her to repeat that ordinance? June had mentioned that the authority to act in God's name had been lost over time. She called it the Apostasy and said that the New Testament was full of references concerning it. Maybe these Elders could help her find an answer.

The next morning Hattie sent the Elders off with a hot breakfast. She caught and prepared one of Mandy's stewing hens and placed it in the oven. She hoped it would cook by suppertime. She reached the store late due to the additional chores. Andy waved to her, but she continued up the stairs to her office. She was soon immersed in shipping schedules and accounts. Andy knocked and entered her office just before noon. He had a worried expression on his face. He said, "Did you realize the two men you hired were Mormons?"

"Yes, is something wrong with that?" she asked, her eyebrows sharpening and rising more than normal.

"If word gets around that we have 'Mormons' working here it might harm our business! Lots of folks think they are Devils!"

Hattie looked at him in astonishment. "Why Andy Dawson are you a bigot? What do you think they will do? Curse the food or something? It seems to me that the Constitution of the United States of America allows for freedom of religion. These poor men are giving up time with their families and friends. They have interrupted their own livelihood just to teach people what they believe. They aren't forcing anyone to join their church."

"Well, they can worship as they please, but I feel funny associating with them. And it could be bad for business! I think we should send them on their way."

"Andy do you remember coming to my home with your hat in your hand asking for a job a couple of years ago?"

"Of course I do. If it wasn't for you and June helping me get started here I don't know how we would have survived."

"You did the books for the first six months we were in partnership didn't you?"

"Of course I do. You were busy setting up the warehouse and distribution system with Murphy and Sam. June and Mandy kept us going that first six months. You know that. All I contributed was my time here as a sales clerk and bookkeeper."

Hattie smiled and said, "Did you know that June and Mandy were Mormons?"

"C'mon Hattie, this is not the time for kidding around. This is serious. We are talking about our business here. June wasn't a Mormon! She was too nice and such a good Christian person. Mormons are just not that way!"

"What way are they?"

"Well I've heard..."

"That's right, you've heard some rumors and some tales spread by jealous people who have let their pride put false words in their mouths and your ears. June was...no is a Mormon. Where did you think she went when she sold out and left last month?" Hattie answered her own question, "The Great Salt Lake Valley!"

"I thought she went back to live with her family in Missouri. All she said to me was she needed to get back with her people. I assumed she meant her family. But that's beside the point. These men are working..."

"What was it you just said? Isn't that what we are looking for right now, workers? How many people have we passed up because they were looking for a paycheck, but didn't want to work for it? Good men have come home from the war. They have chosen to head west where they can apply their skills and knowledge toward building something for themselves. Many of those that remain are unwilling to use their time, energy, or talents to contribute any meaningful service to the community. They want the community to contribute to them."

"I agree these men are working. I meant to add before being interrupted, they are here in our store where people can see them, and they are talking in homes and on street corners in the evening after work. Telling folks about their beliefs."

Hattie moved over to a shelf and took down the accounts payable ledger. She opened it to a random month and placed her finger on a line item. She looked at Andy and asked, "What is the title of this line item in our own ledger?"

"It says advertising. But, that's different." Andy grumbled.

"What's so different? Why do we spend money on advertising?"

"To get people to come in the store, and buy things they need."

"If they need them why don't they just come on in?"

"They don't know we have them. We get in new products all the time. We have the best prices and the best deals on things. We need to get them in the store so they will look at them..."

"All right Hattie I see where you are going with this. These men need to show people that they have something new to offer. In order to do that they need to talk to them, but what happens when they get enough members to vote changes in our laws about freedom to worship. They can change the way I want to worship!"

"I don't think it concerns numbers. They are not about being the biggest church. They just believe they have found the restored truth and they want to share the good news with others. They believe everyone comes to this earth to work out their own salvation. I think they would be the last ones to coerce anyone to do anything. So, unless you find something wrong with the work they do for us they will stay on the job until we get caught up or they decide to move on."

A couple days later at supper Elder Jones asked, "Hattie, would it be all right if we held a cottage meeting here in your home on Sunday evening? We think there may be six to ten people who want to know more about The Book of Mormon and the Restored Gospel of Jesus Christ."

"Would I be allowed to listen? I have some questions that June was unable to answer."

Elder Groves looked at her with surprise and elation. "We would love to have you sit in and listen to what we have to say. What particular questions do you have?"

"Well, I am concerned about this restored thing and why that is important. June kept mentioning Priesthood Authority. Isn't every pastor authorized to preach the good word of God? Why should that be such an issue with you folks? Why, your preachers hold down full time jobs, support their families, and do their preaching on the side. How can they be better than someone who spends all his time learning, studying, and preaching? Someone who has gone to school to really study the Bible should be more qualified to teach and preach than a person that does it as a sideline."

Elder Groves looked at Hattie. "Between now and Sunday night I would like you to ponder this question. Would you rather study a problem out for yourself and then follow a plan based on your own research, or would you prefer to blindly follow what someone else says?" Hattie already knew what she would do, but she just nodded.

The following day, Hattie called on some of her friends and was able to locate a woman who would come in and help her clean and cook.

Martha started the very next day. She even agreed to make and serve refreshments for the Sunday night meeting. Hattie breathed a sigh of relief. She really wasn't good at domestic chores. She was glad that others were.

On Saturday afternoon, Hattie found time to relax at home. She played the piano for a while, but found that depressing—too many memories of times with Sam, June, and Mandy kept intruding. Thoughts of Margaret and Eliza Flower also plagued her as well. Her fingers made mistakes following her befuddled brain.

She decided to make some notes and questions for discussion with the Elders on Sunday evening. As she was leafing through the book looking for the passages where she had marked questions, she came upon the passage in Moroni 10: 3-5. June had underlined it for her and called it the "Promise." She began to read it again.

Words in verse 4 leaped out at her, "If ye shall ask with a sincere heart, with real intent, having faith in Christ, he will manifest the truth of it unto you, by the power of the Holy Ghost."

Had she really ever asked with a sincere heart or with real intent? She had read this book the same way she had read hundreds of others. She liked searching for facts. Feelings had never entered her mind. She knelt beside her chair, placed her hands on the book, and prayed.

The Sunday night meeting went well in Hattie's opinion. A friendly atmosphere prevailed. She especially enjoyed the opportunity to entertain in her home again. The Elders were not as happy. No one indicated that they wished to learn more. Hattie decided to let them in on her decision to be baptized and to join the Church. She had wanted to hold out a little longer and have a few good-natured arguments with them, but she just couldn't face their disappointment any longer. She really had felt the Spirit. She told them she had decided to become baptized before they left town.

Hattie learned that she would have to travel to Baltimore or Washington, D.C. to attend church services. There were members living in Baltimore who helped immigrants who had joined the Church in Europe or England and were awaiting transportation to the Great Salt Lake Valley. She would make the trip by train at least once a month to meet with them. The remainder of the time, she would have to study alone. She would write to

Mandy and invite her to attend her baptism. Maybe she could go to church with her.

She felt excited about joining the Church, but was dismayed to discover that others were not. Murphy and the Dawsons expressed real concerns. Murphy indicated that his priest wanted him to sell out rather than continue in business with her. Was that an excuse or were feelings really that strong against her? Relationships between former friends became strained. Trust evaporated as they began to talk about splitting up the business.

Finally, Hattie could stand it no longer. She invited Andy and Murphy to her home one night and announced she was open to a reasonable offer for her share of the business. Neither one of them could come up with the cash to buy her out. The banks would not loan them the money either. They were wise enough to realize that with Hattie's knowledge and expertise gone the store might go under as well.

Hattie began to feel pressure from others in the community. Business began to drop off. Hattie lowered her sell-out price subject to an agreement to take merchandise as partial payment. She could transport a large portion of the store's inventory to Great Salt Lake City by train and open a store there. Certain purchasing concessions were made. Murphy used his influence with the railroad to get her a five-year freight contract that would greatly reduce her transportation costs.

They finally reached an agreement in late July. Hattie tried to reach Sam and let him know what was happening. She discovered that he was living in St. Louis. He had found a young woman there and they had married. He had opened a store and Hattie was able to add him to her freight contract with the railroad. She had hoped to leave him a better legacy, but it was the best she could do.

Hattie telegraphed June the news that she had joined the Church and was moving to the Great Salt Lake Valley. She told June that all her luggage and store supplies would arrive addressed to her in care of June. She struggled with her packing. She remembered how difficult it had been to sort things when June left.

She glanced through the many journals she had filled over the years. Tears threatened to flood as she placed them in the box. Each one brought back memories of people dear to her heart, now gone but not forgotten. A letter arrived from June a week later as Hattie was making final negotiations and loading boxcars with merchandise.

The letter indicated that June had found a good man who loved her. She would wait for Hattie to arrive so she could be her Matron of Honor. Mandy was already visiting in Salt Lake and would become a bridesmaid.

On a hot dusty afternoon in early August, Hattie boarded the train to start the journey west. She had shipped all her goods to the address June had given her. No one was there to see her off at the station. She looked around remembering all her work, mercy treatments, and lives saved during the war years. Had others really forgotten how she loved and cared for them? Had the stories circulated by a few self-serving individuals bent on retaining their influence and power really turned people against her? She had always believed that a Christian was a disciple of Christ, someone who followed His teachings, so where was all this persecution coming from?

Maybe, the best thing to do was to follow Jesus and turn the other cheek. Only death could bring true understanding and quell the debate raging in the hearts and minds of friends and neighbors. She couldn't wait for that to happen. She settled back in her seat and tried to think happy, positive thoughts. Maybe God let this happen, so she might reach for a higher level of happiness. She was going toward a people who would love and care about her. The toil, tears, and turmoil associated with life in Hagerstown faded into happy memories as the miles passed. She picked up the rhythm of the rails as the train sped along.

Hattie-rise-up. Hattie-rise-up. Hattie-rise-up.

Made in the USA
San Bernardino, CA
13 October 2016